Praise for
Gifted

"Take a break to read this arresting new novel by Nikita Lalwani . . . Her sensitivity to the pressures felt by Indian immigrants calls to mind the work of such novelists as Zadie Smith and Monica Ali, writers who hear the humor amid the anxiety of integration. What's particularly interesting in *Gifted* is the way Lalwani forces her characters to contend with cultural stereotypes . . . Lalwani does a number of things extremely well here. She won't let us settle back in comfortable judgment on this family . . . The result is a tragic coming of age story full of the mingled love and anger that animate families of every culture."
—RON CHARLES, *The Washington Post Book World*

"Lalwani's debut novel imbues the melodrama of teen-age rebellion with humor [and] . . . wry observations." —*The New Yorker*

"In her compelling debut novel, British author Lalwani subverts the standard immigrant-identity cliches with surprises that bring everything tumbling down." —*Booklist*

"Lalwani's impressive debut exhibits deep empathy for her characters' cultural and emotional displacements." —*Kirkus Reviews*

gifted

GIFTED

a novel

NIKITA LALWANI

RANDOM HOUSE TRADE PAPERBACKS

NEW YORK

2008 Random House Trade Paperback Edition

Copyright © 2007 by Nikita Lalwani

Reading group guide copyright © 2008 by Random House, Inc.

All rights reserved.

Published in the United States by Random House Trade Paperbacks,
an imprint of The Random House Publishing Group,
a division of Random House, Inc., New York.

RANDOM HOUSE TRADE PAPERBACKS and colophon
are trademarks of Random House, Inc.

RANDOM HOUSE READER'S CIRCLE and colophon
are trademarks of Random House, Inc.

Published in hardcover in the United States by Random House, an imprint of
The Random House Publishing Group, a division of Random House, Inc., in 2007.

Originally published in Great Britain by Viking, a division of Penguin UK, London.

Grateful acknowledgment is made to Special Rider Music for permission to reprint
an excerpt from "My Back Pages" by Bob Dylan, copyright © 1964
and copyright renewed 1992 by Special Rider Music. All rights reserved.
International copyright secured. Reprinted by permission.

LIBRARY OF CONGRESS CATALOGING-IN-PUBLICATION DATA
Lalwani, Nikita.
Gifted : a novel / Nikita Lalwani.
p. cm.
ISBN 978-0-8129-7794-3
1. Gifted girls—Fiction. 2. Mathematics—Fiction. 3. Immigrants—Wales—
Fiction. 4. East Indians—Wales—Fiction. 5. Children of immigrants—Family
relationships—Wales—Fiction. 6. Culture conflict—Fiction. 7. Cardiff
(Wales)—Fiction. I. Title.
PR6112.A49G54 2007
823'.92—dc22   2006037620

Printed in the United States of America on acid-free paper

www.therandomhousereaderscircle.com

2 4 6 8 9 7 5 3 1

Book design by Lauren Dong

For Vik, my *jaanum*, in the name of all that love

"Equality," I spoke the word
As if a wedding vow.
Ah, but I was so much older then,
I'm younger than that now.

"MY BACK PAGES," BOB DYLAN,
Another Side of Bob Dylan, 1964

part 1

1

$\sim\!\!\diamond\!\!\sim$

mahesh is sitting in his office, marking. He looks up at the arc of the window as a train rushes past, its urgency left behind in diesel scent and echoing clacks. The dank hush of autumn is settling into his room like a foregone conclusion. It is the eleventh season of its kind in his experience in the UK. The fourth of its kind in this room. Mahesh looks up. There are charts and pictures on the wall. The map of the world sits at an awkward angle, blue ocean disappearing behind the iron bookshelf. Books bulge in huge rows, pressing together files and papers, orange foolscap running in chunky alternation with black, white and gray. In the left corner of the room, by the whiteboard, the bumpy illustration of Gandhi peers out at him. In his mind there is an annoyance that delicately attacks his thoughts every few minutes.

Why did Rumi write that in her exercise book? This is the question that hooks into his conscience periodically: a tiny dental tool piercing soft gum. Why did she write it?

I went to play with Sharon Rafferty and Julie Harris and Leanne Roper in the woods. They let me play softball which is like rounders but with only two bases. Sharon said "let's go and get the softball and racquets from my house." When we got to her place we stood outside the gate and Sharon said "I just have to check you can come in Rumi because my mum doesn't like colored people." Then she went in with the others and I waited outside.

Thank goodness she came back and said it was OK. Then we went in and had pop ices and got the racquets. Mrs. Rafferty was sunbathing in the garden and looked red. We took the racquets and played softball in the woods.

"Colored." The word had made him think of a crayon spreading a thick grainy brown over a round face, the kind of awkward pictures Rumi used to draw under duress when she was younger.

Again he looks at Gandhi, wizened and unflinching, in the corner of his room. What would they make of this back in college, cocooned as they had been in the company of ideas? Trotskyites, Gandhian Communists—they had found plenty of names for themselves back then, chewing betel, relishing the bitter stain on their lips and debating whether class war was compatible with nonviolence. What would they think of this name? What would they think of the conversation he had attempted with Rumi after reading it?

"Do you like your school, Rumi?"

"I don't like the bullies."

"What do you mean, bullies?"

"People who aren't nice to me."

"Do not let these things affect you. You are ten years old now."

"What?"

"You should be like a tiger in the jungle. Like Shere Khan in *The Jungle Book*."

"What do you mean, Daddy?"

"If someone hits you, then hit them back. If they hit you once, hit them twice."

The words had come out of his mouth, as honest as a shotgun, and he had looked away when her eyes jumped. If you are shocked, so am I, he'd thought. But you are not going to be a victim. That I will not allow.

What would they think of this—the Hyderabad college collective—this world that he had chosen to inhabit, placing a solitary, all-important offspring right at the center? Come to that, what about Whitefoot, his current friend, colleague from the PhD course at Cardiff, Marxist himself—what would he think?

Another train goes past, carrying a heavy rattle inside it, dense as a migraine. The tremble of the room seems to jolt the Gandhi picture slightly. He can see a square of evening light on the glass, obscuring part of Gandhi's face. Colored? Why did she write it?

It is four p.m., an early end to his day. He has marked four papers, and the room has lost most of its light. Mahesh screws the lid onto his fountain pen and places it in the outer pocket of his blazer so that the brushed steel is visible against the brown polyester mix. The pen had been a present from Shreene, bought with cash carefully siphoned from her first few paychecks, when she had begun to work after the birth. It is almost exactly the same age as Rumi. After ten years it still feels smooth to the touch, cool, not a single visible scratch or dent on the whole body of the piece. There is still that sensation of guilty pleasure at this luxury when he thinks about what it signifies, a tool of learning and wisdom—but a flamboyant one. He buttons up and puts the exam papers to one side, releasing the blind at his window before he locks up for the day, tucking two MSc dissertations under his arm to look at when he gets home.

FIVE YEARS EARLIER, Rumi had come home one day and announced that Mrs. Gold wanted to come round and meet her parents. She was just five years old, in her first class at school. Mahesh and Shreene had arranged to leave work early on the appointed day, and were home by three thirty. Shreene began to fry some bhajis, while Mahesh descended into a deep silence, waiting in his shirt and tie in the living room. When Mrs. Gold walked in, Rumi was holding her hand.

"What a lovely walk home we've had together, Mr. and Mrs. Vasi," she said, letting Rumi go in ahead of her.

Rumi squirmed and went suddenly quiet, looking up at her father. Mahesh stared at the teacher's peroxide coiffure—whipped and sprayed into rounded peaks and troughs, like a butterscotch dessert. He was confused. Mentally he fought against relaxing, a natural response to the large smile exuded by Mrs. Gold.

"Is it possible to talk to you and your wife together?" she asked.

Shreene had brought in the snacks and joined him, sitting with her hands in her lap, still formal in her work wear, tights and heels. There was an alertness about her: she kept looking covertly at Mahesh, as if to say, "Give me the signal and I'll go ahead with whatever it is we need to do."

"What is it you wanted to talk about?" Mahesh said to Mrs. Gold, feeling the accented curves of his voice as though for the first time. "Is something wrong?"

"No . . . far from it, Mr. Vasi. I wanted to give you some news that I think will make you very proud parents."

"And that is?"

"Rumi is a gifted child!" Mrs. Gold declared, unleashing the words with a thrilled upward turn of the mouth.

Mahesh looked at Shreene, who was biting at the dry skin on her lower lip—a sign that she was tense. He looked at Rumi, who was staring at the floor, waiting for him to decipher the words. And then he cast his gaze back toward Mrs. Gold, and her radiant lines of teeth. "You mean she is doing well at school?"

"I mean more than that, Mr. Vasi," said Mrs. Gold. "I mean that she is special. Different. Gifted."

At this, Rumi started to fidget, scratching her nose and kicking her feet, looking from side to side, first at her mother, then at her father, her movements uncertain, exaggerated by the silence. Mahesh noticed that she had a scratch on her knee just below the hem of her corduroy dress, above the tight line of white sock gripping her calf. Shreene twitched her forehead at her daughter. Mahesh smiled at Mrs. Gold again, and softened his voice, aware that his daughter was listening to each word as he spoke. He tried to keep the pressure out of the sentences he began to create.

"Myself and my wife take . . . Rumika's education very seriously. We are pleased that she is doing well in her studies and that her hard work has paid off. I am an academic myself—"

Mrs. Gold shook her head, interrupting. "With due respect, Mr. and Mrs. Vasi, I'm talking about something else. I am talking about a gift. Something that only comes along now and then. Rumi is a gifted mathematician!"

They were plunged into silence once more. Rumi moved her legs back and forth, pushing them rhythmically against the velour of the sofa. Mahesh registered vaguely that she was repeating the movement in batches of four, then pausing, like a physical chant. He watched her support one of her chubby little cheeks with a hand, which she made into a fist, balancing her elbow on her thigh. She was still staring at the floor.

"I am also a mathematician and I am glad that she is doing well in this subject, as you say. I have placed emphasis on it because it is my area of speciality," said Mahesh, trying to maintain an amiable expression on his face.

"We at Summerfield believe that Rumi deserves to have this gift nurtured," said Mrs. Gold. She leaned in, pulling her skirt together so that the pleat at the front disappeared neatly inside itself. She paused significantly, as though she was about to say something serious, possibly untoward. Rumi also leaned in automatically to listen, her swaying legs forcing themselves to halt, pressing a temporary dent into the sofa front. Even Shreene moved her body forward, raising her eyebrows expectantly.

"Have you heard of a place called Mensa?" said Mrs. Gold.

Mahesh felt exasperated. He had seen all the same adverts as her. The ads for this place she named with such careful tedium, as though she was rolling a diamond round her mouth. "Mensa." He'd seen their childish IQ tests, fooled around with filling them out in the Sunday papers. He knew what Mensa was, for goodness' sake. What did she take him for? And why was she so surprised that he and his daughter could string numbers together with reasonable panache? They were hardly shopkeepers.

He was "peed off," as they said here: irritated. He tried to think of more slang, enjoying the taste of righteousness, dousing each word with it. He was "hacked off," "cheesed off," "not pleased." What did she think? That he was some third-rate charlatan, preening his feathers under the banner of academia? He felt a rumble in his stomach as the bhajis fermented, rising as though to validate his sense of pique. Oddly, the sensation cheered him. He felt like making a grand statement to this woman, one that Rumi would witness, about how it was possible through strength and discipline to create your own destiny using the power of thought: through marks, percentages, papers, exams, numbers that had added up, in his case, to a big sum in small hands—a scholarship across the ocean.

He surveyed Mrs. Gold's darting eyes. She was watching his wife as she sipped her tea. Shreene was returning her gaze, looking round the room at intervals. What preconceptions did she bring with her—this queer-spoken woman with her little smiles and polite contradictions? He was not going to make a grand statement. It would only confuse things. But, if he could, he would tell her everything. He'd tell her he'd got into all their universities—all the bloody jewels they treasured so exclusively in this country: that he had been offered a place at their Cambridge and their University College of London. He had ended up in Cardiff because they had offered the cash—several thousand pounds of it, a sum that no one could deny for its totality. Full fees. They had wanted him here, a foreigner with no more than five pounds in his pocket and a slip of a wife, bare-toed and shivering. That was how he had got off the plane with Shreene in 1972, newly wed and aware, dignified by the patronage of their redbrick institutions, sure as a compass, leading the way for them both.

He had not been among the thirty thousand Asians hemorrhaging out of the ugly scar in Uganda's belly that same year, seeping into the dark spaces of Britain, afloat in the soiled bath water of Amin's shake-up: the crawling masses who had fallen into the pockets of Leicester and Wembley. He was not going to be dissolved into the rivers of blood, among Enoch Powell's armies of bacteria, defecating in people's nightmares on the landscape of their precious country.

He was Dr. Mahesh Vasi, PhD, a man who had begun his maths career repeating times tables under a large tree in Patiala with fifteen schoolmates, embossed with dust and driven by the pure heat of numbers. Now he was here, working just over an hour's commute away, speaking to a room of one hundred students each week, employed in name by the University of Swansea, subset of the University of Wales itself. What about that, then?

Mahesh cleared his throat and considered how to proceed. He uncrossed, then recrossed his legs with an air of what he hoped was leisurely contemplation. He still had to learn how to relax, uncoil the ritual desire to please. It was a shameful habit, nothing else, he told himself.

Shreene offered Mrs. Gold the plate of snacks. The vegetables shone through the batter with glistening heat: dark purple eggplant skins and green zucchini, pushing their thick curves through the fried covering. "Please—have one," she said, smiling and pressing a paper napkin into the teacher's hand. "Do you like spicy food?"

Mahesh took the opportunity to interject. "I know Mensa very well, Mrs. Gold. I'm happy to go there with Rumika and see what it is like."

IN THE TWO weeks that followed, running up to Rumi's entrance exam for Mensa, Mahesh enforced a routine that was not dissimilar to the one he had made Shreene follow in the first year of their marriage during her pregnancy.

He had been very attracted to the volcanic quality of his new wife back then: the huge blue eyes (an exotic aberration of color in her family, which she regarded with much pride) that seemed to yell out of their sockets when she was angry, the trickle of black curls that lay sensually against the moist olive of her forehead. But he had worried about the stereotypical elements of their union—the fact that they were essentially strangers, having met only once before marriage, conception occurring within a month of wedlock, as hoped for by their parents back home.

At that time they had lived in a student bed-sit, the kitchen breathing and squeaking its gaseous smells into the room where they slept. Money was tight: Mahesh was working in the university post office to supplement his sponsorship, and he was militant about saving. "If we earn two pounds we save one of them," he was fond of saying. "I will not be someone who struggles to find coins for the heater. If we choose to go without, so be it. It can never be forced upon us if we have our own savings."

At weekends Shreene went with him to the university sports club to shower in hot luxury; during the week she made do with the decrepit shared bathroom on the floor below. She spent the day trying to bring some sense of what she understood as family life to the single room they lived in, deflecting her loneliness with the necessity of housekeeping, finding her place among the steel trays and folded saris that she had brought from her parental home.

He came home late in the evenings, weary with the remote universe of his PhD, and would begin what Shreene (first jokingly and later with a bitter regularity) called "the police-camp procedures." He had taken her out of the rich bustle of her world: interrupted the round stretchings of chapattis, the powdery rainbow of her spices, and punctured her pride at exactly seven thirty each evening, forcing her to sit down at their hobbling plastic table, and run through the events of the day. He could not subscribe to something as transient as a daily newspaper, but he requested that Shreene make a single trip every lunchtime, to read the paper in the local library. She was free to read whichever she chose; all he asked was that they have a one-hour conversation dissecting it before dinner each day. When Shreene retaliated, her proud eyes steaming with humiliation, saying that this was not the way she was used to being treated—that she had not bargained on being insulted like this by her husband—he spelled out very clearly the positive outcomes that made this a logical course of action:

1. He would be able to converse with her on matters other than the drama and intrigue of their extended families. This could only be beneficial in the long run.

2. It would improve her English, thereby enabling her to work as soon as the baby was born. She was a Delhi Univer-

sity graduate; her degree had covered literature, philosophy and fine art, albeit in Hindi. There was no reason why she should not be able to contribute to the household's income. In fact, it was imperative that she did, considering that soon there would be three people in the family.

3. The trip to the library was both thrifty and empowering. It would thrust her into the world, thereby forcing her to inter-act with locals—again, beneficial for her assimilation into the society they were now living in—rather than succumb to the temptation to hanker for and idealize the society she inhab-ited back home.

4. The trip outdoors would be good exercise for her, espe-cially in her current state.

5. The whole regime would prevent her losing her mental abilities through lack of usage, especially during this critical period in her life—pregnancy.

This last point particularly angered Shreene. But she bit back her indignation and proceeded as he deemed fit. For a while it seemed almost to work—she would list the plane crashes and hijackings, the earthquakes, the bombs and the shoot-outs in Ireland. If she wasn't able to pronounce the names of the places, then she made sure to give an indication of the numbers involved in each case, gathering the digits in her memory to create a vast array of weaponry. Some-times she made up events, in unnamed places, a plane almost going down in the Indian Ocean due to a tiny error on the part of the pilot, or small riots in a mosque on the border with Pakistan; a slow news day led to an esteemed guru rousing thousands of disciples in Gujarat, like a latter-day prophet.

Those tales invariably found their way back to the subcontinent. Mahesh forbade her to dwell on her past, but sometimes when she came up with these fabrications he found her unbearably cute. He battled with his heart, which was softening like a marshmallow on a fire, and tried to maintain perspective. "Are you sure?" he would ask, curbing a smile. And so they continued, until Shreene began to crack, splintering into tantrums, losing control. Eventually, one day, dissatisfied with the figures, Mahesh asked her to give an opinion on Heath's plans for dealing with unemployment. She erupted. There were screams, plates were banged on the worktops, teeth were gritted, and she trashed the ritual once and for all.

"We're never going back, are we?" she said, propositioning him with the words, urging him to deny them. "This is all I have to look forward to now. You told me it was just for the PhD but I'm never going to see my family again. You lied to me, didn't you? This is it!"

"What has that got to do with anything?" asked Mahesh. "And, anyway, surely we make the decision that is most appropriate when the time comes? Why call it lying?"

"When you interviewed me for marriage you asked me if I wanted to live abroad," said Shreene, swallowing. "I told you then, 'No, I am Indian, my heart is desi.' Just three years, you said."

By the time Rumi was five, though, and the Mensa equation was assembling before them, Shreene was a fully established working woman. The police-camp procedures were a distant memory for Mahesh, doused with the innocence of their early years.

Inevitably Rumi had to observe a more intensive timetable than other children at her school, and this had to be implemented at home, outside school hours. But in spite of, or maybe because of, her youth, at five, she had been a willing student. She displayed genuine excitement when it came to the numbers game: the figures he threw at her found their mark time and time again, and she would bat them back with a ravenous energy that simultaneously thrilled him and unnerved Shreene.

For those two weeks, Mahesh picked Rumi up from school every day at three forty-five on the dot, and at home, after refreshment and a few basic yoga exercises, they began the preparation. As well as a basic diet that was nutritionally balanced, Shreene provided Rumi's favorite foods at set intervals. These included a small number of biscuits—Jammie Dodgers or custard creams—and a jam doughnut or chocolate ice cream late in the evening. Every two hours they took a short break of fifteen minutes, stretching or taking a walk together round the block. The journey began with their exit through the back gate. Their home was at the center of ten similar houses that stretched up the left of a hilly road, terra-cotta blocks, checkered with creamy beige sealant, and graphite-colored roofs with tiny pipe chimneys, repeating in vision and matching the houses on the opposite side.

Mahesh watched Rumi's pigtails bobbing in front of him as they walked together in the evening dusk, and felt close to his daughter. At the top of the hill, the tributary of their footpath joined a wider pavement, set against a main road with occasional traffic pushing through. As Mahesh progressed like this, tracing a steady circuit past the houses, registering the trio of shops across the road each time (newsagent, launderette and general hardware), immersed in the rich smell of pollution and domestic greenery, he felt bound to Rumi in the mystery of silence, hypnotized by the question-and-answer sessions they had been through. Every question had an answer. For every one he asked, after she had thought, battled, tried things out, she would come up with it. This was their interaction. Even Shreene was focused during this period, attuned to the schedule and ready to prepare Rumi for bed with her bath and nighttime milk, stirred through with crushed almonds.

On the day itself, he wanted Shreene to come with them but she bowed out, claiming she would only mess it up for him if he wanted to get into serious conversation with anyone. Much better for him to take Rumi alone. He drove Rumi to the community center where the local branch of the society was meeting that month. Shreene had dressed her in a matte satin frock, found in a secondhand shop: gray background imprinted with large red flowers that looked like poppies. It had a floppy bow that tied in the middle of Rumi's back. Mahesh looked at his five-year-old daughter, sitting next to him when he stopped at the traffic lights, and had a brief moment of panic. Did she look as if she was going to a wedding? Would they appear uncouth? He dismissed the thought with a blink. If there was one thing he did know, it was that these things mattered least of all. It was important to hold on to this. The simplicity of the proceedings.

However, no one had prepared him for the possibility that he would be driving back within minutes, seconds, even, of entering the hall. They were late, true enough, and this had confused him, made him wonder why he had not been sure of their timings. (Had he done this on purpose? Mahesh wondered later. If so, what did it mean?) But, still, no one could explain the chill that went through him when the person at the microphone had stopped delivering his address to look at the two of them at the back of the hall. Rumi had squeezed his hand as the five rows of people turned round, the speaker calling to them to sit at the front. But Mahesh hadn't sat down among the sea of white faces. (Why the color? He couldn't explain it now, even.) Instead, with a tight grip on Rumi's hand, he had turned and left the room so swiftly that it was only when they were getting into the car that she managed to speak.

"Where are we going, Daddy?" she asked, as he buckled her in, feverishly adjusting the mirror and pulling his own seat forward.

We'll do it ourselves, he said, in silent response, feeling unnatural heat saturate his forehead. He shivered. We don't need them, he thought, while he reversed, checking the mirror in case Mrs. Gold should show up, late herself.

2

Rumi glanced at her watch. She was 10 years, 4 months, 13 days, 2 hours, 42 minutes and 6 seconds old.

Leaning against a Portakabin near the school gate, looking out for her father through the high fence, she wondered how much longer it would be before he arrived. A shiver went through her: the numb bite in the air unsettled her carefully arranged obscurity, ruffling her senses, so that she felt in danger of being noticed. She gathered herself, and stood as quietly as she could. The howls and shrieks of the playground were being funneled slowly down the main path and out through the gate. She was waiting away from the entrance, where the school was pouring its inhabitants down onto the road, because it would be too embarrassing if anyone saw Mahesh pick her up.

She felt as if she had a continual reminder of her own embarrassment now that she was ten, a swinging arrow that rose to point very high, very quickly, like the arrow on a *Blue Peter* charity appeal. She didn't understand why, but she knew that the sight of her father getting out of his car, his beige raincoat belted tightly at the waist, the black beard contaminated with gray wires, eyes as serious as the end of the world—the thought of this in front of everyone—shamed her. And if he spoke, in that slow way, as though something very bad had happened, the voice he reserved for being serious, if he spoke like that in front of everyone, she wouldn't be able to bear it.

"Your dad's so scary," Sharon Rafferty had said once, when she had been doing Julie Harris's hair at lunchtime in the playground. "Does he ever smile? He's like a Dalek."

Rafferty had seen her father only from a distance, at parents' evening, but it had been enough to make him part of her vocabulary.

It was as though he had leaked a funny smell, and now he was fair game for mockery.

Rumi frowned and scratched the bump on her nose made by her glasses. Her father was a teacher, or a "lecturer," as they called it at the university, but her schoolmates didn't know that. So it had to be something else. They made her feel useless. Not just Rafferty and Harris, the popular ones, but all the girls in her class. It wasn't just that Rumi was barely allowed out to play—maybe once a week, for a couple of hours, if that—it was that she always had to ask if she could join in when people like Rafferty and Harris, who lived nearby, were playing, as though it was a special favor. Lately, since they had all started hanging about near the local shop instead of going to the woods, it had got worse. They hadn't played softball since that first time with Sharon, Julie and Leanne. It made her mad. It was more than embarrassing. It was a horrible feeling.

If the whole friends thing was like a Venn diagram, she wasn't even inside the outer circle. It was not like India, where everyone had wanted to play with her, or asked to know everything about her. In the whole of Cardiff, no one wanted to talk to her (you couldn't count your parents in this, and even if you could count your brother, Nibu couldn't speak properly yet), except Simon Bridgeman and Christopher Palmer, also dismissed as "brainboxes." Even they could speak to her only outside the school boundaries or they ran the risk of being ridiculed, as though she was a girlfriend or something. She was lonely. But it wasn't only her father's fault. If she stood at the gates right now, for example, she knew she would embarrass herself just by being there, freakishly dressed in a lacy frock and thick woolen tights, her long hair falling out of the gold slide that Shreene clipped into the right-hand side daily.

Rumi was not allowed to choose her clothes. For budgetary reasons, according to Mahesh, she had to wear outfits that had been made for her during the India Trip, two years previously, stitched in various sizes so that she could grow into them. That was the only bad outcome of a trip that had been otherwise, without doubt, the best time she had experienced in her whole life. But the clothes meant that she was cold most of the time and, unable to wear jeans, derided constantly for her particular form of fashion; the thick National Health Service glasses and the shiny wardrobe of Indian synthetics completed the long list of reasons to be embarrassed. In the cut-and-thrust of playground survival, these things mattered. They all want to be identical, she thought. Identikit identi ident dent-ers irritating girls. Identical dentiski. Skident. It hurt. And Rumi had removed herself from the pool, preferring instead to plan the world through the triumphant and logical completion of books like *Peak Maths,* a series in which she was at least seven books ahead of anyone else in her year.

She looked at her watch again. Now she was 10 years, 4 months, 13 days, 2 hours, 48 minutes and 4 seconds old. She sang the num-bers song in her head. It was almost a lullaby, one she had known since she was a child, the tune working like a step graph with a line that rose and rose, then flattened out when it got to sixteen, ending with a comforting monotone. The wind continued to chop at her, throwing her off balance, but she clung to the melody like a life jacket, letting the numbers warm her with their familiarity. 1 and 1 are 2. 2 and 2 are 4. 4 and 4 are 8. 8 and 8 are 16—and 16 and 16 are 32. The figures continued in her head, as she extended the song for her own purposes, loving its simplicity. They were wholesome, even numbers, created through doubling alone. 32 and 32 are 64 . . . 128 . . . 256 . . . 512. Five hundred and twelve was a lovely number. Really friendly. It made her think of her dad's big, warm, open hands, the lined palms in which she used to put her face on Sunday mornings when he and her mum were in bed. He used to pretend those hands were crocodile jaws waiting to gobble her up. That had been when he wasn't so obsessed with mental arithmetic and getting the right answer. He had played silly games with her, fresh and lazy with weekend yawns.

The car appeared round the corner, hovering at the traffic lights. She picked up her bag and walked quickly to meet it, keeping her gaze on the ground.

Now that Nibu was in the university crèche, no one was at home to look after Rumi so every day she was supposed to go to the library and work from four until six o'clock on twenty problems set by her father. From Rumi's point of view there were many pluses to the proposed new regime. First of all, it exponentially increased the probability of her walking home with John Kemble, the most fancied boy in the class. Her own status meant that there was no chance of talking to him unless they were on their own, when he was apt to be much friendlier. Kemble lived near the library, so in future, depending on whether they were at the gate at around the same time, Rumi had a good chance of walking with him for at least six minutes. She considered it. Well, it was probably a 2 in 7 chance. Or maybe 3 in 14, otherwise known as 3 over 14. If you thought about it, 1 over 14 would be point 0714 so 3 times that came to point 2142. She frowned. Hadn't realized it was that small, she thought.

Today, however, it was the first day of the new plan so Mahesh was going to take her there himself, to the library in Maelfa shopping center. He ran through the rules again on the way there, as he drove through the darkening afternoon with his habitual caution. Rumi listened, her face against the window, watching rain droplets slide into each other. She knew the rules by heart by now.

1. The most important rule. No speaking to anyone. Not even if she should recognize someone from school, who might be in the library. In fact, should the latter happen, she should be especially silent and turn away, avoiding eye contact.

2. No reference to her library routine to be made at any point—not to classmates or teachers, or anyone else who might ask her where she went at home-time.

3. No leaving the library after she had entered it at four p.m. She was to stay at her desk, working on the problems, and use the library lavatory if need be. No wandering around the shopping center, or the small park nearby. She was to stay at the desk and that was that. Mahesh had threatened to make

spot checks at any time: he would return early or at random to check on her. That was to be her deterrent.

4. The librarian to be the only exception to this rule—spoken to in emergencies. In that instance Rumi was to give the librarian the telephone numbers and contact details that had been written in the back of her maths exercise book.

5. She would not carry money on her person. (That was easy enough, thought Rumi. She didn't have pocket money, like other children.) And she would not carry food either: according to Mahesh, hunger sharpened the mind, allowing deeper concentration. She would wait to eat her evening meal with the family at eight thirty. But she would carry a single ten-pence coin in her anorak pocket for a telephone call, to be used only in an extreme emergency when there was no other option. (Rumi wondered what kind of scenario this special emergency might be—presumably if the librarian died or was abducted.)

6. All time in the library to be spent on maths, that being the purpose of this period of preparation. No loss of focus, and especially no time to be wasted in the reading of novels, even though it might be tempting. It was important that Rumi should enforce self-discipline. This was a planned period of sustained study, after all, in which she would build stamina for the coming year: the start of secondary school.

They arrived at the shopping center. The library was just to the side of the entrance, the dirty russet bricks visible through the windscreen as they parked beside it. Mahesh locked the car and took Rumi in, smiling at the librarian as they entered. Although she knew the space well, the multiplicity of the rows and desks, the anonymity of the people, each sitting alone, enclosed in the padding of silence, made her feel nervous.

"Come on, now," said Mahesh. "Let us choose your desk."

They found an area toward the front, directly in the line of vision of the loans desk. Rumi set up her maths-tools box and unloaded her bag, while Mahesh went to speak to the lady who was arranging books behind the counter. After a couple of minutes he returned. "Are you ready?" he asked, inclining his head in her direction, as a gesture of support.

Rumi nodded, not knowing how to react.

"I will leave now and return at six," he said, tightening the belt of his coat. "Or maybe earlier—who knows? There may be a spot check—or there may not."

She nodded again, wondering whether she was supposed to do or say something.

"Today is good practice for you," he said, smiling encouragingly. "From tomorrow you will be making the journey here alone, so if you need to talk to me about the rules we can do that this evening after I have marked your paper."

She watched him walk out, the room ballooning round her, the ceiling rushing up and away, making her head spin.

FOR MANY WEEKS, after that first afternoon, the routine worked as planned. Her father usually picked Nibu up from the crèche, then came and got her between six and six thirty. He would start by surveying her exercises, checking the number of new workings on the page, moving on to his daily conversation with whichever librarian was on duty. After that they all went together in the car to collect Shreene from the British Telecom center where she worked. Sometimes, depending on how well the sums had gone, they stopped at the baker's for the reduced end-of-day cakes and Rumi would get a cream éclair as a treat.

Rumi did not mention how much she hated the new routine because she knew it was good for her, if she was going to be serious about her maths. After all, she was the one who had asked to do the O level next year. "I can do it too, Dad," she'd said, incensed by the idea that the boy on the telly had been two years younger than she was.

But that didn't take away the sodden misery of the whole thing. Rumi took her assigned place across from the librarian each day, crossing her legs in a labored tension as she sat in the dead air, scribbling out the useless sums on the page, remembering to move her feet after a good half-hour only to discover they had been stabbed a hundred times with pins and needles while she wasn't looking. She stared at the librarian between each portion of time, with a dull observatory interest, like a surveillance camera twisting to follow its target—watching her stamp the books and rearrange the index-card box. But the librarian did not watch her back. Eventually, in the fifth week, Rumi left her desk and read fifteen pages of an Enid Blyton book at the back of the room, then returned. The librarian did not comment. In fact, she didn't seem to register Rumi's absence. Eight weeks in, and Rumi had created a new routine, which included breaking several rules each day.

It began with her arrival. After she had set up her kit on the table she went to the back of the library and read a Malory Towers or Pippi Longstocking book for half an hour. She enjoyed this part, despite the out-and-out ban on fiction, but it was always a pleasure soaked in guilt. There was something dirty about it. Then she went for a distracted walk in the shopping center for about twenty minutes, stopping to look in the toy shop at bright plastic contraptions that Nibu might like, checking in with the budgies and the goldfish at the pet shop, examining the numerous gadgets and seeds in the hardware and gardening shop. After this, it went downhill. She often stood outside the library door watching litter being hurled about by the wind, feeling her gut do a similar dance. It was the lying that got her down. They make me lie all the time, she thought. She felt anger at the lack of cash, the single ten-pence coin smoldering like an insult in the pocket at her chest. And she was angry about the hunger she often felt, churning its way through her thoughts, like a roadrunner through the desert, sounding a constant buzz of discipline, a never-ending reminder. She imagined running away and joining a place like Malory Towers or the Chalet School, learning to ski, staying up all night for midnight feasts. Then she would pull herself together, and force herself to walk inside for an hour of maths, plus ten minutes' break.

In the tenth week, things changed, with a single incident—one that released so much guilt that it stained its way through her, like the ink from the broken pens in her pockets. She was sure her mum and dad could see it in her face, although they never said anything.

It had happened during the maths section of the evening. Under the burning tube lights, she attacked the numbers with speed and ferocity, as though she was playing Space Invaders, devouring the figures with the hunger in her belly and spitting out the remains. She worked feverishly, chewing pen tops down to sharp points. Then she had looked up—looked at the bored librarian at her desk, at the old man reading the paper—seen the thin tall rectangle of black sky through the doors and trembled with loneliness. She pinched her arm, like they did in stories, to make sure she was there, and got up. She walked out of the library and straight to the sweet shop round the corner.

There, she loitered by the entrance, pretending to look at magazines, as though she was deciding which one to buy. Two people came in, a mother and daughter, both wearing stripy scarves. Rumi maneuvered her way to the penny-sweets section on her left and stared intensely at the marshmallows and white candy cigarettes. Out of the corner of her eye, she could see the pair at the counter, talking to the woman at the till. The girl was very little, about six years old, scarf covering her mouth and half of her nose. The mother ordered a quarter of pear drops and bent down to wipe the child's nose. Rumi's right hand dived into the box of cola bottles and scooped a batch into her anorak pocket. She stood very quietly, hand shaking in her pocket against the wet zip, then turned and walked out of the door, holding her breath. She was a criminal. This was something that could not be reversed.

She ate the cola bottles in the foyer of the library, chewing the sticky rubber and swallowing it in big chunks before she could taste it properly. Then she sat back at her desk and worked madly to catch up. When Mahesh arrived, a few minutes later, it was a shock to see him towering above her, with Nibu squealing and smiling in his arms. If he had left his office any earlier, he would have caught her. But he never got there before six, in spite of the threat of spot checks.

Soon she was stealing sweets every day, alternating between the four shops that sold confectionery in the shopping center, entering a fantasy world like the one in the book about the chocolate factory, where goldfish gobstoppers lived alongside giant jelly strawberries and white mice. And she enjoyed relying on her wits, using her cunning to slip sweets into her pocket when the moment was perfect— a momentary chat about the weather between two grown-ups at the front, a gap in surveillance when the attendant left to find a fishing magazine for an old man. If she waited for long enough the moment always came. Although she had worked out that the probability of being caught was relatively high, given that none of the shops was populated with more than two or three customers at any time, she was still unprepared for the day when a hand clamped itself on her shoulder, making her jump, her own hand unclasping to scatter a mess of sherbet lollies and red licorice bootlaces over the floor.

"Show me what's in your other pocket, young lady," said the shopkeeper, a sturdy woman with a face like a tortoise, the lines and grooves giving her a fearsome authority. Rumi pulled out her pocket, showing the dusty material with a shaking hand, her head hurting, as though she had been punched.

"I'll let you off this time," said the woman, sniffing as she collected the sweets together. "If you want to buy anything, join the queue and pay like everyone else. If not, push off."

Instead of leaving then and there, Rumi had turned to look at the "queue," which consisted of two boys at the counter, who were staring at her. She picked up a single sherbet lolly, a single white mouse to join it, and stood behind them, heart thudding ominously, as though it was threatening to bash its way right through her ribs and out of her body. I'll show her, she thought, paying for the sweets with half of the emergency ten pence and replacing the five-pence change in her anorak. I can pay. I've got money.

After she was caught, the glamour seeped noiselessly out of the world beyond the library, and the shopping center had a deflated quality, reminding Rumi of her own wrongdoing. She fell into a slump of self-loathing and mentally chained her body to the desk in the library, banning herself from leaving the seat even to go to the toilet—crushing her thighs together with a disciplined mania whenever the desire to urinate came upon her. Instead of physical adventures, her mind wandered through a series of daydreams, mostly revolving around moving to India.

She'd arrange it in the next India Trip, she thought; make her parents agree to it somehow. And then it would be announced in Assembly, how she was leaving them behind—Rafferty, Harris, the lot of them. She'd get her hair cut in advance, with a big fringe that spiked up a bit, and somehow get hold of a ra-ra skirt. When the list was read out at the end for football, table tennis and all that extracurricular stuff, she'd raise her hand.

She'd get up and say, "Yes, I have an announcement. I'm moving to a country where people laugh and have fun and aren't cruel and rude and don't make a joke of you, and where they are more intelligent than people here, especially at maths like me. And I'm never coming back. And also, by the way, my mum and dad say that British people stole all these stones from people in India, the rubies and diamonds in the precious buildings, before they stopped ruling it, and that represents how they stole the sparkle out of Indian people's lives. So it doesn't make much sense for me to live here, to be honest, because I don't agree with it. I'm going back to where I came from."

She knew that she would have to make sure she was in a place where she could look at Simon Bridgeman and Christopher Palmer during this last bit, to give them a signal so they didn't take it personally. Or maybe she'd warn them in advance, so that the shock of what she was about to reveal, about their own history as British people, didn't upset them too much.

3

⁂

Rumi's main memory of the India Trip was linked inextricably with the mythology of the Vasi household. Even her father, usually so suspicious of his wife's growing flirtation with superstition and emotional recall, was influential in nurturing the story's development. It was almost as though missing the trip had liberated him, allowing him to enjoy the cozy folds of legend without feeling the pressure to hack at it with analysis. In this way the story grew till it exuded a paranormal warmth, enclosing Rumi's thoughts like an electric blanket whenever she thought of it.

Rumi had been eight years old when she made the trip, which had begun with the funeral of Shreene's father; the intervening two years since had accentuated its mystique. Often she would ask her mother for more information, which she added to the picture in broad brushstrokes, wild sun blotches heating the events with an intensity she craved but did not understand. Sometimes when she went to sleep she worried she might forget it, that it would turn into a dream and disappear, leaving her at the start, having to begin all over again. Mostly, she wanted to live up to the memory so that when Nibu was older she could pass it on to him.

The story had four parts, which Rumi referred to privately as

1. The Arrival (and the biscuits)

2. The Palm Reader (and the prediction)

3. The Train Journey (and escaping death)

4. The Mountain Top (and the wish that came true)

The first image is one Rumi cherishes, imbuing it with a kind of romantic nostalgia for the trip as a whole. She sees two slender arms, creamy beige, barely haired, adorned with two gold bangles, hanging heavily over scented wrists. Nobody, not even the rain, has such small hands. This is something Rumi has read in the book of poems that Elga, the wife of her father's boss, gave them at Christmas. She likes the sound of the words, shaped together in the only page that she can read in the book. This string of short words creeps into her head whenever she thinks of her mum's hands, tiny and soft, waiting at the luggage counter in Delhi airport.

In the picture, each hand reaches up to pull a suitcase off the conveyor belt. The bags are so heavy that Rumi worries her mum's wrists will snap, loudly and completely, splitting the flesh of her arm and releasing the yellow-gold circles to fall onto the floor. Instead, Shreene lifts each bag with the tense hope of a bodybuilder, breathing heavily and taking ten paces each time, then setting them down to regain her breath. This is how they progress, with a slow but staccato rhythm toward the sign marked "Customs." The exit is framed lazily by khaki-clad guards, who chew paan and stare freely at them.

Rumi looks around her at the sea of Indian faces dressed in colors and clothing from all around the world. Mixed through are people who have traveled with them from the UK, strapped with cameras and pouches and wheelie suitcases. They are like the irregular white stones she finds when she cleans lentils for her mother to cook, arranging them in a pattern on the worktop so they don't find their way into the pan. There are girls in saris, skirts and pleated trousers. There are reedy men in blue uniforms trying to help with luggage. Shreene ignores them and Rumi clenches her fists resolutely when they approach. At the same time she is aware of a thick smog pouncing up her nostrils, a smell that she can only describe as hot; a taste that is like cotton wool in her mouth every time she breathes in. Everywhere she looks people seem to be looking back at them. As they walk she can hear airport announcements every couple of minutes. They are excitingly alien: the female voices soft but certain, the male ones blunt but reassuring. Rumi cannot understand the Hindi because Mahesh has decided that English should be the only language spoken at home, but she likes the sound of the words—the undulating dialogue of Hindi films, the secret text in the lullabies Shreene sings to Nibu when Mahesh is not around.

Shreene will not allow Rumi to help but she does ask her to count: "One two three." Each time she says a figure out loud, Rumi echoes it with three more in her head and multiplies them so her head trails with numbers, snaking through the guilty silence between each moment of speech. Every time she gets close to nine she can feel her mother's sweat, urgency and relief before the crashing break of the suitcases hitting the floor. There are no trolleys to be seen, and the bags contain twenty-three large boxes of Fox's Caramel Crunch biscuits with buttercream filling, with a clock radio and toiletries. Their clothes are in a small holdall, which Rumi carries easily and unhappily.

"Mum, why did we bring so many biscuits? What's the point?" she asks, as Shreene heaves for air, bent over the cases, her hands pushing her up from the handles. "Why do we have to be so weird?" It isn't the first time she has brought it up.

"Look, why don't you be a good girl and help me, Rumika, instead of making it more difficult? Why are you asking this now?"

"But I don't know why we need all these biscuits. Why do we?" Rumi says.

"They are presents, as you well know, for your uncles and aunties and your little brothers and sisters, their children."

"Why do they want biscuits?"

"They don't want anything, Rumi. They don't have biscuits like this here. You are such a lucky girl, eating these delicious biscuits whenever you want, but imagine if you had never tasted something like this. They are so good. 'Mmmm . . . yummy,' you say, when you eat them. I want them to taste what we taste so they can feel it too. Don't you want that?"

"Uh . . ." Rumi trails off uncertainly.

"Don't you want them to enjoy what we enjoy? Are you so selfish?"

She has said the word Rumi hates. "I'm not selfish. Mum, I'm not."

"You are selfish. You are like your dad. You don't realize it sometimes, but you are. You think only of yourself."

"No, I'm not. I'm not selfish. I wasn't selfish!"

"Well, then, help me now and try not to be, OK?"

They begin the next ten paces. Rumi is grumpy, counting out loud resentfully. She idly lets other numbers have their way . . . 23 times 0.79 is . . . 18 pounds and 17 on biscuits. Even after they have got through Customs successfully, her mother smiling sweetly at the guards, answering questions with a tight laugh, Rumi refuses to celebrate. When they walk through the glass walls, the line of watching people leaning on the other side animates into a mixture of hugs and chatter. They scoop Rumi up, kiss her, teasing, and she realizes they must be her family.

THE PALM-READER EVENT took place in the marble hallway of Shreene's family home, two weeks into the stay. Rumi can see the setting clearly when she thinks of it, hear the sound track, textured with Shreene's voice: her mum's translations chattering round the ornate space. The house is immensely exotic to Rumi, a wide area marked with artifacts: wooden carvings of luscious goddesses, wistful chandeliers, Moghul paintings on silk and a marble model of the Taj Mahal that lights up at night with an orange fire glow. The side doors open to a veranda where the honk and blare of traffic and people can seep through, stained with dust, the fine particles spreading through the air in sepia. Occasionally a scooter whizzes past, its patterned horn unique to the model, causing a jitter of excitement in Rumi as she hears the repetition. Sometimes she can see a cow in this memory, languorous on the road, stopping to chew the bush in the neighbor's garden, then disappearing with a shake of its tail into the smoky distance.

At this point, the funeral is over and the most distant relatives have disbanded back round the country. Shreene is seated on a thickly woven charpoy with Rumi. Next to them is Shreene's older sister, known as Badi, or the Big One. Badi is a good fifteen years older than Shreene. To Rumi, she is timeless: angular and intense, sharp cheekbones exposed by a tight gray bun, natural pink shadowing her eyes, which protrude, like her teeth, eagerly when she speaks. Around Badi, Shreene seems so young to Rumi. She acts like a daughter rather than a mother, nodding when Badi asks her if the fan is too harsh for her, and curling up in her blanket when they sleep, Badi folding it so it doubles over Rumi and Shreene together.

They have just woken up, and sit, blinking under the fan, taking in the sticky smell of tea brewing in the kitchen. It is late afternoon and the rest of the home's inhabitants—Shreene's brothers, their wives, the kids—are still sleeping. They wait, semi-alert, the three of them, for the priest to arrive. They do not look each other in the eye, respectful of the transition into full wakefulness. Shreene seems embalmed by the quiet of this limbo period, immune from past and present, untouched by the crying of recent weeks or the uncertainty to come.

They hear a greeting given in the hallway, the maid responding, and Badi gets up to meet their guest. Rumi watches her mother straighten and prepare for his arrival, following her lead on how to behave. The priest enters the room and Shreene reaches down to touch his feet respectfully. She gestures to Rumi to get off the bed and sit on the floor. Badi helps the priest walk across to the charpoy and sit down, his veiny old hand shaking in the hook of a dark walking stick. Rumi twitches her nose under her glasses and pulls her skirt down so it covers her knees, as she sits cross-legged on the floor. Shreene hands the priest a glass of tea on a steel saucer, and they begin.

His reading is kind and questioning. Shreene translates for Rumi, with a voice that is deeper than normal, laying her words down like a protective lining in the background of the room. First he does Badi, taking her hand as she kneels in her lilac salwar kameez, making a smile squeeze girlishly onto her face. He tells her she is the noble one of the family, the one who is responsible for making sure everything fits together. He urges her to think about starting the search for her daughter's marriage partner, although it will be later than is best when it does happen. He warns that her money worries will deepen with the forthcoming years. And he soothes her with the assurance that her son will bring happiness to mitigate the bad times.

When he takes Shreene's hand, he smiles at her and examines her face in a way that would be indecent were it not for his advanced years. He looks into her eyes till she crinkles them with embarrassment. Shreene is told that she is a fiery one, with anger and love devouring her energy. He tells her she should wear a large opal set in silver so that the stone touches the skin of the middle finger on her left hand.

"Are you from abroad?" he asks, and when Shreene translates it into English, Rumi breathes in sharply. She leans forward, supporting her face with her hands so her cheeks roll up, pressing the bottom of her eyes under the specs and blurring her vision. Shreene smiles at her daughter and nods, yes.

"You have been very lucky since her birth," the priest says, pointing to Rumi. "She has brought auspiciousness into your house. And there is more to come, if you control your hot side." Shreene smiles, her cheeks rushing with blood. His final words make her jump. "Although you have suffered loss recently, you are not alone," he says. "You will experience a change very soon that will bring the happiness you seek."

He tells Shreene she should make a pilgrimage to Mansadevi, the place of wishes, at the foothills of the Himalayas, and listen to her heart, ask for something big. Shreene takes this news and almost bows, confused, as she gets up to make room for her daughter. She urges Rumi to touch the old man's feet with her right hand and skim her fingertips against her forehead. Rumi follows the actions and sits attentively.

At this point in the telling of the story, Shreene usually mimicked the face of the priest when he first saw Rumi's hand. The look teetered between comedy and horror, moving from frown to smile, narrow eyes opening out, then crushed to a quivering slit of focus.

"We were terrified," Shreene said, "Badi and I. Can you imagine? We didn't know what he would say. That you would die, or something so bad was going to happen? You don't know with these palm readings. Sometimes they see such horrible things."

Every time she heard it, Rumi would ask the same question, willing herself to believe that her mum's version of what took place next was true.

"And what did he say, Mum?"

"He said that he had never seen anything like it. That he was looking at the hand of a genius. That it was so full of buddhi—knowledge—he didn't know how to tell us. He said that you would become known for this. Your name would be known."

In the train-journey scene her mother's details merged with Rumi's own memories to create a humid picture drenched in melodrama and fatigue. Rumi remembered the heat trapping her thoughts so that she could not speak. She remembered the feeling of being suffocated by her own breath as she lay on the bench in the second-class carriage. She didn't remember when the train had broken down, or the conversation between her mother and the newlywed couple sitting opposite had disintegrated. As for the panic, the nasty daydreams, the way she was supposed to have muttered about water and ice cream, pleading and babbling nonsense at her mother, Rumi was pretty sure she had been told all this afterward. Either way, every time she thought about the experience, the horror rose in her throat: bittersweet, dark, like black licorice swallowed whole, returning undigested to color her mouth.

In the story, they are on the way to Mansadevi when people realize the train has stopped. It is the culmination of a day of slow wheezes and pauses, the train inching and braking with unbearable sloth. Tiffins have been emptied, masala crisps gorged, flasks sucked dry of sterilized water. They are fifteen hours behind schedule and have only mango pickle and a small packet of peanuts left between them. Rumi thinks about the nuts hidden in the small foil package, bathed in salt, nauseating. Allocating 91 square mm for each peanut half (7 by 13), in a packet that is around, say, 12 cm by 18 cm, she estimates 237 pieces to be in the packet (if you were to round it down). There are 4 of them in the compartment, meaning they could eat 59 pieces each, and have 1 left over, when the time comes. And then there will be nothing. She wonders if she should share this information with her mum.

Without the movement of the train, the heat is free to smother the carriage, entering the static space and hanging like a slow, wet fog in the travelers' faces. The meshed fans in the ceiling no longer move: deprived of the power supplied by the engine they have been colonized by flies, buzzing round the blades. Rumi lies on the bench and stares through the bars of the window at the tracks and sky outside. She sees grass, flowers, trees sliced through with metal. The brown paint is peeling on the solid bars, causing her to contract her eyes, shifting her focus between inside and out like a game. At intervals she feels little whispers of touch over her face: mosquitoes causing her to shudder and scratch her cheeks and lips in a frenzy until she collapses back into stillness. She thinks about how she might die. Maybe it will be due to lack of food or water. Or a bite from a dangerous mosquito. Or maybe they will faint one by one in the carriage, and just die from fainting.

On the other side of the track there is a hut hooded in black plastic. Next to it sit two little girls in pinafore frocks having their hair unplaited, oiled and checked for nits by an older girl, who could be fourteen or fifteen. She has two fat bunches of black hair skimming her shoulders, white flowers coiled at the root where each bunch sprouts from her head. Rumi watches the whole procedure, sees the sun glinting on their teeth, black kajol thick on their lower eyelids. One of the little ones laughs, and the pink and blue bangles lined up her arms shake down to the elbows and back. Rumi imagines a river nearby where they will go and play next, wading through and drinking the water, cupping it in their hands. She wants to wave at them, shout, but her throat is blocked with indefinite air, her body suspended.

Shreene is the one who reacts to the sound of the ticket inspector first, a few booths down. His voice is nasal, pitched at a tempo that tries to remain constant in spite of the sounds attacking it. People urge him to give them information, send water, let them know what kind of bribe he is expecting. They ask what measures have been taken, how long they can expect to carry on like this, whether he has any idea of how aging mothers, toddlers, diabetics can cope with the conditions. Shreene sits up, tucking the strands of hair round her face back into her ponytail. Her movements seem to inspire the newlyweds to action—the husband takes charge of straightening them both, crooking his arm round the shoulders of his wife and stroking the silver border of her weighty silk sari.

The inspector is brusque, sweat stains hollowing out large concave shapes down the side of his shirt. Rumi tries not to stare at him too much, looking upward from the bench, but all eyes in the carriage are on him as he mutters at Shreene. Unlike the newlyweds, he is saying, Shreene and Rumi are not reserved on the sleeper bunks even though they have tickets. This means they owe him money. He talks to Shreene in English, his syllables squashed together in a rich, jagged rhythm.

"Madam, you are owing the following berths, as I say. We are waiting further dispensation from, as you know, the commissioner sahib. Now if you would, please, reimburse me to the amount owing, I would be fully gratified."

He smiles at Rumi, his mustache slick with sweat, side parting cleanly splitting his head into a third and two thirds respectively.

"Baby is OK, I take it?" he asks, gesturing at Rumi by making his eyebrows jump in her direction. Shreene responds by smiling and looking directly at him, bashfully.

"Well, I would like to give her some water if there is any chance, bhai-sahib?" she says.

"Madam, seems to me you are from abroad, am I right?" he says.

"Yes."

"And you are only drinking bottled water in that case I am imagining—Bisleri, Aqua, these kinds of brands. You are used to something that is only available in a bottle for safety for your stomach, madam, am I right? Otherwise you fear diarrhea, loose motions, maybe choleric infection, right?"

"Yes."

"Or might be you drink cold drinks—Mrinda, Thumbs Up, Gold Spot, Limca . . . For baby perhaps she is preferring this?"

"Yes," says Shreene.

"In that case, madam, how can I help you? You understand that we are stuck in an isolated place. There is no soft-drinks stand here!"

His face twinkles and he emits a short, abrupt laugh, gesturing at the newlyweds to join in. They look at Shreene awkwardly.

"You agree with me, madam, we are not in the Lessisster Square of London, are we?"

"No, bhai-sahib, I know we are not," Shreene says. "But anything you can do I will appreciate."

At this point the story was blurred in Rumi's mind. She knew the inspector had been trying to do some sums as he was carrying money from five different carriages, payments for which he had no change. According to Shreene, Rumi had got involved, asking him to show her exactly how many notes and coins he had. Then, with a quick shuffle, including their own contribution, she had neatly distributed the change so that nearly every transaction could be completed. Apparently this had been enough to put him in a good mood; he had chuckled at Rumi's demonstration and cheekiness, pleased by the entertainment, but also the outcome.

"Baby is indeed very brainy," he said. "We must feed this brain so it doesn't dry up!"

And that was how they left the compartment, making their apologies to the bewildered newlyweds, who looked pleased for them but understandably irate. That was how they ended up in first class for the rest of the journey, soaked in cool wonder, a dedicated generator purring in the corridor of their cabin and electrifying the air with a magic chill. That was how tall bottles of Bisleri water appeared miraculously for "the little maharani" to drink as soon as they transferred to where Rumi lay on the cushioned gray seats and looked out of the vacuum-sealed windows in silence.

The Mountain Top is the section of the story that is most disheveled in Rumi's mind. Even though they had gone there at noon, steamy green rising to infuse the clouds as they walked up to the peak, Rumi can't remember all of the elements that fit together to make that day. The main image itself is abiding: the tree. She can see that clearly enough: towering in the mist, and laden with a million straggling threads. It looks to her like the Faraway Tree on the cover of her book about the enchanted wood: a tree that comes alive at night with secret inhabitants, their lives intertwined in moonshine as they hop from branch to branch.

Rumi had a sense of the events and conversations, but it was Shreene who had painted in the rest, picking out moments in careful detail. So, now Rumi can see herself in a troupe of four, carrying saffron flowers, tiffins and water between them, wearing a cotton pinafore with her fringe pinned back and sweat kissing her forehead. She is walking on a path thick with dust, feeling joyous—so happy she skips now and then, curling her toes in her sandals and socks for the sheer brilliance of it all. She is on a real pilgrimage, taking a dirt track that curls round a real mountain right to the top. They are all going to make a wish. And everyone in the gang seems to think that dreams can come true, otherwise they wouldn't be doing it. It doesn't get better than this.

The group includes Badi and her eighteen-year-old son, Jagdish. The hill that leads to the Mansadevi shrine is just outside Haridwar, their hometown, which is sacred because the river Ganges flows through it. Rumi watches her cousin as he walks, twirling a stick in his hand like a magician, batting away flies and encroaching plants. He wears a cotton shirt in dark red, tucked into pale jeans, or "jean-pant" as Badi Auntie calls them. She has bought him a new jean-pant to celebrate his recent news: he has been admitted to Delhi University to study engineering. This means that Jaggi is in the top two percent in the country. It also means that instead of graduating on to run the family wholesale store, selling sweetmeats with his father in Haridwar, he has bought himself some freedom. Rumi venerates him, giggling when he talks and flushing with excitement when he teases her. He is tall, curly-haired, with her mum's olive skin and blue eyes. She always calls him Bhaiya, as she has been taught, enjoying the mixture of intimacy and formality that comes with the use of this title: Elder Brother. He calls her Minnie, as in Minnie Mouse. Today he is mischievous, and ready to play.

"Mansa means mind or wish," Jaggi Bhaiya is saying. "And Devi, as you know, means goddess. So Mansadevi, whom we are visiting, is the goddess of wishes. But also the goddess of thought. Mansadevi will know your mind when you stand before her, Minnie."

"But what if there are too many thoughts messing up your mind, Bhaiya?" asks Rumi.

"At that moment you must stand extremely still and your heart will release one wish into your mind, like a bluebird into the sky. If you are very still, this bluebird will speak for you, and when it speaks it will be a pure sound."

Rumi skips ahead, running and laughing for five meters, then waits for them to catch up. The air is hazy with possibility. There are no right answers today. No one is going to say, "Don't be silly," or "Think again." Anything may happen. Who knows what their combined wishes will create, soaring uncontrolled in the mist at the top of the mountain, once they stand before the goddess?

Two-thirds of the way up they stop for lunch under a tree, throwing out the peacock-print sheet that Badi has brought. Rumi sits cross-legged with Jaggi Bhaiya and asks him to time her as she does the Rubik's cube. They have been doing this periodically since she arrived in India. Her scores have varied, occasionally putting up a good fight against the current record of 26.04 seconds. She loves the ritual, and watches him now as he conscientiously confuses the colors, his fingers and thumbs fluttering in the sun. Then he makes the sign for her to get ready, and brings his arm down fast as though signaling for the start of a rally. The beginning always shocks her.

"And STOP!" shouts Rumi, holding up the completed article.

Jaggi Bhaiya examines his digital watch, peering closely at the surface.

"What is it, then?" asks Rumi.

"Looks like thirty-four point six three," he replies, showing her the time.

"Not bad," says Rumi, putting the puzzle on the ground. She looks at the beautiful gloss of pure red, orange and yellow, the unbroken plates of color that shine out from the cube as it sits on the sheet. In the heat the black lines between each square are blurring stickily in her vision.

Rumi and Jaggi Bhaiya talk about world records, in particular about Shakuntala Devi, the maths genius who multiplied two thirteen-digit numbers in twenty-eight seconds the year before. Rumi has seen Shakuntala Devi on TV, her kindly smile gracing the airwaves like the most favorite auntie you can imagine, big red bindi shining out from the center of her forehead with the super-force of blood. Rumi has a funny feeling when she sees Shakuntala Devi on the screen. It is as though she is related to her. Or something. Even her mum and dad are charged and excited when they see her on the box, thrilled by the contradictions of cotton sari, center parting, blond hair-sprayed host and acrobatic maths.

"But why did they treat her like that? In itself, it is proof of the superiority complex that the West has over us," Jaggi Bhaiya is saying.

"What is superiority complex?" Rumi asks.

"When a culture thinks they are better than you. The British still think they are better than us, that we are dirty, cheating scoundrels. That is why they insulted Shakuntala Devi in this way. You cannot deny it!"

He is referring to the text added next to the entry in *The Guinness Book of Records*. Rumi knows the words, having heard Jaggi recite them and having read them in her own edition: "Some experts on calculating prodigies refuse to give credence to the above—largely on the grounds that it is so vastly superior to the calculating feats of any other invigilated prodigy."

Jaggi Bhaiya quotes the entry in *The Limca Book of Records,* India's soft-drink-sponsored equivalent. He seems to know it by heart: "'We respectfully point out that Mrs. Devi has been invigilated a number of times, has appeared on numerous live television shows, performing "new" calculations based on the works of various mathematics professors, and has consistently performed at the level indicated in her record-breaking performance. We support Mrs. Devi in her natural excellence, and hope that researchers will increasingly realize that their amazement and amusement should lie not in the outstanding excellence of any human mental performance, but in the rarity of similar performances.'"

Rumi knows what these lines mean because Jaggi has explained them to her. She still feels the unfairness of it, on cue, when she hears the two entries compared. But she only really enjoys the bit about "amazement and amusement," picturing her parents' eyes widening in bewilderment and creasing into laughter in time with the phrase. Shakuntala Devi multiplied 2,465,099,754,779 by 7,686,369,774,870 in twenty-eight seconds. This is something that never fails to make Rumi's heart miss a beat when she thinks about it. And she didn't even go to school, let alone university. Her father was a trapeze artist and human cannonball. She grew up in the circus, memorizing card packs, making money from it at the age of three. By the time she was five, her whole family was surviving on her earnings. These facts make goosebumps swirl across Rumi's skin and dance to the beat of the words "amazement and amusement." Jaggi carries on the argument, his mother passing him a plastic hand-fan as the passion rises.

"The point is, in 1977, only four years ago, she won a standing ovation from a whole room of mathematicians when she did that extraction. It was the twenty-third root of a two-hundred-and-one-digit number. This is not a joke, yaar. She solved it in fifty seconds flat and everyone knows that their fastest computer took sixty-two seconds. So, how is she cheating? Just tell me."

Rumi nods, frowning and trying to understand why Norris McWhirter, the man who presents the TV show, would say Shakuntala Devi is a liar. It doesn't add up. He seems so friendly with his gray puff of hair and soothing tones, his soft pats on the back for pogo-stickers and baked-bean eaters round the world. Her forehead is covered with a dense constellation of sweat drops. She feels worried about how angry Jaggi Bhaiya gets when he talks about this particular subject. And she feels guilty, for a reason she can't locate. She goes to remove her socks but Shreene notices and forbids it with a shake of the head—she is worried about the many mosquito bites Rumi has accumulated on her feet during the visit.

"The point is, Shakuntala Devi does it again and again, with countless controls, and they say these 'experts' refuse to believe it," Jaggi continues. "I mean, she herself says it is because of her devotion mostly to Lord Ganesh—she closes her eyes and the answer flashes into her mind. This is something they are not willing to believe. It terrifies them, the power of faith."

"Is Shakuntala Devi also a goddess?" asks Rumi.

"Well, no . . ."

"But she has Devi next to her name."

"Devi can also be a middle name. But she does have spiritual powers, for sure. That much is certain," replies Jaggi.

Near the top of the hill they are caught in the engorgement of people who press together in the closeness of the end. There is a line of stalls at either side with sellers who create the rhythmic sound track to the final ascent.

"Madam, madam, souvenir, madam?"

"Photo, madam, photo memory of baby?"

"Tip-top guide, madam, fifteen minutes' history of Mansadevi."

"Flowers, coconut, sweets. Food of the gods. Offerings for Devi to bless."

Shreene stops and buys a coconut broken into six pieces that are still connected at the base, the center filled with red and white rose petals. Rumi takes a sample, clutches it in her left hand and clings to her mother's with the right. They squash through to the first entrance of a caved area where they take off their shoes. Badi is the first to move in and rings a large gold bell above her head, letting the chime trickle through the mesh of other bells being rung at the same time. She walks through and stands with her hands together in na-maste in front of the stone carving inset in the wall of the cave. Jaggi Bhaiya goes next. He rings the bell loud and clear, then picks up Rumi and holds her above his shoulders. She is worried her glasses will slip down her nose and onto the floor, and embarrassed to be the only one in socks. When she sounds the bell and feels it resonate through her hand like a mini thunderstorm, she trembles. Jaggi puts her down.

They join Badi at the altar and Rumi leans forward over the rail-ing to see Mansadevi. She spots a tiny triangle of gold leaf. When she leans closer, she sees it is crowning a string of five minuscule faces engraved in the rock. Draped round this is a pyramid of red chiffon fringed with gold. A lavish bundle of three garlands almost sub-merges the deity with curling saffron marigolds. Rumi breathes in and looks up at Jaggi Bhaiya. He is standing still, focusing his lean body in the direction of the goddess as though he wants to catch an invisible beam coming from her. Rumi whispers, "Is it now that I do it? Is it now that I ask the Devi?"

"Just offer your respects here," he whispers back. "Wait till you get to the tree outside."

They are moved on elegantly by a priest, who wafts a blessing gathered from a prayer flame over each of their heads. Then Rumi walks through the arch at the other end of the cave into the hazy vapor of the world outside and sees the tree.

"Now is the time," says Jaggi Bhaiya.

Rumi takes the red thread that he gives her and walks forward alone till she is standing in front of the tower of leaves and threads that zoom above to infinity. She knows what to do. The branches are layered with thousands of lines of red, wrapped round themselves like never-ending caterpillars. She closes her eyes, focuses on the space between them in the dark, takes a deep breath and holds it, waiting.

4

Nibu appeared in Shreene's belly when her father died, in the summer of 1981, but she didn't realize he was there until a few months later. When he made himself known, she couldn't resist the popular interpretation that Papa had sent himself back, reincarnated, to look after her. In fact, it was Badi who came up with this idea, written in fast, slanting blue, the ink bleeding through airmail paper in a letter full of news. She wrote about the will, the feuds and especially the rivalry that had insinuated itself into their lives, as inevitable as nightfall, after Papa's death. And then she dropped her bomb: "At least you have Papa within you, Shree," she wrote. "You are the one he came back to be with. You were always his favorite, even though you went so far away. You were always the lucky one." Although she knew Mahesh wouldn't approve, Shreene grasped at this idea with both hands. There was no denying that Nibu was a gesture of goodwill from above, sent to her in her time of need. In this new desert, where her estrangement seemed so complete, Nibu glinted and tingled in her stomach, like a jewel in velvet.

That year Shreene was thirty and the trip to her father's funeral had been her first back home after nine years' separation. When she arrived at Delhi airport, even though the grief clamped her throat so that her gullet swelled through a vise with each breath, Shreene had been mesmerized by the smell of pollution and dust fighting through the sweaty air-conditioning. She breathed it in, captured it in her gut and tried to solidify it to stem the hunger. Because even though she was there, she still craved it for the imminent future. She knew her arrival home meant only one thing: that she would have to leave. She looked at Rumi, sitting limply on the baggage trolley, faint in the heat, and wondered if she understood the significance of the moment. In Shreene's head, trees swayed to a Raj Kapoor dusk on a sixties film set. Outside the auto-rickshaws sang in harmony, soothing her with their horns and curves. Her papa had died. He hadn't seen her for nine years. There was no way to tell him anything now. It was not possible to lay her head on his lap, and explain it all bit by bit. But in the cruel beauty of the moment, just standing there, after so many years of exile, she realized that everything was the same.

On the day Nibu was born, Rumi revealed to her, incredulous as she stared into his cot in the hospital, that she had wished for a baby brother in the final leg of their trip, at the Mansadevi shrine. And Shreene's own memory of the trip intensified super-fast, multiplying its significance till it was almost unbearably sentimental, bound up as it was with the end of a father and the beginning of a son.

THE LAST TIME Shreene had spoken to her father was in a phone box in Splott, on the dodgy side of town. Rumi had been just seven, walking back with her from the Sunday market. They were carrying plastic bags of batteries, vegetables and cutlery, shortcutting through side streets, tired but content after the day's events. It was early evening, already dark, spitting with rain, the drops covering their faces with a light spray. Rumi was humming and kicking along, her white socks rolled down to her ankles, a grazed bruise marking her knee where she had fallen over near the homewares stall. Shreene was trying to get her back as soon as possible, in time for a couple of hours' maths practice, slotted in from seven till nine in Rumi's timetable.

She was also aware that, in a few moments, it would be too late to be caught among these run-down streets, the pebble-dashed fronts of the houses blending into the wretched shade of gray that seemed to own the sky in this part of the world. Ahead of her, a crossroads parting into spidery legs—more streets, filled with more identical dwelling places, semi-illuminated by dirty lights through net curtains—residential roads that were mostly empty, save for lone stragglers. On the corner a couple of teenagers were kicking a ball against a boarded-up shop. It smacked against the wet planks, hitting multicolored expletives and crude shapes that had been marked out with spray paint. One of the boys looked at Shreene as she approached, his eyes almost invisible in the shadow formed by the peak of his cap. She crossed to the other side and pulled Rumi close to her.

Even though it was not hot, something about the warmth, the rain and the moon was tugging at Shreene's heart, making an echo of yearning, a feeling she couldn't identify. She tried to locate it. The sense was of warm rain, being outdoors, children in the street. Then it swamped her. Monsoon. She froze, feeling her body betray her. It was the sudden desolation that often overtook her without warning, come back to ruin her on the way home, bleaching her surroundings with white cold, licking every street, house and passerby into numb caricatures of their incarnations just thirty seconds previously. Although she was used to this feeling, right now it caused her immense strain; it was as if her heart would pop in the silence. They walked past a telephone box and Shreene diverted into it, taking Rumi inside.

"What is it, Mum?" Rumi asked. Her voice held a wary tension.

"Nothing, Rumi, don't worry." Shreene fumbled in her purse for change. She found two coins, ten pence each. Mahesh would not approve of this kind of weakness if he found out: succumbing like this to such a melodramatic tug of the heart. But, then, he would not know. Although he controlled the finances, and the activities for which they might be used, she still had twenty pence, which could easily be lost in the day's purchases. She dialed the number, trying to control her breathing. Such a long number with all those zeros and ones added on to it. Such an amazing number, as Rumi would say. It felt so strange that the same number could still exist, untampered with—familiar from Shreene's college days in her parental home. When the pips went the first time, she pressed the button to return the coin, confused and worried that it might go through. She stood next to the phone and looked at the world through the telephone box, raindrops on the glass spotting the unwieldy trees outside in a blur.

"What's wrong, Mum? Who are you calling?" Rumi asked.

"Nobody," Shreene replied, a forceful note creeping into her voice.

"But, Mum, why won't you tell me? What's going on?"

Rumi's voice was edged with a high pitch, nervous and irritable. Shreene put the coins in again and dialed the number. This time the pips went for a long time, she counted fifteen. Then it started to ring with a faraway Toy Town ring that echoed each time it sang. "It's ringing! Rumi, it's ringing!" Shreene gripped her daughter's hand and smiled at her through the sound.

At the other end she heard the phone click, and then the voice: "Hello?" Before she could speak, it came again. "Hello? Kaun? Hello?"

When she spoke, the word rang feebly against the prickly burr of a dead line. "Papa!" she said, too late, and leaned against the body of the phone, her frame collapsing out of sync. She felt foolish.

"Mum, what's wrong?" said Rumi.

Shreene couldn't respond. She pressed her cheek against the receiver and stared at the graffiti written into the side of the machine. "I luv robbie J" traced out in Tipp-Ex. The letters were strong and fierce.

"Mummy, please tell me . . . Why are you crying, Mum?" Rumi pulled her mother's hand and tried to get her to turn round. "Mummy, please? What happened?"

Shreene knew she had responsibilities. She knew there was a way to behave in a lone phone box in Splott with your seven-year-old daughter and the sky dangerously dark around you. But the tears were tumbling through a simple rip in her control. She willed them to stop, as her body wobbled silently. "I spoke to my papa, beti," she said, choking with sobs. "I heard his voice but then the money ran out." Now her voice was strangled. "I miss him, beti."

Rumi put her arms round her mother, reaching up to her shoulders. She hugged her as best she could, but as though she expected to be pushed away. Instead Shreene put her hand on Rumi's head and pulled her close. "Don't tell Daddy," she said, stroking Rumi's hair.

For a good few minutes Rumi stayed like that, her cheeks pressed hard on her glasses against her mother's chest, until they gathered their things and left.

Now THAT THINGS were starting to worry her, Shreene often thought about that hug Rumi had given her, three years ago. The anxiety wasn't just because her daughter was growing up in a foreign country. It was more to do with Rumi's lack of femininity, her awkwardness and her general . . . *croadh*. She considered how to translate this word into English. It was an old-fashioned word. A *Mahabharata,* gods-and-demons type of word. But not a word Rumi would understand. The communication gap caused Shreene an almost physical pain when she thought of it. Even after years of working the phone lines, talking to strangers every day, she could not express herself happily to her own daughter. Instead she came out with platitudes. Awkward generalities.

"This country has messed everything up," she would hear herself saying, when they were alone in the kitchen. "Confused you. You don't even know who your parents are. What your country is. You are becoming like the goré. The white people. How will we find a boy for you? You don't apply gram flour and yogurt to your face, so it stays patchy and dark. And you don't wear your slippers, so your feet are growing out of control. Soon they will be too big for shoes and then who will marry you? You don't listen to your mother and you will regret it, you'll see."

In fact, she often regretted it when she descended to that level, using the archaic warnings that had infuriated her when she was growing up. It was a low shot. She had hated the emphasis on physical perfection when she had been up for her own marriage. They had made her walk through the old house in Delhi with books on her head, oil her hair and plait it methodically with jasmine, carry tea in for potential suitors. She had felt demeaned and ridiculed, producing her sewing diploma and bachelor's degree as equal receipts for mothers-in-law to examine. And she couldn't deny that, during that period, she had resented her father. The worst had been when she had come home from college, aged twenty, waving her application for pre-med school at him while he was drinking his evening rose milkshake on the veranda. She was breathless and excited, having learned that her arts background was no barrier to sitting the pre-med exam. But Papa had dismissed her genially. "If you become a doctor, how will we find a doctor for you to marry? You will be over-the-top qualified, beti. It is time for you to get married now."

He had kissed her, ruffled her hair and broken her heart. And so Shreene had found herself living in a cinematic cliché, the too-modern girl disturbing the fine balance of Indian harmony. In the end she had been reduced to arguing with her parents for the next best thing, demanding that they find her someone intelligent to marry, instead of a vulgar businessman. "Brains not money!" she had squealed, in the tortured nightly debates, crying like an infant when she thought of her future, the roulette wheel of parental contacts that would dictate who came knocking on her door first. Everyone knew that if she rejected more than one or two boys, or vice versa, word would spread and no one would want her.

Rumi thought these things happened only in Hindi films. Some part of Shreene wanted Rumi to know that her maths and long words and storybooks weren't going to save her when she grew up. She worried about her daughter's routine. If she wasn't studying, she was eating. If she wasn't eating she hungered for television, demanding access to her weekly two-and-a-half-hour allowance of programs. If she wasn't allowed TV, she wanted books. The girl didn't talk, or seem to want to make conversation with anyone, even in her breaks—she just wanted to absorb all these make-believe stories, these kysas, sagas of other lives. Why were they so important to her? Shreene had taken literature as part of her own degree, but she had never been reliant on novels in this strange way—and what good had it done her anyway, spending her precious university years studying all those useless, fictional worlds?

She had even discovered Rumi reading with a flashlight under her duvet, late into the night, devouring her latest acquisitions from the library—books that, alarmingly, seemed to change their covers almost every day. At these moments, when Shreene pulled back the quilt, Rumi looked up, her face asking Shreene not to reveal the shame of her overindulgence for fear of losing her library card to Mahesh's fury. And Shreene consented, also wordlessly, to keep it between them. She felt sorry for her daughter's addiction. She didn't understand the need for these books, but she understood Rumi's need for . . . well, something.

Still, Shreene didn't know how to get close to her daughter. Over the past few years, Mahesh had become so obsessed with Rumi's routine and their responsibility as a household to uphold it that they didn't see any of their original circle of friends anymore: he worried too much about the disruption. Not only was this lonely for someone as lively as Shreene, she argued with Mahesh that it was a staggering loss for the family. Their friends had been from the sub-continent—Indian, Sri Lankan, even Bangladeshi students from Mahesh's early years at the university, when they had cooked for each other in rotation, shared their stories and hopes for the future over simple daals and rotis. But now not only were they bereft of friends, Mahesh's single-minded regime meant that there was no one Indian in Rumi's life other than her immediate family. Occasionally, once every couple of months, he rented a video player and a Hindi movie for them to watch together as a family. But it wasn't enough.

Shreene wanted to explain to Rumi that even though she was only ten she wasn't immune. It would all be over so soon. When the time came for marriage, she feared her daughter would be rejected left, right and center for her gawky gait, thick glasses, her generally antisocial behavior, and the thready clumps of hair that fringed her messy complexion. They would make life hell for her, and she would become a joke—asexual and foreign; like a eunuch, neither this nor that, neither here nor there. It was her mother's responsibility to steer her and show her how to be a girl, an Indian girl at that.

But instead it was as though she embarrassed Rumi. Lately Mahesh had agreed that she should try for promotion and Shreene had started wearing the full works to the office: satin blouses—pink,

black-and-white check or leopard print from Marks & Spencer—
tight knee-length pencil skirts, ten-denier tights and pointed sling-
backs that hurt her feet. Hair spray and mascara to go with kohl and
lipstick. This was all new. But it wasn't enough. Rumi had said she
looked "glamorous and amazing" on the first day, yet after that, the
usual disdain. Now Shreene barely recognized herself in the hall
mirror before she left in the morning for work. And life seemed to
get more and more complicated. Sometimes, when she thought
about all these things, she made herself cry. Mahesh used to say he
loved her eyes, blue and wild. Now he said she was "making a drama
out of small things."

"My father said, 'If one tear escapes my daughter's eye it is like a
precious stone—you cannot let it get away,' " she used to say to Mahesh, when they were newlyweds, and he had craved her every
thought and move, lying so close to her in bed and stroking her hair
as she talked. But now even her tears had ceased to be relevant to
them. Only Nibu was young enough to gobble her up, kissing away
her heart's hysteria, blinking his long black lashes with giggles and
burps.

5

Shreene heated some oil at the bottom of a large steel pan, her face glistening with pleasure. "Watch this!" she said to Rumi, who was sitting on a stool, balancing Nibu on the worktop and feeding him milk from a plastic mug emblazoned with a picture of He-Man. The superhero was brandishing a sword toward a turbulent sky, stretching his torso up and away from his metal pants, muscles straining vehemently as though desperate to explode out of the breastplate that crossed his chest. Nibu was sucking the milk intently through the spout at the top of the mug, looking at the picture as he did so, with a meditative stare that made his eyes point inward.

Shreene tipped a large batch of corn kernels into the heart of the pan and watched as they cascaded into hard, popping fountains, shooting bullets off the ceiling, sounding a violent *ra-ta-ta-ta-ta*. A couple of pieces jumped out and hit her forehead, bouncing their polystyrene curves down her face, then falling to the floor. Rumi gave a little shriek of excitement. "Mum, are you all right?"

"Oh, I am very all right, thank you very much, little monkey," said Shreene, shaking her hips and head in a comic manner, feigning espionage-style acrobatics, as though she was dodging the kernels that were now flying out of the pan and landing in the mesh of the cooker's grate and on the kitchen floor. She giggled, and took the pan off the hob.

"Taste these, little bandar!" she said, pinching Rumi's waist and popping two pieces into her mouth. Rumi looked into the pan and saw a mass of inflated white, a snowstorm of fluff, puffed out like the wool of storybook sheep, each piece indented with an orange center, a hard ball of corn. Nibu laughed and did a little dance, his bare feet pressed against the marbled swirl of the worktop.

"And for you, little maharajah!" said Shreene, inserting a piece into his mouth. There was a squeal as he tried to negotiate the alien element, chewing clumsily and steadying himself with a hand on Rumi's head, his fingers pulling her hairclip, causing her to lose her balance.

"Nibu, stop it!" said Rumi, laughing, her face angled upward as he pulled her hair.

"Go and get ready now," commanded Shreene. "We mustn't be late. Papa is on his way home with the tickets."

"What's it like in the cinema, Mum?" asked Rumi. She could feel a thrilling tingle exploring her arms to her fingers since she had said "cinema," this previously marginal word—a word that now had something to do with them. She was covered with a warm flicker from head to foot, a thick line of fire traced round her body.

"Oh, it will be great, just you see," said Shreene, picking up Nibu and holding the mug to his lips. "You will learn all about your own past. Our own past. This film is about the greatest man who ever lived. Mahatma Gandhi. The father of the nation. It is no joke, what you are about to find out, I can tell you!"

Rumi stood in the doorway, pulling her socks up. "Mum, what is it like in the cinema, though?"

"Oh, it is very exciting. You know, in India I used to go to the cinema when I was growing up. It was much cheaper than it is here."

"Were you allowed to go whenever you wanted?"

"Come on, beti, now isn't the time for this. You have to get ready!"

"Go on, Mum, just quickly, and then I'll go." Rumi pushed her glasses and stabilized them at the highest point of her nose. "Go on, then," she said.

"It wasn't come-and-go-as-you-please to the picture hall. There were many things that would affect it—like the cost, or how long we were allowed to be out of the house. Especially when I got to a certain age and then there was so much housework. From us four, we sisters, only one of us was allowed to go each week. So whoever went would come back and, while we were working in the kitchen, it would be her responsibility to tell us the whole story!"

"Like memorizing it?"

"Oh, yes. And not just the story. For example, Badi would come home and she would start with the music, and it would be like this: here I am, for example, cleaning the daal, and then I say, 'What were Dimple Kapadia and Rishi Kapoor wearing?' and she will explain like this, saying, 'Her kameez dress top came to here, and then it was, oh, so tight on the chest, very daring, and her sleeves were cut like this, exposing the arms so prettily.' Then she will tell a bit of the story and throw in particularly strong dialogues like this." Shreene assumed a booming, angst-ridden voice: " 'What is the sense in life without you?' " She continued in a shrill wilder one: " 'You have broken my heart, Krishan!' " She giggled and emptied the pan, using the sleeve of her shirt to wipe her forehead. "Then one of us will ask, 'Oh, Badi, sing us one of the songs at least,' and Badi will have to sing and do the dance round the trees with all the latest moves, and show how the hero gazed at the heroine as if he was going to die without her, and how the heroine turns away with shyness and runs through a field, the pallu of her sari flying behind her, just like this, you know."

Rumi chuckled as Shreene took on the pose of a dazzling maiden, her head thrown back and right arm flung out to the side.

"It was quite a good acting job, I can tell you. Now go and get ready. Your father will not be pleased if we aren't ready when he returns. And you need to be vigilant, as he says. This is a true story we are going to see. Something very important."

They walked to the cinema in a short cross of a foursome: Mahesh striding ahead with purpose while Rumi trailed behind Shreene and Nibu, studiously documenting her environment. It was late afternoon, a Sunday "matnee" as Shreene kept calling it. They were walking through Queen Street, a built-up area where the pavement was made up of large concrete blocks separated only by drains, at fourteen-slab intervals, counted and double-checked for symmetry by Rumi, who also made sure to walk inside each rectangular plate and not touch the dividing lines with her shoes. She could see a few trees, planted next to lampposts in large transparent plastic boxes, raised so that their roots disappeared into a mass of earth that began at the height of her shoulders. An assortment of closed shops lined each side, clothes hanging sadly in the gray half-light of the windows, stragglers stopping to stare at the display models, the toffee-colored smoothness of the mannequins' faces so empty of expression that they looked as though at any minute they might topple over and die of boredom.

We are not bored today, thought Rumi, as she stopped with Shreene to admire a display of mother-and-daughter statuettes dressed in full ski regalia. We are doing something really important. She surveyed the lime green outfit worn by the daughter (who looked about her age), magnetized by the large cards at the front of the window, words like "Salopettes!" brandishing their exclamation marks at her with an urgency that demanded she do something. Hat! £2.99. Jacket! £33.99 (so expensive . . .). Salopettes! £19.99 (quite a lot, these things were . . .). Scarf! £4.99. Sweater! £9.99. Even Socks! were £1.99. The full amount, 73 pounds and 94 pence, was a huge amount of money. Almost too large to visualize. Somehow the number didn't do it justice. Rumi wondered what the shop was like when it was open, imagining supremely rich gusts of customers, women like the ones in *Dynasty,* flashing their gold chains and greasy red lips at the attendants, perfume saturating the air drunkenly as they bagged their 73-pound-94 outfits for all the family.

Mahesh turned and walked back, moving stiffly to stand with them by the window. He cleared his throat lavishly, making the sound stagger over several notes. "You know everything in this shop is made in India?"

Rumi shook her head, running her tongue over her front lower gum, confronted yet again with the return of the quiver in her skin, the excitement of the event yet to come, the memory of India as a word set in the clouds, far, far away.

Shreene sniffed. "These winter clothes?" she said.

"Yes. If you check the labels you'll see everything is made in India. And you know what else? They pay the workers hardly anything, a few rupees, tiny children forced into labor, barely making enough to eat and live. And then here they make the prices so much—all that profit they cream off for themselves so shamelessly. It is abysmal. An internationally sanctioned theft of human rights and liberty." He snorted and looked at Shreene, awaiting a response.

Rumi gazed guiltily up at the towering letters drawn in a swirl of rainbow colors, a huge "C" and "A" linked with a (and now somehow perverse) curly flourish: "&."

"Well, I was only looking," said Shreene, pulling Nibu's hand and walking primly ahead. "What are you saying? It's not as though we're going to have to stop our big spending sprees now we have this knowledge, is it? Still, every penny ends up in your precious savings accounts. What are you telling me all this for, making this point to me?"

She laughed, a bitter rind to the sound. Rumi held her breath in her chest and looked at Mahesh, fearful that it was all going to come tumbling down, that they would now sit in the cinema in silence, Shreene's mouth curdled with irritation, immersed in a cycle of resentment that there was no way to break. If this was the beginning of one of Shreene's moods it would start with the silent treatment, her mother possibly abstaining from food and drink not only in the cinema but until Mahesh said sorry (which, from experience, could be very late at night or even, terrifyingly, the next day). Rumi's mind juddered. Why doesn't he do something? It's all going to be spoiled now, she thought. Instead he walked beside her, horribly relaxed, stopping to study the interest rates in the window of the bank next to the shop.

"Which one is the Indian flag, Rumi?" he asked, flicking his head toward the large black board in the window, plastic white digits inserted into grooves next to tiny multicolored banners, the figures looking hard and crunchable, like numeric Polo mints.

She scanned the board, biting her lip, angry but powerless to do anything about it. "It isn't there."

"That is because Indian currency is self-sufficient. India is not dependent on trade with the U.S. and the United Kingdom—India is independent as Gandhi wanted—so its currency is going to be—?" He said "be" on an upward note and waited for her to fill in the blank.

Rumi nodded, trying desperately not to look away from the board, although anxiety about how far her mother had gone down the road was making her feel sick.

"Self-sufficient," she said, on cue.

Starting a line of questioning indicated that Mahesh was in a good mood. But Rumi only felt more anger. Why does he have to ask me all these things every time we go anywhere? she thought. Why can't we just go and see the film and have fun without all this stuff? She scraped her right shoe against the ground, scratching the black patent willfully.

"So what is the rate of, let's say . . . Germany at the moment?" he asked.

She had played this game before. And luckily, because it was his favorite, she knew what to do. If he had asked her about Italy or a country she didn't know, she would have been in trouble. It should have been a relief but instead she felt sad. This was delaying every-thing, delaying the inevitable end: the end of all fun, the end of her mum's happiness and the end of anything good. It was all rubbish.

"Depends if it is East or West Germany," she said.

"That is correct. So if you have, say, a hundred and seventy-three West German Deutschmarks, how many pounds does that make?"

"Come on now. We don't want to miss it, do we?" Shreene's voice trailed back toward them on the wind.

Rumi breathed with a rush of release. She could hear the sparkle back, the popcorn cheer, the we're-going-to-the-cinema joy that had twinkled through the day. It was going to be OK. She stretched her body imperceptibly, releasing her shoulders, and walked on with Mahesh, watching her mother from behind. Shreene's lustrous kameez was sashaying immaculately, two beats after each step, the pale pink of the satin rustling in waves through the strings of blue leaves printed round the border. There was something about the color that seemed magical to Rumi, like a rouged Indian sunset, the blushing hint of romance, a caressing song ready to leak out of the clouds at any moment. Shreene was a film star today, her small back supporting the long undulation of thick hair, unleashed for the afternoon, hanging right down to her hips. Eventually she stopped and turned, holding Nibu up to wave as they stood in front of the vast expanse of glass and steel, letters forming the word ODEON plunging down above them, a thin rectangle of glossy shapes set in blocks of navy, standing out majestically against the sky.

MAHESH TOOK RUMI to the ticket counter so that she could queue and see the exchange, which, he announced, would be "good experience" for her. The queue was bunchy, growing in a disorderly fashion at various points to accommodate Indian families who looked around them, reflecting Rumi's own curiosity. Mahesh waved at a couple who were right at the front. Rumi recognized them as Uncle Rohit and Auntie Smita, parental friends who had not come round for a long time. "Shall I go and tell Mum?" she whispered.

Mahesh shook his head. "Today we have to concentrate and focus on what is before us. Don't let your mind wander around." His voice was affectionate. "Look at that poster there," he said, gesturing at a lit placard placed directly opposite them. "Now, who is that on it?"

"Mahatma Gandhi," said Rumi.

"Good. And what is this film about?"

"Him."

"And?"

"Oh, and our own history."

"And how is it about our own history?"

"Because we are Indian."

"Yes, that is true," said Mahesh, smiling. "But also because this story is about what happened in India when Mum and I were very young. Now, there are two other people you need to take note of in this film, two important people. One is called Nehru. He is Hindu like us. The other is called Jinnah. He is Muslim—"

"Partition," said Rumi, remembering the alien word as though it was a marble that had rolled round her head, stopping at the forefront of her mind, hopefully in time for the jackpot.

"Yes, Partition. The parting of—" Mahesh stretched out his hand so that the palm bent itself in an elegant curve, fingers stretched at a right angle to the thumb. He lifted the hand and brought it down with a cheerful ebullience, unleashing a karate chop on the space before him. "The parting of India when the British left, becoming India and Pakistan. That is called the . . . ?"

"Partition. Can I get some Minstrels?"

"No, Rumika. Mum has brought all kinds of tasty treats with her. Try to focus."

INSIDE THE CINEMA hall, they were led through the dark by an attendant with a flashlight. He glided telepathically up the side of the hall to arrive at their row with a graceful disinterest. The food began almost instantly, minutes after sitting down, a constant stream of snacks passed up and down their compact family row of three and a half. Rumi sat between her father and mother, Nibu a moving variable, who stayed mainly between his own chair and Shreene's lap, occasionally venturing farther. Rumi imagined looking down on their little row from the soaring ceiling, a line of 4 inside a series of 47 seats, part of an oblong that was probably just over 100 seats long, raised up in space so that the seats got higher and higher as you reached the back. A hypotenuse down the middle of 110-point-something seats. Probably 110.5ish would be near enough, she thought, or more like 110.48. In front of her a huge drape of red velvet shrouded the screen, pulling back for various false starts that produced a rippling hush throughout the hall each time until at last the screen illuminated to reveal a crazed spin of adverts and trailers, dubbed with zany, larger-than-life voices. In between, the lights came on for a break, revealing the carnival of people munching and talking in the multiple rows of blue seats stretching out before them. Rumi ate happily. Every time there was a lull of some kind, Shreene produced more snacks from a bag that could have been bottomless for all the pakoras, bananas, apples, biscuits, peanuts, bhajis, dhoklas, sweetmeats, crackers and, of course, popcorn it yielded.

Once the film began, however, the room was lulled into stillness, the screen becoming the only reality, synchronizing all eyes toward its expansive light and movement. Rumi looked around every few seconds, shocked to realize that no one was interested in anything else now, that she was alone in not understanding what was going on. Like Nibu, she found it hard to keep her eyes open. But she couldn't fall asleep like him, feeling bound to fight her growing lethargy for fear of causing offense and wasting her ticket. She couldn't work it out, though. There were no love scenes. There was no dancing round trees or dynamite songs or dashing outfits. Instead, there was a series of angry men, cruel men with mustaches and helmets (all white-skinned), who beat up crowds (all brown-skinned) with sticks and guns, killing and snarling every time they appeared onscreen. There were also long, serious discussions between smartly dressed Indian men, with similar mustaches, that she couldn't understand.

She recognized India, though, in all its rushing, dusty glory, and was hugged by the desire to run into the screen and live among it. Just like that. Halfway through she got a bit excited when she recognized that the main character had turned into Gandhi, shorn of his hair and three-piece suits, a white cloth wrapped round his spindly form to present him recognizably as the person on the poster. But it was not enough. And so, finally, she succumbed, her head lolling forward, mouth open, her mind, even while feeling asleep, fighting to open again to the world.

When she woke, toward the end, the first thing she noticed was Shreene's tears, wept heavily into a cotton handkerchief embroidered with green triangles. Even Mahesh's eyes had a swollen gleam, visible beneath the rich sheen of light superimposed on the lenses of his glasses. And, of course, Nibu was crying, mainly because of the abrupt nature of Shreene's breakdowns.

The light was dying as they traveled home, a chunk of a half-moon making itself known in the sky, hovering above bushy clouds. Rumi watched it follow their journey from the car window, clinging to the silence round her, and assigning different diameters to the line that sealed the visible semicircle of white, snug in the sky, working out the circumference for the curve each time.

6

When they got home, Shreene busied herself with unloading casserole dishes from the fridge, prepared in advance for that evening's meal. It was a semi-special occasion, marked by the monthly guest appearance of Mark Whitefoot, Mahesh's main friend from his time at Cardiff University. Whitefoot made a regular visit to the Vasi household on the third Sunday of each month to play chess, and Shreene used it as an excuse to lay on a spread.

Mahesh had met Whitefoot through the university postgraduate Marxist Club in his first week in the UK. He had been drawn in by Whitefoot's provocative banter, the barbs he launched at anyone who came near him, testing the boundaries under the protection of what he termed his "honest Scots working-class roots." He had found himself fascinated by Whitefoot's free and easy use of the C-word, naming university bureaucracy as "barren elitist cunts," fellow Marxist Club members as "champagne-socialist cunts," and even Mahesh himself as a "wannabe coconut cunt," the aforementioned fruit/nut being brown on the outside and white within. Instead of taking offense, Mahesh had been oddly attracted to their exchanges, envying Whitefoot's hunger, his need to "fight the good fight," the idealism hidden in the mossy dirt of his language.

They formed a grudging friendship, based on antagonism, spending long hours in the greasy-spoon café on Crwys Road near the department, debating the finer points of Marxism as a viable way of life. And so, in this charged terrain, a constant state of attack and defense, their affection grew. They continued to meet and argue after they had finished their respective PhDs, and Mahesh had taken up the job in Swansea. Finally Whitefoot suggested that they play chess and formalize the arrangement. "I'll come round to yer house on

Sunday and give you a run for yer money in exchange for some of that food you live off, you lucky bastard," he had said. "It's either the master game or I start beating you up. You need me around to prevent you going senile. I'm yer conscience, man, you cannae forget that!"

And so the monthly meetings had begun. Whitefoot came round and berated Mahesh for leaving the lights on upstairs and radiators on in his toilets (he was also a voracious advocate of "saving energy"), for having a Scrabble set ("bourgeois nonsense, you should be ashamed of yourself!") and for living in the suburbs. He loved Rumi with a gruff tenderness, giving her a Sherbet Dab each time he visited, and performing card tricks for her when she came to say goodnight in the living room before she went to bed. He brought beer with him, usually a six-pack, which he shared with Mahesh at a ratio of two to one, consuming four cans himself over the evening. Mahesh drank more slowly, relishing the occasional indulgence of alcohol, and, depending on the state of relations, pressing Shreene to join them for half a glass at the end of the evening, which she did, shyly, retreating as soon as was deemed polite.

Shreene usually cooked a basic thrifty daal-pilau-raita combination with one vegetable treat. Today this was her own treasured version of sag aloo, the spinach rich with garlic and fenugreek seeds, the potatoes steaming with turmeric against the sludgy bed of delicious greens.

She liked Whitefoot, although he couldn't look her in the eye, due to some kind of awkward tic that, she suspected, prevented him meeting the gaze of other women too. She was interested in his past and often questioned Mahesh with regard to Whitefoot's personal history. But he was a man without a past, or a past that had been silenced of his own volition; this much she had noticed. When questioned, he changed the subject or gave answers too vague to reveal anything other than the most mundane occurrences. Yet he had mortality in his face, which Shreene was convinced could only have been the result of playing for huge odds in love and losing everything.

Mahesh would not be drawn into Shreene's desire to know more. "Let him be," he would say. "What is it to us?" But she had managed to distill two reasonable conclusions from the information she had found hidden in conversations over the years:

1. He had once lived with a woman in Glasgow.

She had gleaned this two years into the friendship when he had sympathized with them over the problematic cost of central heating, referring to a boiler that "we had to get fixed when I was living in Glasgow." Shreene had leapt in with uncharacteristic familiarity: "So you were not living alone?"

He had replied, mainly to fill the silence, not used to direct questions from her, his eyes averted, reluctant to the last, but with no option: "No, I was living with a . . . girl . . . yeah, a girlfriend."

Shreene had left it there, using the silence to give Mahesh a victorious smile as she left the room.

2. He was committed to a life of bachelorhood.

This particular "fact" was one that Shreene had deduced mainly from the omission of female characters in Whitefoot's narratives. Second, he did not seem to put himself into the arenas that she had noted were reserved for Western courtship and discussed keenly by girls at her workplace—"parties," "discotheques," "nightclubs"; these words were also conspicuously absent from his vocabulary. He had to be over forty, his face pockmarked and well-worn, hair obliterated in what he called a "level one" for maximum "lack of botheration." This disinterest in his own aging and desirability, and the fact that he was well above the natural limit for marriage, even for a man, in Shreene's book, were key indicators to her that Whitefoot had been so destroyed by his experiences on the battlefield of love that he would never risk his heart again.

He arrived later than usual, well past eight o'clock, his face shining with the aftereffects of drizzle. Mahesh welcomed him in, shaking his umbrella and opening it to stand in the hall. Whitefoot was wearing a football shirt over loose jeans, a battered leather jacket hanging loosely over his hips, carrying the regulation six-pack in a plastic bag.

They settled into the living room, Mahesh fetching a small bowl of cashews and two glasses for the beer.

"So, how have you been, then?" asked Whitefoot, as Mahesh unpacked the chess pieces. Each was small and perfectly formed, carved from Mysore sandalwood; the set was one of the few superfluous possessions that Mahesh had carried with him when he had first traveled to Cardiff. He was proud of his honorable battalions, deeply Indian in design and scent. The set's only downfall was its size: it opened out to well under a foot square; it was extremely compact. They sat on the floor on two cushions, the board between them. Mahesh took a pawn from each color and juggled them behind his back, offering closed fists to Whitefoot.

"I'll take this," said Whitefoot, pointing at Mahesh's right hand. It revealed a delicate black pawn, with an ornate head hooking over the top like a sea lion, tiny in Mahesh's lined palm.

"I'm fine," said Mahesh. "Went to see this film—*Gandhi*—this afternoon."

He pronounced the word with a strong accent on the "dhi," using the heavy reverberation peculiar to the Hindi lettering of the name.

"Ah, I've seen it!" said Whitefoot, with interest. "What do you reckon, eh?"

"I knew you had seen it," said Mahesh, rubbing his beard. Whitefoot had used a new opening move, one that seemed to him to indicate temporary insanity: two steps forward for his rook pawn. Very strange behavior indeed. "I was looking forward to talking to you about it."

"Father of the nation and all that. Mahatma means 'saint,' right? I get it. What I want to know is, how were they justifying the sinister undertones, the anti-Muslim stuff? What do I know, eh?" Whitefoot spoke in an excited patter, speeding up characteristically, as though he had important things to say and wanted to avoid being interrupted. "But, you know, I'm interested in this stuff. I thought, What's Vash going to think of it?"

He took a lengthy guzzle from his can and settled into his argument.

"I just thought it was so up-front it was kind of embarrassing. Take Jinnah, for example. I mean, the guy's always shown brooding with his cigars like a kind of serial killer waiting for his moment. There's all this sinister music following him around, telling us he's about to become the destroyer of worlds, and Gandy's like some kind of benevolent hippie spirit, beyond religion or something, don't you think? It was like he'd been sanitized, all his Hinduism airbrushed down with this idea that it was a secular cause, while the Muslims are portrayed as these rabid primitive tribals, right? But what followed after Partition was a holy war on both sides. Am I correct or am I correct?"

Mahesh made his move and frowned. "On the contrary," he said, continuing to stare at the board, wondering how Whitefoot could provoke him so effortlessly, "I don't believe they truly explored the self-interest and greed that were clearly behind Jinnah's despicable separatism. The man was selfish beyond belief with disastrous consequences. How you can even take his name in the same sentence as the Mahatma?"

"Look, I'm not doing the guy down," said Whitefoot, chuckling as Mahesh flinched on the word "guy." "I'm just saying why don't they show a bit more of how it was, essentially with the Muslims feeling marginalized, forgotten, no sense of belonging, no part in Gandy's 'Hare rams' and 'Jai Shivas' or whatever he said, when he was off leading the masses and his beloved cows to make salt from the sea or clean toilets or whatever he wanted them to do?"

Mahesh looked at the board. He felt anger rocket through his body, isolated specifically in Whitefoot's pronunciation of Gandhi's name.

"You know the government of India financed almost all of that film?" Whitefoot continued. "You got to explore the propaganda element, right? Suits them to show it in black-and-white terms. Evil

English guys beating up the natives—fine, fair enough. Good Gandy guy—nonviolence and homespun garments win freedom—fine also, I buy it. It's the movies. But what about evil Muslim leader ruining everything because he's . . . just some kind of psycho in that 'quintessential' Muslim way . . . er . . . Not on surely?"

Whitefoot neatly nipped Mahesh's bishop with his knight, causing Mahesh to flinch again. "Sorry about that, mate," he said, winking, as he placed the bishop on top of the box. "Got you under duress. Anyway, the point is—"

"You are forgetting," said Mahesh, bristling, his face clenching, "that I was there at the time. This film you are discussing is more than just a—a playground for your usual cynicism. This film is about my life, Mark, and Shreene's too. It is ridiculous that you can just sit there and make your pronouncements on events that mean nothing to you. There are some things that are beyond your experience. Even you have to accept that. The basics seem to elude you. The Mahatma was opposed to Partition: he wanted Hindus and Muslims to live side by side for a start, without problems, without violence. This is basic, I mean, really. Where are you getting your facts from?"

"I don't understand why you're so offended. It's not like it's a sacred text or something, is it? The guy who directed it's called Attenborough, eh? It doesn't get more English, old boy, than that. Gandy-ji, 'the father of the nation,' 'Bapu,' whatever you want to call him, is played by a guy called Ben. I mean, come on!"

At that point Rumi entered the room, carrying a plate of fried numpkin, a fatty sheen spread over the semolina threads. She put it on the table and turned to leave.

"Hey, you have to see this, Rumi, yer pap's being thrashed and we're only ten minutes in," said Whitefoot, coaxing her over with his arm, still coated with leather, a grin on his face that made her look away. She eyed the carpet.

Mahesh nodded to signify that Rumi should sit down. She crossed her legs and sat at a right angle to them, supporting her face with her hands, balancing her elbows on her calves. He looked at the board. In spite of his early loss, he had managed to create something approaching a Slav defense, lining his pawns in a neat diagonal. But it was a feeble start. Whitefoot was annoying him, and it was filtering through to his play, making him emotional, vulnerability manifesting itself in his choices. He went for an aggressive attack, throwing his queen out into the wide-open space of the board, letting her stand alone, hoping it would seem threatening.

"Look, if you want me to explain, I can," Mahesh said. "If you are interested, that is. But you sound like you've got the whole thing worked out fully and, might I add, in your mind, so—"

"Calm down, mate!" said Whitefoot, using his knight to create a fork, simultaneously attacking Mahesh's other bishop and his queen. "Calm yerself down! Of course I want to know. MKG is the real deal, man, Mohandas K. Gandy, the don, the number one. He's the original gangster without guns, he's the—"

"OK, OK, fine," interrupted Mahesh, feeling the whiplash of his own stupidity. He was now about to lose his other bishop in a juvenile case of flamboyance. And his queen was also open to attack, sheer idiocy. He felt like a teenager. Carefully, he removed the queen from danger, letting Whitefoot knock over the bishop and whip it from the board.

"OK, look," said Mahesh, meeting Whitefoot's eyes sternly. "This is how it is." He cleared his throat violently, the sound filling the air. "Basically what do you want me to say? That I was four years old when the whole thing happened? That my mother, pregnant with my sister, carried me over the border in a suitcase because the Muslims were not just setting fire to trains, they were going around stabbing children and fathers, raping the mothers, leaving them to be 'defiled, childless widows,' in their words. Direct translation. That she fed me milk, my mother, in a bottle through the corner of the suitcase, separated from her husband, fearful for her life. These kinds of details you find enjoyable? They add a certain 'color' to your film? Mass cremations, burning bodies, train carriages full of flesh?" He was shaking, his voice escalating, splitting with a high-pitched anxiety, his throat thick.

"Look, man," said Whitefoot, "I didn't—"

"No. No, let me fill you in. What else?" said Mahesh, crashing over Whitefoot's words. "That we lived in a refugee camp in Gurgaon? You enjoy the sound of the word 'refugee,' it has an honest ring for you. I know that appeals. That we lived on one chapatti twice a day, yogurt once a week, nothing else, months of trying to find a way to survive, hungry, Whitefoot, imagine that—hungry, starving, pregnant, barely alive. Good, honest, poor, dying people. Hearing about everyone else who didn't make it—my aunt who was kidnapped, my father's uncle who was castrated by 'friends,' three streets from us, in the road itself, his children watching."

"Listen, man, all I meant was that the Hindus were on the rampage too. It wasn't just one way. I didn't mean to—"

"What? It takes 'two to tango' or some other such trite phrase of your language?" said Mahesh. "It's everyone's fault? No one's fault? Tell that to my father whom they came to find, in our hometown, so pleased with their new country 'Pakistan.' Let's think about how he hid himself in his own basement, shaking like a dog. You think these stories are just in films or something? Rousing anecdotes for a party political broadcast? When my father finally got out of Gujranwala, somehow made it across the border and found us, my mother didn't recognize him. In fact, she ran for her life because he was wearing the vilest outfit you can imagine, the pure incarnation of filth—he dressed in the black robes of a Muslim to get through safely and he did it. We went from living with Muslims in our daily life, at my school, on our road, from sharing lives to nothing, over, bang, that's it. We had no Muslim friends after that. You find that surprising? That we would—*I* would—rather die of thirst than drink one drop of water in a Muslim's house?"

Whitefoot took a gulp of beer and looked at Rumi over the can as he did so. "Are you saying yer a racist, man?" he said, his voice carefully paced.

Mahesh looked back at him directly, heaving with air, his breathing scratchy. "That word is irrelevant in this context."

"I'm sorry to say this, man, but I want to know. Are you saying that you don't believe the Hindus were massacring too? It was civil war. You're an academic, you know the score—someone starts it and retribution runs the rest. Come on, you can't—"

"Again, irrelevant."

"I had no idea," said Whitefoot, finishing his can and pressing it so that the metal creaked quietly. "You really went through—"

"Forget it," said Mahesh, moving his queen aggressively and knocking over one of Whitefoot's pawns by accident. He returned the pieces to their rightful places. "Don't patronize me."

Whitefoot moved his bishop two steps, removing Mahesh's queen. "Sorry, man," he said, putting it next to the other pieces and opening another can.

They played in a space devoid of words, watched by Rumi. Finally, after about five minutes, Mahesh spoke. "Look, there's no point in my playing without a queen, is there? It is useless," he said.

"Listen," said Whitefoot. "You know it's religion that gets me. Any kind. That's how this started. It was about that. Hate it all."

Mahesh stared at the board as though he couldn't hear anything.

"Remember I told you once, years ago, that gal I lived with back home, she was unfaithful to me? Don't know if you remember . . ."

Mahesh looked up, his face communicating disbelief at the irrelevance of Whitefoot's new train of thought.

"She kept slipping off to these secret meetings and I found out where she'd been going."

Rumi pushed herself up from the floor and went. Mahesh let her leave without comment.

"Anyway, look, the point is this," said Whitefoot. "I found out where she was going and it was the worst kind of betrayal. Worse than being with another man."

Mahesh looked at him, his expression waning into something approaching amusement.

"It was the church, man," said Whitefoot. "It was the church, even though she knew how I felt, even though we had spent years—"

"And that was why it ended?"

Whitefoot nodded, swigging from his can with a pained expression, as though he was suffering from trapped wind.

A brief exhalation of laughter left Mahesh's throat, a puff of a giggle. "Hence your obsession with that Graham Greene book?" he said.

A smile curled at the corners of Whitefoot's wide mouth. "*The End of the Affair,*" he said, raising his can in a solitary toast.

"Interesting," said Mahesh, emptying the board and setting up the pieces from scratch.

7

the next day, Rumi stood by the side of the pitch at lunchtime and watched the boys play football as she ate her sandwiches. At the back of the field she could see Bridgeman struggling to keep up with the pack, headed by John Kemble as main striker. Bridgeman was loping along, waiting as though he was trying to convince someone to pass him the ball through the power of his mind alone, without actually shouting for it. His pale face was wide open with concentration, big eyes looming in a tiny moon space under dark fringes of hair. It seemed pretty impressive that he had managed to get on to the pitch at all, and he looked as if he knew what a precarious position he would be in if he didn't demonstrate some prowess during the match.

In the afternoon she sat at her usual table with Bridgeman as they worked on grammar. Mrs. Pemberton sat dozily behind her desk at the front of the class, a large rhombus of sunlight warming her face and the blackboard behind her. The chair between Rumi and Bridgeman was empty because Palmer had gone on holiday: his parents had taken him to Torquay for a week to stay in a seaside camp. Bridgeman seemed unsure of himself without his best friend.

"What did you think of the break dancing in the playground yesterday?" Rumi asked, sharpening a pencil in a new device she had begged Mahesh to buy on their last trip to the stationery shop. It was a sharpener that had been made to look like a Rubik's cube—one that retained its own shavings inside the block.

He turned toward her with a slight frown. "Bit rubbish. Why was everyone going over the top about it?"

Rumi felt an inward sigh of relief. "I dunno. I thought I'd missed something," she said, taking out the pencil and admiring the newly pointed tip. It was perfectly sharp. She almost didn't want to use it.

"Where were you anyway?" Bridgeman asked, the same moody quality in his voice.

"Doing maths."

"You're always doing maths now . . ." he said, leaving his statement open as though he was clearing the way for her to provide more information.

"Well, I sort of . . . have to." She felt herself grimace. That wasn't the right answer. She tried again. "I want to do my O level soon, see," she said, trying to sound casual.

Bridgeman's shock was mixed with envy. His face was like the litmus papers Rumi had read about. Right now, his eyes were glowing with wonder. "Omigod, seriously?" he said, quiet awe in his voice. "Does Mrs. Pemberton know?"

Rumi looked at their teacher, who was barely awake. Mrs. Pemberton's auburn hair fell weightily in long, straight lines at either side of her face, divided by a center part. She looked as if her thoughts had hammered themselves into serrated lines on her forehead.

"Yes," she whispered. "But you're not supposed to know. No one else does. I'm going to do it next year when we go to high school."

Bridgeman nodded, as though he was thinking about the implications of this. "I won't tell anyone," he said.

Rumi put her finger against her lips and closed her eyes meaningfully, then opened them again.

They worked for another ten minutes. Then Bridgeman broke the silence: "Listen, I've got this amazing book for my BBC Micro. It's really lush."

"What is it?" asked Rumi.

"It has all these programs, one on each page, and you write them into the computer with all the commands and everything, then you run it and each one is a different battleship game that you can play."

"Oh, wow!" Rumi was genuinely excited. "Can I borrow it for mine?"

Mahesh had brought home a computer a year ago, a machine discarded from the new department being set up at the university. She had developed a passion for it, playing games like Bug Blaster and Asteroids in her breaks, Nibu watching her every move. Her allowance was an hour and a half each week, so she wouldn't get addicted. It was time that had a special currency all of its own, like chocolate coins wrapped in gold foil.

"You can come over and try it if you want," said Bridgeman.

Rumi swallowed. "I won't really be . . . like, allowed . . ."

"I can ask my mum and you can stay for tea."

"I just . . ." It was so tempting. She wished she could tell Bridgeman about the library routine. Maybe he would be allowed to come and keep her company there sometime. But telling him would be going too far. And she wouldn't be allowed out at the weekend, which was now timetabled to the maximum, the days compartmentalized into breaks and study like the black and white keys on a piano. "Guess what I read about the other day," she said, to change the subject.

"What?"

"If there are sixty people in a room there is a ninety-nine percent chance that two of them will have the same birthday."

Bridgeman looked at her. "What?" he said, rubbing his nose, an eraser in his hand.

"It's called the Birthday Paradox. There's all these really difficult sums to prove it, loads of them."

"How do you know it's true?"

"It's true," she insisted. "My dad showed me it in a book."

"Like Palmer and Sheldon have the same birthday?" Bridgeman used his thumb to gesture toward Sheldon, at the back of the class.

"Yes, like that. But there are only thirty-one of us in this class so the probability is lower."

"But they have the same birthday, though," he said, rubbing out a word on the page, holding his book down.

Rumi sighed, and finished her exercise, then got up to empty the Rubik's cube sharpener into the class bin.

8

Shreene was lying in the bath. She looked at herself, horizontal in the water, and felt the shame of her own gaze. Her body seemed so overtly displayed, the landscape of her physical form so present. It was not something to which she was accustomed. This was only the second time that she had taken a bath in the British sense. In India, like her sisters, she had worn underwear, launching dollops of water over her head and chest, submerging the jug every few seconds in a steel bucket that rattled with a continual waterfall, narrow but intense, from a tap in the wall. She had shivered as the water slapped her back, then felt goosebumps as the natural humid world around her rebalanced the warmth in her blood. This was how she had bathed until she was married—a fully grown woman at Delhi University, a city chick, drenched in her knickers, soaping her body like a child, blissfully unaware of the contours that shaped her.

Or, at least, that was how she now saw it. That was her memory. Today was the second "bath" in her life, and it had come about for a reason—in an attempt to banish the rash that had been troubling her. She looked down at the space of skin below her stomach, stubbling and leering with short hair. A fortnight ago she had shaved there for the first time. It had taken an article in a woman's magazine, read in her lunch break at work, to galvanize her desire to do it. Something had come over her: what had started as an attempt to replicate the "bikini wax" shaping guidelines in the magazine had turned into a minor mania. The more she eliminated from either side, the more she became convinced that she needed to go further, increase the amount she shaved to achieve symmetry on either side.

Suddenly it felt like the most hygienic practice one could possibly undertake, and she performed the task urgently, gripped with self-loathing at her own ineptitude in letting it grow like this for all these years. The words from the magazine rang in her ears with a lazy sneer: "Although you will have your preferred way of doing your bikini line, the summer calls for extra diligence, allowing you freedom of choice when it comes to high legs and high ties." Shreene had never worn a bathing costume either, but that was not part of this decision. Eventually she had looked down at herself, nude in the way that only a child can be, but devoid of the innocence, the black curls stuck to the sides of the bathtub, a red spray of tenderness adorning each thigh, the razor glinting clinically in her hand.

Now the slow return of hair was harsh, both visually and to the touch. It reminded her of Mahesh's crawling beard that had re-turned each fortnight in the first year of their marriage. Back then she had pleaded with him to shave, and he would laugh and put his hand on her cheek, threatening to go for a fully bearded look in the style of a true academic. It was a game between them of power and affection—at times comic, at times angry. Usually it was more than ten days before he surrendered, ending the daily sparring with a dra-matic bow upon emerging from the bathroom, his face suddenly los-ing a decade, the smile at once sweet and teasing, curled knowingly in the smooth skin of his cheeks. Mahesh had never understood the extremity of her relief on these occasions, the way in which she seemed almost to collapse with shyness. Indeed, she felt that, during those fortnights, as the spread darkened over his face, so did his spirit—he seemed murkier, more controlling, almost violent in his outlook as the days went on. If they argued, she saw only thunder in his eyes and the crease of his face, her tolerance of anything that might be construed as humor debilitated by the sight of his features in shadow.

Now his beard was a thick, nonnegotiable carpet, stretching in criss-cross vagueness over his face. It had stayed put for years; he trimmed it occasionally, but not much. She didn't remember the moment when the game had gone stale, the desire to peel off this outer face and have the clean-shaven freshness of her husband back. It had disappeared without her realizing it. Shreene looked down at the open area between her legs again. The view repelled her. An ugly, old man's beard growing wildly across her skin. She shuddered.

When she had first come to the country, they had asked if she was his daughter. It must have been a bit sickening for him, she thought, being only eight years older, just thirty. But in stature he had towered over her, his huge form dwarfing her skinny outline, his confidence and vocabulary throwing her into panic. She had experienced fear as he spoke to her in English, the large, ponderous syllables combining to give her memory loss: the conversational English she had confirmed at their first and only meeting before marriage was suddenly gouged out of her brain, leaving her thoughts stranded in a vacuum. It was the fear that strangled her, fear that it had been a mistake, that they would not fit together like two spoons in a drawer, in the way her parents had claimed all wedded couples did, fated to be together from birth, astrological charts allowing. What if she was part of some skewed hole in the universe, a mistake on the part of kismet, unable to interlock seamlessly with this man because they were both the wrong shape? What if she was returned by him, days, weeks or even months later, a disheveled failure with the inky blot of shame stamped indelibly on her forehead?

Shreene took the plug out of the bath and felt the pressure of the water draining round her. The fear had subsided, she thought. For a while he had even fallen madly in love with her. Just like the films.

But during her own fortnight, just elapsed, he hadn't noticed the altered space between her legs. They were now more private than they had been before they began.

Later, Shreene worked on the menu for the following day. Mahesh had received a small rise in his salary, the first for a number of years, and she had insisted the family be allowed to celebrate with a grander meal than usual, particularly given that occasions like Diwali were allowed to come and go without acknowledgment.

She was ripping open a chicken for a curry, plunging her hands, covered with gloves the texture of clingfilm, into the mass of guts and flesh. Rumi sat on the worktop adjacent, holding a mound of green lentils on an oval plate, her fingers pushing seven grains to the side every few seconds, checking for stones. Her lips moved silently in tandem with the action of her fingers, as though she was counting prayer beads. Her legs swayed against the pale green cabinets below, bare heels skimming the doors. Shreene looked at her, feeling a strange suffusion of love, as though seeing her child anew, with fresh eyes. There were three hours before Mahesh was due to return, at least. And this Rumi, with her hair tied back in a ponytail, looking at her with such innocence, peeking through her glasses, was friendly, sweet, ready to listen to her mother without scorn.

"Mum?" Rumi's voice was relaxed, almost careless.

Shreene gathered the entrails, holding the wet shapes against the thin glove in the palm of her hand, and threw them into the bin under the sink, her nose quivering at the smell. "What is it, beti?"

"When are we going to go to India again?"

"You have to focus on your studies, you know that, but if you are a good girl, who knows?"

"I wonder what Jaggi Bhaiya is doing there at the moment . . ."

Shreene was used to this. On these afternoons, when Mahesh was away and there was cooking to be done, Rumi invariably turned the conversation to India, finding ways to stay in the kitchen so that she could get through a seemingly endless route of questioning.

"Well, I'm sure he thinks about his little sister over here, and he would be excited if you were to visit."

"Mum?"

"Yes?"

"When you were my age, did you do maths?"

"Yes, I did, and a lot of other subjects. But I was also very good at sports."

"Were you popular?"

"Popular in what sense? I wasn't unpopular."

"With people at school?"

"Well, I was very good at the javelin. I used to win medals for that."

"Really?"

"Yes."

"That's amazing."

Shreene moved on to the chapatti flour, which she needed to turn into a solid, elastic dough that would keep overnight with the addition of a small amount of oil. She left the kitchen with a large bowl to scoop three cups of flour from the large sack in the store-room. When she returned, Rumi began again, with the same slide down and up through the single syllable of her question.

"Mu-um?"

"Yes?"

"What was it like when you got married?"

"You know what it was like. I've told you before."

"I mean, was it weird that you hadn't seen Dad before?"

"Only people here will call it 'weird,' as you say. For us it is nor-mal. That is what usually happens. At least your daddy and I had met once when he came to see what I was like. And we wrote to each other before our marriage. Some people don't even do that. Can you imagine it?"

"What was it like when Dad came to see you?"

"Well, he did a typical Dad thing. He wanted to catch me un-awares so he came a day early, with your daadi, his mother, and I came home from college—in through the back, all hot and sweaty from traveling—and they all crowded round me, Badi Auntie, your nanny, and they all were so overexcited. I was so irritated! 'I mean, what is the big deal?' I kept saying, and I was so annoyed. 'Why are you all going mad like this, as if the King and Queen have come to visit?' "

"So what did you do?"

"I changed into my home clothes, my old salwar kameez for hanging around the house, and started washing the dishes, with my sleeves rolled up, sitting on the floor."

"Why were you on the floor?"

"Because that was how we used to wash dishes there, under a tap. You sat on a wooden stool on the floor and scrubbed and rinsed each plate under the tap. All the water drained into the floor, you see. It was not like it is here, when you wash dishes with a sponge and Fairy Liquid."

"And what did Nanny say?"

"She said, 'Are you mad?' Paagal, she called me—you know that means 'mad'? Pagli is the mad girl. She said to Badi Auntie and Pushpa Auntie, 'God help me, my daughter has been taken over by insanity! I have given birth to a pagli!' And she put her hand on her forehead like this and shook her head . . ."

Shreene did the motion, flecking chapatti flour on the side strands of hair above her ear, which were escaping from the plaited mass.

Rumi chuckled. "Mum?"

"Yes?"

"Didn't you worry that Daadi and Dad might come in and see you?"

"Let them see me! It is their loss. If they will come in a day early then what can they expect? Just because he is fancying himself as so studious and educated it doesn't mean he can go about doing what he wants, isn't it?"

"So what happened then? Did they see you?"

"No. Eventually my father came into the kitchen. And he never did that, really. I got up immediately, feeling shy to sit there crouched like that in front of him."

"Why did you feel shy to sit there like that in front—"

"Because a grown daughter doesn't sit with her legs all over the place in front of her father, silly. Sometimes you can be such a bud-dhu."

"What's budoo?"

"A foolish person. For someone who is so brainy you ask some silly questions, don't you?"

"But why doesn't a daughter sit like that in front of her father? Tell me."

"You are getting off the point. Do you want to know the story or not?"

"Yes, I want to know the story."

"So then I said, 'Papa, what is it?' and he looked at me like only my papa could look at someone, with the purest of hearts shining lovingly through his eyes, and he said, 'Beti, what are you doing here? We have been graced by a visit in your honor. I am a proud father today. Now go and put on your most beautiful suit and make me even more proud.' And he touched my cheek like this and pinched it."

Shreene performed the action on Rumi, and her eyes welled. She turned away.

"Mum, don't cry," said Rumi.

"I'm not." Shreene pulled forward her shirt cuff and dabbed her eyes. "It's just onions."

"Mum, there aren't any onions. You fried them ages ago. I'm not budoo!" said Rumi, playfully, taking her mother's elbow and turning her round.

Shreene laughed and looked up at her. "Little buddhu," she said tweaking Rumi's nose.

"So did you do it?"

"Of course I did it. I am not going to disobey my father, am I? Especially when he asks so lovingly, like that. Could you refuse such a sweet request from your father?"

Rumi's face was pensive, as though she was trying to give serious consideration to whether or not it was possible for her father to say such a thing. After a few seconds she returned to the daal, scissoring her fingers between the two mounds. "And then what happened?"

"Well, I got changed and I came into the living room and your daddy, he did his interview-shinterview. And so did your daadi for that matter."

"Did you have to bring in the tray of tea, like in Hindi films?"

"Oh, yes. And you will have to do the same, won't you? And carry it oh-so-gently like this, with perfect timing, elegance and grace. And your future mother-in-law will examine how you walk and how you pour the tea, just like Daadi did to me."

"Mum! I'm not going to get married."

"I used to say that at your age. Just you wait. You'll be doing all this before you know it, you cheeky monkey!"

"Mum! Stop it."

"Oh, I can stop it very well but you will need to be prepared—"

"Anyway, what did they ask you in the interview?"

"Oh, very proper interview questions. Your father asked me what my qualifications were. Daadi asked my father to produce my certificates. As if he would lie! That was very annoying."

"And what else did Dad ask you?"

"He said he had moved abroad and did I want to live abroad? I said, 'No, I want to live in India. I am an Indian girl.' "

"So did you fall in love with him at first sight?"

Shreene flared her eyes at Rumi mischievously, a big smile on her face. "You have been watching too many Hindi films, naughty girl!"

"But did you? Did you think, I love you, when you saw him?"

"No, I didn't. And, anyway, where we come from, love grows after marriage. Only here do they expect to 'fall in love,' as they call it. And where does that get you? Divorce is where it gets you."

"But in the Hindi films . . ."

"Those are films, beti. What are you talking about? Anyway, I thought, You think a lot of yourself. Definitely not 'I love you' business. But he did think something like that. In fact, he went a little paagal himself."

"How do you mean?"

"He decided he was going to have me whatever happened, even though I said I wouldn't go abroad because I didn't want to have a menial job, as I'd heard our people were forced to do—all these things. Still, he started writing to me, even though I had given negative answers to lots of his questions. He wasn't having any of it. It was as though he had lost his senses. He used to write me these long letters in English, with poems in them and all sorts of logical arguments and everything."

"Dad wrote poems?"

"Oh, yes. And all kinds of things. Long lines about my blue eyes like 'shocking sapphires' and my shining skin and all that sort of non-sense."

"And did you write back?"

"Oh, no, I didn't for a long time. But you can't fight whatever is written in your kismet. And so, eventually, when my father asked me to write back to him, I did."

"And then what happened?"

"We got married. And I saw how wonderfully high-thinking your father is, such a mind, not like those whiskey-drinking businessmen that so many of my brothers' friends were but a high-minded intellectual who cared about important things in life, not just looking good in front of people or being rich. And I prayed for a child who could be as intelligent, if not more intelligent even, than him. I prayed and prayed and then you were born."

"And did you have sexual intercourse so that I would be born?"

Shreene stopped bang-center in the middle of kneading, her fist leaving knuckle marks deep in the grainy ball of dough. She did not turn round, just stood in silence, her shoulders wrenched back in a freeze. "What did you say?"

Rumi flushed and began to count the lentils as fast as she could, her fingers clumsily negotiating the terrain of green. "Nothing."

Shreene left the dough, wiped her right hand on her apron and slowly turned to face Rumi. When she spoke it was with sinister clarity. "What did you say?"

Rumi continued to move the lentils, her fingers tripping insanely over each olive bead.

"Stop that," said Shreene.

Rumi slowed down but continued a lethargic form of the same action, making a big show of removing a gray stone in the midst of the rhythmic movement. Shreene walked over and abruptly pulled the plate out of her hand. The two separate mounds of cleaned and unclean daal slid easily into one.

"Mum!" said Rumi, "I just did all that . . ." She didn't look up.

"Repeat what you said, Rumi, or I'm warning you, you will be getting two tight slaps right now."

"It's only because they taught us at school. They said it was called that and it was how everyone has babies. Why are you so angry?"

"Listen to me and listen to me clearly. Look at me now."

Rumi continued to stare at the floor, jutting her jaw with a resentful immobility.

"Look at me!" Shreene took Rumi's chin in her hand and maneuvered it up so that Rumi had no option but to meet her eyes. Even then her pupils danced away every time Shreene tried to hold her gaze.

"That is not how our babies are born. Only white people have sex."

At this, Rumi shook her head, looking up directly at her mother. "But in science we were told—"

"Forget science. That is their science, for white people. We do not do that."

"So where do they come from?"

"Through prayer. Like you did."

9

the end of that term contained a surprise change in fortune, a period of pure happiness for Rumi that came out of nowhere, like a benevolent asteroid, the kind that comes bearing good tidings. It began with the abolition of the library routine and ended with the stamps.

The stimulus for the change carried a more complicated emotion with it. Mahesh had increased the amount of work that Rumi was expected to complete, due to the proposed O level, which blazed on the horizon like a signal flare. But she had not been performing: according to Mahesh, her work was getting sloppy and lacked commitment. He attributed this to the fact that books surrounded her in the library, and that her attention was wandering into the avenues of fiction instead of staying focused at her desk. He was quite right. Rumi was now on book fifty-one in the Chalet School series, and she spent less and less time catching up on the problems before her pickup at six thirty. She had even got used to the hunger. So, Mahesh had decided that it was time to change approach by allowing her to have a key to the house, which she could wear as a necklace. This way, both he and Shreene would be able to phone her during the two-hour block and check on her progress.

It was a liberation that at first she couldn't believe. One of the greatest benefits was being able to walk home from school with Simon Bridgeman and Christopher Palmer, which she did daily, newly joyful, caressed by the hot weather and easy playfulness that existed between them. Once, they had ambled back together, carrying their newly done school photos, joking about how awful they were. Rumi was hiding hers safely in her bag, swerving away whenever either boy tried to convince her to show it. Finally they had done a deal, each revealing their own photo after a three-two-one countdown, holding it against the chest and turning it round at the same moment, so that the huge rectangle of cardboard broadcast itself from the center of their bodies. Rumi remembered being astounded that she was willing to do such a thing. After she had recovered from their mutual collapse into laughter, she had pushed the photo back into her bag and walked on ahead.

Bridgeman had yelled after her, "Oi! Do you know what I'm going to say?"

"Leave it out, will you?" she had said, suddenly frosty.

"You look even better in it than you do in real life," he said.

And Rumi had taken the photo home and stared at herself, smiling behind cellophane in a gray and white frock with lace trim, spectacles removed at the request of the photographer, tiny gold hoops curling in her ears.

The gang had begun stamp collecting together. Rumi had brought back a bunch of impressive-looking stamps from the India Trip, salvaged from old letters in different relatives' houses, which she now produced to start them off. Each stamp sat against the ripped border of an Indian envelope: a thin white that looked as if it had been dipped in lilac, the kind of paper that had its own special scent. She had a full spectrum of colors, ranging from the standard one-rupee indigo print to a shockingly beautiful special edition of a tiger growling in the sun. That one was quite rare, according to Christopher's book, and grew to be a prized possession, set in sticky plastic hooks on its own page. Her small but intriguing collection had led to their weekly meetings at which the boys would pool and swap from the bags of mail-order stamps they had bought with their pocket money.

Rumi also brought her own international stamps from other countries, still on their envelopes. These were culled from her father's office, scrawled with the writing of diploma students from places like Ghana, Singapore and once, memorably, Papua New Guinea. The meetings had moved from lunchtime to after school and, one day a week, unbelievably, Rumi met them at Bridgeman's home. Strangely enough, although Shreene hadn't been too happy about it, Mahesh hadn't seemed to mind. He thought it was good for her to have a hobby: it had a "motivating function" so long as it was only a couple of hours and just once a week. Shreene was disgruntled at his attitude. She thought it was odd in the extreme for a girl of Rumi's age to be consorting with two boys so regularly (and white boys at that), but Mahesh stood his ground. It was ultimately an intellectual pursuit, he said, geographical in nature. They had to allow for Rumi's growing need to socialize, as total exclusion could have a negative effect. This was a positive, controlled outlet, and she would benefit from being with other intelligent children, in moderation, of course.

And then Rumi had ruined it. The new after-school rules included absolute secrecy, just like the library ones that had gone before them. On the days when it wasn't Stamp Club, she went home and promised not to open the door to anyone or leave the house. Her mother and father both called her every half-hour from their respective offices to check that she was there. She spent a quarter of her time on the maths and the rest on TV. As the weeks progressed, she began to explore the house and play on her own, reading adult books from the shelves—the *Happy Heart Cookbook, An Illustrated Travel Guide to Germany*—and building models and games from TV programs. Sometimes she created hypnotic chants: speaking out loud, repeating the theme tunes and catchphrases from the daily shows. Finally, feeling bolder because of her new control and daily routine, she decided to hold Stamp Club at her own home one Wednesday, and informed the boys accordingly.

On the day in question she walked back on her own and invited them to come half an hour later than normal so she could get things ready. She filled small bowls with peanuts, Bombay mix and mishri, the hard cubes of sugared cardamom that her mother put out when guests came round. She made three glasses of orange squash and arranged them on the table, for their arrival. For one dark moment, when she heard the doorbell, she felt her heart contract with guilt. But then she pressed her hair down with her fingers and walked toward the two shapes: Christopher's fidgety length and Simon's smaller frame, equally amorphous in the light behind the marbled glass at the front.

They had been surprised for sure that she was there alone. But the mishri had gone down a treat, both boys filling their pockets with it at her request, once she had realized they thought it was a kind of penny sweet, like the cola bottles or gobstoppers at the local newsagent. They had sat at the dining table and talked about which stamps they desired above all others, looking at the empty pages in their albums and reading about the countries they wanted: Zambia for Christopher, Nicaragua for Simon and Indonesia for Rumi. When the phone rang, Rumi ssshed them quiet and went to deal with it.

Eventually she asked if they'd like a tour of the house, thinking it would be a good way to pass the time. Mildly interested, they agreed and trooped upstairs behind her. First stop was her parents' room. She let them into the bedroom, feeling very grown-up. They stood in the doorway and stared at the large bed, with its beige velvet headboard and flowery covers: pink and green strewn over white in a repeated pattern of petals and leaves. Suddenly Rumi got the giggles. This was fun. "Let's play a game!" she said.

"What?" replied Simon. He screwed up his nose like a rabbit, as though the room contained an unfamiliar smell.

"You know, 'Let's Pretend.' Let's play it."

"But what, though?" asked Christopher. He was looking at the cupboards and dressing table fitted into the wall, a confused expression on his face as though he couldn't imagine "Let's Pretend" in that environment.

Rumi got into the bed and pushed herself under the covers.

"I know. Why don't we do this? Let's say I'm married to you, Christopher, and you go outside the door, then Simon gets in the bed here and starts cuddling me, and then Christopher walks in and discovers us having an affair and he goes mad and shouts and has a fight with Simon and one of you dies."

Simon looked at her, shifting uncomfortably in his shoes. Christopher was jiggling the mishri in his pockets and glanced sideways at Simon.

"You know, like in *Dallas* or something," Rumi said.

"No, I don't want to play it," said Simon.

Christopher hastily joined in. "Me neither."

"But why not?" asked Rumi. She could feel some heat in her cheeks, a sign of shame. "I don't get it. It was just to be funny. What game do you want to play?"

"I think I'm going to go home," said Simon, looking down at the carpet.

"Me too," said Christopher.

Rumi pulled the cover over her head and felt the tension collect in the hot black space before her. Gradually she began to sense the light seeping through the edges of the quilt: a flower-stained light, stale and unreal. It was difficult to believe that this was the same light that had been in the room just minutes before, transforming her parents' normality into a thrilling Wendy house, encouraging her to jump into the bed without a care in the world. The excitement still bubbled in her chest, but now it caused her pain, made her screw up her eyes and press her cheek into the pillow, so that the edge of her spectacles burned into the skin on her nose, creating a ridge that she deepened by pushing her face down farther, as hard as she could.

She heard Simon and Christopher murmuring outside the world of the duvet, shadowy and uncertain, as though they didn't know how to use their voices. And then the cumbersome shuffle of their footsteps as they left the room, clomping down the stairs without a pause, each step making her screw up her eyes even tighter. They were leaving her. She had dreamed of them running round her house, dreamed of John Kemble and Sharon Rafferty and Julie Harris, Simon, Christopher, all of them, running round the garden and falling over on the grass, getting up and running some more. It was a dream she had experienced several times, waking up and blinking for a few minutes, the bumps on her bedroom ceiling distilling themselves into focus as she realized that no one had been in the house, that she had imagined it. In the dream they had been wearing white towels, tied neatly around their chests as though they had just come out of the shower. Even though they ran and shouted and played all kinds of games, the towels never came undone. Now they were here, in reality, Simon Bridgeman and Christopher Palmer, banging heavily down the stairs.

A few minutes later, Simon called up the stairs: "Rumi?"

She lay still, multiplying the first numbers that came into her head: 1467 times 1235. Before she could finish, she heard Christopher's voice: "Er . . . Rumi?"

Rumi removed the quilt from her head and let the air sit on her face: a cold mask that fitted neatly, like one of the transparent face packs she had seen her mother use. She waited for them to call again.

"Rumi? The thing is . . . we can't get out. The door's locked . . ." Christopher said.

"Can you come and unlock it?" said Simon.

"Er . . . please?" said Christopher. He had lowered his voice so that it mixed with Simon's in a nervous hush.

Rumi pushed herself up and looked into the mirror of the dressing table opposite. Her golden side-clip had come undone, releasing her hair in a tangled mess onto her shoulders. She stiffened, hearing a quiet growl and the familiar crunch of gravel as a car pulled into the space at the front of their house. A lacy curtain split the window on the side of the bed: two arcs touching each other gingerly for a few centimeters of their circumference. In the glass space between the join she could see the machine bring itself right up to the front window of the dining room, a huge red robot ready to eat the house: eyes sparkling in headlights, teeth ready in the mesh of the grille. It felt so large that even the houses in their street seemed to cower in response. Elderly Mrs. Schwartz's proud blue door, on the left, appeared to be rumbling on its hinges. Even the washing hanging to the front of the house on the right (belonging to the unnamed and unfriendly family of five) was trembling on its hexagonal frame, as if in terror. Rumi stared at the plate on the front of the car, the letters and numbers unmistakable.

"R380 6TQ. R380 6TQ," she whispered, under her breath. Too late, she saw her father look up and catch her in the window, and too late she bobbed down, pressing her head into the quilt so that she almost went into a headstand, cursing herself for her stupidity.

"R380 6TQ," she whispered frenetically. "R380 6TQ! R380 6TQ!"

"Ruuuuu-mi!" the boys called up together, timed as though they had set their voices to collide and double in strength.

Rumi shivered and pushed herself off the bed. "Coming!" she replied, pulling the quilt over the side and tucking it under the pillow. Her heart was lurching with each beat. How would she explain being in their bedroom? How would she get rid of the boys? She would have to let them out of the back door, but would they understand in time? She skidded down the stairs, slipping on the carpet, then regaining her balance.

At the bottom she encountered them standing together in their coats, clutching their stamp albums. Simon's face showed the most relief, his dark eyes widening. "Can you—" he began.

"We've got to hide! We've got to go in the back," she babbled, using one hand to push the shoulder of each boy.

"But we have to go home!" said Christopher, shrugging her off.

Simon was plainly bewildered. "We don't want to play Let's Pretend," he said. "We came here to do Stamp Club."

"But my mum and dad will kill us! You don't get it!" Rumi said.

She scrabbled for words but Simon was already looking over her shoulder down the hallway at the door. The metallic sound of the key carved into the silence as it scraped in the lock. Rumi turned to see dark shapes looming behind the door. She tried to turn the boys in the direction of the kitchen, but she knew it was hopeless. They continued to stand like zombies, staring straight ahead.

Shreene was in first, holding Nibu, who began to burble when he saw his sister, as if on cue. Rumi looked at her mother, pressing her hair behind her ear. But Shreene did not hand Nibu to Rumi, even though he was clamoring for her, his little arms outstretched, fingers clasping the air. Instead, she glanced over her shoulder and gestured, with a lilt of the head, to Mahesh to hurry in. He walked through the porch door, mountainous in his raincoat and scarf, his forehead furrowed into a sharp valley of annoyance when he encountered the scene.

"What is going on?" His voice was slow and sad. It made Rumi feel like crying. She wanted to bat it away, break it into pieces and make another voice come out of his mouth. The folds of skin round his cheeks, covered with beard, seemed to sink deep into rigid lines on his face as he spoke, freezing like scars, run over with blackness, the short hairs standing alert and prickly.

"Dad, I . . ." Rumi said.

Simon and Christopher moved closer together. Christopher dropped his album, and knelt down to pick it up, his long, bendy legs folded in two. Nibu spluttered, giggling in the silence, as though at a horrible, rude joke.

"Explain what has happened, Rumika," continued her father, pronouncing each word very clearly. He stood absolutely still.

"Dad, it was Stamp Club," she said. "I thought I'd do it here. I know I . . . I made a mistake . . . I . . ."

Mahesh looked at his daughter and raised his lip so it jutted out under his nose. Rumi felt fear enter the back of her throat.

Shreene gestured at Simon and Christopher with her spare hand and said, "You two are going home now?" They nodded. She took them into the kitchen, leaving Rumi and her father standing alone in the hallway, Rumi staring at her feet and counting for her life.

LATER THAT EVENING, Shreene brought Rumi some biscuits on a little plate and set them down on her desk while she was working.

"Look," she said, "these are your favorites. Bourbon ones. Chocolate."

Rumi did not look up at her. Instead she stared at her desk and held the compass tight in her hand, the pointy end pressing against the flesh under her little finger. She had decided never to speak to either of her parents ever again.

"Beti, you knew it was wrong, didn't you?" Shreene said. "You know that when you are in the house you are supposed to work on your timetable, and the rules are important. No one is allowed in here."

Rumi fixed her body in a pose and held it tight so there was no chance of any movement. The slightest shake might be interpreted as communication.

"It is for your own good, Rumi. What will happen if people find out you are here on your own? Anyone could come. All kinds of bad people are out there and what you did was very, very dangerous."

Rumi felt the compass tip. It was finding its way deeper into the flesh of her hand, pressing but not yet puncturing the surface skin.

"What is it, Rumi?" asked Shreene. "Is it because he hit you?"

Rumi frowned at the mention of the word. It wasn't because she had been smacked. She couldn't explain why this time it was different. Why the slow journey up the stairs and the chill in the air as they had sat in her bedroom, her father explaining that he would have to enforce discipline on her, for her own safety, was so unbearable.

There were some things you couldn't work out. Like why, for instance, she had been given time to plead and ask for forgiveness before it happened—a request that had become more and more high-pitched, ending in a desperate wail. It had made it so much worse. When he had finally hit her, smacking her back with a ruler from her desk, she had thrown herself onto the floor, trying to grab his feet like a reformed villain in a Hindi film. Then he had knelt and hit her ten times, holding her down with his left hand as she rolled from side to side and squealed. She couldn't explain this now to Shreene: why the ruler made it unforgivable, why the guilt in his eyes at having been driven to this made her feel disgusting, why there was no way out, nothing would ever be the same again.

part 2

10

~~~

He is standing outside the school gates, rain dripping off his nose and lips, a thin Elastoplast of purple hood suckering his forehead. Rumi sits expectantly on the shallow brick wall over the road, watching him. In her pocket is a small black plastic cylinder, a camera-film case. It is full to the brim with needly brown seeds. Her right index finger jabs inside the case, then enters her mouth—once every five seconds. She is barely aware of the timing. Each time, her tongue twists to receive the seed covering, ritually licking, crushing and swallowing the chaff of the cumin. The seeds slide off her gums and down her throat, releasing their bitterness to line her stomach. She continues to focus on Simon Bridgeman. He is waiting for the rest of the chess team and Mr. Roberts. Today is important. She just has to get through the first twenty-five grams before everyone has arrived and it is time to leave. The tournament is three hours away. She has spearmint chewing gum in her pocket to disperse the smell.

RUMI NOW ATE 100 grams of raw cumin each day. Sometimes, depending on the rate at which she worked, this would change. If she was studying in the early hours in her room, her back cramped irreversibly over her desk, she would resort to more. At those times the bulb in her table lamp loomed out at her, forcing purple, blue and pink clouds onto her retinas. In this hazy stain of integers, statistics and shifting light, she began the procedure again. The crushing of cumin with her molars had become routine. One day, at three in the morning, she knocked over her stash, stored in an old paracetamol pot, and the seeds scattered over the carpet, hiding themselves in the battered swirls and dots. It had taken ten minutes of jabbing at the nylon forest, on her knees, finding them, collecting them in the pot, removing the hairs and dust clumps, before she realized what she was doing. She recoiled as she ate them, but she did eat them. It was as though she was addicted but that wasn't possible. They were cumin seeds. She was fourteen. It was too embarrassing even to think about.

The first time she had eaten them on her own it had been quite innocent. She was on the phone to Shreene in the two-hour block before both parents came home from work. Nibu was watching his favorite program in the living room, fed and watered. It was the main period of freedom before the night's vigil began at six forty when her parents got in. There were six months to go before the A level exams, and countless problems throttling the veins in her brain, stemming the blood and clotting her thoughts. Sitting on the kitchen worktop, phone cradled in her neck, she leaned down and opened a unit, explored with her hand for something to eat and settled on the jar of cumin. She knew it was an odd thing to do. A bit like eating raw garlic or raw green chillies. Something weird. She licked her finger and dipped it deep into the jar. Pulling it out, she stared at the long shaft, pressed over with a thousand tiny seeds, then engulfed it with her mouth, right down to its root, the tip of her nail feathering a tonsil. The sour flavor had unnerved her. So had the knowledge that she liked it.

Now she was held to ransom by cumin. She craved the multiplied pressure against the tip of her tongue, and the tingling sensation when it exploded against enamel and gum. Over time she had finished the jar in the kitchen, not responding one evening when Shreene had crashed into her bedroom demanding an explanation. "You're supposed to knock," Rumi said, slamming shut a drawer in her desk.

"Don't talk to me like that. What is this?" Shreene held up the tub in which she stored monstrous amounts of cumin, bought in bulk from the wholesale shop in town. "What have you been doing? You are mad. A mad girl. How can you eat so much jeera? It is inhuman! Rumika, what is wrong with you? *Kya* problem *hai tere mein?*"

Shreene was very pretty. Everyone said so. Even when they went to the ashram in London, little kids would come up to Rumi after the service and say shyly, "Your mum has beautiful eyes." Shreene said that Mahesh used to joke that she was more beautiful when she was angry, like Basanthi, the alluring, if verbose, female horse-and-cart driver in the film *Sholay*. Just as well, thought Rumi, as she seemed to be angry a lot. She preferred it when her mum's face was not twisted in fury. At this moment chapatti flour dusted Shreene's elbows and the front of her maroon salwar kameez. Her hands were covered with sticky dough. She had been interrupted in full kneading nirvana. Rumi looked away and studied the picture of Tom Cruise on her wall, counting backward in sevens from a thousand in her head. It was a still shot from *Top Gun*. He was in a plump leather jacket, patched over with badges, like the baseball jacket John Kemble wore to school on top of his uniform. 986 . . . 979 . . . 972 . . . 965. Cruise's smile gleamed in rows like a kind of reflective beacon. They had called him "the man with a million-dollar smile" on the new chat show Rumi had started watching. She focused on his mouth and tried to separate out each tooth.

Shreene started to panic, presumably at the lack of reaction. "Soono!"

Even after fifteen years of marriage she still did not refer to him by his first name. It was a kind of joke that Nibu thought Mahesh's name was "Listen" in Hindi—"Soono." Rumi heard the characteristic thump move slowly up the stairs and watched Mahesh enter the room. He's knackered, she thought, and now he gets to enter the twilight zone. Her right hand changed the page of her textbook discreetly. She had been doodling on the title page, adding to the existing graffiti, and had drawn a big heart which had RV 4 JK encircled with an arrow through it. The gray in Mahesh's beard had spread, she noticed, forming a padded underlayer of whitening color. There were exam papers in his left hand and a fountain pen in his right. When he frowned, his thick eyebrows pushed against each other, creating a roof above his nose.

"What happened?" he asked.

"Look at this. Have you seen it?" Shreene shook the paltry number of seeds left in the jar. They rattled weakly against the plastic.

Pathetic, thought Rumi. She's right, I am a weirdo. She felt a muscle at the base of her spine contract, and shifted from one crooked position to another, leaning forward on her elbows to try to relieve the pain, familiar by now.

Shreene shook the jar again. "This is your daughter's doing," she said.

"Have you eaten these?" he asked. "Why, Rumi? Why so many? Please explain."

The ensuing "serious conversation" with her mother and father had not yielded any answers, because there were none. They locked away the remaining sack in their bedroom. It took Rumi five afternoons to find the key to the room, and it was a fortnight before her mother checked the sack and found it depleted to the bare minimum. Rumi had used logic to get her through those days—it had been almost enjoyable, like a treasure hunt. The maze of possibility had a thrill that took the edge off her desperation. She left school at a quarter to four every day, picked Nibu up and took him home. Once in, she got him out of his uniform, warmed his milk and made his toast. He was full of five-year-old growl, running up and down the stairs in white undershirt and shorts, jumping off the third step into her arms at the bottom. She loved him like this, singing out nicknames to rev him up: "little maharajah," "imp in the white short pants" and "wig-head" were among her favorites. He often challenged her to a wrestling match or a shootout with holsters and pistols. Usually she obliged for the first half-hour at least, but that week she settled him in front of the TV as soon as they got in. Then she'd begin the hunt.

It wasn't too bad for the first three days—adrenaline spurred her on—but by the morning of the fourth there was a constant patter in her stomach, like a squirrel scratching the fleshy walls begging to be fed. She dreamed of seeds soothing the aching wounds on her tongue, the split white sores that had come when she had started eating them. When she discovered the key, snug between Rajasthani quilts in the airing cupboard, she shouted with relief. It was as though she had punctured the balloon she had been living in and started her life again—to breathe real air, do real maths, find real answers.

After the second exposé, she had to make trips to the city center to source it herself. She went on a Tuesday afternoon instead of to PE, giving the excuse that she had to go to hospital for hydrotherapy on her back. As lies went, this one had truth on its side so the guilt was muted. She did go to the hospital for this reason but only once a month. Now, her strange-shaped need for cumin drew her into the heart of Cardiff with magnetic precision. Once a week she walked to the local station and took a train into town. She was usually the only person on the platform at that time, and solitary in the carriage too, watching the world flake by the window in a mess of gray and green. In town, she would find her way to the built-up area and enter the health-food shop in the Morgan arcade. There, she spent her lunch money on cumin seeds, bought in small packets of 100 grams, at sixty-nine pence each. Standing on the platform of Queen Street station, waiting for the train back, she tried to work out a solution to the problem of cost. She never had enough money for full supplies, as she was supposed to go home for lunch at least three days a week. This was a nonabating problem. No matter how she put the figures, the net result was always the same.

RUMI CLOSES HER umbrella and gets into the minibus. She hasn't counted on rain. Her body is sheathed in new clothes, allowed as a treat to celebrate the end of the exams. The chess tournament is part of the deal. Shreene chose the outfit with her a week ago, in Bridgend, at some shop that was linked to a person she knew from the ashram. At the time Rumi had been tense. Doubt had slowed down every move she tried to make. Finally she had settled on tight calf-length white trousers in stretchy ribbed material, flat white pointed shoes and a long white viscose shirt almost to her knees, blotched with "shocking pink" polka dots.

She is wearing the shirt baggy, pulled in at the waist with a white plastic belt, three inches wide. The outfit is completed with pink jewelry—a shiny bangle, triangular earrings and circular beads at the neck. Her hair, recently layered, is boyish and choppy, and refuses to do anything cool. She has applied pink eye shadow and lipstick, borrowed from her mum's room, and the new contact lenses have been forced in ruthlessly. Now she feels exposed, sitting on the narrow gray rubber in the back of the minibus as the boys try not to stare at her. Milky Boy keeps glancing at her out of the corner of his eye, like he has a tic or something. Even Mr. Roberts stares at her. The foundation on her face is "full cover," also gleaned from Shreene's dressing table. She feels as if she has dipped her face in cement.

Bridgeman is mostly quiet on the way to Marlborough. She offers to play a game but he says he doesn't want to lose focus. What does he mean? she wonders. He's so infuriating. One day he's showing you his latest opening move and laughing at your jokes, the next he's avoiding eye contact, let alone dialogue. She tries to register his reaction to her outfit but he remains distant, slouching his thin body and looking out of the window silently, long dark lashes almost sealing his eyes shut, his skin as pale as creamed coconut. He stays aloof, even when Mr. Roberts gets everyone singing along to "By the Rivers of Babylon," shouting the chorus awfully and brilliantly. When they zoom over the Severn Bridge they curse the English and cheer for Wales. As the bus pushes through into the gaping turfed fields littered with boys and noticeboards, blocks of classrooms with chessboards in the windows, she feels the excitement rising in her like sickly cherry fizz. The bus stops and she runs to the loo.

RUMI WINS THE first three games without a problem. Although she doesn't like playing to time, the clocks on the desk make her take risks and push each game to its conclusion. So far, so bad. There's no talent to speak of: a pimply red-headed midget, a bespectacled pubescent blonde who takes forever to make a move, and a straight-A type complete with downy mustache, side part and constant frown. It's depressing. She reconsiders her optimism. She has been too obsessed with the idea that this chess tournament would provide some kind of alternative universe, with her as leading lady: intelligent, sophisticated over the chessboard. Then she sees the exception to the rule that all those who play chess must live on the margins of school society. He is a huge tree of a guy with floppy dark hair and a cheeky grin. He is her fourth game; she is already sitting at the table.

They play extremely slowly. He keeps getting up and walking round the room, stretching and yawning. The clock doesn't seem to bother him. "I like to move my body between moves," he says, returning to the table. "Helps me get my order sussed. I hope you don't mind."

The smile he unleashes is blazing. She is unstrategic, losing not pieces but board space. She can barely put a sentence together to speak to him. He has to be at least fifteen, maybe even in the lower sixth. Early on, Mr. Roberts had walked by and winked at her, signifying that she was in a good position. Halfway into the hour-long allocation, she is drowning, the board crammed full and her mind agitated. Her queen has been tricked into submission. Whatever she moves on the board, Rumi is going to lose her. She calculates the possible outcomes over and over again, although she knows it's futile. Her head is spinning. Bridgeman walks over just as the guy comes back from another of his extended trips round the room. He watches them play.

"So, where are you from, then?" says the tree. "Rumi's a nice name."

She realizes that he's expecting some kind of answer. Her cheeks flush, as she waits for Bridgeman to leave.

"Oh, sorry, love. Don't mean to put you off your game," the tree says, letting out a throaty chuckle. "Although it's a pleasure to play with a lovely lady like yourself."

Rumi curses under her breath and stares at her knight, a glossy plastic specimen, copious scratches adorning the lashings of mane carved down its back. Why is he making fun of her like this? Because

Bridgeman's around, she thinks. It isn't fair. And who says "lovely lady" other than people down Cardiff fruit market, with fingerless gloves and leathery faces? She ignores him and counts the square root of seven upward on itself. After making her move she looks up at Bridgeman. He walks off to the other end of the room. 2401 times 2401 is . . . She sticks with it, computing the numbers before they turn to sludge . . . 5764801 and out.

After losing, she goes to the loo and gets out the next pot of cumin. It is teatime and disappointment hits her. She has a bad head-ache. The game was a washout. At the end the guy had got up and walked off, whistling, after he had shaken her hand and winked. She sucks the seeds hard from her fingertip, biting into the top layer of skin. This means she is now out of the main tournament and into some kind of "novice" round for losers and primary-school kids. It's humiliating. God knows what Bridgeman will think. For the first time that day, she remembers the A level. She wonders what she will get. If she ends up with a B, will they still consider her for Oxford next year? Did she screw up the last question? It had been tortuous sitting alone after school with Mrs. Powell to do the mock statistics paper at Christmas. She had known that the seeds were twisting her breath and staining the air through her polyester sweater, but she was powerless to curb the speed with which she ate as she wrote. She ate for her life during that exam, using her left hand to dip into the pot on her lap every few seconds. Now, chewing her way through the mounds of brown seeds, sitting cross-legged on the shiny loo seat, she is filled with self-loathing. She has run out of spearmint gum.

The hallway is dark when she emerges, lit in odd pockets. She has been inside for a while. Bridgeman is standing by the men's, hands in anorak, kicking his feet against the wall. His face is pure cream, like the color of the wall behind him. Rumi notices how his eyes seem different, dark brown pupils diluted to amber. They seem softer, and so big she can see the tube lights reflected in them. Why is he so awkward? she thinks. Always so intense. Like an owl: watching, waiting, thinking. Bridgeman is so weird. But magic, in a way. He always has been.

"Where have you been?" he asks.

"Um, in the loo."

"Are you feeling all right?"

"Yeah, why?"

"You looked a bit upset during that game."

"Uh . . . did I?"

"And then you disappeared."

"How do you know?"

He looks at the floor, then takes a coin out of his pocket and presses the edge into the wall.

"Where's your glasses anyway?"

Rumi flinches. "I hate them."

"I thought they were nice. What's the big deal?"

"You're taking the piss. Thanks a lot, Bridgeman."

"Whatever. Do you want to go for a walk or something?"

"What, now?"

"Yeah. Get out of this weird place or something?"

"Don't you have a game to play?"

"It's the break."

"OK."

THEY WALK IN the grounds side by side. Each time they step forward they continue not to speak. Rumi is trying not to breathe too loudly. She looks at the sky. The moon is becoming clearer with each step they take, a bitten disc of white. There are no stars. An image flashes into her head of an Indian film, the two of them dancing round floodlit trees, werewolf sounds melded into the sound track. She feels ridiculous. A tremor in her throat is wobbling its way to the surface. He won't look at her. His eyelashes are pressed down as he stares at the ground. If only it could be a moment. Her whole body shivers. She feels like throwing them both down and rolling on the grass in an endless soft cylinder. The thought is shocking. She shivers again.

They get to a quiet area of thicket, human sounds murmuring on the periphery. The ground is still preened lawn, but above them wild trees are outlined with thick marker ink against a gray, dying sky. It makes her think of the end of *The Jungle Book,* when Mowgli is sucked through the border from forest to mankind. Bridgeman is in shadow, walking in time with her. He puts his hand into the pocket of her trousers and takes hold of her first three fingers, forcing her to stop. This is Simon Bridgeman. She is paralyzed. Rumi wants him to kiss her. She wants him to walk over the line that has been between them for years, painted solid and hard on the playground. She wants it more than the whole world, with its half-bitten moon and its starless sky, she knows that much. But when he moves toward her she shifts violently, as if she's broken a limb. Her mouth is too rotten. It is peeled out with cumin. She runs hard, wind chafing her eyes, shredding her.

11

Shreene unscrewed the thermos and poured some water. It was the end of the day, and the tea bag floated quietly in the plastic cup that formed the cover of the flask, slightly bloated but otherwise seemingly unaffected by the action. It was only in the first cup of the day that the tea bag reacted attractively, with a satisfying and hearty leakage of brown in response to the heat of the water. This was the fifth and last cup, inevitably lukewarm. It always aroused despondency in her, the time around five o'clock—half an hour to go before she would leave for home. There was a kind of defeat in the air, a sense that nothing much had changed with the unfolding of the previous eight hours.

She could hear Mary and Cerys in the office kitchen, their whispers and giggles grating on her nerves. They were often like this on a Monday, restless with stories from their respective Saturday-night adventures, showy and overexcitable, boringly exclusive. You'd think they'd have got it all out in their lunchtime, thought Shreene, but by this time of day, instead of calming down, it was as though they were slightly drunk, intoxicated by the power of their own storytelling.

"You're joking?" cackled Mary, lifting her head from its slouched position so that it bobbed above the back of the couch. "Seriously? You're having me on, you slapper!" She turned round and gave the office a quick once-over. Shreene looked up and caught her eye by accident, instantly annoyed with herself for appearing as though she cared to know what they were talking about. Mary raised her eyebrows and laughed, shrugged before turning back and slipping lower so that she was out of vision. The conversation continued in softer tones.

Shreene put the letters she hadn't dealt with back into the TO DO tray on her desk. It had been a slow day. A retired nurse who couldn't get her phone to link up to her new answer-machine. A miserable customer from Blaenau Ffestiniog, still disconnected after six days. Some lonely posh man who said she had a beautiful voice when Shreene had called him back as requested to discuss his direct-debit payments. Nothing to write home about, as the saying went. What was worth writing home about, though? She wrote to Badi every couple of weeks and she attempted to make the letters mean something—but she was only too aware of the space between the questions Badi asked and the responses Shreene found herself giving.

She heard a snort from the kitchen and some strained gulps of laughter. Mary and Cerys "got together" with someone new every couple of months, celebrating the romantic entanglement with several days of discussion. Sometimes Shreene joined them at lunch, relaxing into the freedom of talking about trivialities: fashion, television, recipes. She was adept at keeping up with the flow even when it covered terrain she did not inhabit. But when the conversation turned to "blokes," Shreene knew she made them self-conscious. It was something understood—they knew how she felt about such things. At some point, after an intensive line of questioning, she had explained her own stance on sex before marriage, and boyfriends in general. They had made interested noises and nodded to show they got the picture, but it had changed the dynamic between the three of them—that much was certain. Since then, they had exercised a patronizing discretion on the subject, saving the real chat for when Shreene went back to her desk, if ever she decided to join them.

Shreene had started bringing in her own thermos for precisely this reason, to avoid having to go into the kitchen again and again throughout the day, interrupting their conversations. It was better to be self-contained, independent, rather than feel like a gooseberry.

Their smugness angered her, though, Badi's ignorance about the realities of British life too. They had no clue what kind of pressure she was under, all these people with their ideas of how things should be. It wasn't easy, keeping values going for Rumi, working out how to do right by her, trying to give her the tools to lead a good life. No wonder she got so distraught, her moody young daughter—no wonder she was more and more rude and difficult to deal with. Sometimes Shreene wished they would all just shut up, Badi with her concerned questions about Rumi's development in preparation for marriage, and the girls in the office, with their stupid, misplaced pity.

She took another sip. The lack of warmth accentuated the bitter quality of the tea, a synthetic aftertaste that you got only with bags. It would be nice if you could boil up proper leaves and cardamom here in the office, some cloves, hot creamy milk, tea as it was meant to be drunk, a treat, rather than a force of habit. But imagine the smell, the comments. Shreene smiled to herself. Maybe she should try it one day, just for the comedy element. Bring in her own saucepan and everything. She tried another swig and shuddered. There was half a cup left, the bag lying soggy and wasted in the corner, but it was undrinkable. She would have to go and rinse it out.

MAHESH TURNED IN TO the space reserved for Shreene in the car park, and switched off the engine. Lying back in his seat, he turned up the radio and closed his eyes. He was a good fifteen minutes early, and as the swell of anonymous classical music filled the air, he felt strangely emotional, almost fragile, for no apparent reason other than the shudder of the instruments—the clash of cymbals, the gentle wheedling of oboes, clarinets. They seemed to touch some nerve deep in his system. He had been feeling odd all day, ever since he had woken from that dream this morning.

The dream was one he had experienced at least ten times over the past few years, a frequency of recurrence that should have made it feel familiar each time it began. It was also based on real events, which, again, should have meant that he recognized the sensory elements each time: the location, the emotions contained within the journey, the weather, even. But instead the dream always felt real, something he lived through anew, waking from it with the trembling sweats that almost proved he had been there and back. That morning he had woken with a shortness of breath, a pain in his ribs as he tried to breathe through it. He had been troubled by the leftover images for the entire day: a slow leak of pictures that trickled into the corners of his consciousness with horrible regularity.

How could a dream set in Disneyland have such a powerful effect? A dream that was pretty much (give or take a few time shifts and artistic interpretations) a straight transcript of reality. It wasn't as though he had been dodging snipers in Vietnam or gagged and tortured by militants in Kashmir. As anxiety dreams went, it was so silly.

When Rumi was eleven, Mahesh had been sent to California for a conference. It was the first foreign trip for which he had been selected in the years since his tenure as a full-time staff member had begun and, to this date, the only one. The invitation included the prestige and luxury of all-inclusive funding for accommodation, travel and meals, allocated by his department. Although Nibu was only two at the time, and Rumi not yet settled into her first term at high school, Shreene had agreed when Mahesh suggested he should go alone. The U.S. was much too expensive to manage as a family. He planned it as a two-week trip (there was no point in being paid to go so far away without taking a few days to see the sights before he returned), put aside ninety percent of his meal budget and used it to subsidize overnight sleeper-bus trips for the week after the conference.

He visited Venice Beach in L.A., the Grand Canyon, San Francisco and, of course, Disneyland. He had washed his face and cleaned his teeth in the toilet cubicle of the bus at six a.m., queued for the world-famous children's theme park from seven fifteen, paid the extortionate price for a day ticket, then apportioned his time diligently, so that it encompassed as many rides as possible. He made sure that everything he saw or did was photographed, expending four rolls of film on that day alone so that he could take the pictures back to Rumi. Every moment was documented—from the most inane (singing monkeys, dancing bears in hula hoops), to the outright sadistic (Hitchcockesque roller coasters and gigantic swinging boats). Even when his stomach was almost giving way, his heart whipping its beat with increasing fear, Mahesh made himself smile, and waved on cue as he passed the person on the ground to whom he had entrusted the camera for that particular shot.

By the time dusk fell and the moment arrived to get on the bus back to L.A., he was spent. With profound and weary relief, he crawled into the cubbyhole of the seat farthest to the back and collapsed into the pure sleep of a baby, the engine shuffling like a lullaby as it warmed up to leave.

The dream always began with the combined chant of hundreds of small dolls, lining both sides of a train track, watched by Mahesh with other tourists as they sat in a string of boats and traveled on water through miniature valleys and mountains, under the blaze of a hot, dry, American sun. "It's a small world! A small, small world!" they sang, their high-pitched voices becoming more and more tuneless as Mahesh's boat disappeared into a tunnel.

"It's a small world! A small, small world!" continued the alarming sound track, as an enormous Mickey Mouse lifted Mahesh out of the boat with huge white-gloved palms, crushing him in a hug and waiting for the click of a camera to release him back onto his seat. "Ssssmall world!" hissed Kaa, Kipling's decadent snake, as he emerged from the blackness and wrapped himself round Mahesh's neck, flickering the scarlet V of his Technicolor tongue over Mahesh's lips.

But most of the dream centered on Rumi's reaction when he returned. He had walked through the door with the two photograph albums under his arm, preprinted and mounted at a budget place on the outskirts of L.A. the day before he flew back. It was dinnertime when he arrived and he entered the house quietly, slipping in unnoticed because of the clamor in the kitchen. Shreene was cooking hot poppadums to go with the meal, pressing them down with a cloth on the tava till they bubbled up crisply, simultaneously issuing orders to Rumi, who was helping to feed a very boisterous Nibu.

Shreene had greeted Mahesh with appropriate warmth, a bit confused and shy after the time apart, but he definitely had the sense that she was pleased to see him. Nibu had yelled and banged his plate with his spoon, a fanfare that made Mahesh smile. Rumi had looked up, locked eyes with him, pressed her glasses to the top of her nose, and then returned to whatever she was doing, wiping daal from Nibu's cheeks.

Mahesh went over to the table. "How are you, Rumika?" he said, aware of the edge in his voice.

"OK," she replied, without looking at him.

"Just OK?" He handed her the albums, frowning in spite of himself. "That is all you have to say?"

She took them dutifully, flicking through the images quickly at first, then hovering over each page with a gradual understanding of what she was looking at. When she glanced up at him, her eyes were shocked, wide with hurt. "This is . . . Disneyland?" she said, pointing at a beaming picture of Mahesh, standing among a sea of giant candy canes, next to a large picture of Winnie-the-Pooh and Tigger. She looked up at him again, waiting, as though she could barely believe her own voice.

The dream always ended with a lingering close-up of Rumi's face, her emotions communicated so unmistakably that Mahesh felt as if he had never known or understood his daughter until that second—a gestalt moment that caused him to feel a paralyzing sense of loss. She had thought it was a punishment for something, not a gift.

That morning he had woken early from the dream, the sky only just starting to lighten. The air was cold and clingy, merciless through the thin cotton of his pajama trousers. He had left Shreene sleeping on the right-hand side of the bed and gone to stand outside Rumi's room, watching her sleep through the crack in the door, feeling the claustrophobic muffle of a love he could not express. He longed to take her in his arms as though she was still at an age to be cradled, hold her against his chest as though that kind of behavior was normal, cry into her hair and say, "I love you, daughter," utter the words with the unhinged extremity of feeling they deserved. But instead he watched her like a fugitive, turning in to the bathroom as soon as she showed signs of stirring.

Now, in the car, he opened his eyes and looked out of the window to see if Shreene was visible in the side mirror. He felt a different-colored version of the same love for his wife—a low crackle of discomfort that made him close his eyes and lean back again, the music swelling to fill the car interior.

the next night, Mahesh took Rumi to the department. She stared through the windscreen at the long road, white lines dissecting the way before them, creating their direction, leading them onward. There was a kind of rain haze, a shallow growth of blurred light as each lamppost came close enough to throw its luminous stain onto the windscreen, yellow flooding the black background. The silence in the car between Rumi and her father was tense, one in which she kept her place by holding her breath for as long as she could, fearful that the audible rhythm of breathing might reveal something, an emotional leakage that would be disastrous.

Am I transparent to him? she wondered. Does he know everything? Everything he despises? The thought caused her unease. She took the next gasp of oxygen carefully, knotting her illicit thoughts together, clenching her fist to hold them in.

Mahesh was driving her to Swansea, to his office. It was six o'clock on a Saturday evening and they were on their way to begin the weekly session: preselected exam questions, covering her week's preparation, under exam conditions in the conference hall next to his room.

Rumi had four sets of thoughts running in parallel. She alternated between them with swift nervousness, like a bird hopping between four lanes of traffic. Some were unpleasant, leading her to adjacent safer lanes; one lane, which she kept open for emergencies, was sweet.

First, she was thinking about Bridgeman and how he had stopped speaking to her since the chess match almost six weeks ago. This was a constant abrasion on her mind, a scouring pad scratching its questions into her dreams by day or night in equal measure. A few times a week at least, if not every morning, she woke from a dream in which Bridgeman was sitting with her on the wall near Nibu's school, waiting for him to come out. In the dream they discussed the misunderstanding and hugged. Bridgeman kissed her cheek, then got up to walk over the road to his house. If she dreamed this in the deep cave of the night, rapid eye movement carrying her through the reunion with an ambrosial urgency, she would always wake with a feeling of well-being. The dream was so convincing that sometimes she wasn't aware that the events had dream status until she saw him at school, playing football, his face averted, or looking over and through her to the distant scuffle of people beyond. Then she felt foolish, gripped with inadequacy, suddenly aware of her own ridiculous body shoved into its awkward skin of uniform, her gait hunched, inhabiting the old space of humiliation. If she dreamed it by day, sitting at her desk, staring out of the classroom window, it was bitter and bitter alone.

Her dislocation at school was the same as ever, only worse, because something odd was happening to Bridgeman . . . He was slowly ascending into the ranks of the unattainable. Something had happened to his hair, a sort of choppy nonchalance inspired by what could only be termed "hair stuff." Gel? Wax? Lacquer? Rumi fumbled for the answer, dreading to find that her own knowledge of this universe sagged badly in comparison. Bridgeman's calves no longer trailed thinly into his socks: they had expanded, as had his thighs, under his shorts, with a kind of confidence. He had even grown a few inches, and his features had taken on a harder, more angular shape as though the soft moon face she'd known all these years had been pulled tightly over new, protruding bones. His eyes were suddenly, immensely, violently blue, an offhand intensity saturating the cool indifference of his face. Whether she liked it or not, she sought him out daily with what she hoped was an air of low-key coincidence—in the library when he had a free period, or just before Assembly, on the stairs before lunch she would try to walk past him, without looking up, at least once a day.

All this since the chess match. It seemed so strange that she had checked repeatedly on her calendar that the match had really been only a month and a half ago. She knew about "growth spurts" but, still, it confused her to see one happen so immediately, animated out of the textbook into her life, most visible, in Bridgeman, in the nimble defiance he exerted on the football pitch. In fact, it hurt her in a way she couldn't place. His status in the muddy crossfire of the school turf was the most wounding indicator that something was up. At worst, he was indulged with affectionate joshing from the other boys when he missed a goal; at best, and most horrifying for Rumi (who feared that the desperation streaking its way through the fibers of her brain at these times was a true sign of madness), he was lauded with giggles from the supporting girls, who idled on the side, watching the matches.

At this point, sitting in the car, she was thinking about how to be alone with him so that she could have "the conversation." But there was no way of getting to that point. The last time she had waited to speak to him after school, dawdling by the gate as he knocked a football round the back field, some of the other boys had noticed. "Your girlfriend wants you," Carl Stephens had mocked, in a tweaky falsetto, shoving Bridgeman till he had to turn round. The blue eyes had met hers, bang on for a second, and he had ducked out of her stare, flushed and untouchable, shoveling the ball with his weight to the opposite side. By the time he was being tackled, crushed in a fray of jovial insult and heaving fists, Rumi realized he was not going to look round again. She waited a moment before leaving, so that she could walk out with dignity, focusing her eyes on the pinstriped socks fringing her ankles.

As she walked she counted to the beat of the clicks from her court shoes, powering up exponents of two with the left and subtracting one with the right each time, creating Mersenne numbers (2 to the power n minus 1). Each time she created a new total she checked to see if it was a composite or prime number, working out possible mutations in her head. Whenever the number was prime, indivisible, it felt like a little stab, a minute betrayal, the tiny catheter of pain insinuating its way into her heart. 2 to the power 7 minus 1 = 127. This was particularly painful. Who knew why? Maybe because it had such promise—carrying all the world in it: the certain 1, the right-now-unbearable 2 and then 7, which would always be lucky and sexy, cheeky and cool. Everything she wasn't. It was only when she was halfway to Nibu's school that the tears had their way and burned through the corners of her eyes, a toxic spillage, unseen but not imaginary, and wiped away as fast as she could by the time she reached the gates.

Rumi took another gasp of night air in the car, locked her knees together and looked at her father. If Mahesh asked her what she was thinking, she didn't know what she would say. How to get round it? This was the most nerve-racking element of the time they now spent together, linked firmly to her second line of thought, into which she skidded with some alarm. She had decided not to lie anymore—to "walk in the valley of truth," as stated in the books that Shreene had added to the new temple in Nibu's bedroom. Rumi had been reading them recently, seeking out a course of action that would guide her through life. She had taken the vow of truth, in some way, to start a clean slate after the Chess Club incident, in which memory she felt her own soiled presence with some anxiety. But the vow was proving more and more difficult to keep without extreme forward planning—to avoid getting into trouble, you had to avoid doing anything that might not be received well when it was revealed.

Sometimes she wondered what it would have been like if she had been born and brought up in her country of origin, a moving dot graduating through the comforting structures and hierarchies of "Mother India," as they referred to it in Hindi films. If you succumbed to urges that didn't lie within the grid reference, you paid for it by being usurped from your ascent through the ranks for a while. It was up to you to assess whether it was a fair trade-off. At least there was a generally agreed idea of right and wrong: you weren't struggling to work it out on your own all the time. There was an acceptance in Hindi films that romance was part of life. But no one expected you to kiss them on the mouth when you were fourteen, or at any time before marriage for that matter, or meet them by the shops at night, with a bottle of cider, as part of the whole thing. Everything was so innocent even when it wasn't. The boys were allowed out, the girls weren't. Boys courted girls by giving them greeting cards and phoning them, or snatching moments with them on the way home from school.

With this in mind, Rumi had gone back to basics, assuming that there had to be a pure answer, ready for access in the tomes of spirituality filling the prayer cupboard under the shrine. Between their perfumed pages there had to be a guide to life, a simple list of dos and don'ts.

The Vasis had newly subscribed to a practice that assumed enlightenment through meditation, called the Self-Realization Fellowship Programme, an international organization that followed the teachings of the guru Paramhansa Yogananda. To this end, Mahesh had purchased several books in English that talked about the discipline and practice of meditation. Rumi had been trying unsuccessfully to meditate for the past year. Sometimes she looked at Nibu and wondered what he saw when he shut his eyes in their family sessions. He was six now, but he managed to sit reasonably still with an air of mystical contemplation for at least ten of the twenty minutes' silence they performed as a family twice a week. Rumi knew this because within seconds she would have opened her eyes, although she struggled to close them. She twitched, scratched and fidgeted.

Now, after reading what she could, she put this down to pollution. Unlike Nibu, she had been intoxicated by all kinds of vices and needed to clear the water in the well. The first and most dramatic step toward purity was to eliminate lying and that was the task to which she had been applying herself.

So far, so good, although there were problems in this new life choice. That morning, after they had returned from the market, Shreene asked Rumi and Nibu who had left the bathroom window open. Instead of feigning lack of memory, Rumi owned up. When asked why, rather than concede that it was a mistake not to be repeated, Rumi forced herself to say that the smell from Shreene's number two that morning had merited leaving it open. When questioned as to whether she was joking, she focused on being as scientific as possible, trying to pin down her thought patterns as truthfully as she could, without slipping into vagueness. In her opinion, the benefits of returning to a bearable bathroom space outweighed the risk of burglary. The smell had activated her gag reflex, leading her to open the window as quickly as possible even though she knew they were leaving the house at that moment. She did not believe that air freshener would have masked the smell, she explained regretfully, such was the intensity of the nausea she had experienced during her brief visit to the bathroom. Shreene had been staggered, thrown off course by Rumi's deadpan delivery. But the outcome was as unmistakable as could be, with Rumi taking the verbal barrage from Shreene with a new, stoic fullness, nodding graciously every time Shreene called her shameless or rude.

As THEY PULLED into the university car park, Rumi took stock of her other trains of thought. The first was functional. She had to work out a way to get to the Christmas party at school. And then there was the nice thought, the reliable one. It was to do with the last time she had tested herself with a past A-level paper, her midweek self-assessment. She had come out with 95 percent, 93 if you didn't count the trigonometry fudge where she'd got to the answer without showing her full workings, running out of time. There was a rumor that the workings were more important than the answer. Either way, her total was good. It made the dream real. It meant that she was in shape for the match ahead. "When Will I Be Famous?" Bros had sung, on *Top of the Pops* in the week just gone, flashing their boxy charm at the camera, shaking their ripped 501s with muscular bite. Nibu had danced along with them in the living room. Rumi was waiting to see herself, fully made-up—and enviably grown-up—first in the *Western Mail,* and then the *Guardian:* "Indian Prodigy Accepted at Oxford Aged Fourteen." It had to be before her birthday. Fifteen was so . . . normal.

They walked to the building together. Mahesh moved slowly and heavily a couple of yards behind Rumi, waiting for her to go on ahead. Each time she waited for him to catch up, he slowed down until he too came to a stop. It was like a weird game of chess in which he was unwilling to lessen the gap between them at her bidding, wanting her to go on, lead the way, take the initiative. And so they walked: two people along the rail track up to the mass of red brick, united by invisible elastic with a slow, reluctant stretch. Rumi was nervous. Was he angry with her? Had he heard her thoughts? Was it the bathroom stuff from this morning? She decided to try out speaking, although it seemed brutish to rock the silence.

"Er . . ." She cleared her throat by accident as she spoke. "Dad . . ."

Mahesh stopped, looked at his briefcase, then raised his face so that his eyes looked at her briefly, moving to just beyond her face.

"Dad," she said again, urging him to speak.

"Yes?" he replied.

"Why won't you talk?"

Mahesh frowned. The corners of his mouth moved downward. He began to walk again, overtaking her this time and jangling the keys for the side entrance to the building. Rumi followed him, dabbing her finger into her pocket to access cumin, chewing it secretly as they walked. They padded through the silent corridors, large squares of light clicking into vision above them, illuminating their progress. Sullenly she found herself absorbing the familiar scene: notices and timetables, drab photographs of lecturers in V-necked or chain-mail sweaters, whiteboards licked with red and green figures, the chemical scent of marker pen and cleaning fluids coating the air.

The coffee machine came into vision as predictably as the rest. Rumi stopped and waited as Mahesh walked farther. She knew that he knew she had stopped, but that he would not. I play chess every lunchtime, she thought. Let's see what you do now. Eventually, Mahesh turned the corner of the corridor without looking behind him. Rumi stood as the squares of light shut down round her, thickening her environment into a virtual black that briefly housed the memory of light, first as a flash on her retinas then an X-ray silhouette of the whiteboard, the notices, the walls, all fading. Finally nothing. She moved her gaze to the machine. Gradually, as her eyes grew accustomed to the dark, she could see the outline of the coffee illustrations, thick brown lines circling white shapes. She focused on a small jug that was printed at a raised angle, tilted to release fluid into a sleek shallow cup. After about a minute, the light at the end of the corridor came on, blinking itself awake before her father walked into view.

Only when he reached her did he speak. "What are you doing?" he said. His lip was raised on the left side, where it trembled almost unnoticeably. But Rumi could see the anger.

"I want a hot chocolate," said Rumi. She kept herself steady.

"What?" said Mahesh, incredulous. "Now?"

"Yes, please. If that's OK."

Mahesh looked at her as though she had belched in public. A loud, fat burp in front of thousands of people, thought Rumi. Well, if only I could. And a big fart too.

"You have not even begun your—"

"It's Saturday night."

"So what if it is Saturday night?" Mahesh's voice was now openly contemptuous. "What does that mean to you? How is that linked to your—"

"It's not fair!" said Rumi.

"Do not interrupt me!"

"It's not fair," she said. "Everyone is at Sharon Rafferty's house for a party tonight and—"

"What does this have to do with your preparation? You are the one who purports to have commitment. To be serious. You want Sharon Rafferty? You want to go to parties, is it? This is your priority?"

"No, I was just saying—" Rumi heard her voice being crushed into a tight squeal as she tried to finish the sentence.

"Saying what? It seems to me you are not ready to take this step. I thought you were advanced. That your discipline in your practice was at such a stage that you had—"

"Dad, it's not fair. They are all out and they will all talk about it on Monday and they're allowed and they'll make fun of me or ignore me, you don't know, and I can't even have a hot chocolate!" Her eyes filmed over.

"What is it you want, Rumika? You have to decide."

"I want . . . to do my exam."

"So, then, you must behave accordingly." His voice widened into an almost consoling tone. "Rumi, you know that the hot chocolate is something that functions as an attraction, something desirable. You have it at the end of the night when we leave to go home."

"I know." Her voice was quiet, but still contained the squeal, buried deep.

"What will you have to look forward to if you remove it from the end of the evening? If you consume it now, what will you keep as the magnet drawing you through to the end? You will become disheartened, won't you?"

"Don't know."

"You want to get through a high-level exam, you want to do an A level and it is not easy. Make no mistake, you have some ability but only through extremely hard work will you achieve what you desire."

"Yes, Dad."

The coffee machine started to crack and shake the silence, a bumpy ride of pipes and drones asserting its inner workings.

"So, come on, now, don't be a silly girl." He put his hand on her shoulder and patted, his hand brushing her neck. Rumi stood with her back curved so that her face pointed down, hands in pockets, body rigid, in a hunchbacked swoop. Mahesh walked back up the corridor.

She counted seven steps before she began to follow him.

LATER, AFTER STRETCHING and meditation, she sat in the conference hall, the papers laid out in front of her, lulled into a numb distraction by the wispy sound of her travel clock ticking through the stillness. Mahesh stayed with her, marking his own undergraduate submissions at the opposite end of the room, sitting beneath the whiteboard as invigilator. Rumi was unable to focus. For one thing it was freezing. Mahesh believed that the atmosphere had to be below body temperature if she was to achieve true focus. So she was down to her T-shirt, shivering in the name of concentration.

"I'm going to the toilet," she said.

Mahesh nodded. "You should go beforehand and only if you really need to during the exam," he said.

She emerged from the cloakroom with a chill covering her arms and neck. Just outside there was a large noticeboard covered with flyers for students. She read the various ads for housemates, band members, counseling services, lightly pricking the flesh of her index finger with the seeds in her pocket and shoving them into the left side of her mouth. The right side of her tongue stung with a kind of citric bruise from all the chewing and sucking of cumin. She must have right bias, because she was right-handed, she thought. These days, she was attempting a left-tongue bias to balance it. Opposite the cloakroom there was a pay phone. On impulse, Rumi went to it, lifted the receiver.

She had no money on her. She found herself dialing 999.

"Emergency," a voice said. Simultaneously she heard the number of the phone she was using, being called back at her. "Zero . . . four . . . four . . . one" said a robotic voice, then a businesslike woman overlapped with it, asking, "Which service do you require?" She dropped the receiver and replaced it. Then she stood in the cove of the phone booth, biting at her cumin. The window framed the moon, which was lopped at the side and embedded in the thick blanket of the sky. She stood like that for some time, staring at the world outside, until she realized that Mahesh was standing in front of her.

"What is going on, Rumika?" he asked.

"Nothing, Dad," she said. Rumi was resigned, standing under the brown plastic hood, in the enclave of the phone.

"You have been away from the examination hall for more than

five minutes. You won't be able to do this in the real thing, you know."

She nodded.

"What have you been doing?"

The valley of truth lay before her. She could choose to walk through it and see blue skies, rinsed clean of pain. Or she could choose the sordid mire of confusion in which she was currently living, the halitosis of her lies. "I made a phone call."

"What? To whom? Do you have cash on you?"

"To the emergency services."

"Pardon?"

"I called nine-nine-nine."

He gave her a look that made her feel mentally deficient. "Why did you do that?" he asked, pulling his face down in a jolt of anger, so that his beard creased into a ripple of flesh, a double chin of furry hair.

"I just . . . wanted to speak to someone," she said, trying to imagine a rope she could hold to keep her balance in the conversation, which was starting to feel more and more slippery.

She hated him. Hate was not a noble emotion. "I was lonely," she said, her voice ricocheting round the empty corridor. There—she'd got it out. She'd told the truth, whatever the repercussions. Surely there would be some reward. It was a step toward enlightenment, at least.

"You are a very silly girl," he said.

They walked back to the hall, Mahesh in front, Rumi following, trying to control her heartbeat, feeling it batter away in her chest.

13

By that Sunday, the atmosphere in the Vasi household was taut. To Shreene, it felt as if the walls of the house were straining perilously against the pressure, mounting with each hour. The tension was a physical presence, at such a level of intensity that she felt it was blocking her ears, building up in the canals, making her dread and desire the kind of violent pop that would send reality rushing back in.

Mahesh and Rumi were mostly silent, speaking in single words and gestures. It was as though the daughter was trying to outdo the father at his own game. Shreene had been shocked to see that Rumi had even developed a new vocabulary of facial grimaces, hovering somewhere between gruesome and, quite simply, ridiculous, as though she wanted to do battle by demonstrating that her snarls and frowns were more versatile and inventive than her father's. She even ate alone now, at her desk, barely responding to Shreene's attempts to massage her shoulders, turning away her head when Shreene suggested that she change her clothes, shrugging off her mother's worry at the disrepair and smell of the T-shirt she wore continuously. Even Nibu had quietened, winding down his energy till it was almost nonexistent, a barely heard whirr and click of life. It was like living in a monastery dedicated to silence but in which inhabitants could communicate all manner of discontent through movement. What was it they said here? thought Shreene. "Actions speak louder than words"? If this was a Western philosophy, she wasn't very keen on it, that was for sure.

Whitefoot was due to come round for the monthly chess face-off that evening. Even though it was dangerously close to Rumi's exam, Shreene had encouraged Mahesh to keep to the arrangement, worried that unless he relaxed, something would give way.

She prepared the food in good time, then went out the back to hang the laundry, beginning with the sheet, which she shook so that it whipped the air like a huge flag. She pegged it to the clothesline, then returned to the basket, stacked to overflowing. She picked out three brassieres next and toppled a pillowcase into the vegetable patch. She watched it flutter in the wind, the crumbly soil skating over it like a spattering of coffee granules. Dusting it down, she smiled. Ten months, and being in her own garden still had a glorious novelty value: the shoulder-high wooden fence that made this small square of concrete and soil their own still appealed with its quaint notion of privacy. The centerpiece, a large willow tree that brushed right up against the fence, had an almost spiritual quality, as though it was a guardian for her family.

Although she had grown up on a diet of assorted Hindu figurines, their new family approach to religion seemed to make a lot more sense to Shreene. Following the SRF program to spiritual enlightenment had only brought them luck, even Mahesh had to admit that, with his promotion to associate lecturer and the purchase of their own terraced house on the nicer side of Llanedeyrn. Everything was changing. And following Paramhansa Yogananda's path seemed to take all the good bits of Hinduism: meditation and purity of thought, for example, without the worship of elephant and monkey gods, so offensive to Mahesh. He had taken to it quite well, attending the meetings with her and helping with the preparations at the ashram in London. Most wonderfully, the speeches and mantras were all in English, which meant that the children could engage. She had overheard Mahesh explaining it to Rumi, talking about the practice being like "Buddhism, but with a God at the end of everything." It was nice to share something with him, she thought. Everywhere, numbers came between them, a noisy layer that separated her from him incontrovertibly, even sandwiching itself between them in bed, making them more lost to each other than they had ever been. He was always tucked away with his books or testing Rumi. Wedded to numbers. More to the point, their devotee. But there was no god or goddess of numbers. At least now they were on a real spiritual journey together, as a family.

She pegged up a pair of Nibu's shorts and took the rest of the basket indoors. Mahesh was in the kitchen, looking for snacks to take up to his study.

"Arre, you will be full for dinner if you do that!" said Shreene. "What are you looking around for, messing up everything? Mark Whitefoot will be here in just twenty minutes."

Mahesh turned to her, his face carrying a storm. "So I want some numpkin. I can't have that in my own house?" he said, voice lowered, crackling with static.

"But—" said Shreene.

"Sssh," he said, making the sound quickly, with a harsh shuffle of air, as though berating a child. He put a finger to his lips and raised his eyebrows to indicate Rumi's room above the kitchen.

"What are you—" said Shreene, infuriated.

Mahesh grimaced, curling his left lip so that it exposed his teeth. He pointed at the ceiling and shook his head in brief dismissal. "She needs absolute silence to focus," he said, in a no-nonsense whisper.

Shreene felt her face strain with a violent rage, so extreme it threatened to throttle her. "Don't you dare speak to me like that!" she said, choking, her voice a loud hiss. "You think I don't know? Do you ever think how hard I work at everything? I am not one of your students!"

Mahesh widened his eyes till they almost bulged, then continued the silent pantomime with a curt shake of his hand as though he was throwing something behind his back, before turning and closing the door firmly behind him.

AFTER DINNER, THE two men went to the pub to play their game of chess. Whitefoot protested, complaining that the six-pack would go to waste, but Mahesh was firm, putting his arm round Whitefoot's shoulders and shepherding him out of the house, explaining as they walked that Rumi could not afford any distractions at this point: however much they subdued their voices, she would still know they were there, and he was not willing to risk it.

After ten minutes they entered the Traveller's Rest, a crumbling old pub that looked as though it was being propped up almost against its will. Whitefoot led them there, assuring Mahesh that there would be no students: it was too low-key. Mahesh was familiar with pubs, mostly at annual events, the departmental Christmas lunch or summer drinks at their local in Swansea. But, inside, the lights were more fluorescent than he had been expecting, while the concoction of pop music, cigarette smoke, fruit-machine trills and sports commentary—from a small portable TV, fixed to a ratchet in the corner above the bar—made him feel dizzy. These places were different when they weren't being used for parties.

He sat at a table by the window and began to set up the board while Whitefoot got the drinks. Mahesh watched his friend and suddenly felt intimidated by his confidence. Whitefoot seemed to be in his element, a barely noticeable swagger adorning his step as he balanced the two pints in front of him, a packet of cheese and onion crisps held with just the little finger on one side, turning back to glance up at the television as he walked.

When he arrived at the table, Mahesh got up to sit in the opposite chair, placing himself so that his back was to the rest of the room, preferring to look at the ambient reflections of people and light that were skimming against the window. He felt small, uncultivated somehow, shrunken with insecurity, and he knew it had something to do with the pub, the easy assurance with which alcohol and sport could connect these unknown people into a community of their own. It was ridiculous. "A little Indian man in the corner." The words came into his head, circled with an imagined note of pity, like the red pen on a student mistake, too quickly for him to feel anything other than shocked. Was this how he saw himself? He made a reprimanding mental note: "If you look down on your own status, you can only expect the same from others. No more of that."

They played the first game with perfunctory respect, Mahesh allowing Whitefoot to take lengthy pauses before moving, Whitefoot allowing Mahesh to take back a move, a second after he'd made it in error. Mahesh won, clearing the board practically and simply, so that

Whitefoot had no option but to resign, outdone by the sheer annihilation of his army. With the second game, they began to talk.

"So what's yer actual aim with Rumi, then?" asked Whitefoot, crunching through a single extraordinarily large crisp, and smiling at a couple of men who were standing by the games machine.

Mahesh turned to look at them. They were burly, heads shaved roughly, wearing rugby shirts that topped off thick stripes with white jersey collars. It looked as if they were watching a match on the TV. "Who are they?" he asked Whitefoot, taking a sip from his beer.

"No idea," said Whitefoot. "Why? Any particular reason?" He bent in and gave Mahesh an interested look, inviting him to spill any beans he might have.

"No reason," said Mahesh. "What were you saying, anyway? About Rumi?"

"Oh, yeah, what's yer plan there? Where's it all going?"

"My plan? There is no plan."

"Come on, Vash, man, you're orchestrating something there, aren't you? This isn't happening by itself, now, is it?"

"Orchestrating," Mahesh said. He paused, then grunted something inaudible.

"What was that?" said Whitefoot, looking entertained. "Are you sulking already? What did you say?"

"Nothing."

"No, go on, tell me. I'd like an insight into the inner workings of the man himself."

Mahesh sighed lengthily, and made his voice sound as dismissive as possible. "Using a word like that is a luxury."

"Oooh. Now we're cooking. Let me have it, Vash, hit me with it."

Mahesh smiled, registering Whitefoot's childlike enthusiasm for a clash and elaborated: "It is a luxury, used only by someone who is deluded enough to think that the world is full of choices, someone who essentially lives their life in a false cocoon of leisure."

"Oh, yeah," said Whitefoot, taking an extended guzzle of his pint and wiping his mouth with the back of his hand. "I like your style—

'a false cocoon of leisure.' " He chuckled, then crunched a crisp greedily. "Explain this theory to me, then. Explain my lack of white man's burden. My blinkered elitism. The rarefied atmosphere I live in. I'd love that." He clicked the back of his throat, signifying that he was ready for action.

"I'm not going to get into a quarrel with you," said Mahesh. "It will only exacerbate your self-indulgence."

They laughed together, Whitefoot feigning outrage, then nodding in a fake bow of respect.

Mahesh continued: "I was pointing out that I am not 'orchestrating' anything. I am merely helping Rumi to fulfill her potential. And if she wants to be taken seriously in this country she will have to do a lot more than just fulfill it, you can be sure of that. But even when you are in a minority, if you apply yourself you can achieve anything in life. However difficult it may seem."

"Bravo," said Whitefoot, clapping. "But what if she gets into university and goes there now, this year, when she turns fifteen—your grand plan, right? I put it to you, sir, that you are a very controlling person, and you are currently doing what is desirable to you. But what about her? Don't you think it's going to screw her up? Where's the need for it?"

"What do you mean, 'need'? If she can do this, and has the ability, why would you want to hold her back? Academic achievement is necessary to success. It is the only quantifiable measure of a life of the mind. Nobody can argue with an objective grading system. Once you achieve certain marks you can carry them with you for life. They are like . . ." Mahesh hesitated, thinking of the right word. "It is like Krishna says in the *Bhagavadgita*—'Always persevere, control your mind. This will be your armor against the fickle nature of the world.' " He sniffed decisively. "The armor, you see," he repeated.

"I hear you, Vash. You've pulled out all the stops there, quoting the holy book and that," said Whitefoot. He peered at the board and took a deep breath, crushing the crisps packet in his hand before making his next move.

"But what about being a normal teenager, man?" he continued. "What about, you know, discovering how to vomit in a straight line on a starlit night after one too many bevvies down the local?" Whitefoot chortled, demonstrably amused by himself. "Dyeing your hair green so you can get the attention of the kid who sits at the front in chemistry. That sort of thing, et cetera."

A loud cheer came from the bar, the two rugby men joining in with the steady escalation of applause and horns from the TV. The sound bellowed through the room, blasting Mahesh's nerves. He retorted loudly, aiming to get Whitefoot's attention back from the screen: "You are mocking my approach to parenting? Does it amuse you to deride the traditions of my culture?"

Whitefoot raised his eyebrows and shook his head vehemently.

"Oh, no, no, no way, I'm not taking that. Not from a man who wears a raincoat with a three-inch-wide belt. You're not telling me you're paying homage to the traditional work wear of your ancestral people with that one, are you?" He feigned a Welsh accent, his voice like a compressed spring. "Got yew a homespun loongi on underneath, have yew? I missed that today, love. Why don't you give us a peek of it later, like?"

Mahesh laughed, in spite of himself. He felt his chest relax, and realized he had been holding himself as though he was literally preparing to do battle. It was a relief, and he let the breath empty out of his body in a large, windy guffaw. "Look, Rumika is not going to be interested in these things as they are not relevant to her journey," he said. "And as far as the opposite sex goes, that decision will be made when she is old enough to take the step of marriage. There is no point getting involved in these things previous to that."

"Jesus, man, you have the ability to descend into the Dark Ages at will, don't you?"

"I fail to understand how licentiousness will enrich her life."

"A bit of licentiousness would enrich *my* life, I can tell you," said Whitefoot, rolling the *r* in "enrich" with a seedy purr. "But, no, I'm destined for a life of monastic servitude to the University of Cardiff. Check, by the way."

Mahesh jumped. A cursory look at the board revealed that his king was indeed under attack from a probing knight. He bristled. Even worse, there was a whole strategic fan of activity that he hadn't noticed: a tightly coordinated army of Whitefoot's pieces waiting inside his own territory on the board. It was as though they had animated out of his own ranks, clones of his army, which had suddenly changed color from black to white, so neat and final was the infiltration.

"This is unfair," he said, glaring at Whitefoot. "You are now two moves from an inevitable checkmate. You confused me, and meanwhile you were planning all this . . ."

"Oh, no, my man," said Whitefoot. "Don't give me the injured-party whine. I've won this fair and square. Now move yer king and let me have it."

Mahesh began to remove the pieces from the board.

"Unfair?" exclaimed Whitefoot. "Denying me the wee pleasure of seeing your king surrounded with nowhere to go? Well, take yer victories where you can. I'm going to the loo."

They played the final game without much discussion. It was an amiable draw, both sides left with only the king and a single other piece. Mahesh went to the bar for last orders, succumbing to Whitefoot's command that he "finally get a round in," keeping his gaze averted from the two men at the pinball machine as he waited for a pint and a glass of water. He had a dizzy head and a shaky stomach from the three pints he had already consumed, way over his usual intake, and the alcohol was confusing him more than it did when he took it in his own home, smudging the sounds around him so they disappeared into a murmuring background. It was only when one of the men yanked the sleeve of his coat, causing him to recoil in self-defense, that he realized they had been trying to get his attention for a while.

". . . need to sit down?" the man in the blue stripes was saying.

Mahesh blinked at him in something close to wonder.

"Just checking, mate," said his friend in the red stripes.

The two stripes looked at each other. Red put his arm on Mahesh's shoulder to balance him. "Propping the bar up, mate?" he said, with a smile. "You've been there a while. Just wondering if you're OK, like?"

Mahesh fell against the bar in a sudden sloppy movement. He felt a heave of nausea in his stomach. The stripes laughed as the room washed round them, twirling madly to a central core, like a whirlpool. He shut his eyes and prayed that he wouldn't drown. He was suddenly, and shamefully, drunk.

"He's going to be out like a light," Red said to Blue. And then, louder and slowly, as though Mahesh was deaf, "ALL RIGHT . . . MATE?" They laughed again, together, causing a rebounding anger in Mahesh as though they had pulled an elastic band and released it to sting his face. He opened his eyes and tried to speak. "Baaaa . . . shaaaaa," he said, wiping his mouth.

"Listen, mate, I'd try to sit down, if I were you," said Red, offering him a stool.

Mahesh stared at him defensively, his eyes tearful with the effort, and forced the word out of his mouth. "You . . . bhen-chott!" he said, straightening and swaying dangerously on the final syllable. It was a word he had not heard since his school days. The queen of all insults. A sister-molester. Strange that this was the official top number-one swear word in India, he thought. He had never used it before and now it sat in his mouth like a decaying paan, leaching its smell into the pub.

"You what?" said Blue, leaning over and frowning. He knocked Mahesh's head, letting his knuckles sound against the bald pate. "Everything all right in there?"

Red giggled.

Mahesh pulled back his arm, balancing himself against the bar with a flourish and prepared to swing his fist forward. He might have been carrying a great big bowling ball, so ponderous and off center was the movement when he attempted it. More snuffling hilarity from the stripes mixed with a ringing noise from the bar. When Whitefoot's voice seeped into this unstable soundscape, Mahesh looked up and saw him negotiating with the stripes, moving them away with a placatory smile so that he could take him out.

On their way home they stopped at a bench placed on a triangle of green. Mahesh threw up in the bushes behind it, then joined Whitefoot, who gave him a piece of chewing gum. Above them the sky was pale gray, overcast with a thin fog, the burned scent of fumes soaking the air. Mahesh felt oddly content as he looked up, points of light coming into focus at rare places in the sky if he squinted for long enough, his mind settling back into lucidity, frame by frame.

14

It was a week before the exam. Rumi sat in her bedroom in a thick clog of numbers, her brain torpid with unbroken equations and statistics. When she moved her head it was as though the swell of the subject shifted itself inside her mind, a fraction of a second behind her conscious movement.

On her desk: a steel bowl half filled with the seeds (accepted now "in moderation" by Mahesh as an aid to concentration), pens, geometry set, a small table lamp, the cream shade stained with a brown burn; an uneven light pierced the scorched hole where it had touched the bulb for too long. Also a selection of chocolate oatmeal biscuits, a broken Galaxy bar and, most enticing, a long finger doughnut crammed with synthetic cream and raspberry jam.

She was in familiar territory—the final stages of exam prep, and Mahesh's quiet panic that she might flag meant she was allowed to eat whatever she liked. She felt dizzy in the soak of sugar, slowly swelling both outwardly and inwardly until one day, pop, a lethargic split, and she would collapse uneventfully, releasing nothing, no hidden wonders, no secrets to the universe. No mind-wrenching discovery of prime-number theorem by the age of fourteen, like Carl Gauss. No terrifyingly brilliant paper on conical sections, like the teenage Pascal. When her brains leaked out they would just be a sugar-coated variety of normality, the same old arithmetic and geometry. A buzz of cheap numbers and symbols that anyone and everyone could memorize, given enough time and imprisonment. End of story.

She had no friends. She did not attend school anymore—had not done so for several months. She did not even feel cold anymore, having acclimatized to the chill that pervaded the house at all times, supposedly keeping her alert. This is what I have chosen, thought Rumi, crunched up at her desk. This is my life. Until I get there. Until I am free.

It was only nine o'clock. She was thinking about transcendental numbers, those chains of mystery: uncountable, numbers that never ended, just went on for ever, like *pi*, the biggest celebrity of them all. There were so many numbers out there and mathematicians had been able to prove that only a handful of them were transcendent, all the time knowing that many more waited to be uncovered, if they only knew how. Rumi imagined them—dark stars dotted through the sky, waiting for their moment, waiting to be lit up. Stars that would never die. Imagine discovering another *pi* or another *e* or another *sin*. Would it mean that you had, in fact, transcended yourself?

Her own attempt at transcendence had disappeared. She was not walking in the valley of truth anymore. Instead she was lying again, and even the desire to speak the truth had waned, so quickly that she wondered if it had ever really been possible to fulfill. The only constant was cumin, which she bit with quick violence, stabbing the flesh of her index finger with her teeth and tongue each time it retraced its route into her mouth.

There were two knocks on the door, a pause and then another. It was a weak version of the knock used by Mahesh to signify his presence, a simple code: two, pause, then one.

"Nibu?" she said, trying to keep her voice stern.

There was a squeal behind the door, a flapping laugh in a little chest.

"Nibu Vasi?" she said.

She walked over to the door and flung it open. Nibu was standing in a white undershirt and shorts, his face squashed into a silent giggle. He put his finger to his lips, curving his eyebrows into a frown, and took a deep breath, expanding his chest. The silence gave his movements a slow-motion quality. "Are you studying, Rumika?" he whispered, deepening his voice and indenting it with an Indian twang.

Rumi leaned against the edge of the door and looked down at her brother. "What do you think?"

"Sssh!" whispered Nibu. "They'll hear!" He pointed at the floor and widened his eyes, nodding solemnly.

"What do you want?" said Rumi.

"Let's play a game." He tried to inveigle his way through the door. Rumi blocked the space, causing him to dissolve into shakes of laughter. He pressed his hand over his lips to block the sound.

"I'm working," said Rumi.

"Go on!" he said.

"What kind of game do you want to play?"

"We could wrestle?" He made his hands into fists and assumed the pose of a seasoned boxer. After flexing his muscles, he jumped to one side, accidentally pushing the door against the wall. The thud made them jump, then cease all movement, fixing their positions. They waited, Rumi glaring at Nibu while he kept himself as still as possible, leaning on one leg, arm up where it had hit the door, barely trembling, as though he was playing Musical Statues. The clatter of dishes continued downstairs.

Rumi relaxed. "What d'you do that for?" she whispered.

Nibu shook his head and put his hands together in a gesture of apology. He went and looked up at her, hands still clasped, a pleading expression stretching over his face.

"All right, all right!" she said, hiding a smile. "You're allowed into my room. But only if you are silent."

Rumi allowed herself ten minutes with Nibu. She began by sitting on her chair and holding out her arm in a rigid line, angled down so that he could run against it repeatedly, throwing the force of his wiry body against her. Then she picked him up, swinging him round, finally laying him on the bed, pressing her little finger to his cheek.

"I can beat you with my little finger, *yesss,*" she said, with a majestic hiss.

Nibu hooted with laughter and thrust his face from side to side, clasping his hands round her wrist and slowly pulling himself up her elbow until he stood, almost matching her height, his feet wavering on the springy mattress.

Rumi pressed the finger of her left hand against his left cheek. "With the power of my little finger, no *lessss*," she continued, enjoying the sibilance of the final word.

"By the power of Grayskull!" said Nibu. His voice sang joyfully through the whisper. "I have the power!"

He battened his arms round her shoulders, squeezing them, and raised himself up as though he was on a climbing frame. Rumi started to walk backward with him hanging from her front, his hands locked at the back of her head, tickling the base of her skull. She turned robotically and lowered him, using her neck, bending her knees to crouch. Jumping off, he pulled her to the floor. Rumi lay down so that Nibu could envelop her in another clenching hug, rolling on her stomach to pin her down. He pressed her arms to her sides and pushed his forehead against her right shoulder, raising himself into the beginnings of a headstand. Slowly the giggles escaped him, rising like bubbles from her chest.

There was a scrape at the door. Mahesh walked in. Nibu jumped up and stood to one side while Rumi gathered herself together.

"It was just now . . ." said Nibu.

"Nibu, leave," said Mahesh. "Rumi, can't I leave you unsupervised at your age?"

Rumi remained silent, her face arranged diametrically opposite the textbook, clutching a pencil in one hand, geometry tools in the other.

"What have you been working on?" asked Mahesh, coming over. He stood behind her and looked over her shoulder. "You have stopped a timed exam to play like a child?"

Her body was rigid, muscles threaded suddenly with pain. Do not succumb, she told herself. Do not speak. Do not look at him.

"How will you know what your capability is in a real sense if you do not have the timings to hand?"

Mahesh sat down on Rumi's bed. She could hear his breathing, rubbing the air like sandpaper, with a light, regular friction.

"I am due to go to the office now. I don't know if I should cancel my plans due to the severity of this situation."

They sat in silence for a few moments, broken only by the movements in the kitchen below.

"You are a very silly girl."

A tiny yelp escaped her. She realized the compass was locked in her hand, that she was pressing its point against the flesh at the base of her little finger.

"Stupid girl," he said.

She attempted to steady herself, her hand shaking with contained force.

"This is stupid behavior, isn't it?"

There was silence. Rumi could hear him waiting for her response. Her focus went to two triangles interlocking in the top third of her exercise book. In her mind, an expression of disgust was warping his mouth in the fissure of his beard.

"It is stupid behavior, isn't it?"

Rumi nodded, aware that it was over.

"I will trust you, Rumi, but I expect to see the completed papers when I return."

He got up and passed his hand over her hair. "Come on now. You can do it." His voice was softer, coaxing. "Be a good girl. Don't jeopardize everything you have been working toward."

After he had closed the door behind him, Rumi looked at her hand. The compass had pierced the start of a dark brown line of pigment that streaked across her palm toward her index finger, the kind of line that was supposed to tell you something about your life. A thin cut was visible, revealing a minute globule of red. She took the compass in her left hand and inserted the pointed end back in the slit, aiming to pull it and extend the cut, imagining that it would follow the trajectory of the line embedded in her flesh, a drip of red superimposed over the long curve. But her skin wouldn't give way, and she didn't force it.

LATER RUMI WENT downstairs to make herself some hot chocolate. Shreene was finishing off in the kitchen, her movements impatient and loud. Rumi filled the kettle, sat on a stool and stared out of the window that stretched across the wall by the sink. She could see the world outside, muted through the double glazing: a peculiar twilight of cloud and garden, the large willow waving its obese mass in the wind. Nibu's swing shook under the branches in a tortured dance, the orange plastic plate jumping against the ropes that held it.

"Mum," she said.

Shreene didn't reply.

"I need a bra," said Rumi.

Shreene turned. She was crouched at the door that led to the garage, emptying the dustbin, her hands deep in the process of disentangling a bulging bag from its container. Her face was simmering with nausea, nose turned away, as she picked up the rotting vegetables that fell to the floor each time she tried to heave the bag out of the bin. She looked at Rumi, weary irritation traced out in her face. "Why are you thinking about these things?"

"Because I need one and it isn't fair."

"Is this what you should be thinking about when your exam is so close?"

"What?"

"When I was your age I would not have asked my mother for something like this. We were so shy of speaking about these things. When my mother took me aside and explained to me that I would need one, I was so embarrassed. It had not occurred to me—I was so innocent—"

"I don't care! I don't care about when you grew up! I want one! I've started my periods, you know that, and you can't stop me asking you—"

Shreene raised her hand abruptly, cutting Rumi short. She knotted the bag of rubbish with furious speed, her hands moving expertly against the black plastic, leaving it to present a perfect knot. "Look how you speak to your mother. Shameless. Without shame. We were so simple at your age, and you, look at you—stripped of any sense of decency. We have lived here so long you are changing color—"

"Mum, I am not going to listen to you. I am not going to listen to you be cruel and nasty. I don't care!"

Rumi rocked unsteadily on the stool as the words came out, and stared at her mother with defiance.

"You are calling me cruel and nasty?" said Shreene, with a mocking laugh. "This is how you talk to your mother? Have you no shame? Do you not have any idea of respect, the way you should respect your mother? Do I have to teach you even this?"

"Cruel, cruel, cruel and nasty!"

Rumi banged her fist on the worktop with each word. Shreene took a step toward her and enclosed her wrist in a tight grip, crushing it against the worktop. "How dare you? Is this my fate, then, to be treated like a dog by husband and daughter? Some kind of servant who is just there for your needs?"

Rumi struggled to pull herself free with her other arm. Shreene pressed down more forcefully. Rumi looked at her hand splayed under the other, a brown spider flailing its legs under the pale elegance of Shreene's skin and bone. Her mother's wedding ring glinted under the chemical light from the tube that split the ceiling above them.

"Stop it!" said Rumi. "Why are you saying all this? Why do you make it all dirty? It's not fair. Why are you so nasty to me?"

"You are telling me how to speak now? How I should tell you things? Like father, like daughter. Is this what he has taught you to do? He has given you too much freedom. It has gone to your head. Let him reap the consequences. Why should I have to deal with this? We have a saying, you wouldn't even know it, in Hindi: 'You should take a droplet of water and be so shameful that you should drown yourself in it.' "

Rumi pulled her wrist free and got up from the stool. Her chest collapsed as sobs arched through her stomach and up to her throat. Her hands flew to her ears, pressing them down to eliminate all sound. She began to wail, tears slipping down her cheeks with each heaving, cavernous release. "Ay-yay-yay-yay! I can't hear you. You can say what you want!"

Shreene came over and tried to peel off her hands. Rumi clasped the sides of her head and pushed as hard as she could, face steaming with the effort, as though she was aiming to make both ears meet in the center of her skull. Her eyelids sealed themselves over her eyes, crinkling taut. "Ay-ay-ay! Yay-yay-yay-yay-aieee! I can't hear you!"

She bent over double, crying with huge, gasping throbs, her hands still clamped to her ears, subduing Shreene's shouts into a distant thrum. At the edge of her vision, her mother's mouth was moving. "I can't hear you!" Rumi sobbed, "I want a bra! It's normal!" She continued to wail, staring at the floor, letting the salty heat gather in the corners of her eyes and dribble down the sides of her nose in tears. Eventually she removed the hands and let the cold landscape of kitchen noise rush back into her head. She waited, steadying her breathing, and began again: "And I want to go to the end-of-year school party."

"What party?"

"The summer party for the end of the year. It's a disco in the church Portakabin. You didn't let me go to the Christmas party but this one is after my exam. I'm going to go."

"What do you mean, 'I am going to go'? What do you think, that after starting your periods you will be allowed to go anywhere? Putting yourself in danger? You don't even know how to behave properly, asking me for a bra like that, so proudly, no shame, not even the hint of it!"

"Shut up! Leave me alone!"

"Don't you dare talk to me like that! What do you want to do at this party? Why are you so desperate to go? Tell me that."

Rumi began to shake. "You're horrible! Why do you talk like that? I hate you!"

"You hate me, do you? You want me to talk differently? You want me to talk in your English way? Not intelligent enough for you? You think so much of yourself now that he has made you believe you are the greatest thing on earth."

Suddenly Rumi bolted, running through the kitchen and down the corridor to the front door. She could hear Shreene coming close behind her as she scrabbled for the key to the porch, pulling it off its hook inside the storeroom door. By the time she had turned round, choking and disoriented, Shreene was standing in front of the door, arms extended, hand over the lock, as though she was held against a crucifix, the gray light of the night outside casting a ghostly outline round the slender lines of her body.

Rumi turned and bolted again, running into the living room and pulling dementedly at the patio door. It was locked. She knew the key was in the kitchen but she pulled anyway, resting her belly on the long plastic handle as she urged the door toward herself. Shreene walked over quickly and pulled her away from the handle. "What are you going to do? Break it?"

Rumi stopped and began to cry, her head against the thick glass, hot breath creating a small patch of steam, filming over the sight of weeds and rosebushes populating the soil outside. Shreene stood by.

This time when she began to run, Rumi shut the living room door behind her to slow Shreene. She clambered up the stairs, using her hands to scale them as though attacking a steep, carpeted mountain, resting her chin on the edge of the last step, then pushing herself up, her hands near her chest. At the top, catching her breath, she saw Nibu come out of his room, a skeleton of a boy, eyes meeting hers briefly then looking to the floor.

"Nibu . . ." she said, faltering. He stood limply, his frame deflated, holding himself at an odd angle, kicking a leg in front of him.

"Nibu, can't you help?" she asked. He retreated into his room, closing the door.

"Nibu?" she called, getting up speed to run into the bathroom. Shreene came up the stairs, her face pink and strained. Rumi ran into the bathroom and got hold of the door, pushing it away from herself to ram it shut. Shreene came up and inserted her whole body into the space between the door and its frame, leaning hard against Rumi's opposing weight. This continued for a few seconds, Rumi easing up every now and then at the fear that she might crush her mother's arm, watching Shreene's angular elbow levering the door open, her feet inching in. Eventually Shreene flung open the door and Rumi threw herself into the bath, letting her legs tumble in so that her feet fell over the plughole.

She lay against the cool ceramic and watched Shreene standing in the dark, breathing uncertainly.

"Get out of the bath," said Shreene.

"No."

"Get out of it now."

"No."

Rumi stood up, and looked into Shreene's eyes. They both shivered. Shreene put her hands on Rumi's shoulders and applied pressure.

"Come on," she said.

"No," said Rumi.

"Come on—what do you want? You want a smack? At your age?"

Rumi leaned against the windowsill. A rectangular window was open at the top, crowning a large frosted pane of glass. She inserted her head directly underneath the opening and began to call out through the space. "Help me. Somebody help me!"

Shreene smacked her neatly on her right cheek, her breath seething, mouth opening to flash an intense gleam of teeth. In the close density of the room, barely there at all, Rumi saw a tear fall, like a whisper, from Shreene's right eye. "You want to humiliate me?" Shreene said.

Rumi buckled under dramatically, took a deep breath and increased the tenor of her voice. "Help me, somebody! Save me from this!"

Shreene froze. She put her finger to her lips and frowned at Rumi, her eyes diverting out of the bathroom. She turned her head, listening for a sound from below. Rumi waited. They heard a key in the garage door and the metallic creak of the door being lifted, the unmistakable footsteps of Mahesh moving across the front yard. Shreene walked out of the bathroom. Rumi stayed for a minute, counting up to 60 in simple whole numbers. Then she returned to her room. She sat at her desk and took the position of study, layering the cumin in her mouth with a tired monotony, biting her finger in a systematic rhythm, stopping only to allow herself to swallow.

15

Rumi wakes at six and looks out of her bedroom window. The light is diffuse, straining through the mesh of the net curtain, hovering in the air like a spring scent of her mother's, lemon-tinted, bracing, not to be ignored. The thick outer curtains stand surely, like guards at either side, pulled half open by her own hands the night before, placed to allow her to be woken up by natural light as early as possible.

It is fifteen minutes before the alarm she has set will go off, the time arranged with an allowance for 3×7 minute presses of the snooze button, getting her out of bed by 6:41 a.m. at the latest. Instead of beginning this series of hurdles, she lies still, alert, and looks at the blurred space that is her room. Her specs are on her desk. There is a permanent shake in the base of her belly, fighting to be acknowledged, which she diverts instead by using short, simple mission statements.

I will not wear contact lenses today, she thinks, even though I have to go to school for this, even though I might meet Bridgeman. Even though it has been three months since I saw anyone, including him. I will wear my glasses and I will tie my hair back from my face, even though there is a pimple at the top of my forehead, like a minute volcano ready to overflow. I will not be vain. I will be humble. My exam is the only truth. My exam is my freedom. And I will not lie, whatever the consequences. Today is too important. Today I have to walk in the valley of truth.

She makes an internal prayer to a faceless entity, scrunching her eyes shut, embracing the sheen of black under the lids. "Today I will be good, God," she whispers. "I will be so good. Please help me." She opens her eyes and turns onto her side. Next to her pillow there is a little plastic sac of cumin, slackly open and containing about an inch of the seeds, which are trailing out of one corner onto her sheet, the tiny brown thorns pricking the white background, sharp among the soft bobbling of the cotton. She licks her index finger and presses it against the sheet, allowing three or four seeds to affix themselves. Chewing them brings no sensation, so familiar is the taste. It is the first day of the A-level papers. She is 14 years, 11 months and 22 days old. Here we go, she thinks. It is time.

THE MORNING WAS spent in a state of unified calm. Even Nibu knew to keep himself to himself, playing his part in the super-shushed expectancy of the household, carrying himself with a dignified distance as he performed his ablutions: cleaning his teeth as quietly as possible, looking away as Rumi walked past the bathroom so as not to distract her. She prepared her kit for the exam, held in a transparent plastic bag as requested by the authorities. Her maths tools and a brand-new set of pens lay together with an adult nonchalance that felt different from the O level. There was a sense of ceremony about the occasion. And, indeed, Shreene performed a short ceremony, giving Rumi a series of white things to eat, to bring her luck, a tradition that she did not feel the need to explain, in spite of Rumi's cheerful bewilderment. She put each item in a steel tray and lit a stick of incense, then took the food and put it into Rumi's mouth. First, a piece of banana. Then a drink of milk from a steel glass. Third, with a laugh and a wink, a Polo mint. And finally, bizarrely, yet not unpleasurably, some shredded coconut and freshly mashed potato, in quick succession.

Mahesh was all smiles today. He made Rumi a pot of tea and sat with her at the breakfast table, asking whether she had slept well, commenting on the weather. It was a sparky morning, and Rumi felt there might be electricity under the clouds, a sunlight made of ions, positively and negatively charged particles rubbing through the atmosphere to land on her skin. She felt very happy, as though she had sucked helium from a balloon and was talking in a squeakier voice than normal. She heard herself making conversation in this voice as she ate her cereal and sat with her father, bathed in electro-sunlight, so friendly, such respect between them, existing in an easy rapport that she wished would never end. Then she left the house, three film cases filled with cumin in her bag, a kiss on the cheek from her mother, an arm round her shoulder from her father, squeezing her before she left. And inevitably, she thought later, in the way that certain things are written in your dreams without your consent, as inevitable as the alarm that never had gone off that morning, three minutes into her walk to school, at the end of her road, she bumped into Bridgeman.

He was trudging along on the pavement parallel to her, down the main hill, a gaping expanse of black tar road between them. His jacket sleeves were rolled up, a thin band of leather spiraling from the wrist upward almost touching his elbow. His hair was ruffled in a wild crop, eyes on the ground signifying deep thought. There was no traffic, just a soundless void, waiting to be filled. A bird chirped, an irritable burble, gone as quickly as it had begun, but it made him look up. As he lifted his face she whipped her glasses into her blazer pocket, cursing herself, suddenly plunging the world into a defocused gray, the air pricking her eyes as though they had been revealed for the very first time. She looked down. Her ankle socks melded with her shoes in a furry mishmash of black and white, and she walked very slowly, praying inside her chest for release.

"Please, God," she whispered. "Please. Please. Please please please. 3.14159265358979323846 is *pi*. Please don't let him see. I can go further if you want . . . 264338 . . ."

She heard his voice behind her, a stabbing noise in the foggy space. I'm blind, she thought. I'm stupid.

He walked alongside, matching her slowness without speaking for a few seconds. "What are you up to?" he said.

She shuffled along, micromanaging her movements, feeling her cheeks burn with a tart heat.

"Why'd you take your glasses off?"

Rumi looked up, carefully retaining her balance, and pretended to meet his eyes, registering only a snowstorm for his face. Her gaze returned to her feet, which she moved as though they belonged to a toy, a doll that might fall over at any minute. Humiliation surged inside her.

"C'mon, what's wrong with you? And where have you been, anyway?" he said.

Water appeared in her eyes, a trickle of tears.

"Why'd you take your glasses off?" he said. "You look nice in glasses. I told you that before. You can't see, can you?"

She stopped walking and wiped the corner of her eye with a lightning movement. Her hand knocked against a cumin pot as she fumbled for the loathed object in her pocket and replaced it on her face. Then she walked at speed, restored to the world of the living, letting her feet hit the pavement with strong regularity, ignoring his voice as it became quieter and quieter behind her, until it was deleted by the air itself, like liquid correction fluid, blotting the page into white.

The small field outside the gym hall was full of sixth formers, something that shouldn't have surprised her, but did. She realized she wasn't mentally prepared for the event. Mrs. Powell, her old maths teacher, walked her through the crowd, ignoring the heads that turned at their entry. Rumi looked round the tall, self-assured mass of students. Dressed casually, they waved at each other, chatted, leaned against bags on the grass, bit their knuckles in mock fear, ruffled their hair. Some glanced at Rumi, drawn in by her red and gray uniform, a familiar posting from their old lives. She registered shock on some faces, as she got closer to the entrance, a stirrup of building panic against her chest when she locked eyes with a trio of older girls. They looked at each other in open confusion as Rumi walked past. Mrs. Powell spoke in a low voice, guiding her to a desk at the front of the hall.

"Don't worry," she said. "You'll be fine."

Rumi nodded. She was hoping that the teacher would leave with minimum fuss so that she could sit down and chew cumin, alone, without scrutiny or more well-wishing. Eventually, after a few more equally inane comments, to which Rumi didn't reply, she left, holding up a hand with 2 × 2 fingers crossed, shaking it encouragingly in the air, the palm facing Rumi as she walked away, almost backward, treading carefully between the grid of desks. From a distance it looked as if she was making the peace sign. The thought was outrageous enough to make Rumi smile. She took a deep gasp, sat down, laughter knotting like a cough in her throat, trapped in phlegm and inhibited air. But it was a cough that wouldn't go away, like the image of the smiling, peace-loving Mrs. Powell. Again it erupted, louder this time, and then again, till the spasms were closer and closer together. Eventually she sat, giggling silently to herself, a hostage to the earthquake of her body, which shook and ground itself in her chair, while she held on to the desk for dear life, staring at the mauled wood in front of her for fear of catching the eyes of the people nearby. Again she saw Mrs. Powell in her mind's eye, holding up an abnormally large hand in a gesture of peace, nodding in slow motion, mouthing, "Peace," her eyes half closed, fingers fused from four to two. Imagine if you had only two fingers. It wasn't funny. Only somehow, right now, it was.

"Are you all right?"

The sound killed her movement as instantly as switching off a TV. She looked up. It was a teacher she didn't know, someone who did only the sixth form. This must be the invigilator, she thought, serious and tall—V-necked gray sweater, blond mustache and red tie combining to give him an aura of sadness, as though he knew his fate for the next three hours was unavoidable. She nodded, and unpacked her pens onto the desk to indicate that she was in control, ready for study. He looked at her blankly, then returned to the front of the room, walking with sloppy boredom, his legs bumping into the sides of the desks as he went. As the papers were distributed she covertly positioned a film case of cumin on the floor, so that she could dip her finger into the murky depths.

SHE LEFT THE hall with a fizzing happiness, the optimism and relief racing with adrenaline in her blood. She had got away with it. She had done it. She was through the first gate. This really could happen. She was going to escape to Oxford. Finally was going to leave Cardiff and her life. She would be free. Or, at least, it felt like it. It was the first paper of five and it had been an amalgam of all the kinds of questions she had been forcing her way through for months. "Last year the employees of a firm received no pay rise, a small pay rise or a large pay rise . . ."; ". . . find the probability that in a string of beads, four or fewer are orange . . ."; "calculate the equation of the regression line of y on x . . ."; ". . . Andrew A, Charles C and Edward E are employed by the Palace Hotel . . ." Statistics. She loved them suddenly with an unbearable passion. Looking out over the field, the grass seemed to shine with a Disneylike radiance. If there are x daisies per square meter, she thought, and y dandelions, what is the probability of any one blade of grass being next to a flower? Her face flushed happily as she walked up the path.

Deflation occurred gradually, as she emerged into the open space close to the entrance of the school and felt the uncertainty of being in the world once more. In front of her, the path went both ways, the right curling round the orange brick of the main building to the harsh wheeze of the playground, the complex sound both alien and nostalgic, the left leading back to the main road and the lone safety of her room. She pressed inside her pocket for stray seeds that had fallen from the film case and chewed them, extracting the odd cotton strand and piece of fluff from her tongue. She waited a couple of minutes, standing there, breathing, her blood still speedy, the exam still unfolding in her head. And then she took the right, feeling a rush as she walked round the corner, as if she was being utterly daring, even though she was just walking back into her own school.

The playground was unchanged, a gray space of concrete adjoining sprawling open turf, padlocked by gates and fence along one side, school buildings on the other. It was lunchtime so the full montage of Llanfedyg High School was out on display. She watched as an observer, her presence irrelevant. Standing with her hands in her pockets, keeping her distance, she scanned the crowds, for whom, exactly, she wasn't sure. Her class formed a conglomerate in the top right-hand corner, same place, same setup, but more mixed up than before. The girls stood near the wall by the Senior Hall, boys slouched round them, talking or kicking a ball. Diagonally behind them, on a small hilly patch of green, sat three people from Chess Club: Milky Boy, Graham and Flug. They were staring at something on the grass, something that was very likely to be a travel chess set.

Her initial reaction was of pleasure, trounced by embarrassment. Getting to them would involve walking through the entire space, exposing herself to potential mishaps—she was likely to be seen, glasses and all. She looked back at the louche gathering from her class, concentrated by the wall, and saw Bridgeman. He was standing apart from the group, talking to a girl with a chocolate bob, kinked through with perm, the hair dried to curl plumply, resting in a perfect orb against her neck. In fact, they were barely talking, muttering the odd phrase and looking about, as though they were attached by some invisible thread but didn't know what to do in each other's vicinity. Occasionally they let their eyes stay linked for a beat. Rumi felt a lurch in what she supposed was her heart, a seasick moment in her chest, which made her turn and walk back out, following the path to the gate.

On the walk home, she saw Rafferty and Harris. They heard her come up behind them, Rafferty turning first and eyeing her as though she was a specimen under a microscope. Rumi went for her spectacles again, a knee-jerk reaction, then moved her hand up to pass through her hair instead, remembering the morning's mess-up.

"Look who it is," said Rafferty. "Well, well, well."

Rumi gave her a weak smile and resigned herself to walking in tandem with them, rather than moving past and being accused of weirdness.

"Your glasses are well thick, aren't they?" said Julie Harris, as if surprised by her own observation. "Thought you didn't wear them anymore."

"Where have you been?" said Rafferty. "Is it true what people have been saying?"

Rumi shrugged, twisting her hand in her pocket.

"Tell us, go on," said Rafferty. "Where've you been hiding away?"

"Just . . ." said Rumi.

"Is it true you're going to do your A level now?" asked Harris.

Rumi thought about it for a second, then nodded.

"Omigod, you are SUCH a complete, unbelievable, total swot!" said Rafferty. "I don't believe it! This is so amazing!"

"But you must be super-brainy to do that," said Harris, pensively, as though she was contemplating her own relative braininess.

"Come on," said Rafferty. "It's like you're the queen of nerds, Rumi Vasi. You're like, the top of the family tree. You've outdone the whole lot of nerds worldwide with this one, haven't you?"

Rumi looked down and counted. Her road was four left turnings away. Not far to go.

"Anyway, are you going out with anyone at the moment?" asked Rafferty, ending the sentence with a sarcastic giggle and looking at Harris, encouraging her to join in. "I guess you know your old 'boyfriend,' your serious 'luvver,' is going out with someone now, don't you?"

Rumi took a deep breath and felt the hurt like a hot outline of pain in her chest, in the same place as before, something that burned and spread when she inhaled.

"Come to get him back off her, 'ave you?" Rafferty winked at Harris. "Going to have a scrap at the back of the gym hall with Clare Williamson, are you?"

So that was who it was. She'd changed her hair. That was the face hidden under the bob. Williamson was bright, pretty, self-assured; her dad was a doctor. The type who might become head girl one day.

"Scrap! Scrap! Scrap!" said Rafferty, acting out the chant that accompanied playground fights. "We want blood! We want blood!" She stopped walking, looking at the ground just ahead of her feet. A small mound of dog's excrement was blocking her way. "Ugh!" she said, sidestepping it and commenting to Harris in a low voice, "Watch out, you might step in some Rumika." They laughed together, Harris more sheepish than Rafferty, who seemed to be enjoying herself.

Rumi had a choice. She could either cave in, let the pain go full blast, or do something. She was not willing to let them see how weak she felt.

She made herself laugh. It was an awkward, fumbling sound, but it was a laugh of sorts.

She tried to make her voice join in with them, subconsciously mimicking their rhythm as though she could see the funny side of the joke.

Rafferty cut short her own leering chuckle, with an abrupt movement. She took Rumi's schoolbag, lifting and shoving the portly satchel so it whacked back against Rumi's hip. "Fuck *off*!" she said, a fierce rasp to her voice.

They walked on, leaving Rumi behind, Rafferty whispering in Harris's ear and looking back, a smirk pasted over her face.

16

they flew to India nine days after the final exam. It was Rumi's birthday. "You are 15, daughter," said the front of the card she opened while they sat in the departure lounge at Heathrow. "0245 a.m. . . . Terminal 3 . . . Please do not leave your luggage unattended . . ." were the words on the rolling banner of scarlet digital letters that wooed them through repetition, like a practical mantra set to keep them awake as they sat in their chairs, waiting for the gate number to be called. Inside, Shreene and Mahesh had written, "We are proud of you on this special day. We know you will retain your high ideals and make us even more proud." Nibu had written, "Happy birthday DIDI you are grrrrrEAT" in a liquid scrawl of orange felt-tip.

Her present was forthcoming: a series of clothes made to her own specifications by a tailor in India, from material of her own choosing, to be purchased in Lajput Nagar market. In her bag she had a series of pictures torn from women's magazines for ideas— long shirts in silken materials belted loosely round the waist, prints of tiny flowers, Indian Paisley, checks and ginghams, hippie skirts in floating cotton with small bells attached to the drawstrings, a pair of velvet hot pants cut with a serrated edge and worn with an oversized T-shirt tied in a knot at the waist. In her mind the shapes and colors shifted in a constantly mutating mosaic: layer upon layer of changeable lengths, sleeves, colors and fabrics. Who knew what she would find in Lajput Nagar? Maybe a roll of maroon lace, stitched through with silver thread. Or a wide slab of thick turquoise cotton, stiff as cardboard, speckled throughout with holes cut in the shape of daisy petals. Maybe even pure silk, luscious and drinkable under the lantern light she remembered so well, the hot spots poised at intervals, ushering her discreetly into the dark alleys, the tight warren of the market.

It was the culmination of three days' furious preparation: present-buying, packing, suitcases-weighing, the shutting down of their home—a whipped sweet confection of excitement building up like the ice-cream peak on a Mr. Softee 99 special. They were going for a whole six weeks. Rumi had never felt so connected to her family, so bound in this new present tense where maths could not exist until they had the results, due in exactly one month's time. Until that moment of release they had no option but collectively to forgo any study, extricate themselves from the grid of routine with a shrug of the shoulders. Even Mahesh had eased up, letting Rumi become Shreene's official helper.

Sitting in the airport, she was still tense about several things, juggling thoughts at the back of her head against the image of the forthcoming trip. But the tension was almost sweet. After seven years they were going to India. That in itself was such an incredible happening, of almost otherworldly significance, so immense an event that it had to offer her protection of some sort from her mundane anxieties. But she continued to worry. First, and most obviously, she couldn't work out what her grade would be for the exam. She had run out of time on two papers, throwing her proofs down in rapid panic, like newspaper on a spillage, for the final problem in each case. She had started with the answer, which she calculated easily enough, through intuition, and worked backward with panicked etchings and suggestions of how she had got there, both times. But she hadn't given it the detail and respect for process that was expected. The question was simple. Was it down to showing how you did it, or was the answer enough? If you didn't explain how your mind worked, would you still make the grade? This vague fear circulated readily in the background of everything she did, like Shreene's anxiety that she might have left the oven on—something that could mean they would return to a soured world in Corbett Road.

Next, and more pressingly, she was worried about the cumin in her shoes. She looked down at the round-toed clumpy blocks, balanced on a thick rubber sole, a silver-plated buckle stitched into the top. The metal reflected the crush and swell of movement round her, human faces magnifying in the steel as they walked past, squashing the tired light with intermittent beats. The decision to put the cumin in her shoes had taken a lot of thought. It had won over the idea of putting the plastic bag in her knickers, like the girl she had seen on the news, now in jail for drugs in the Far East somewhere. Although she knew there was no way she could be searched in that exact place, the idea of placing it in such an intimate area was too harrowing. What if the bag split and she felt the seeds running down the leg of her trousers and hitting the floor in full vision? The shame of it. What if they realized she had touched herself there so practically, hiding her wares in that space as though it was a normal part of her body? And what if she aroused suspicion because of the way she walked—being taken aside by a female security guard, then made to strip down and clumsily expose her awful-shaped figure? There was all of this to fear if she didn't make the right choice.

And so the cumin had been enclosed in two thin plastic sandwich bags, knotted and inserted into the center of her shoes, covered by the heart of each foot, the arch of her sole fitting neatly over the mound. She pressed her shoes into the floor and felt the mass inside them. There had been no choice. There had to be cumin on the plane: it was a nine-hour flight. And if she carried it overtly in her pocket, she would be forced to put it in the X-ray with her purse and glasses case. They would suspect it was some other drug, an illegal one, and she would have to go through a whole embarrassing breakdown and explanation, her parents shocked and repelled by her dependence on the substance, maybe even missing their flight while the guards analyzed it in their labs or whatever they did.

More thoughts. Would her contact lenses dry up on the flight? Should she send Bridgeman a postcard from the plane, saying, "Sorry for any weirdness . . . by the way I just wanted to say I'll always . . . xxxx you"? Maybe she should cut it out of her heart once and for all and paste it on the page, a homemade greeting sent back flying through the biosphere at the wrong time of year for Valentines to arrive on his doormat in Justine Close. When he opened it, she wondered if she would be suddenly and mysteriously released from the dead weight in each word, the beefy vowels and consonants that she had carried in a slump at the back of her mind for so long. "By the way . . . in case you didn't know . . ."

And what would happen to her now? Now that the hard corners of her school self were melting into this new, indefinable person, clad in tan waistcoat, stonewashed jeans and silk scarf—a person with no postscript attached, the years of swotting evaporating with each breath she took. She could be anyone, really. Would someone lock eyes with her on the plane? Only if she managed to keep her contact lenses in, thereby limiting her ability to sleep. But worth it, if she could get away with it. Her first kiss—would it be at the back of the flight cabin, the sky reeling by in drunken fits of cloud and exhaust? Or in India? All the boys there would be Indian, after all . . .

It was early evening when they began the descent into Delhi. Rumi pressed her face to the window and consumed the lolloping puffs of white, the caramel-hued horizon and the dizzy map of emerging land with covetous pleasure. The whistle in her ears was magnifying into a suitably intense sound, a trumpeting arrival. This is it, she thought, eardrums buzzing with a dangerous thrill. I'm back!

"You're excited?" asked Shreene, shifting sleepily in her chair. "Put your seatbelt on now."

Rumi did as instructed, and checked Nibu's, which covered him loosely as he slept. Mahesh was reading the paper at the end of their row, his eyes drooping, a hand massaging his temples as though the drone of the plane was getting to him. Rumi checked her watch. It had been 8 hours and 34 minutes so far. Not bad. She had worn her contact lenses for the final hour of the journey, and applied makeup forty-three minutes before the descent. Shreene let her borrow her foundation as a special treat. Rumi had returned from the loo seventeen minutes later, beige eye shadow highlighting the skin from lashes to eyebrows, a thick layer of mascara applied, third time lucky, after infecting her lenses with a streaky black during the first two attempts, a small comb-clip pulling one side of her hair back and pinning it behind her ear.

Shreene had coshed her gently on the cheek as she settled back into her chair. "Looking nice, eh?" she said to her daughter. "Looking sweet. Glamorous." She winked, then narrowed her eyes in mock seriousness. "Maybe you look a bit too nice, though . . . Good job you aren't smuggling gold in secretly, isn't it? You might attract attention when we go through Customs, eh, little bandar?"

Rumi looked at the floor, feeling a sudden reaction to the word "smuggling."

"Don't you worry, silly!" said Shreene, laughing and stroking the top of Rumi's head. "It's nice to make yourself look pretty. You are of that age, you know. There is this cream in India called Fair and Lovely. You can't get it in the UK. We can try it, if you want. You are becoming a young woman."

Rumi smoldered, hiding her face in the corner of her chair, and watched the universe roller-coaster past. One light-year equals the distance light travels in a year, she thought. At the rate of 300,000 kilometers per second (671 million miles per hour), one light-year is equivalent to a figure that comes close to six trillion miles. Six trillion. She remembered first finding this information, then cautiously expanding her mind to try to understand what it meant. Bridgeman would always be "light-years away" from her now, she thought. She realized why people used that phrase: it made you think of how distant two people can become, rocketing away from each other like dying stars. In fact, they were now so separate from each other that they could surely use parsecs, or "parallax seconds." One parsec was equal to 3.26 light-years, i.e., well over 19 trillion miles. "Trillion" was such an overwhelming word, though, all those zeros hurtling away into the universe. Not sad enough to express the Bridgeman feeling. How many parsecs would it take to capture their difference? She had not sent Bridgeman a postcard, although Mahesh, horrifyingly, had made her write one to her class, as though she was ten years old. She had replaced it with a blank card when the air hostess came round, handing over the pile (which included post-cards to Nibu's class and Mahesh's department) and collapsing the offending item in her right hand, then shoving it into her rucksack.

They passed through the airport in a soporific haze, Rumi relishing the familiar smell of air-conditioning, the beloved feeling of heat that thickened the transitions between rooms, the perfume of pollution and unknown spice that insinuated itself into pockets of the airport landscape. She had a warm sense of her own instant belonging in a world of brown faces. These feelings were as she remembered, and as she had anticipated. But it was not long before she noticed the changes—specifically one change, something that was not part of the India Trip memory as it stood in her mind. It came at her in many forms.

"Ch-ch-ch-ch-ch-ch-chhhhhhh . . ." This was the sound from a man staring at her with two friends, standing outside the lavatory.

"Soo-sooo-so-so-soooo . . ." came a shining hiss as she walked past four men sitting on their suitcases, waiting for the rest of their luggage.

"Tut-tut-tut-tut"—the wet click of a tongue on the roof of a security guard's mouth as she rolled her bag by the customer service stall. And it was not just housed in sound, it was also communicated in looks.

"Come on, now, hurry up," urged Shreene, who was waiting by a coffee stall as Mahesh went to collect the remaining bags. He walked off holding Nibu's hand, pointing out and explaining how the process of emptying luggage from a plane's storage compartments worked.

"Mum?" Rumi whispered, when she caught up.

"What is it?" asked Shreene.

"Why is everyone looking at me?"

"Who is looking at you?" said Shreene, her voice chopped with annoyance as she attempted to balance the weighty hand luggage on their trolley. "Come here, hold this now." She made Rumi crouch and balance a wheelie suitcase on its side, as a base on which to build the rest of the bags.

"Everyone, Mum, all these men—look."

Rumi pointed at three men sniggering beside the adjacent conveyor belt, at a huddle of Customs officials, who were looking in her direction and muttering to each other, at youths in the arrivals area on the other side, a man in a flowered safari shirt, who winked and grimaced at her through the transparent wall while his friends balanced their arms on his shoulders, sharing his amusement.

"Don't point at them, you silly girl!" said Shreene, lowering her voice. "Why are you so interested in them anyway? Don't look at them. Stop it now. Silly girl!"

Mahesh returned with the suitcases and they made their way out. Nibu was chattering, suddenly awake to the playground element of the airport. "Mummy, look," he said, pointing at a man in a dhoti, the white cloth wrapped neatly between his legs and pinned at the waist, sturdy leather chappals cradling his feet. "Is that man wearing a skirt, Mum?" he said. "Where are we going now?"

Rumi walked slowly, acclimatizing to the net of interest that seemed to surround her, this scattered male gaze that multiplied further when she was outside the airport, her eyes colliding accidentally with those of two sellers behind a bookstall, two more crouched by a stove, fanning the hot embers of roasting corncobs as they watched her. She felt her cheeks leak a humid blush. There it came again, that sound, like crickets in the dust, as she walked through the crowd to the taxi on the other side of the road. "Ch-ch-ch-ch-ch-ch-chhhhhh . . . Sh-sh-sh-sh-ssssssssh . . ." She looked up toward the sky and locked eyes with the buxom heroine on a film poster, caught dancing in the rain, her twisting torso painted in fruity yellows and oranges, her eyes a swivel of black lines and suspense. It seemed as though they could see something Rumi couldn't, these men around her—the nakedness under her clothes. Their teasing glances had a Superman-style confidence, the lewd knowledge that came with X-ray vision. She looked down at her body. Her shirt was buttoned just below the base of her throat, the mushroom color impermeable in thick, braided cotton. She glanced at her jeans, the flies zipped appropriately and hidden under the shirt. She was so confused that it was only halfway on their journey into the city, as they stopped at traffic lights, a disheveled boy and girl scratching on her window, undershirts stained as brown as their coffee-colored skin, stretching out their palms, that she realized she had got through, the cumin still in her shoes, untouched. She was safe and dry.

THEY WERE STAYING at Hashi Chacha and Bina Chaachi's flat in Azad-pur, a semirural suburb that was new to Rumi. Shreene had not stayed there during the India Trip seven years previously, using the opportu-nity of a solitary visit, and a funereal one at that, to remain with her own family rather than observe daughter-in-law duties by staying in the extended network of her marital home. After an hour of driving through traffic, they entered an earthy enclave of honeycomb-colored dust, and trees with pink and white blossoms, the road trailed by a rivulet running down the left-hand side, following the journey of the car. They slowed down.

"We've reached Ashok Nagar," said Shreene.

" 'Chacha' means father's brother," Mahesh explained to Nibu, who was taking in his surroundings. A cow walked in front of the car, its long tail swaying lethally, an idle whip in the wind.

"Hep!" said the taxi driver from his window, smacking the animal on the rump to move it on. Nibu watched in wonder as the cow set-tled down in the middle of the road, yawning with a loud groan and shaking its head.

" 'Chaachi' means 'father's brother's wife,' " continued Mahesh, ignoring Nibu's anxiety. "Now, what are their names?"

Nibu responded, his eyes mesmerized by the cow. "Hashi Chaachi and Been Chacha," he said.

"No," said Mahesh. " 'Chaachi' is the feminine—it applies to the wife of the father's brother."

Rumi had one memory of meeting Hashi Chacha and Bina Chaachi. She had eaten roasted cashews and sat with them in almost perfect silence in Ama's living room, after the funeral. They had two children: Honey and Bunny, given nicknames that still defined them in the home, and which, according to Shreene, would stick for life, or at least until they were married. In the lead-up to this particular holiday, Rumi had been presented with a vast array of names of cousins: they lay before her like darts in front of a board, each carrying the hope of friendship. But the names themselves were a sugary catalog of absurdity: Sweetie, Rinku, Pinkie, Chinky, Minky, Lucky, Bunty—the list went on. Most were of Rumi's age or older, of both sexes, and yet, inconceivably to her, apparently answered to these names well into their twenties. When questioned, Shreene had explained that the "proper" names of Indian children were used only at school and, hence, of interest only to the children and their teachers.

"But Honey is my age and he's a boy!" Rumi had responded, incredulous. "And Bunny is almost seventeen! Are you serious that they don't find it stupid that everyone calls them these names, everyone they know?"

"What stupid?" Shreene had snapped. "Another Angrezi type of thing, these concepts you come up with. Why would somebody find sweet words offered by their family, in love only, as stupid? Sometimes, Rumi, you really go overboard."

So Honey and Bunny they had been and, no doubt, Honey and Bunny they remained. They were even sketchier in Rumi's memory than their parents—two quiet, clean children who sat between their mother and father and refused the cashews, Bunny with her hair in plaits so tight that they seemed to pull on the roots of her hair, and Honey with a sleek basin haircut that lay close to his head, as though it was permanently damp.

THE FLAT WAS the top half of a pink concrete building, flat-roofed and pronged with a veranda that stretched out from middle like a deep tray. From a distance it looked like a doll's house, the candyfloss paint peeling at the sides as it came into vision. A blocky staircase took them up to the entrance, where they were greeted by Bina Chaachi, large and excitable, her curves wobbling inside a jade green housecoat.

"Arre Baap re!" she said, pulling Rumi and Nibu into her chest. "Finally you come and the light has gone!"

An electricity failure had turned the space into a candlelit wonderland. The flat shimmered with the reflection of small points of fire, oil-doused wicks arranged six apiece in steel trays, scattered in the bedrooms, on top of the fridge in the main hallway and on the polished stone worktop in the kitchen. In the living room there were four trays on the dining table, twenty-four points of barely dancing flame that threw an amber light onto a large mural: a plunging waterfall that adorned the whole of the main wall. Next to this striking photographic ode to nature sat Hashi Chacha, drinking from a cut-glass tumbler.

"Mashu bhai!" he said to Mahesh, nodding semidrunkenly in their direction. "It is like Diwali for your comeback. The Festival of Lights, yaar. You are like Ram in the *Ramayana,* come back from exile to tell us how to do it, heh?"

THE ADULTS MOVED into the main bedroom, clustering near the generator, which was powering the only cooler in the flat. Nibu was given a bottle of Thumbs Up cola. He lay contentedly on the bed near Shreene, reveling in the rare taste of a fully caffeinated drink. Rumi was whisked to the balcony by an enthusiastic Bunny, who was accompanied by another girl, introduced as her friend. Bunny was now a confident and speedy talker, large eyes opening innocently out of a face that shone immaculately with a deep chocolate sheen, glossy curls pinned back at the nape of her neck.

"Honey is on his way home from the shop—he'll be so pleased to see you. Wow, you've changed so much. I hear you're majoring in maths and coming first in your class. Is that true? Do you like it here? What do you think of India?"

Rumi struggled to put some words together, shocked by the

beauty in Bunny's features and the rapid animation of her movements. "I really . . . love it," she said.

Bunny nodded and steam-rollered on. Her rich voice was like
am papad, the sweet and sour sticky pulp made from dried mango,
chewed by Rumi on her last visit.

"I am majoring in art. I intend to apply to Delhi University—to
study fine art, that is. I am specifically interested in examining how
faith has historically been depicted in North Indian art, particularly
Hinduism, and I am doing a series entitled 'Expressions of the Holy
Light.' That is my proposal for my undergraduate project when I get
into university. I can show you some of my pictures later, if you
want. I have already had some interest when I worked for a design
company as my out-of-school work placement. In India what you
study is dictated by your grades. Over ninety is medicine, over
eighty is engineering, over seventy natural sciences, et cetera. I
achieved over ninety but I am studying art because I believe it is my
calling."

Rumi nodded. Bunny's enthusiasm was dizzying. She knew that
Bina Chaachi had studied art before marriage and had shown her
paintings as part of the interview to be Hashi Chacha's wife. She also
knew that Hashi Chacha didn't believe that women should study science. She wondered what he thought of her own maths journey and
felt a little faint. Bunny had a minute black mole placed exactly in
the center of her forehead, like a chaste bindi, the type worn by
maidens in the years before marriage. To Rumi, it seemed as though
Bunny had been touched by the hand of God, with a sign that was in-
controvertible through its very symmetry of place.

"Rumika has a nice personality, no?" said Bunny's friend, a
cheeky-faced girl with a long ponytail of silky hair that swung round
to lie sensually against the curve of her neck.

"What?" Rumi said, looking at her cousin.

"This is Mintoo," said Bunny, as if that explained anything that
might need explaining.

They leaned against the balcony wall, the mashed heat hanging in
the ebony vessel of nightfall, a murmuring quiet holding them to-

gether as they waited for the lights to return. Rumi watched a yellow and black auto-rickshaw purr up to a paan seller below, like a lazy bumblebee. The driver got out, a lean man with a hyperactive gait. He took a comb from his back pocket and carved it through his hair before speaking to the seller in a low whisper; then, suddenly, two ribbons of smoke were curling up toward the sky, accompanied by the heady bass of male laughter. For a second she hoped that the lights would never come back, that the whole trip from this point forward could be conducted in the muted flicker of candles and dark spaces, these boxes of black velvet that she watched from a distance and seemed to envelop her.

Mintoo pointed at Rumi's breasts and then her hips, making the shape of a semicircle in the air and finishing with an up-and-down movement of her hand, as though she was flattening a panel of air against Rumi's body. "Personality," she said.

"How do you know my personality?" asked Rumi, stepping back involuntarily. "We've only just met."

Mintoo looked at her as though it was a trick question. "I can see your personality!" she said, laughing and waiting for Rumi to relax into the joke. The confusion remained on Rumi's face. Bunny eyed Mintoo with disapproval. "What are you talking, yaar?" said Mintoo, giggling into a handkerchief, which she then used to wipe sweat from her forehead.

Bunny turned and leaned against the balcony.

"Personality means this here," she said, gesturing at her own frame in a graceful wave from head to toe. "Height, body," she said, moving her head in a swirl from left to right, then back again, repeating the movement rapidly, a figure eight on its side, like a line drawing going back over itself again and again. She waited for Rumi to nod in acknowledgment. "Height, body?" she repeated, coming to a stop.

Rumi squinted, attempting to divert a droplet of sweat that was crawling down her nose. She wondered if she should ask for a handkerchief. There was no toilet paper in the lavatory; she'd seen that earlier. The way Bunny said "body," like the way she said most things, was very innocent. More innocent than Rumi felt she could ever be. Aeons of it, a never-ending tunnel of truth. It was strange to listen to someone like this, and in turn to realize you were charting your own innocence in relation to them. But that was what Bunny did to you. Speaking to her was like looking into a dirty mirror. Somehow the very enchantment and grace of her movements, the lucid conviction of her speech, the proud purity of her mind combined to present you with a shabby and much murkier picture of yourself. Rumi looked into Bunny's eyes, black and voluminous in the heat. She could see a tiny picture of herself reflected in a small square of light in each pupil, a distorted face spread out like a ghoulish hallucination. She thought about the cricket sound that had whirred the salute to her arrival in India, the whisper of lust that now hung in the air she was breathing, the shape of its memory filtering through the sky like a droplet of herb in a homeopathic remedy. She hadn't entirely disliked it.

WHEN SHE LOOKED back on the next three hours, something she would do many times, Rumi read the impression of the story like the outline of a faint carbon copy, traced faithfully but subject to a thousand interpretations, depending on which words, which letters were the most visible at any particular time. In the end she would remember a makeshift timetable of events that cataloged the happenings that came with the arrival of Honey, attempting to limit it to facts but having to include certain moments that were supposition. This timetable of imagined precision was the only way she could make sense of that night in Azadpur, a tear in the fabric of her understanding that happened so quickly she had to plot it out in hours and minutes, work out when and how it could have all happened.

9:40 P.M.

A second auto-rickshaw below the flat. A lanky boy with a shiny puff of black hair steps out. Bunny calls out to him to look up: "Honey, dekho! Look!" He stands just beneath the balcony. Rumi can't see his face in the dark but she gets the sense that he can see her.

"Hi," he says. It sounds as if he is smiling.

9:50 P.M.

He emerges from the lavatory and washes his hands and face in the hallway basin. Their eyes hook together in the mirror. He grins, eyes crinkling at the corners, making him look older, as though some wisdom is conferred upon him each time he goes through the act of smiling. He turns to her, rubbing his neck and hair with a towel in the shadows. "So?" he says, as though they know each other.

He is pretty, like a fifties Bombay matinee idol, girlish lashes trimming what Rumi assumes are the reference point for "puppy-dog eyes." The shape of his face is slashed at both sides by a jawline that makes a V-shape, coming to a point under his chin, strong lines that are at odds with the feminine hustle of his lips and lashes. He should have been in black and white.

"Where have you come back from?" she says.

"Shop," he says, looking amused that she should ask.

"Did you enjoy yourself?" she asks, taking the piss, not knowing why.

He laughs. "Yes, I enjoyed. *Bahut zyaada mazza ayaa.* I enjoyed a lot."

10:00 P.M.

They all eat together, two families rolled into one big oval perimeter, bordering the large polished table in the living room, the room full of a waxy glow, a nimbus of cloying heat. Bina Chaachi and the two girls are in charge of bringing hot chapattis for the rest of them, straight from the tava, the volatile wheat blooming with hot air and deflating as each one slides onto the plates. Hashi Chacha asks a lot of questions about Mahesh's job. Mahesh asks a lot of questions about the family business and the rest of his family, who are scattered around Punjab. Shreene is involved in a seesaw of manners with Bina Chaachi, regularly getting up to help her, then being ferried back to her seat by one of the girls. Rumi does not look at Honey. She barely eats.

10:25 P.M.

Rumi goes to wash her hands at the basin. Honey meets her there. He stands behind her, waiting for her to finish. She is overcome with a sudden desire, which catapults through her body like a shooting star, to lie back against his chest and place her cheek in the crook of his neck.

"Do you want to go for a walk?" she says, looking at him in the mirror.

He shrugs, his eyes linked to her own like magnets. "Yes, OK."

10:27 P.M.

Rumi goes back into the dining room and asks Shreene if she can go for a walk with Honey. Shreene glances at her watch. "It's a bit late, beti."

"Just round the block, Mum."

Bina Chaachi comes in with some pistachio-flavored milk.

"What is it, Bhabhi?" she says, addressing Shreene.

"Nothing, Bina," says Shreene. "Children are thinking of going for a walk. I am wondering if it is safe at this time . . ."

"Oh, what all is that, Bhabhi? It is so safe here. It is like a village. Honey, come, take your little sister for a walk, take her to the Mukhi market, feed her some ice cream, some gulab jamun. After-dinner walk helps digestion. Anyway, you must spoil her! Actually, is she your little sister or are you her little brother?" She laughs. "It is close, na?"

Shreene shakes her head. "Rumika is born in June, three months after Honey. Don't you even remember that much, Bina?" she says, pretending to be shocked.

"So, you are her older brother by three months," says Bina Chaachi, crossing into Hindi and thrusting a fifty-rupee note into Honey's hand. "So be it. Don't let her come back without sweetening her mouth. Today there is much to celebrate."

1 0 : 3 5 P.M.

Rumi and Honey leave for their walk. Rumi walks with a lightness that makes her feel as if she has dissolved into the gentle winds that buffet them on their journey. Ahead, the roads are covered in a bricky dust, which rises like sand to cloud the air a few centimeters above the path. She wishes she could walk barefoot. To each side the large trees wave their thin branches, a greeting that relaxes her as they pass. They do not speak much. He says his English is not so good. She tries Hindi, surprised by her fearlessness, and realizes she can speak in a way that he can understand. These strands of broken Hindi-English entwine their long silences like warm arms.

"You are in school?" he asks.

"Yes," says Rumi. "You work at . . . shop?"

"I left school," he says, nodding. "You like it there or here?"

"Where?"

"UK . . . or India?" He looks at her, mischief hidden in his smile. "Are you Angrez or Indian?"

Rumi waits. A lot seems to hang on the answer she gives. But she is also weightless, apparently beyond mortal cares. "Both, yaar!" she says, the unrolled *r* in the final word betraying her lack of Indian accent.

They laugh together.

"I see," he says. "But which one first?"

Rumi shakes her head and they walk on once more without words. Once or twice his arm brushes against her own. The contact induces a slight panic in her. They arrive at a crossroads, a sign for "Azadpur" lying low at the corner. Above them the sky, a welter of brooding clouds, no visible moon, haunted by the witchlike scent of blossom, suddenly all-pervading, inescapable.

"You want ice cream?" he asks. "You want to go to the market?"

She looks at her watch. It is 11:15 p.m. The panic intensifies. "We go . . . back?" she says, stumbling for the Hindi in the last word. "Waapas . . . ?"

They walk more quickly than before, retracing the recent experience. Rumi feels nervous. "What does 'Azadpur' mean?" she asks.

" 'Pur' is, like, 'place.' 'Azad' is, like . . ." He falters. "Like Azaadi?"

"Means?"

"Azaadi. Like Indian Independence Day. Means, like, India was azad on that day."

"Oh, OK," says Rumi.

11:45 P.M.

They ring the bell outside the flat, standing before the spiraling outer grate. Shreene opens the inside door and fumbles with the second lock. "Bit late?" she says, letting them in. "Over one hour? It is nearly midnight."

"Sorry," says Rumi, walking past her. "Didn't realize what time it was."

Preparations for bed have begun. Nibu is already asleep in the room allocated to the visitors. Shreene has declined the invitation for their family to take the room with the cooler, declaring that they are Indian, after all, and can deal with any kind of heat.

Rumi changes into pajamas in the lavatory and thinks about what has happened. In essence, nothing. Nothing has happened, she thinks. She emerges from the bathroom and bumps into Honey. "Where are you going to sleep?" he asks.

"In there," says Rumi, pointing at the room, a shake of her shoulders signifying "obviously."

"It is too hot in there," he says. "The cooler is in our room. Sleep there."

12:05 A.M.

Shreene has agreed to Rumi's request to sleep in the cooler room because of the overpowering heat, nodding at the question while rubbing night cream into her cheeks. Mahesh is falling asleep next to Nibu, contented, a local newspaper fanned out next to him on the guest bed. Bunny is sleeping with Mintoo in the living room. In the cooler room, Hashi Chacha is lying on the bed alone. Bina Chaachi is sitting on the floor next to him, talking quietly. Rumi and

Honey form a right angle on the floor, a point arising from their heads, which are close together. Honey's body stretches back to parallel the foot of the bed. Rumi's body follows the left-hand side of the bed, her feet pointing toward the headboard. They talk about what they are going to do the next day. Rumi is starting on a cross-country journey round India, taking a train to Rajpura in the Punjab. Honey is going to the shop.

Bina Chaachi and Hashi Chacha chat for a while, enclosed by the shadow of a low candle that burns in the corner of the room. Then Bina Chaachi blows it out and lies down on the other side of Rumi, her body close to the door.

"Good night, beti," she says, stroking Rumi's head, then pulling a light sheet over their bodies. "After so long we are seeing you. It is such a good thing." She turns over, her back to Rumi, moving her lavish hips against the thin mattress.

I 2:20 A.M.

Honey turns his face and balances his chin on his hands so that he is looking at Rumi. He asks if she is awake. Rumi giggles silently. They begin a whispered dialogue in which Rumi tells him to sleep, and he makes funny faces, suggesting an inability to understand her, encouraging her laughter. Rumi turns and looks at Bina Chaachi. Not only is she fast asleep but she is emitting violent snores, heaving them out at regular intervals as she lies on her back. Rumi mimes horror, putting her hands over her ears, and Honey's face folds into laughter.

I 2:30 A.M.

Rumi is lying turned toward Honey's face, her cheek on the pillow. He reaches out and touches her hair, sending his fingers in deep, until they press against her skull. "You have beautiful hair," he says, in Hindi.

Rumi understands the words for "beautiful" and "hair." She shivers.

He takes her face and pulls it toward him, reaching his mouth to meet hers.

"What are you doing?" Rumi hisses, in Hindi, disentangling her head, a war cry punching her temples as she lies back on the pillow.

"Kiss me," he says.

"Are you mad?" She glares at him. "We are like brother and sister!"

Bina Chaachi sends out a vehement snort and turns on her side, her chest rising and falling in perfect deep sleep.

"I love you," he says, in English, taking her hand and kissing her palm over and over again. Rumi feels her own body lose control with the sensation of his burning mouth in the center of her hand. It is like a heated mug pressed on the surface of a table: a burned scar, the temperature changing the color and texture of the wood forever.

She turns over, presenting the back of her head to him, as though she is going to sleep.

1 2 : 4 5 A . M .

His hand is on her head again, stroking it. She turns back to face him. "I love you," he whispers, his eyes wide globes of liquid brown in the dark.

"You've only just met me," she says, "and you are my father's brother's son. This is wrong. You know it is wrong."

"That was our starting stick," he says, leaning over and kissing her cheek.

"Our what?"

"Starting stick. Where it starts." His mouth is on her hand again. He begins to trace a line with his lips from the pulse in her wrist along the entire length of her arm. When he reaches the flesh on the inside of her elbow, she trembles and finally leans over to feel her lips on his face, raining kisses on his cheeks. He turns his mouth up to kiss hers. Again, she retreats.

"No," she says, falling back to the floor and taking a scampering breath, trying to recover. "Our parents would throw us out on the street," she says. "We are supposed to be brother and sister, not like Muslims, who marry their own cousins."

"Don't worry about it," he says, his face serious with intent as he kisses her at the point where her cheek meets the corner of her mouth.

1:00 A.M.

The silence is intact when he begins to kiss the palm of her hand once more, and move her head toward his, more feverish than before. Only the clang of Rumi's bangle against the floor—a furious reaction to pressure applied by him in an attempt to link their mouths—breaks it. He continues to caress her, until the main light comes on, a shock that makes Rumi crush her eyelids together and bury her head in her pillow. She hears him being told to sleep on the bed with his father, Bina's voice so low it might have been inaudible, but Rumi can hear it. And when he gets up and lies on the bed, taking his sheet with him, she knows what has happened.

THE NEXT DAY he didn't look at her. And, other than the most polite offerings of coffee and breakfast, neither did Bina Chaachi. Rumi cried in the lavatory every half-hour, returning there to clutch Honey's T-shirt, which she had found hanging on the back of the door, sucking up the scent as if it was an asthma inhaler. Once or twice she tried to accost him, getting in his way, but he found a way to get round her, slipping away as though she was a stranger who had bumped into him at a busy crossing. Finally she wrote him a note, a stricken request to go for a walk so that they could talk for just five minutes. He was sitting on the balcony, eating his breakfast, when she put the tiny square of folded paper into the pocket of his shirt. Almost instantaneously he lifted it and threw it over the balcony, continuing to eat as before.

THE DAY AFTER, Rumi left for a six-week trip round India.

She inhabited the days, places and families of their journey without really living inside them. The experience with Honey became an

Arabian night in her memory, a night of a thousand moments, one in which each second held the potential for a lifetime of contemplation. She yearned for him day and night, carrying the painful joy like a child against her chest—kicking and chuckling, hungry and wailing.

But her rite of passage had given her a new status: one that found its way into her dealings with the catalog of unseen cousins. The way she saw herself—a heartbroken, illicit sweetheart—conferred upon her an important new power: empathy. Recognizing the symptoms in each new environment, she became a confidante, almost instantly with each new cousinly meeting. Ten minutes into sitting with Chinky in her bedroom in Ludhiana, as they listened to Madonna on a hammering tape player, she asked, "Do you miss someone?" Five minutes on the back of a scooter in Chandigarh, light rain falling like warm snowflakes round them, she asked Bunty, "Is there someone you are thinking about now?"

And they told her their stories. Especially the older ones. It was as though they had been waiting all this time for her to come along, so that they could share them. In this way her trip round India revealed the love and lust fighting for breath in each pocket of the country of her origin. She plugged herself into this hidden voltage and let herself be the carrier of all untold stories. In Kanpur she stayed up a whole night, listening sympathetically to the story of Rinku's love for a boy of Gujarati origin, her own Punjabi background making her unsuitable for marriage in spite of three years of secret meetings and a padlocked cabinet of several hundred love letters and cards—unlocked hysterically for Rumi, as though she was opening a coffin. Rinku told Rumi that she was halfway through a ten-day fast, in the hope that her own courage would inspire her lover to take action and stand up to his father. In Kurukshetra it was the oldest story in the book: Minky's own family had been living in denial of his love for the girl in the house opposite, begun at the age of twelve through stolen gazes, their sign language intercepting the respective curtains, their differing social backgrounds irrelevant. Now, after eleven years, her family's relative lack of wealth and his own parents' outright refusal to accept her into their home meant that he was planning to elope, if only he could work out how to survive financially.

This patchwork of broken passion, held by the stitching of love, revealed itself to her like a join-the-dots puzzle, each geographical region more emotive and less surprising than the last. She learned many words for love in Hindi: from the basic "pyaar," to the poetic and fatalistic "ishq," the heartfelt "mohabbat," and the somewhat enigmatic "mehboob." But she could not reveal her own story. Because, of course, they were all related to him in some way. He was not anonymous.

Sometimes she sat outside and wept for Honey in the evening, the sky like a big green blackboard, with its chalkings and dots of stars. She scratched her hand with her nails to wring out the feel of his lips. She repeated to herself, over and over, single lines of Indian love songs, as though her brain had gone soft, wondering at how she finally understood everything—the Hindi, the music, the maddening phrases.

Mera khoya hua rangeen nazaara de de,
Mere mehboob, tujhe
Meri mohabbat ki kasam.

Give me back the lost color in my gaze,
My sweetheart, for you
I swear upon my love.

And everywhere the sound of crickets, following at her heels like the dust hardening over the back of her feet, until the time came for them to fly back to Britain.

AT THE AIRPORT on the way home, Rumi bought two tubes of Fair and Lovely with Shreene. It turned out to be a "skin-lightening cream" proven to deliver "one to three shades of change in most people, for radiant fairness!" A small board next to the stack of tubes showed the before-and-after of a young Indian woman, the "before" capturing her despair at seeing her own dusky reflection in a bathroom mirror, the "after" showing her crying with happiness, walking round a wedding fire, her fresh vanilla face glowing from the folds of a red and gold pallu, draped regally over her head. Rumi did not argue. Instead she let her mother spread the cream over her face and rested her forehead against Shreene's shoulder as she slept through the long journey home.

PART 3

17

the discussions on how it would all work had been protracted, with Mahesh alternating between stabs of euphoria and extreme anxiety. On the day that the phone call came through, Shreene had passed the receiver to him, but the tutor had asked for Rumi. It had been a voice that was clearly carrying good tidings but, still, he hadn't been prepared for the moment when his daughter nodded, her face automatically turning to Nibu, bewildered eyes darting to Mahesh a moment later.

"Thank you" were her last words as she put down the phone before Mahesh could take the receiver.

"They said they would call back to speak to you," she explained to him. "They said I was supposed to share the news with you now and think about what I wanted to do or something."

Nibu jumped up and grabbed Rumi's arm. "What happened?" he yelled.

"I got in!" Rumi said, the words fighting their way out of her throat.

"Hooray!" said Nibu, taking her arms and attempting to jump up and down in unison with her. After a few seconds, Shreene rushed over and crushed them to her chest. Mahesh's reaction was even more delayed, a good while after the rest of his family had disentangled.

He stroked the top of Rumi's head and murmured, "I don't believe it, beti," a fuzzy pain starting up in his forehead. "Can't believe it. You have really done it, it seems . . ."

MAHESH CARRIED THIS diffuse sense of unease for all of the ensuing weeks, right up to Rumi's first day at Oxford. It took the form of a headache that wouldn't go away. On one level he felt like jumping and shouting for joy, a repeated desire to punch the sky, mark the moment with a loud verbal and physical gesture. He felt such a strong sense of elation when he thought about what had happened that he struggled for a way to celebrate it. What could they do to commemorate this? Was there anything? How did people mark these things? How *should* one rejoice in a satisfying style? It confused him, this inarticulate feeling that lay pressured in his chest, pushed further and further down as the days went by. Was he supposed to go to a restaurant with the three of them? It seemed inadequate and somehow irrelevant what they ate. Food just went into your body and came out the other side, after all. It would be over in three hours and cost a fortnight's food budget. Was he supposed to take them to the cinema? But staring at a screen in silent agreement, watching fictional characters in a fictional world, how was this supposed to achieve anything, or be of any significance?

When he had these thoughts, the elation would diminish, to be replaced by depression. Is that all there was in life, then? You fought hard, marshaled yourself and strained every fiber you had to climb the mountain, and when you got to the top there was nothing to do, no one to tell. He could tell Whitefoot, of course, but that would only take two minutes. Then what would happen? It was hardly as if the sky would split open when he uttered the words. He could call India and tell his brothers, his mother. But what would they say, other than that it sounded good? It wasn't as if he was announcing Rumi's engagement, where there was a set procedure of joint celebration. Suddenly he felt the absence of ritual in his life. It had always seemed meaningless to him. Until now.

In the end, thirteen days after the phone call, he ordered Chinese takeaway and allowed the children to watch game shows on the Saturday night as they ate it.

In reality, of course, he had a lot more to worry about than the mysterious nature of contemporary celebrations. The practicalities were so tricky that they threatened to jeopardize the whole thing.

But he had to make them work. He was in regular dialogue with the college, at one point receiving phone calls daily from all manner of staff. It was a female college, so that at least was dealt with. In the past, he was informed, underage students had lived with an immediate family member in a house separate from the student lodgings. But those parents had given up their jobs to become full-time guardians. Mahesh knew that there was no way he could do that. For a start there was the financial problem—they needed the money. Then there was Nibu. He could not bring up Nibu without Shreene, and she could not uproot him from his school and take him to Oxford. That would be absurd.

Further investigation revealed that Rumi's main tutorials and a decent proportion of her lectures fell within a weekly three-day period, necessitating her to be there for two nights only at a time. But, still, he could not ask for that amount of time off each week. He was a full-time lecturer himself, bound by terms and timetables. An exhausting conversation with the principal of Somerville College revealed no solution. The college could not employ a full-time guardian for Rumi. She would have to live with an immediate family member as her guardian, apparently, because that was university protocol when dealing with the delicate issue of taking on an underage student. They would attract enough media attention as it was, without publicly exposing Rumi to a clearly visible accelerated lifestyle.

Who had these people been, thought Mahesh, that they could afford to throw in their livelihoods to live at university with their children? Like anyone else who watched the news and kept abreast of current affairs, he had seen the pictures of Ruth Lawrence, riding a bicycle-for-two with her father through cobbled Oxford streets. But he had not thought through the implications for himself. He could not do that. He simply couldn't.

And so it was that after much deliberation and many long nights sitting at the dining table, he and Shreene, having driven themselves mad with long-distance phone calls and questions, came up with their own solution: an "aunt" who lived in Didcot, otherwise known as Mrs. Mukherjee, a.k.a. the widowed niece of the cousin of the husband of Shreene's brother's mother-in-law's best friend. Rumi would live there as a "paying guest," or PG, as they called it in India, a lodger who would eat and sleep under the protection of the home-owner, with an agreed curfew, for the two nights of the week that she was required to remain in Oxford. They would have to pass off Mrs. Mukherjee as Shreene's sister to get through the bureaucracy. It took only one phone call and the confirmed offer of twenty pounds a week to seal the deal.

Mahesh had been a PG when he was doing his master's in Hyder-abad—in his early twenties. He had eaten with the family and stud-ied in his room each night, with a strict curfew of eight thirty p.m. unless arranged otherwise for special occasions such as college func-tions. He had become friendly with the children of the family he was staying with—at six and eight years of age they were pretty unavoid-able—but not the parents. The memories of the experience were fond, though, of the narrow room where, although under curfew, he had felt free. When he thought of the inanimate trinity of single bed, desk and window that had been the central points of his simple uni-verse, he had a sense of secure warmth.

And now his own daughter was to be a PG at the age of fifteen.

The thrumming in his temples relented slightly once this aspect of the arrangements had been sorted out, and he allowed the news-paper interviews to commence, having avoided them until that point. The *Cardiff Post* had already included a little item on Rumi without any input from her family. It was unauthorized but inoffen-sive enough, just a five-line piece and a standard photo of the school, stating her grades and perceived start date at Oxford. "Cardiff Girl—Maths Genius" was the headline.

A week later Mahesh took four prearranged phone interviews on Monday morning, and allowed three different reporters from na-tional newspapers into their home during the afternoon—two male and one female—allocating them an hour each. He worked through the interviews systematically, with a manner that was friendly but not overly personal. Rumi sat with him but barely spoke, preferring to let him deal with it as safely as possible—most of the questions were addressed to him anyway. Shreene and Nibu sat with them for each hour, with appropriate roles. Nibu worked on drawing a circle and dividing it into fractions while Shreene provided general solidarity, helping Nibu, volunteering information on their lifestyle (mentioning her own job, education and input as a parent at discreet intervals so that they would not be seen as a stereotypical patriarchal family), as well as sorting out food and drinks. Mahesh was, he hoped, dignified, straightforward and principled. Calmly he got across the main points he had prepared:

1. Rumi was like any other teenager—lively, social, with her own hobbies and interests (chess, music and Indian cinema). But instead of being plugged into the superficial banalities of popular culture, she had learned to channel her energies into the search for knowledge, in all its forms.

2. Her success in mathematics was merely the result of application and living an alert, stimulated life—too many people, these days, were sleep-walking through their days, barely fulfilling a fraction of their capabilities. As a family, they believed that the mental and spiritual lives went hand in hand, and that feeding one area should enrich the other.

3. This idea of studying and guidance of one's own child was something that any parent could apply to their own situation. It was about creating a currency of values and a climate of idea exchange within the home. It was about application, hard work and stretching one's boundaries.

4. The label "gifted" was meaningless to them as a family and, in Mahesh's opinion, a damaging idea to perpetuate in the population as a whole. They believed that any child could achieve this kind of knowledge and success rate, given the right developmental approach by the parents.

Mahesh delivered the answers with relatively few interruptions. He also stayed strong in the face of questions he had not anticipated, maintaining his calm, delivering a casual reaction of surprise and a dismissive shrug of the shoulders when asked about his personal views in the following areas:

1. Religion.

2. India's long love affair with mathematics.

3. The Indian immigrant's particularly intense drive to achieve.

4. Rumi's evident entry into adolescence, and potential love affairs of the future.

He finished with a quote by Gandhi, which he had written out and kept stuck to his desk throughout his life as a student. It put him in a good mood as he said it, a twang of nostalgia reverberating in his voice that only he could hear: "Men often become what they believe themselves to be. If I believe I cannot do something, it makes me incapable of doing it. But when I believe I can, then I acquire the ability to do it even if I didn't have it in the beginning."

And that was that. Each reporter took their leave at the end of the agreed hour, seemingly pleased with the sound bites they had accumulated.

THE PROCESS OF taking Rumi to Didcot and settling her in was simpler, although the headache returned on the way, a mind-numbing friction that confused Mahesh's vision as he drove the whole family there, strapped between suitcases and plastic bags, inching down the motorway through the bleary autumn evening. He had seen White-foot for the monthly chess stand-off two days previously. Amid an expected mixture of congratulations and jibes, his friend had given him a good route to follow, stating proudly that he went to Oxford at least two or three times a year for conferences.

But the journey was not easy. Nibu was fractious and agitated, his need to get tangled up in everything making Mahesh snap. "Sit down and behave yourself," he said, when Nibu was trying to find the roasted peanuts at the bottom of the food bag Shreene had prepared.

"Stop getting overexcited" was his curt intervention when his son started to repeat a number-plate that contained the word BOOM; it was on the back of a large truck that had blocked their progress for more than ten minutes.

Mahesh looked at Shreene. She was busy trying to rearrange her purse. Then, leaning down, she got out the nuts and tore a little piece of foil off the top of the bag. "Give me your hand," she said to Nibu. He stretched out his palm and let her empty a few onto it. She seemed not only immune to annoyance when it came to Nibu but so casual about his behavior, thought Mahesh. Why did she have no awareness that it might be putting off the driver? What about Nibu's stamina? Was it good just to give him things whenever he asked? Mahesh frowned as he overtook a large truck, nervously feeling the incongruity of moving the car in such a dramatic way as he sat bound in his seat, motionless. Maybe, with all of the recent developments, he thought, he had not been paying enough attention to Nibu's care. He would have to watch his son's relationship with Shreene. Nibu needed to build some emotional muscle—for his own sake more than anything else.

After a few crunches on the nuts, Nibu started on Rumi, pulling her hand to play Paper, Scissors, Stone and complaining in a singsong voice at her lack of response: "Do-ooooh it! . . . Play it—play it! . . . Play it now—you have to!" he said, attempting to uncurl the fingers of Rumi's right hand, which were locked into a fist.

He sounded like a baby, a mawkish, whining, effeminate weakling, and suddenly, to Mahesh it felt like a personal affront, this lack of control—an embarrassing display of neediness. Where had Nibu learned to forgo his dignity like that? What was he playing at?

"*Dooooob* it!" complained Nibu.

"Be quiet now or you will see, you SILLY BOY!" shouted Mahesh, barking the words so that they shattered the air, like a stone through a window.

Nibu started to cry, muting the sound so that it came from the back of his throat, dragging it out in an endless mournful drone. Mahesh pulled onto the hard shoulder and turned to his children in the back. Rumi was staring out of the window.

"You are six years old," Mahesh said, with distaste, his top lip curled upward, leaving no doubt as to the seriousness of the situation. Nibu went quiet. The sound of spitting rain flicked against the silence in the car. Mahesh continued to look at his son.

"Come on, then!" said Shreene, after they had sat there for almost a minute.

Mahesh waited a few more seconds, then turned round and drove on.

MRS. MUKHERJEE WAS dissimilar from the picture that the voice on the phone had suggested. Neatly turned out in tapered black trousers, buckled loafers and a thick cream sweater, knitted in a diamond pattern, her age was not immediately apparent, confused by her girlish features and twiggy form. Her hair was cut in a pageboy layer, which stayed in place as she nodded at Mahesh and Shreene, guiding them as they brought the weighty bags up the stairs. She moved in and out of corners and round doors with a sparrowy rigor, waiting for them to finish each bout of unloading, then leading them back to the car. Shreene exchanged words with her about the household routine—meals, bedtime and cleaning procedures. Mrs. Mukherjee responded to her questions affably, but did not encourage the conversation or speak unnecessarily.

When Mahesh introduced Rumi, Mrs. Mukherjee twitched her lips in a brief allusion to a smile, nodding with the same decorum that suggested everything was taken care of—and, more to the point, seemed to be proceeding according to a preordained plan,

Mahesh thought, so unruffled and incurious was Rumi's new guardian. It seemed almost Oriental to him, this lack of discussion and polite display of hospitality. She certainly wasn't trying to bond with them on the basis of their shared Indian background, like most of the self-proclaimed NRIs, the Non-Resident Indians that Mahesh and Shreene had met during their time in the UK. None of the usual "Where is Vasi from, then? It is not immediately apparent. I am from Punjab/Gujarat/Sindh/UP," with the subsequent slide, through tentative slang, into Hindi. But he didn't dislike the fact that personal intimacy was not her agenda. In fact, he thought it was probably for the best, considering the nature of their arrangement. What mattered was that she seemed professional, the place was clean, she would treat Rumi's curfew as important, and would be available in emergencies. Her house was a modest end-of-terrace council place, which peaked in a gray slate roof like the rest of the row, diminutive but functional, on a well-lit street. He and Shreene had no idea of the circumstances that had led to her lone status and he felt it was best not to ask too many questions.

Mrs. Mukherjee went downstairs to make tea, leaving them standing in Rumi's room. It was reassuringly basic, not far from how Mahesh had imagined it, with a desk, window and single bed populating the space, not so different from the picture in his own PG memory.

Shreene unzipped a large soft travel bag full of clothes, while Nibu sat on the bed. She pointed at a small plastic suitcase. "Unpack your toiletries," she said to Rumi. "Make sure that you are hygienic by starting with the basics. You must always be clean, in body and in surroundings."

Rumi made a face and slouched over the suitcase to click open a buckle. "Mum," she said, her irritation defusing into teasing, "I'm not Nibu's age, am I?" Proudly she clicked open the other buckle. The top of the suitcase sprang back to reveal a botched mess of clothes, soap, washing-powder sachets, hair products, various brushes, including some strands of hair, a statuette of an Indian goddess, some beads and other indistinguishable artifacts.

"I don't care what you say," said Shreene. "You are still a child. Look at that. You think you are mature?" She laughed and went over to Rumi, knelt down beside her and put her arm round her daughter, mimicking the frown on Rumi's face. She pinched Rumi's cheek and shook her head. "Little baby," she said. "Moody, ha?"

Rumi gave a long-suffering sigh and rolled her eyes.

"Think you are so grown-up?" said Shreene. "You can start with being grown-up at least by looking after your things like a more adult girl, can't you?" She sniffed and squeezed Rumi's shoulders. A resigned expression came over Shreene's face as she extracted identifiable pieces from the jumble. Rumi gave another sigh, sucking in her breath, then letting it slide out theatrically.

Nibu stirred with interest. "Oh-ho . . . Oooooooh," he said, rolling his eyes and doing his own version.

"You are only coming here for two nights a week, you know that," Shreene said to Rumi. "Don't start acting like you're something you're not."

Mahesh watched them. It occurred to him, with a shock, that Rumi was now taller than Shreene. On a conscious level he had known that of course, but had he ever really seen what it meant before? He could see some of Shreene's personality delineating itself in Rumi's wheatish face: the stubbornly high cheekbones and plump lips. Even her eyes seemed different—would one say larger? Did that happen to eyes? Of course it must. Why should they be different from the other elements of the body? But wider eyes? What? Older? He studied mother and daughter kneeling by the suitcase. The density of the overhead light gave them both a haggard look, scoping out the dark shadows under their eyes, another genetic legacy that Shreene seemed to have passed on to Rumi. The purplish shading of the skin pushing up under their lower lashes made them seem so dramatic, Shreene's like a tragic film heroine's, Rumi's like a kid playing dress-up with her mother's kohl stick. He watched Rumi move, her puppyish form seeming suddenly more . . . would one say "ladylike"? Womanly? Curvaceous, even? She was fifteen. The number of her age came before him visually. It seemed suddenly so British, Western——it carried a whole gamut of Caucasian significance. He had a brief image of Whitefoot smirking in his uniquely annoying way.

"You are wearing the contact lenses?" Mahesh said abruptly to Rumi.

"Yes," said Rumi, stuffing some shampoo into a plastic bag along with a bar of soap.

"There was no need," he said almost instantly, out of habit.

"I just thought I would," she said, continuing with the motion. She didn't look up.

"They are only for special occasions, you know that," Mahesh said halfheartedly.

"I thought I could . . . unpack more easily," said Rumi, picking up the plastic bag and leaving for the bathroom.

He let it pass. He was exhausted. Shreene spoke to him in Hindi while Rumi was out of the room. Had he brought some money for Rumi? Mahesh replied that he had a five-pound note. Shreene thought he should give more, in case. Mahesh refused, just in time, as Rumi came back into the room.

"Where did you go?" said Nibu, who was lying on the bed kicking his feet off the side.

"Nowhere," said Rumi.

"Did you bring your you-know-whats?" said Shreene, in a lower voice, although it was loud enough for everyone to hear. She looked at Rumi and raised her eyebrows, as though reminding her of a shared secret.

"Mum!" said Rumi, throwing the empty plastic bag onto the floor so that it floated on its side across the carpet, stopping at a pile of sweaters.

"What's wrong now?" said Shreene, with an indignant glare. "What is the problem, I ask you?" Then she said to Mahesh, "Why is she talking to me like this now?"

Mahesh shut his eyes and shook his head at Shreene in the manner of a holy man—maybe a wandering pandit or sadhu, he thought—then opened them and moved his head diagonally from one side to the other, then back again. It was a uniquely soothing motion, both for the person doing it and, hopefully, the person witnessing it. He remembered his own father using it on him. Somehow Mahesh had found himself employing an adapted version, these days, to respond to any hysteria that came his way.

"You are giving her all this freedom," said Shreene to Mahesh. "You are the one she respects."

"Mum, don't say that!" said Rumi.

"I know you want to get rid of me," said Shreene. "You have never loved me. Even when you were a little girl you used to wipe my kisses off your cheek—don't you remember that? Only before age five did you show me love."

"Come on, Shreene," said Mahesh.

"Mum!" said Rumi.

Shreene's eyes filled and her bottom lip quivered fiercely, as though she was holding in an unspeakable pain. She met her daughter's gaze. There was a look of exaggerated bewilderment on Rumi's face, her mouth falling open as though in shock, self-righteous horror in her stare. Almost on cue, as though acknowledging how absurd they both looked, they let out a simultaneous laugh, an involuntary chuckle from Shreene mixing with a giggle from Rumi. Mahesh felt a sensation of relief.

"Anyway," said Shreene, using her shirt cuff to dab her eyes, "you must make sure you are well prepared each month with the you-know-whats as this is not your bed with your sheets. It's time to go now. It is a long drive home for your father."

18

Rumi lies in bed and stares at the thick fingers of orange that are heating the bedroom through the night, six bars on an electric fire. There is a shadow blotting the wall opposite, quashing a rectangle of white light every time a car drives past outside. She is listening to the Golden Hour on Fox FM. Three buttons are pressed down on the clock radio cassette section, record, play and pause, in case anything comes on that she may want to tape. She releases the pause button as the DJ introduces the next song. Randy Crawford drifts through the space, singing of escape, lending it an air of clenched sweet sadness. The room is unreal. It feels as taut as her heart, swollen with anticipation. There is an armchair in the corner, which looks like a cartoon version of itself, drawn with an insecure hand, the olive cushions splitting to reveal yellow sponge. A wooden desk looms at the foot of her bed. Rumi is 15 years 4 months and 8 hours old. It is her first night at university and she is awake for the full length of it.

AT FIVE THIRTY Rumi stirred. The house was silent, except for certain swells and creaks, a scratchy rhythm that formed a temperamental backdrop to her thoughts, scraping and filling the hours since she had switched off the radio. Even though she had been technically awake, she had not moved for what had seemed like a very long time. Now she could sense the shift of the night's dark block into a thin mist of Parma violet dye that was dissolving through the air, rousing her to action. She began with the movement of the fingers in her right hand, raising them one by one and trickling through them in a wave, aware of their rise and fall in slow motion. She felt each finger as an entity in itself. In the ashram's teachings they always talked about this stuff, she thought: "I walk, I am mindful of walking. I eat the apple and I know I am eating the apple. I am happy to know this." Those were the kind of examples they used to hint at a life in which the lucky inhabitant could experience everything in the present moment. Gradually, her body moved inside the kaftan that Shreene had given her, rippling with a slow momentum as though she was a fantastical creature coming to life, her body hostage to some devilish djinn that had taken possession and was now breathing through her.

I shake myself and my belly wobbles, she thought. I am aware of the wobble of my belly. I am mindful of it. I am happy to know this. She giggled, a sneeze shuffling the air through her nose. Her limbs curled to support her as she knelt up, resting her bottom on her heels. She held the quilt at her neck and pressed it to her chest with her chin. Then she brought both arms through the gaping armholes of the kaftan so that they rested against the skin of her breasts and stomach. She dipped her head and lifted the neck of the kaftan so that her face joined the rest of her inside the thin purple material, camping inside the tented drapes. She inhaled the scent of her body and made out the shape of her bra, the triangular pale cotton glowing in the confined space. She pressed her breasts together with her arms and put her lips against the soft skin. I kiss my flesh, I am mindful of this, she thought.

Rumi pushed up out of bed, feeling the cold gloss of the atmosphere on the vulnerable parts of her body—her ankles, under her arms, round her neck. On impulse she jumped up and thudded down onto the floor, exclaiming to herself in a sharp whisper: "Yeah!" She waited to see if there was any sound from the rest of the house, then jumped again, landed first on tiptoe, then collapsed onto her soles in front of the mirror on the wall, letting out another strangled exclamation: "Yeah!" She looked at herself in the mirror. Then she screwed up her nose and made another sound, a groan pressed out from deep in her stomach.

"Yeah!" Her voice sounded like a man's. "Yeah, you . . . you . . ."

She glared at herself in the mirror and opened her mouth in a tight circle, crinkling her nose. "Yeah, you . . . you . . . fuckers!" she wheezed, with a cowboy snarl.

She stared at herself and made another face, jutting her lips to the right and opening her eyes so that they bulged. "You . . . you . . . cunts!" she said, a falsetto squeal tucked inside a hiss.

She changed tack, and used a posh voice with a deep vibrato. "You . . . you fucking cunts!" she said, screwing her eyes shut and opening them again four times. "Oh, no, you cunts!"

After the last pronouncement she watched herself cautiously in the mirror. "What I am doing?" she said, in a quiet, very normal voice. "I am mad.

"You are mad," she said, to her reflection, in a stern reprimand. "You weirdo. Fucked-up weirdo. Fucking weirdo." She frowned at herself. "Stop it now," she said. "Stop it."

She walked over to her wardrobe and opened it to reveal the respectfully ordered piles of clothes that Shreene had put there. She picked up a set of turquoise satin shorts and a blouse, among the recent Indian creations, embroidered with flowers at the borders in gold and crimson. The shorts were too long. She unfolded a long black skirt, tailored in an A-line, cut to fall to mid-calf, and held it against her waist. Also too long. Shreene had insisted that nothing should be above the knee in all of Rumi's personally designed clothes. She had been allowed short sleeves and shaped garments but no low necks on the tops she had tried to design (everything came up in an embarrassing scoop or square shape just below her clavicles, barely allowing a short necklace to nestle at her throat).

The time had come to cut up her skirt ready for the first day, slice off the excess length, she thought. But she had no scissors. She glanced at the clock. The digital figures had dulled to matte sticks of red in the new light. It was 5:46 a.m. Suddenly everything felt a lot less threatening.

She got downstairs relatively quietly, treading barefoot on the thick peppermint carpet that covered most of the house. At one point she slipped on the stairs, but her hand steadied her, pressing against the textured wallpaper. The kitchen was basic enough and easy to navigate. She opened a drawer as quietly as she could, wincing at the gruffness of the sound as it came out. It was full of cutlery. She opened the cupboard below and saw a stack of steel saucepans in various sizes. Her next attempt was more careless. She opened two drawers swiftly, with a simultaneous brandish on both sides, hoping to eliminate the sound with speed. But one of the drawers came out in her hand, the side hitting her foot and making her shout in pain. Tools and serving implements clattered to the floor. She saw the scissors among them and crouched to pick them up.

"What do you need?" The voice was quiet but clear.

Rumi turned and saw Mrs. Mukherjee standing in a velvet dressing gown, belted over jersey pajamas, the thick line pulling in her waist and accentuating the slight curves above and below. Rumi imagined how she must look to the women, dwarfed by the spreading endlessness of her kaftan, which seemed to have got mixed up with the contents of the drawer. I am in a kaftan and she is in pajamas, thought Rumi. I observe this. I am mindful of it! She giggled, feeling the nerves start up inside her again.

Mrs. Mukherjee waited politely.

Rumi began to clear up. "I wanted some . . . scissors," she said.

Mrs. Mukherjee bent down and deftly began to replace and rearrange the items that Rumi was negotiating. She extricated a small pair of metallic scissors and handed them to her. "For?" she asked.

"Um . . ." Rumi stood up, trying to pick up her shorts and skirt as inconspicuously as possible. "Just to cut some . . ." She looked at the scissors. It was important to end this and get out of the kitchen as soon as possible. They looked blunt, pretty useless, but she would have to think of something for which they could be used. "For my . . . maths?" she said.

Mrs. Mukherjee nodded. "You can prepare your morning's toilette now," she said. "I will prepare breakfast. The shower is as I explained yesterday. You may leave your wet towel in the linen basket. And hairs that are dislodged into the bath can be wiped up using a tissue paper. We shall leave at seven forty-five a.m. as arranged."

Her manner was perfunctory, as though she was reeling off a shopping list. As she spoke she completed the ordering of the utensils and stood up, lifting the drawer and pushing it into the hollow space of its origin with a quiet "Hmph," a pert sound that signified a mixture of effort and satisfaction as it slotted neatly into place. Then she began to busy herself in the kitchen, picking up a small cloth, wetting it and wiping the drawer's front and the worktop above it.

Rumi waited for Mrs. Mukherjee to look at her, but after a minute of watching her open and close kitchen storage units she realized that wasn't going to happen. "Yes, Mrs. . . . Mukherjee," she said uncertainly, by the door. "I'll . . . er . . . do that, then."

THEY DROVE TO Oxford at the preordained time. Rumi sat in a newly slashed skirt, cobweb threads of the black cotton straggling out onto her tights with amateur defiance. In the end she had used the scissors, which had been as blunt as they looked, and battled against the stubborn fabric with building frustration. It was no good. She had felt along the blades with her index finger but there was nothing of any danger. Only when she ran her tongue lightly over the bitter metal did she find an area at the farthermost point of the join between the two blades that was sharp. She devised a style of cutting that worked, albeit slowly and clumsily, using this section of the scissors. It forced her to cut in one-inch sections, so the line of the hem was visibly jagged when it was done, a demented irregularity cramping the whole shape and causing it to sag toward her right knee when she put it on. But it was shorter, no one could deny it—and that was enough for Rumi.

Mrs. Mukherjee was driving steadily, hands arranged precisely on the wheel, looking through the windscreen at the road ahead. Her face was impassive, devoid of clues. Rumi kept staring at her, against her will. Every time she looked away she felt the urge to look back. But the stares were not returned. There was nothing hidden in the clean, broad forehead and languid eyes, which were now watching the road. She was driving, thought Rumi, and maybe that was what she was thinking about. But how could it be? Surely everyone hid their thoughts. What was Mrs. Mukherjee thinking about? What did she care about? She tried to understand her fascination with her new guardian. When she had come down the stairs wearing the sawn-up skirt, Mrs. Mukherjee had not commented, and Rumi had felt a sensation that was almost disappointment. But she couldn't understand why. It seemed perverse, somehow. This was what she had hoped for, after all—to escape the unbearable scrutiny of her life.

They had eaten their breakfast in relative silence, broken only by two questions from Mrs. Mukherjee—what were the names of Rumi's different courses, she asked, and what was the name of the principal of the college, to whom she was scheduled to deliver Rumi at eight thirty? She had received Rumi's replies to both questions with a brief "Mm-hm?" of acknowledgment, and an abrupt twitch of her head, as though receiving the answers meant she could dismiss the solved questions like flies that had been buzzing round her face. She had read a newspaper throughout the meal. Rumi did not ask any questions.

This lack of interest in her activities was new to Rumi. She was used to silence with Mahesh, but he had always been acutely aware of her every move. So much so that she had sometimes wondered if he could hear her thoughts. Mrs. Mukherjee was not like a parent or relative, or any grown-up—at least, not one with whom Rumi had ever had contact. She was, officially, an equation with no answer. A minus figure with no square root. Rumi named her, then and there, Mrs. Minus the Enigma.

The procedure of arriving at the college, feeling herself materialize gradually to inhabit this new, peculiar, romantic world, was one that Rumi moved through with an intoxication that might have been mistaken for laziness, so slow were her movements and so dazed her responses. The absence of Mahesh left her off center, nervous and hungry for the rush of feelings that crept into her unmonitored heart with each new stimulus. She was freed from the guiding signals of his face, the expressions of affirmation, suspicion and disapproval, that had been her barometer for so long.

Rumi crossed the road while Mrs. M found a place to park, and walked through traffic toward the college gates. Part of her thought she would fall over, unable to get to the other side alone, lie mangled beneath a car, unidentifiable for days, a dumpy crush of stained flesh and bone. She reached the opposite pavement and said to herself, in a low voice, "Why did the chicken cross the road? To get to the other side." When she entered the courtyard, and was confronted by a prickling quad of grass, bordered with the corpulent old buildings of prospectuses, she stood at the sign that said, "Visitors Report to the Porter's Lodge," felt the heave in her stomach and pictured the unceremonious vomit launching itself out of her innards and onto the specific word "Porter's."

Girls rushed round her—manes of yellow, brown, black and strawberry—important minds and bodies that designed the space with their movements: grown-up girls with bikes and suitcases, trunks and musical instruments, girls who looked as if they had never been to a high school, never been called swots or nerds, cool or classy, regardless of their specs or their perms, the line of their jackets or jeans, the amount of cleavage hinted at by the swell of a V-neck sweater. These girls were above such terminology, with serious business to attend to. They floated round Rumi, part of the same world plan as the trees, which seemed to rattle their branches in a husky whisper of complicity, and the veiny orange and red leaves that danced out in tangents on the ground, thrown by the wind into the corners of stone and green. A stocky man in a uniform came out of the porter's lodge, walked up to her and winked, putting his hand on her shoulder. A smile spread genially across his milky face as he looked her in the eye and said, "Rumika Vasi, I presume?" The sensation she felt, hot in her flesh, was familiar. It was shame.

THAT WAS RUMI's last precise memory, in real, existing time, for quite a while. The next twenty-four hours passed in a craze of events and introductions. She met the principal of the college, a frail crisp of a woman with a thin covering of yellowed hair on her head, like the frosted coating on a posh biscuit. Rumi was assigned a "college mum," a maths student in the year above her: twenty-year-old Serena, who turned out to be a bored waif in black leggings and a green blazer. Her face was so angular that Rumi could imagine the skull beneath the skin, the hollows where her large eyes lay supported, the jutting bones that combined to push her lips into a perpetual pout, teeth that protruded in unison, but had been clamped down with a brace. They went to meet her maths tutor—Serena, Mrs. M and Rumi—in an orderly trio that creaked up the stairs of an old house in the garden of another college and into a room containing a coal fire, leather chairs and a bald-headed man with a backward fringe of lengthy silver hair that licked its way down his neck so that he looked like an aging musician. He turned out to be Mr. Mountford, one of the people who had been in the room when she was interviewed all those months ago. He was very well thought-of at Oxford, an "absolute legend," according to Serena, who had decided that Mr. Mountford, and Rumi's acquisition of him as a personal tutor, were actually topics that merited her speaking. His legendary status did not make him easy to talk to, though. Now he questioned Rumi again, as though it was still possible for her to be sent home, about her intentions, her aims. He asked her, with a doubtful expression on his face, what she thought of maths in general—"what the purpose of it could conceivably be." She replied, "To try to quantify the world," an answer that Mahesh had given her for exactly such an eventuality, ready and waiting like the ten-pence coins zipped now, as always, into the side of her bag for phone-box emergencies.

The meeting and greeting continued with gusto. It spiraled, multiplied, whorled along the stem of the day. They were busy. Serena had been given a long list of people to get through. Rumi met the college domestic bursar, the librarian and the canteen manager. Mr. Mountford took them round the maths department, the maths library, the empty maths lecture theaters, and Rumi met more people, walked among more books, tons of them—leatherbound, varnished or split at the seams, books that flooded in rows, rows that were bent into ovals, connected in squares, stacked high toward domed ceilings, reaching up to the vulnerable undersides of slatted roofs. She left the maths compound with Serena and Mrs. Minus and they continued their travels.

They walked down stony backstreets, over moist grass and mud, and passed an abundance of students on cycles: a steady stream of limbs, rucksacks and wheels that refreshed and renewed itself wherever they went. They climbed hills and staircases, entered halls, ornate and functional, "Victorian" and "Newly Built." Rumi went to the student's union with them—her near-mute gang of two—and was aware of their detached presence, standing at either side of her as she signed a plastic card, which told her she was a member for life. She did not share with them the thrill she felt. There she saw the black-and-white photos of world leaders, framed in gilt, charting the ascent of the curved stairs. She hovered halfway up, having sought out the pictures of Benazir Bhutto and Indira Gandhi, secretly smiling at them. In a way she was alone in those moments between meetings, even though she was not unaccompanied. She watched public-school boys rush past her with floppy hair and long college scarves that swished their stripes against the carpets. She stared, and people stared at her too.

Later she went back to Didcot with Mrs. Minus, ate a microwave meal of cauliflower cheese, called Mahesh at exactly eight p.m., went up to lie in the bed, and came back in the morning for more of the same.

And then, at four fifty-six p.m. on the second day, Mrs. M put Rumi on a train.

On the way home, Rumi wondered how she would ever speak to her parents or Nibu again. It seemed impossible to experience so much, to soak in this world and all its possibilities so passively and completely that its remnants now lay like grime in her skin, an undefined guilt, for who knew what, and then to go back to the past like an interloper, wash her hands and eat dinner with them, as though it was all the same. She watched the trees and fields cantering past her window, peered through the graying wash of light in the space between the glass and the world outside, and tried maybe fifty times, maybe more, to imagine the moment when she would get off the train and walk with her father to the car.

19

Over the next month, Rumi worked slowly to separate herself into two different people, with two exclusive sets of personal characteristics. She stored these covert signs of her personalities in separate parts of her brain: instead of having a right/left divide for science and arts, she reshaped it, creating a new split that was much more functional, two new compartments, top and bottom. This meant that the top could contain all of the information that was supposed to define her at any one time, leaving the bottom to safeguard everything that needed to be kept hidden. The duality of her life had started to take its toll on her, the feeling that she had always to be on her toes, that either there was always something missing from her conversation or that she was oversharing information, especially during the subtle questioning from Mahesh or the girls at college, so much so that she had distilled the anxieties—the soup of manic thoughts that could start frothing unbidden, confusing her in either place—into a simple list of basic dos and don'ts.

On the first of November, the morning of her fifth visit to Oxford, Rumi woke and realized she had stopped eating the seeds. This thought was present as she lay and watched, without her glasses, a fuzzy shape move across the skirting board under the wardrobe, near an old cup of coffee. She had started going to bed so late that she now showered at night and got into the next day's clothes before she slept at three or four a.m., applying foundation and thick eyeliner in these lethargic hours, leaving her lips bare for a slick of red on waking.

Mrs. Minus did not wake her or tell her to sleep—she did not seem to consider that her role—but she was always ready to leave when Rumi came running downstairs, flushed with the shame of being late, pinning up her hair and tousling strands out as she raced through the hallway to the car with her books, scratching a woozy head. Even then, Mrs. Minus was not ruffled—she did not emanate anything that was even close to judgmental about Rumi's way of being. It was as though displaying even the lightest hint of that kind of subjectivity was either alien or distasteful to her.

A month in, and Rumi still did not know a thing. She was no closer to finding the root of this most deceptively simple number: Mrs. Minus. In fact, every week it was almost like the first time they'd met, bar the polite introductions to the various rooms of the house. Other than that, they spoke as if they had no history together, even though Rumi felt that each week, each day, even, was adding to her own personal history with vast significance. When interviewed by newspapers, thought Rumi, Mrs. Minus would have genuinely "no comment." Her interior world was utterly separate from Rumi's, and anything which suggested that this state of affairs might change (if Rumi stayed in the kitchen for too long after a meal, or started washing the dishes) made her visibly nervous.

Presumably she's watching me as she drives off, thought Rumi, as she ran to the newsagent opposite the Oxford drop-off point, by the college gates, to buy an outsize Yorkie for breakfast, a hulking chocolate brick that she sucked agitatedly as she pushed herself down the winding roads to get to her morning tutorial.

On this day, 1st November, she stopped for breath near Keble College and wondered at the recurring thought that the two-kilo bag of cumin in her room was still unopened. It was such an incredible idea that she had to sit down, on a pavement bench, and watch people walk past. They crowded the foreground in a painting dominated by gangling old buildings and embossed archways. Rumi considered the world for fifteen minutes—a beautiful world in which it was possible to live without cumin.

She reached her tutorial seven minutes late and ran into the room. She dumped her coat on a pile by the door, then joined the other three students, puffing as she sat in the empty chair and attempted to assume the air of attentiveness that dominated the tutorial, moving her body to continue the smooth parabola of the three boys who leaned in toward Mr. Mountford. The dotted sound of chalk on the small blackboard punctuated the constant voice of Mr. Mountford, an audio commentary that lumbered along in a determinedly measured fashion, in spite of the disruptive arrival of his youngest student. Rumi pushed her hand around in her bag, full of the crackle of confectionery wrappers and the rustle of college society leaflets. She tried to find a pen, continuing the noisy foray, until she realized with a sickening slowness that, clearly, she had forgotten to pack one in.

"Can I . . . ?" she whispered to the boy next to her, Marty Chambers, an American boy with a giant preppy innocence who had a peculiarly divine relationship with maths, a hunger for the right answer and a sincerity that Rumi found impenetrable. He watched Mr. Mountford through the rimless lenses of his glasses, sealed in an evangelical bubble.

"Please, Marty . . ." said Rumi, thickening her voice in the hope that he hadn't heard her. He twitched and leaned forward, clutching the edge of his sleeve.

"Let a be an element of the group G," droned Mr. Mountford. "If there exists a positive integer n such that $a^n = e$, then a is said to have finite order, and the smallest such positive integer, as you know, is called the order of a, denoted by $o(a)$."

Mr. Mountford sniffed and took out a large handkerchief into which he blew his nose, a sound that turned out mostly to consist of high-pitched air. Rumi felt panic in the base of her stomach. Mr. Mountford looked at her for a beat, then back at the board. The sunlight pouring through the grand glass pane behind him gave the chalk dust an ultraviolet gleam, the numbers and letters shining with space-age confidence, as though together they linked to make an elite formula, something that was the secret to the heart of the universe. No wonder Marty was transfixed, thought Rumi. There was something going on in this room, something very important, and she wasn't part of it.

The truth was, Rumi didn't know what Mr. Mountford was talking about. In fact, she hadn't understood the steady rotation of numbers and letters being paraded in front of her at Oxford for quite some time, whether in the deceptively intimate interchanges of the weekly tutorials or in the huge, vaulted latitude of the lecture theaters.

She had not been studying in Cardiff, in spite of the weight of her new endeavor, and Mahesh was none the wiser. He had relaxed his inspections, presuming that she was now safely in the care of the most prestigious academic institution in the world. But she was not working. She was unable to understand this new stuff over which she had no control—the lectures that came at her in a fuzz of white noise, a cold cloud that cloaked itself round her for eight hours each week and disintegrated as seamlessly as it had arrived.

Instead of learning maths, she preferred to read novels at her desk, borrowed from the Eng. Lit. section of the Bodleian Library, hiding the slabs of fiction under the weight of her algebra textbook. She also listened to the radio in her room, taping songs onto old cassettes from which she would write down lyrics, one finger poised over the "sleep" button in case she should hear steps on the stairs. In this way she had built up a small library of lined paper, torn from the back of exercise books and scrawled on with new pens bought from the stationery section of the bookshop on Magdalen Road: green, violet or turquoise inks that trickled their colors out with juicy care into the rhyming unity of chart-topping love songs. These sheets of paper she stored in the bottom drawer of her desk, underneath the stout security of a first-year core text entitled *Vibrations and Waves*. The stash of songs was, by its nature, extremely private, in an almost bodily way—it was as though writing out a song gave Rumi ownership of its words, as well as committing them to her memory. It was quite a diverse list, including, as special favorites, among its ranks the lyrics from "Baby Can I Hold You" by Tracy Chapman, "Nothing Compares 2 U" by Sinéad O'Connor, and "Push It" by Salt-N-Pepa (the words of the last song being particularly repetitive but somehow deeply powerful, especially when Rumi looked at them over and over again on the page).

The natural rhythm of this daily life of deception had begun to worry her; the identity she had built up as a "genius" was sliding with shocking ease into a fudged land of nonsense, a burble of algebraic imagery that leapt and belched through her dreams, with a taunting disregard for her feelings. She woke throughout the night, and kept the unease during the day, pretending to understand, skittering over the surface of this ever-increasing sign language. Regularly, and awkwardly, she was on the back foot. And no one knew about it, except Mr. Mountford and the boys in her tutorial. How long would it be before Mr. Mountford blew the whistle on her? Did he care enough to let her secret out into the departmental ether so that it could drift home over the mist till it arrived, frostbitten and unpardonable, at her father's ears?

How can I be here, like this, again? she thought. She sat in the tutorial, tapping the side of her knee manically and looking down at her blank exercise book, a penless hand simmering over the lower right quarter of the right-hand page. How am I here, stupid, empty, not knowing anything again? How do I know nothing now? How did I fool everyone? Please, God, don't let him ask me. Please, God, she said to herself, tapping her index finger against the bone protruding in a circular shape over her knee, knocking it in a tripping pattern of four, pausing her breath in time with her finger. I promise I'll be good again. She felt the Yorkie emulsifying in her stomach, a vat of lazy greed, oozing with brown waste.

"What would denote an infinite order for a?" said Mr. Mountford, nodding in the direction of Rumi and Marty. She jumped, choking without sound.

Marty spoke, almost instantaneously, taking advantage of the fact that the nod had been aimed at the space between his and Rumi's heads.

"If there does not exist a positive integer n such that $a^n = e$," said Marty, in a hasty rush of speech, "then a is said to have infinite order."

Rumi felt the air collapse back into her lungs.

Mr. Mountford grunted and wiped the markings on the board. He wrote something new. She tried to make contact with Marty out of the corner of her eye, wanting to thank him, but he remained fixed, his shoulder turned away from her, the devout stare now channeled in the direction of the blackboard. She nudged him gently and he reacted again by clutching the ends of his sleeves, both of them this time, moving imperceptibly away from her and toward their tutor.

"Let G_1 and G_2 be groups, and let $\theta : G_1 \rightarrow G_2$ be a function," said Mr. Mountford, sniffing as he chalked, and chalking exactly the symbols he spoke, an interlinking of movements and speech that would have felt almost poetic to Rumi if she hadn't found his presence so intimidating. "Then, as you know," he continued, "θ is said to be a group isomorphism if, (i) θ is one-to-one and onto and (ii) $\theta(ab) = \theta(a)\,\theta(b)$ for all $a,b \in G_1$. In this case," he said, "what is the relation of G_1 to G_2? And how is this denoted?"

He turned and looked at Rumi this time, a laser flicker lightening his eyes as they focused on her. She swallowed, and the chocolate melt squirted dangerously in her belly. "Rumika?" he said.

She blinked several times, feeling a sting in her eyes, reacting to the clinical quality of his gaze. The silence that followed in the room was morbidly long, interrupted only by the windy whistle of a bird outside, then a short series of clicks—a brief conversation on the lawn below.

"Rumika?" he asked again, the voice sturdy, with a questioning upturn at the end of her name.

"I need to go to the toilet," said Rumi, looking at the floor as she stood up, holding the book. She stood, waiting for a response, some kind of permission, staring at her bag, which was slumped by her chair, maintaining her physical balance.

"Please may I go to the . . ." she said, feathering the words with an erratic breath, walking out at an angle, fearful of fully turning her back on them as she left the room.

This is what Dad calls fight-or-flight instinct, she thought, and sat, with her knickers down, trying to cry the feeling out in the small rectangular cubicle, looking up at the raised coving on the ceiling, the high, inverted mound of plaster that linked the long walls round her. She shook violently, feeling the wetness of the rain that had spattered her that morning, as though it was lying trapped under her skin. This is fight or flight, she thought. A chemical has been released in my veins now, making my body move like this, like a mad person's. Suddenly, and awfully, she hankered for Nibu, craved his struggling little body for its wholesome warmth and simplicity. He came to mind embroiled in a play-fight—she found herself choreographing the scene in her mind—one of the twirling wrestles that had bound them for years, almost since the age when he had begun walking. He was too old for that now. Her hands huddled round her, hugging her front. There was a frosted quality to the air, causing her exposed thighs to quiver. She forced herself to think it through. Something was released in my body, then, which meant I had to escape—it helped me to escape. Does that mean Mr. Mountford is a predator? Did I think he was . . . Was he actually about to destroy me? Why else would I have run like that, like . . . run for my life?

When she returned she was grateful that a tacit agreement had been reached to ignore her for what little was left of the tutorial. At the end as she got up to leave, hoping to get out of the door before the boys, wanting to avoid the awkward walk through the college grounds, she heard Mr. Mountford cough and speak her name, muttering as he turned to wipe the board. His voice continued to emanate from behind his broad, curved back as he moved the duster against the board. Rumi could see his famous silver hair lying in long, lank strips against the back of his neck, trailing from its roots round the central circle of baldness. She strained to pick up the words, but the rest of his sentence was inaudible.

"Sorry . . . sir?" she said. "Pardon me?"

"I'd like you to stay behind," said Mr. Mountford, returning to his domicile in the large old armchair, and pressing his head against the velvet backrest.

He waited until the others had left, then blew into his handkerchief ponderously, as though he was heralding an announcement of some significance.

"How are you . . . finding it here?" he asked.

"Good," said Rumi, quickly and categorically.

"Are you . . . experiencing . . ." He paused, frowned. "Are you . . ." He stopped again, the frown deepening as his eyebrows came together. "Is there something . . ." he said.

Rumi wondered if she was supposed to finish the sentence. She decided to go for it. Anything was better than waiting like this: what if the fight-or-flight stuff took hold of her again? She could already feel the thwack and loop of her heart changing its speed in her chest.

"Are you in—" he began again.

"—joying abstract algebra?" tried Rumi, her voice hysterical.

Mr. Mountford jerked his head back, eyes opening in surprise.

"No," he said, with a slow shake of the head. "No," he said again, more firmly.

Rumi waited for a signal, eyeing him.

"Are you in trouble?" he asked.

She froze.

"Are you finding this . . ." He looked at the empty blackboard and gestured at the space around him. "Is it difficult?"

She did not respond, and began to count internally, a series of hopping numbers that increased in gulps but made no sense: 34 . . . 76 . . . 98 . . . 1126 . . . 123654 . . . They formed a loose tower of gibberish in her mind.

"Do you . . . want to . . . be at Oxford?" said Mr. Mountford, as though he was translating a foreign language.

Rumi nodded. She repeated the action. 37 . . . 3 . . . 99 . . . 010 . . . 54.769823185 . . . The tower collapsed into absolute, hellish randomness.

"Do you want help?" said Mr. Mountford.

She looked at him in open panic.

"Look," said Mr. Mountford, "we here in the department . . ." He blew his nose again, but in a thwarted fashion. The sound was verging on pathetic—there was nothing to blow out this time. It was a gesture robbed of its previous power.

"Insofar as . . ." he continued. "We are . . . I am . . . pleased to have you in our care . . . and we do not want to . . . jeopardize this . . . this . . . prestigious liaison with yourself . . . um . . . this positive acquisition for the university . . . an important event . . ."

An ambulance siren slithered by. Mr. Mountford stopped speaking and examined Rumi for some sign of recognition. "But I have to confess some . . . anxiety . . ." he continued.

"Please don't tell my father," said Rumi.

He leaned forward. "Sorry?" he said.

"I said, please don't tell my father," said Rumi.

"Tell your father . . . what, exactly?"

She waited, unable to reply.

"Why would that be . . . er . . . of concern to you?" he asked.

"He won't like it," said Rumi. She kept her voice in line but her face was giving way. "Please don't tell him," she said, tears rising to her eyes.

"I . . . ah . . ." said Mr. Mountford, clearly disturbed by the new turn of events.

Rumi wiped both eyes in a lightning movement, a diagonal slide of her index finger from the corner of each eye to the side of her head, transferring the dampness over her skin and up to her hair.

Mr. Mountford sighed. "Look . . ." he said gently, ". . . I have to make sure that I'm not seen to be . . . er . . . failing my duty in any way. You have to . . . understand the basics before you can . . . er . . . There is a long way to go . . . to the first-year exams and already . . . you . . . I mean . . . Imagine if you don't manage to . . . I mean . . . you see . . . the risk of embarrassment . . . for myself . . ."

"I promise," said Rumi, looking at the floor. "Just don't . . . please?"

He winced, got up and walked over to the window so that his back was turned toward her again. "Have you heard of Penal Collections?" he asked.

Rumi cleared her throat. Was this a trick question? She could give it a shot but she felt so inadequate, she didn't have the confidence to make a go of it. Differential equations? Calculus? The probability of getting the right subject area was too slight to bear. It sounded, well, rude, but he didn't seem to be . . .

He turned his head and looked at her over his shoulder.

"Penal Collections are a particular form of exam, set at the discretion of a personal tutor, to bring those students who are showing signs of lagging behind up to the level required by the curriculum. This form of assessment is universitywide and the results are transparent—they will be visible to your collegiate superiors as well as departmental heads, should your personal tutor feel it appropriate."

Rumi shut her eyes in sync, a painful swell behind them. She craved for him to stop talking.

"I am hereby notifying you of a Penal Collection, a month from today, to be held at a location that I will confirm in writing, timed and invigilated by myself—"

"Please don't—" said Rumi.

"You need not worry," said Mr. Mountford. "I will not tell your father at this point."

20

the hall was crammed with an assortment of gifted weirdos of all shapes and sizes. In truth, that was the only way Rumi could think to describe it. Although she acknowledged that it was a cruel use of vocabulary, a word that had been the cause of much pain in her own life, "weirdo" was the only term that came close to defining the crowd. They ranged from the doddery enthusiasts who had organized "Reading Between the Lines—A Convention of Gifted Children," to the parents, who included the fawning strokers sitting in front of her at either side of a docile seven-year-old boy, whom they had dressed in a three-piece suit (pin-striped, jacket unbuttoned to reveal a tightly tailored waistcoat and chunky black tie). And then there were the children, an unsightly jamboree of, well, weirdos, whose eyes she couldn't meet, because of her own feelings of revulsion. Rumi sat at her assigned place in the third row from the back, wearing a badge that displayed her name and reason for being there ("Gifted fifteen-year-old maths undergraduate, Oxford University"). She took a deep breath and attempted to control the feeling that she was an out-and-out fraud.

In fact, she was lucky, she thought. Lucky in many ways. She was lucky that Mrs. Minus had believed that this convention would go on until ten p.m. and that Rumi would stay there. Lucky to have a guardian who did not want to come in with her, who seemed relieved that all she had to do was pick Rumi up at the assigned time. Lucky, indeed, that Mahesh had displayed a pretty visible emotional tug-of-war when she had told him about the event—he had wanted her to go, of course, but for some reason (probably the same reason that lay behind his aversion to Mensa), he had not wanted to come with her. But most of all, in a flush of luck, she had found a parentally justifiable event to go to in the evening—more than that, one that coincided joyously (with the kind of euphoric synchronicity that suggested she was, indeed, lucky, exactly as the pandit had predicted in India all those years ago) with an event run by the Oxford University Asian Society.

She had collected the various society leaflets at the freshers' fair, at the start of term, when she had still had Serena, her ironically named "mum," in tow. It was before they had agreed that they could help each other by not spending time together, preferring to be free of the bind, except when public appearances demanded it—for example, at maths lectures, where a few hours spent sitting together was a small price to pay for the freedom of other days. During these lectures, Rumi actually appreciated Serena, whose cool diffidence acted as a shield against the nakedly curious stares and whispers that she still attracted from the rest of the crowd.

At the freshers' fair, however, Serena had been tiring of her responsibility, especially when the differing nature of their interests had become clear, Rumi hovering by the Astrology, Dungeons and Dragons Role-Playing Society, Poetry and Magic Circle Society stalls among others. For financial reasons, Rumi had joined only one group, and the clearest contender was the Asian Society, it being the outright winner, according to her most important criterion: "society most likely to provide reciprocal love interest via social events and type of members." The fun-and-games societies, unfortunately, had to wait. The OAS also had links to Black Caucus, the Anti-Racism League Society, at which table Rumi had stopped indefinitely, losing Serena after ten minutes of slow leaflet-reading and careful absorption of their material. She had paid her three pounds annual membership fee to the Asian Society, and collected information on all the events she could find, hiding the printouts in the inner zip pocket of her satchel.

Now she had to find an appropriate moment at which to leave the convention. She looked at her watch. It was 6:23 p.m., and The Jazz and Samosas Night was due to begin at seven in a room at a college called St. Hugh's on the Banbury Road at the other end of town. She had a long walk ahead of her, maybe forty-five minutes, longer, even, if she got lost—she would have to read the map in her pocket by streetlights as she walked there. Her exit would have to be swift and soon. A swagger of applause went through the audience and a short woman in a blocky woolen dress took the stage. Rumi was aware of someone pushing through the row ahead of her, aiming to get to three empty seats farther up to her left. "Sorry," came a husky whisper. "Sorry . . . I just need to . . . Sorry, thanks." She looked up and saw a matronly woman with a shaven man's face, the words "former nationally renowned child prodigy" clasped to the curved lapel of her dress, a funnel of rich perfume moving ahead of her. Rumi waited for the seed of memory in her mind to germinate. She recognized the face. But how? "Jane Green" was the name on the lapel. Who was Jane Green? "Sorry," said Ms. Green, dealing graciously with the second row. "Hi, Becky," she whispered, to a blond head in the front row.

The girl she had addressed turned round and whispered, "Hi, Johnny!" Rumi recognized another face—a grown-up and chillingly distant Rebecca Lazenby, subject of countless daydreams, the youngest in her lifetime to have got to university (age twelve for her maths degree), owner of the familiar features that had dominated Rumi's childhood—as relevant as a relative, remote as a mannequin.

Rumi watched Ms. Green disappear down the row, then made her way out. She had understood. Jane Green was Johnny Green, a child prodigy from Swansea, who was never mentioned in the Vasi household. He had changed his sex after presenting an extremely popular television quiz show for almost five years, only to be ditched after puberty robbed him of his cuteness and rendered him unmarketable. Johnny Green was possibly the most loved and ridiculed prodigy Rumi had ever heard of, praised and pushed by an adoring public, then rejected by the very same.

In the foyer, Rumi stopped under the mosaic of flat blocks in the ceiling, a large but feeble source of off-white light, and looked at a prominent noticeboard by the entrance. There was yet another familiar face. This time, cut and pasted among press clippings and listings, she came eye to eye with Shakuntala Devi, goddess of numbers, wonder woman of number crunchers, the original superpower, demimortal human calculator, circus-auntie herself. She had been shorn of her huge bun, her large bindi had been dissolved off her forehead, and instead she had been styled with a French bob, unruly but groomed, clad in a square-shouldered navy jacket and skirt, and photographed holding a book entitled *Awaken the Maths Genius in Your Child.* Rumi reached out and touched each eye of Shakuntala Devi in the way that, as a family, they asked for blessings from the photograph of their guru at home. She touched the tips of her fingers back to her own eyes to transfer the blessing, skimming them over the lids. Then she walked out of the building, trying to outstep her mind, not wanting to understand any of it.

The moon was with her as she walked, hands deep in her pockets, collar drawn up to combat the nuzzle of cold round her neck. In the air, a wayward expansion of hope seemed to carry the wind forward, fortifying her breath, which came out as hot balloons of steam, in a steady symbiosis with the dark sky around her.

"Push it!" she whispered, the lyric lacing her breath like a confession, then louder, as her walk turned into a skip, the pavement under her feet strengthening into a secure runway, a track that would lead unquestionably to her destination. She sang it again. Then she ran, the cold rubbing into a burn against her cheeks as she opened her mouth and let rip: a medley of song titles, hoarded in the bottom section of her mind, jumping up and out through her voice, into the world, to commemorate this, her first solitary nighttime walk. "Baby Can I HO-OLD You Tonight?" she heard, rebounding into the ether as she threw back her head and shouted up to a black sky, streaked with sherbet stars. "Angel of Harlem!" she belted, her vocals effortless against the traffic. "All I Want Is You!" she yelped, as she ran over a zebra crossing, swerving past a kebab shop at the end of Cowley Road, the long tail of her coat flying out behind her as she rocked to the blue jangle of electric guitars in her head. "Boys Don't Cry!" she quivered baggily, as she tripped over Magdalen Bridge and into the illuminated old postcard stretch of walls and spires. "Kiss Me. Kiss Me. Kiss Me! Close to Me!" she lamented, finally slowing down, taking deep bulky breaths to refill her lungs, coming to a stop by the spotlit window of a shop selling woolen keepsakes, embroidered with a variety of coats of arms. "Oooooh, oh!" she sang, bending over her knees and wheezing, her face wrinkling with the ardent sincerity of a rock star. She raised her voice into a soprano. "Hey . . . That's No Way to Say Good-bye," she crooned, straightening, then walking to join the brawling collision of people and lights in the center.

THE PARTY WAS visually an anticlimax, consisting of fewer than thirty people standing in a room with nothing to do. This was something that pleased Rumi: it meant she could slip in, aimless and friendless, without fear of ridicule. It was also reasonably badly dressed, with a good mix of classic socially malodorous Oxford geeks. They diluted the effect of the small but potent measures of impossibly smooth, mocha-tinted girls, standing together in impervious cliques. Set in a boxy room in a "new" wing of the college (a room not dissimilar to the conference room at Swansea University, where Mahesh had arranged Rumi's mock exams), it was full of the embarrassed deflation of a failed birthday party, the kind at which the parents haven't realized that their child has outgrown them.

There was jazz, for sure, tinned in a small tape recorder, placed at the end of a chain of tables, which had been lined up to create a kind of "bar" under the large whiteboard on the wall. And there were samosas, arranged in fans of five: peas and potatoes enclosed in greasy pastry, which etched transparent silhouettes on the paper plates. There was even a tray of red and white wine poured equally into a series of plastic cups from two wine boxes, dispensed through black taps that reached out over the edge of the table and dribbled drops of purple and pale yellow onto the floor.

Rumi stood alone, relishing the anonymity, feeling the rarity of being in a place where she had no context. There didn't seem to be any maths freshers here—at least, none she knew by sight. She could experience being ageless, decategorized, for a finite amount of luxuriant time. She lounged against the wall, aping the achingly bored look that was Serena's hallmark, and took a large gulp of red wine. It tangoed through her, a rabid, tart taste that was nothing like the dense black currant nectar she'd imagined. She grimaced, hoping the action would ditch the sourness, and help get her back to being urbane and enigmatic.

"Are you all right?"

Rumi looked up at a boy with a rough goatee, thick hair languishing in a sloppy fringe and streaming down into messy sideburns. She frowned, hoping to give off an air of flippancy, as though she didn't understand what he was talking about. "Pardon?" she said, clearing her throat. It felt like a long time since she had used her mouth for conversation.

"Oh, parr-don?" he said, in a croaky Indian accent.

She giggled, snorting by accident.

"What could he be referring to?" he said, deepening the sound and staggering the words, so that they took on a raplike quality. "What—indeed—is—he—talking about?"

Rumi rolled her eyes, and pretended to take another sip of wine, tipping the cup so that the bitter liquid splashed lavishly against her lips, then letting it slip back.

He laughed—a ticklish sound that was unexpected, more infantile than she'd imagined.

"Come on, man," he said, in an accent that Rumi could only place as London. "You don't have to pretend in front of me. At least you gave it a shot, eh? I salute that at least." He looked round the room. "Most of the eighteen-year-old girls here are too fresh from Ama and Papa. They wouldn't be caught dead with shameless sharaab in their hands, not for another couple of months at least."

"You're mad," said Rumi.

"And you're . . . endowed with the most beautiful . . . eyes," he said.

"What are you like!" said Rumi.

"I am 'like' serious," he said, in a grand voice. "Fall-into-left-right-and-center-style eyes. Drown-in-if-you're-not-careful eyes. Oh-don't-look-at-me-like-that eyes. Will-someone-give-me-my-head-back eyes."

"OK, OK, don't take the piss!" said Rumi, flushing.

"Far from it," he said. "I'm being serious." He nodded in a gesture of respect, a semibow, and let his eyes linger on hers.

Rumi felt a quick trill of excitement. She glanced round the room. Not only was no one looking at them, it seemed as if the others were in another picture, drinking and talking in a different era. She thought quickly for some words—a joke, a line to parry back. " 'If I Said You Had, er . . .' " she said.

He waited, a smile at his lips.

" '. . . a Beautiful . . . er . . .' "

His eyes widened with obvious interest. Rumi giggled with boiling discomfiture. She caught his eye and saw his bewilderment. It set off new, wilder laughter, coming all the way from her gut. She held her sides to try to stop the attack, fighting to regain some semblance of dignity.

"Go on," he said. "I'm intrigued to see what you're going to do here."

She tried to say the word but the giggles prevented her.

" '. . . a Beautiful . . . B-B-B—' " The sentence crumbled into another laugh.

"Please," he said. "I can't take the suspense."

" 'If I said you had a beautiful body,' " said Rumi, " 'would you hold it against me?' "

He laughed, a genuine, rocketing noise that Rumi loved for its sheer wholeheartedness. It was so large a sound that the three girls standing near them stopped speaking and turned to look in their direction.

"Oh, I do like your style," he said, taking Rumi's hand and enclosing it between his palms. "What say we get out of this tragic joint and hit the road?"

FAREED AGREED EASILY to stop off at the convention center for Rumi to run in and pick up her wallet after she had "discovered" it wasn't in her bag. The simplicity of convincing him saddened her. She had opened her satchel, waved her hand inside it, let out a little squeal of recognition while he was starting the car in a quiet street at the back of the college, then acted out the shocked realization that she'd left it behind somewhere.

"It must have been at that maths workshop," she said apologetically, aware of how easily the lie formed as she spoke. "It was an out-of-town speaker . . . I hope you don't mind . . . Thank you so much."

He smiled at her and winked, delaying the moment of looking away, leaving the brown eyes on her again for an unerring moment. It was an intimate thrill, as though he was an actor who had come offstage, pausing between acts. Rumi had a sudden irrational vision of two large warm hands on her breasts, like these eyes of his, which were covering her now. She felt a quickening in the car. The air was clotting beyond inhalation—it felt much too dense and hot for them both. She felt guilt heat her thoughts, a sordid guilt that squashed her joy at being present in a moment with someone as she had desired. Guilt at her lies, and guilt at the thought of Mahesh and Shreene, who would have been inconsolably hurt if they could have seen her now. As he drove, she gave directions and tap-danced over his questions, barely audible, her hearing frayed with the fear that they would pass Mrs. Minus somewhere, anywhere. She looked out of the window to her side, rubbing through the condensation and watching each car for the telltale navy curves of the vehicle that belonged to her guardian. Fareed's assumption that she was telling the truth was achingly perfect, thought Rumi. But it only underlined the fact that she was a liar. She was too good at bending the information at hand into these perfectly circular lies. The water in her well was not pure in any way. In reality it was . . . putrid, diseased . . . infected. She shuddered.

"Funny," Fareed said, as they neared the building, which was, happily, still lit up, a few people straggling near the entrance. "You don't look like the maths-geek type," he continued, indicating that he was about to turn. "What do you guys get up to at these gigs, then?"

Rumi opened the door as he was slowing down to enter the driveway, and let her feet hit the moving road, as though the friction of her soles would be enough to stop the car, like the last moments of a dodgem ride.

"Hey, take it easy!" he said, braking instantly. "What's the problem, man?"

"Don't worry. Wait here," she said, jumping out, then running up the vast gravel expanse, hearing the dashing rhythm of her feet against the tiny stones, breathing in the chilly mist as fast as she could. His name flashed into her head unbidden. Fareed = fact. Fareed = something: an old thought, something borrowed, remembered, known, but presenting itself as new. Fareed = Muslim. Quite clearly. No ambiguity. Whether you rearranged the letters or assigned to each one a different value, the word was pretty much unequivocal.

Rumi saw Mrs. Minus sitting in the car, positioned, wonderfully, at the point farthest away from her, on the left-hand corner of the entrance. It was magical. It would seem as if she had come out of the entrance as arranged. She picked up her pace even more and ran, carefully, to try to avoid appearing in the car's rearview mirror. When she poked her head into the passenger side, Mrs. Minus looked up.

"Hello, Mrs. Mukherjee," said Rumi.

Mrs. Minus waited. She shivered pointedly to get Rumi to shut the car door.

"The thing is," said Rumi, pulling the door in as narrowly as she could, feeling the slicing contrast between the top part of her body—plunged into the artificial heat of the car—and the bottom half, her legs furring over like a centaur's, due to the freeze surrounding them.

"Basically," said Rumi, chattering the words out at speed, "I have to stay because the conference isn't over and it's OK because the parents of another child, Jane Green, are going to give me a lift home in a few hours, but don't worry, they've put dinner on for us here and it's fine, so I'll be dropped home by them, and if you're asleep I'll be really quiet and I won't wake you if you can leave the key under the mat."

She paused and took a diplomatic gulp of breath, attempting to cover any desperation in her voice. Mrs. Minus, true to her nature, did not reveal anything. A moment passed, and then another. Rumi looked into the woman's eyes for a sign of condemnation, disagreement . . . suspicion? She saw nothing. They were the eyes of a master at work, just watching, as though she was waiting for Rumi to betray herself, no more.

"And, er, it means we can't ring home tonight to say goodnight but that's OK because I'll explain it to Dad tomorrow," said Rumi.

Still no reaction. Mrs. Minus looked at Rumi over the top frame of her glasses, blinking as a sudden gust pumped more cold into the car.

A few more beats passed, a holding stalemate as they eyed each other, waiting.

"OK, then. Bye-eee!" said Rumi, with a cheerful shimmy in her voice. She pushed the door shut and walked into the building, joining the vociferous crowd of parents and children who were saying their good-byes. They flapped leaflets, nodded and whirred, exchanging sentences in various states of fatigue. She stood to the side of the main doors and peered through to see Mrs. Minus reverse and leave, feeling the heady intoxication of having pulled off some kind of heist. The car disappeared down the driveway, slowing down to overtake others, its exhaust hanging as a shadow in the air each time it spurted forward.

Rumi turned and looked at the board featuring Shakuntala Devi.

Even though the placard was surrounded by a group of five people, she could still see Devi's heavily made-up eyes peeping through. Rumi touched her own briefly again, a rushed move with an absence of delicacy. The thin wedge of a nail scraped the surface of her left eyeball.

"Sorry," she whispered, blinking and pressing her eyelid to squash out the pain, releasing a viscous concoction of tears and liquid eyeliner. "Sorry, Shakuntala Devi," she said again, bowing her head and wiping the corner of her eye, limiting the damage, before she ran back down the gravel, the piercing grit softening into a billowy smoothness under the soles of her boots till she felt as if she was running along a mattress, a springy cushion that might launch her into the sky and off into the galaxy, powered by the sheer immensity of mind over matter, like a levitating disciple, or a broomless witch . . . off, up and away she would go, the fear and guilt dripping away, shedding its weight as she moved higher and higher.

He pressed a button and the music released itself into the car exactly as they turned in to the dark hollow of the motorway. Rumi leaned forward hungrily, the rain-kissed windscreen opening out in her vision like the slow reveal of a screen in a cinema. She was held by the road's repetition, the way it hurtled its long central tongues of white at her, raising them from darkness out of the bruised wet throat of the night. Let this moment stay longer, she said to herself. Let it stay like this for longer before everything goes wrong. She shut her eyes and let her senses capture it, hoping to imprint it on her memory: the two of them shooting into the future with no words, nothing, just the stringy violence of the music, the singer's torrid voice wringing their souls out on the stereo.

"Amazing, isn't it?" he said, his eyes on the road.

"It's beautiful," she said.

"Bob Dylan," he said. "You can't argue with this guy."

"I love it," said Rumi, wistfully. "It's unbearably beautiful."

He chuckled.

"Are you for real?" he said, turning to look at her. "You're dangerously cute."

They talked. He was from London but had spent his early teens in Canada. He was twenty, in his second year. He had been on a "gap year" before university, during which he had planted trees in Tanzania. He was studying politics, philosophy and economics at Balliol College, a place that bored him with its male/female ratio of seven to one, "a lot of senseless testosterone, all dressed up with nowhere to go." He had "been schooled" at Merchant Taylor's in London, but she shouldn't hold that against him. He was the product of hardworking Pakistani parents: a doctor and a social worker. He had visited Pakistan once, when he was seven, but still had to "resolve some conflicting feelings" by going there as an adult. His brother was two years older and a lot more "trad" than him. He wanted to work "in development" when he left Oxford, and "get his hands dirty."

Rumi had never met anyone like him. She didn't even understand some of the things he said. She struggled as he spoke, in fear of being found out, working out things she could say in response to sound even momentarily as impressive.

"You ask a lot of questions," he said. "How about letting me have a go, ma petite inquisitor?"

She answered his questions. She was studying maths because she was good at it, she had come straight from school (no "gap" year), she loved Suzanne Vega and U2, her favorite books were *The Rainbow* by D. H. Lawrence and *Dr. Zhivago* by Boris Pasternak; she also adored an Indian poet called Sujata Bhatt. She agreed that she looked young for eighteen, but said he shouldn't let that bother him. (On cue he laughed, submerging her with happiness.) She was living as a lodger in a house, and not in halls because she had . . . joined the college late, a last-minute thing. She had visited India twice and . . . it was in her veins, "inescapable." Her parents were . . . Her father ran a corner shop with her mother—actually, it was a pharmacy: they were both chemists who had met on the job. She had been to a comprehensive school and then to sixth-form college. And, yes, she had been in love, once.

This last question caught her out—and she gave an uncensored answer—slung as it had been out of a relatively harmless biographical Q and A. But she backtracked simply, treating it in the spirit in which it had been asked and laughing it off, running two fingers over her lips to signal that she was zipping them shut after the admission.

They parked outside a large iron gate, backlit by a permeation of moonish floodlight. Inside she could see a grand sweep of path, disappearing into a murky collage of foliage, dominated by a bulbous topping: a selection of boozy clouds in a mauve sky.

"Where are we?" said Rumi.

"This is Blenheim Palace," he said, turning to look at her.

"Wow," said Rumi, unsure of the next move.

"It's locked up for the night but we could . . . try to get in," he said.

She felt warmth circling under the collar of her blouse. What would he expect? "Yeah, let's do it!" she said.

"Sure?" he said, lowering his head conspiratorially, so that, looking at him, she could mostly see black, a sensuous overlay of choppy hair covering his head and slipping down the sides of his cheeks. She looked at his lips and imagined the moment. It seemed out of her league, terrifying, entirely hopeless that she could hope to match his lips with her own, link them together.

"It's pretty cold, you know," he said, implying that he wouldn't be disappointed if she declined.

"I know!" said Rumi.

"You're game, then? Might be fun."

"Have you ever done it before?" she asked.

"What? Broken into Blenheim Palace?"

"Yes. Have you, like, done it before?"

"Sure, I come here every week and camp out with someone," he said.

She flicked a look at him, feeling the burn intensify, a scarlet line branding itself round her neck.

"I've got a whole tent-and-stove combo in the back," he said. "Along with a good selection of classic lines for . . . conversational dead ends." He grinned and mimicked her Welsh accent. "What are you like?"

She bristled, as though she had been jabbed with a tiny needle, and looked at the glove compartment.

"Look, you joker, no, I haven't broken into Blenheim Palace before," he said, putting a hand on her shoulder. "I had the idea now. I'm just . . . going with the flow. I'm thinking, let's have an adventure, just like, hopefully, you are too. Or am I totally off course here? If so, I'm sorry."

Rumi stared at the floor, kicking the rubber mat that covered the area in front of her, trying uselessly to fit the curved toe of her boot into one of the squares. She gave him an embarrassed smile. "I just meant . . ." she said. "As in, like, I just thought . . ."

HE CLIMBED OVER the gate first, heaving his limbs up till he stood crouched over the spikes at the top, like a misshapen chess piece. Rumi recoiled as she watched him jump off, his body thudding onto the turf, feet failing to steady him on the ground.

"Aaah!" he said, as he fell onto his side and rolled over.

Rumi tried to decipher the sound, worried that it contained real pain. "Are you OK?" she yelled. "Are you all right?"

He came to the gate and stood before her, his face directly opposite her own through the bars so that a prickly light outlined the edgy length of his hair. His eyes were scoped out in shadow. Rumi watched him dust down each arm. He put his hand between two bars and took hers. "This is very *Kabhi Kabhi,*" he said, moving his index finger across her palm.

"You know that film?" said Rumi, shivering.

"Yes I know that film," he said. "I'm not a complete coconut."

"But I love . . ." said Rumi, realizing how lame it sounded before she said it again, "I love that film."

He created footholds for her through the gate, interlinking his hands so that she could step into them, and haul her way up. She protested, feeling the debasing weight of her body push down on the linked mesh of his fingers, so fleshly and vulnerable in comparison to her mannish boots. The higher she got, the heavier she felt, swaying with each movement, assailed by a biting terror of falling.

"Don't look at me!" she said, as the sole of her right foot slipped down, threatening to mash his hand against the metal. "Look away or something. I can do this bit alone."

"Come on!" he urged. "Do you think I'm going to give up now? Imagine the headline: 'Fareed Hussain Caught in Welsh-Maths-Broken-Bones-in-Stately-Gardens Shocker.' Hey, look, you've done it, anyway, you classy bird!"

She tried to stand up, clutching the metal column on her right for dear life, one foot trapped, immobile, between two spikes, the other hovering with nowhere to go. He held out his arms. "Go on, jump!" he said.

She balked at his face. He looked so friendly and natural. She imagined the moment of impact: his denting collapse, the crushing sound of bones inside his body, and eventual loss of consciousness under her bulk.

"But I'll . . . I'll hurt you," she said, faltering as she saw there was no alternative. The ground was a long way down.

"Don't be ridiculous," he said. "Come on, baby, fall into my arms!"

She stood like that for a few moments, trapped in a confused asymmetry, her loose leg threatening to drag her down, retracing the way she'd climbed up. Horror rose in her, a poisonous fear of being found out, the fact that she was not what he thought, transmitted in the indisputable fact of her body hitting him. A layer of tears seeped into her eyes. She blinked furiously, looking aside to stall the whole thing.

"Come on," he said. "Don't be scared. I'll look after you."

She jumped when he was least expecting it, as though somehow she expected to dodge him and approach the ground poetically, in a seamless arc. Instead she fell poundingly into him so that they broke into a cumbersome tangle, hitting the lawn with wild cries: her chest pinning his head down, one of his arms launched between her legs, her foot kicking his stomach as they struggled for breath. She squealed: a single, continuous, absurdly girlish note that mingled complicatedly with his yelps of pain.

"I'm alive!" he said, a muffled joviality emerging from beneath her breasts. "And how!" he said, shaking his head from side to side. "Woo-hoo!"

Rumi pushed herself back, as though she had brushed against an electrified fence. She shut her eyes in panic. This is like Nibu, she thought, when he used to think shutting his eyes in times of trouble made him invisible to everyone round him.

He kissed her before she could speak, a wet heat in the cushion of his lips as they pressed against her own. She responded, her body turning to lie inside his arm so that they were up against each other, her arm moving round the leather of his jacket, her hand reaching up to touch the back of his neck, the moves strangely natural, as if she had lived a whole life of this kind of feverish rough-and-tumble. When she felt his tongue slide into her mouth, her own met it in a violent friction, that brought the mirroring of their bodies closer and closer until she could feel his hands pressing on the back of her hips, his pelvis moving to fit into the space between her legs. She pulled away, her head flooded, a hole scorched through her breathing.

"This is funny," he said. "I didn't think we'd be horizontal quite so soon."

She laughed hastily, fear shortening the sound into a series of hiccuping exhalations.

They looked at each other for a while. He kissed her again, a series of light butterfly kisses that started at one corner of her mouth and moved through the track of her lips, then over her cheek, down past her jawline. She jumped, letting out a giggle, at the ticklish feel of his stubble as it scraped her neck.

"Well, at least we know our bodies fit together," he said.

She stared at him, wanting to kiss the unexpected places: over his eyelids, the thick hairline on his forehead, the central bump of his chin.

"You're beautiful, baby," he said, his voice low in the dark. "That was beautiful. A luscious drop of honey. Trickling onto my tongue."

He kissed her again, and slid his hand down the V-necked front of her blouse, into her bra, rounding the palm over her breast so that the tips of his fingers skimmed the nipple. He let out a small sigh, a scrape of a groan, barely heard before it was over.

Rumi felt a cavernous vortex of guilt as her nipples hardened, a pinpoint lust that wired through her, like a telegram to her brain. She pulled herself back, taking his hand out of her top, and holding it up against the grass, between their two faces. "Do you really think we fit together?" she said.

"Don't you?" he said, breathing scratchily, moving to whisper in her ear, "The evidence, my friend."

"Like amicable numbers," she said.

He put his lips over the central swirl of her ear and kissed it with a sucking languor, his tongue moving fatly over the thin skin. Rumi giggled and shuddered, her body awake with the same ticklish desire.

He moved back.

"Amicable numbers are . . . like, numbers that go together," she said.

"Go on."

"I think it was the Middle Ages, or something, when they first discovered them, a really long time ago, yes. You know, say you have two numbers, like 220 and 284?"

He laughed. "Say it was those numbers, yes . . . then?" he said.

"It's like they're a pair because all the numbers that each one can be divided by, those numbers add up to make the other in each case."

"Er . . . go again, please. I like the sound of it, though, you gorgeous, mad boffin. I think I kind of know what you mean . . . but explain again?"

"Like 220? The numbers it can be divided by are 1, 2, 4, 5, 10, 11 obviously, then there's also . . . 20, 22, 44, 55, 110."

He nodded, slowly.

"So if you add all those numbers up, you get 284. And the perfect thing is, if you do the same thing with 284—its divisors are 1, 2, 4, 71, 142, then if you add those up, they make 220."

He seemed to be considering the information.

"So 220 and 284 are always linked in a pair. They fit together," she said.

He cradled her cheek with his hand.

"No shit?" he said.

She nodded.

"Pretty amazing," he said, chuckling. "Maths poetry, eh? You're something else, aren't you? Kind of beautiful crazy."

21

When she returned home the next day Mahesh wasn't on the platform. After exiting the station alone, Rumi looked over the road and saw him at the wheel, sitting upright in his latest beige raincoat—a variation on the others by virtue of a tartan lining, visible at the collar. Late evening traffic was reflected in the window on his side, the flicker of crimson and white lights making him look as if he was in some arty photo about sadness and desolation. Why did he look like that, she thought, when his face was at rest? He can't see that I'm watching him. He must be at rest, surely? His lips were twisted almost in a snarl, more like a sneer. A very sad sneer or snarl, whatever it was. Like the sign for approximation. Rumi considered it. When you approximate, you can err on the side of more or less than the actual answer. It's not the real answer, though. Dad is approximately . . . not happy with the way the world is turning out? Was it just the way his mouth had shaped itself, or was he angry? Even worse, was he sad? If he was sad because of her . . . This idea hurt like a suddenly open sore, as though she had kept the painful thought bandaged and hidden but it was now exposed through her own negligence. He must know all about me, thought Rumi. But, obviously, he can't. Then the world would end. He wouldn't be sitting in his car. Everything would be over.

She thought back to Fareed as she crossed the road, let her mind feel through the experience tangibly, like fingertips on Braille, to remind herself of the information: the ways in which it might have been discovered, the horrific repercussions, the events themselves. It was not something she had allowed herself to do more than once every hour since he had driven her back to Didcot, at one thirty the previous night because the result was this—a staccato heartbeat battering

hard in her body. Was that it? Did her father hate her now? Was it because she hadn't called at the assigned time? Did she carry the stale
scent of loose behavior about her person, a degraded aura of sexual-
ity? Maybe, hopefully, it was something more innocent . . . Had her
mum found out about the skirt she had slashed? But Mrs. Minus
wouldn't have told them . . . Did she look too different, too happy to
have been away from them? But she felt so miserable and confused to
be back. Ah. Was she supposed to show joy at her return to her parents? Maybe that was it. Of course it was. She was an idiot. She
cleared her throat and forced a bright smile onto her face.

"It's . . . good to be . . . home," she said, looking sideways at
Mahesh. He didn't respond.

WHEN SHE REACHED home and entered the kitchen she realized it
was something else. Four newspapers lay on the table, all opened to
a page featuring similar photos of Rumi taken against the patterned
wallpaper in the living room, the raised swellings of lilac flowers and
stems forming a domesticated pattern round her face. A whole three
months later, and the articles were finally out.

She didn't look too bad—a bit of a geeky smile unfortunately:
her eyes had lolled into a half-shut daze each time the flash had
blasted her. Mahesh hadn't allowed her to wear any makeup, but it
could have been a lot worse—at least she was wearing her contact
lenses, and a black polo-neck with a metallic zip that ran right
through the neck. A tabloid-size newspaper dominated, with a red
pen lying in the fold; she could see it had been used to underline the
text at various points. It was the kind of paper Rumi had only ever
seen at the dentist's or the doctor's, and she felt a momentary confusion. She looked closer and saw the headline: "THE BRAINIEST
TEENAGERS IN BRITAIN." Underneath, she saw a photograph of the
packed conference at Oxford, as well as portraits of individual
prodigies. There was a little surge of heightened feeling in her
blood, a small summit of excitement, as she read the words "Rumi
Vasi" next to her face. Maybe Bridgeman had seen it. She went on to

the next line: "Taught by her father, who rejects everything we believe in!"

The article was polite, but vicious, quoting Mahesh's comments about "the West" with veiled surprise. "Mr. Vasi believes that we are a decadent nation, which has lost the ability to do what is best for its children," read Rumi. "He believes we are a country of sleepwalkers who need to wake up!"

She looked farther down the page at another heavily underlined paragraph.

> The child in question, Rumika Vasi, was eerily silent for most of the interview. She let her father do the talking and appeared very much off-limits when it came to the few questions I put to her. It remains an enigma as to whether she agrees with her father's approach to life and shares his controversial feelings about her own destiny. Although Mr. Vasi claims that she is a "completely normal teenager," her behavior was clearly very controlled, much more pacified than that of an average girl, just fifteen years old!

Rumi felt nauseous. She looked round the kitchen. Shreene and Nibu were upstairs; Mahesh was nowhere to be seen. She forced herself to read the final paragraph, boxed in a wobbly red rectangle of ink.

> "Intellect is a spiritual matter," says Mr. Vasi. "I don't believe in the concept of giftedness. I believe that we all have an inherent duty to nurture and develop this internal ability. Rumika's time at Oxford will only develop her natural curiosity; there is no way that it can work against her. She knows this is a valuable opportunity, which she will not treat lightly."

Underneath the quote, set on a line on their own, were two words from the interviewer, to close the article: "Heaven forbid!"

The rest of the day was impossibly slow. She sat in her room, feeling too big for it, a giantess stuck in a dream from the past. Nibu came to see her three times in an hour, exhorting her, making threats and challenging her to a duel every time she asked him to leave. Eventually she exiled him, barricading herself inside by placing a freestanding bookshelf in front of the entrance to thwart his continual reappearances. Even then he threw himself against the door to try to topple it, a waifish brutality to the sound of his body hitting the wood, over and over again, followed by a guffaw.

" 'My wings are like a shield of steel!' " he said, quoting his favorite cartoon as he ran up, gathering speed, and whacked his lean form against the central panel.

" 'My supersonic sonar radar will help me!' " he said, pushing both hands against the barrier and applying maximum force.

It was only when Shreene came up and shooed him away that he relented.

Shreene knocked on the door, realizing it was blocked, and Rumi took a plate of food through a small gap. The bookcase stayed in place all day and all night, Nibu being the excuse.

Having found a way to simulate a private space, Rumi relaxed the ruling she had instigated during the lengthy hours since the event, and allowed herself to think about Fareed for more than a single moment.

The light fell away from the sky in stages, placid clouds rocked by the wind visible through her bedroom window. She sat at her desk, listening to songs on the radio. She wrote out their lyrics in a fever, as though she was searching for a single inarticulate truth—a nearly academic hunting for words and phrases that could summarize the storm she was feeling inside. "Someone's Got a Hold of My Heart," she wrote, in black felt-tip, the dark width of the words fully masculine, reminding her of the brusque stubble against her face, the insistent shape of his body moving to press against her mounds and hollows, the almost imagined sound of his moan, so low it could have been indistinguishable from the general murmur of the night around them.

He had not pushed things farther after the amicable-numbers

conversation. They had lain together for a few more minutes, watching each other, their faces motionless against the grass, then got up and walked into the grounds. He had held her hand, so naturally, and she had felt blessed.

The fear of Mrs. Minus, latent during their tussle on the ground, returned with a consuming angst as they walked until it could be ignored no longer. Rumi forced herself to ask him to take her home, and he had agreed, after a short attempt at persuading her to "abandon yourself to the proceedings." Instead, she had pulled him behind her, laughing, as she walked to the car.

"Come on!" he said, urging her to stand still by shaking her hand. He laughed, then sang, with a gruff American accent, "Show a little faith, there's magic in the night. You ain't a beauty but, eh, you're all right!"

She turned and thumped him softly, squealing with outrage, then found herself running away, shrieking with laughter as he pursued her, until he caught up, forcing her to stop, trapping both her arms in a bear hug.

The drive was over much too quickly. She had anticipated his surprise that the place was in Didcot not Oxford, but it didn't affect the intensity of his goodnight kiss when they got there. He grappled with her comically over the gearbox and laughed as she pulled away.

"You're a mysterious girl," he said. "I didn't expect this at the Oxford University Asian Society inaugural Jazz and Samosas evening, Michaelmas term, 1988."

Rumi snuffled a giggle, feeling wobbly at the thought of the ensuing good-bye. She gathered all her tension: her teetering fear of rejection, the terrible desire to stay with him and hold him against her, like a shield, saying the L-word over and over again, like a psychopath. She put it all on hold for a single moment. More than anything, she had to sound grown-up when she left the car.

"I'll drop you a note through pigeon-post," she said, as casually as she could, getting out of the car before she could see his reaction.

"Oi!" he said, winding down his window.

She raised her hand in a backward wave, walking up the street to Mrs. Minus's house.

"$E = mc$ squared, baby!" he shouted euphorically, starting up the engine and reversing.

In spite of herself Rumi laughed and turned to wave properly, squinting in the headlights as the vehicle backed down the road.

Now, IN HER bedroom in Cardiff, she was gouged out with a desire to hear his voice, see a photo of him, anything to confirm the reality of his existence and the truth of the events. The very cells of her body felt saturated with guilt: it was a squalid sensation that she worked hard to ignore. Instead she focused on the next step. Pigeon-post was the twice-daily flow of letters between Oxford colleges, a free-exchange fluttering of notes that were collected in sacks and emptied into pigeonholes. Rumi had never received anything personal in hers, only society leaflets and JCR announcements. The only handwritten note to come her way had been deeply disappointing—she had noted the blue jottings excitedly, reading her name in wonder, fascinated by the wiry indecipherability of the words, then realized it was from Mr. Mountford, confirming the date and time of her Penal Collection.

There were four days and four nights to get through before she could next conceivably see him. And she had to get the letter off in the morning (by normal post from Cardiff, but hopefully he wouldn't take much notice of the stamp on the front) to ensure that he had it in time to see her on one of her three assigned days in Oxford. But there were things to consider, so many flapping thoughts, fears and kicks, oscillating like disco lights in her head. It was so confusing that Rumi fought to separate them.

1. Would he want to see her?

She had sidestepped this whole issue by saying she would be the one to contact him. This had also avoided the issue of her own contact details. But now she was haunted by the fear that he wouldn't want to see her. And she couldn't get involved in an exchange of phone numbers for obvious reasons. What did he think? What in hell did he think?

2. Would he expect her to go further the next time they met?

The idea was insatiable: it came back at her again and again, in different pictures, so that she bit her hand to still the demonic imagery, paced the room, opened the door of her wardrobe and breathed a hot mist on the mirror, which she then kissed, letting her tongue lie on the glass between her lips. She lay on the bed imagining his presence. In this room, joined from wall to wall by the brown-patterned carpet of her youth, he was like a phantom, a substanceless image. She could hardly believe he existed, but if he did, the sex issue would have to be tackled at some point. She couldn't have sex with him. It was so wrong. Oh, God, she thought, what if he expects it? He's going to expect it and he'll think I'm so tragic when I stop it happening. It'll change everything.

3. If he did want to be her boyfriend (the word was as luxurious as a foreign chocolate in her mouth—a Belgian truffle or an Amaretto slice—so alien, yet so hankered after), should she tell him about her situation?

There was so much to get through, so many hurdles to leap, if they were to start meeting. So many more lies. But if he got even the slightest whiff of her life . . . He didn't seem like someone who had to hide things from his parents. It would seem contemptuous to him, surely, obscene, even.

SHE WAS ON the fifth draft of the letter when Mahesh walked into her bedroom. She had missed his footstep on the stairs because of the music, having set the volume louder than normal. The bookshelf was standing away from the door—she had left it off-center after a recent trip to the lavatory. When he walked in, her hand went automatically to the open drawer at the bottom of her desk, which contained the tome of *Vibrations and Waves* and slotted the latest version under its weight, a deft movement that took a fraction of a second. As this happened with her left hand, she wrote out a formula from the textbook in front of her with the right, assuming an expression of involved analysis.

"What are you working on?" he asked. His voice was pretty even. It didn't seem to be weighted in any way to suggest that he had seen anything.

"Mechanics," said Rumi, feeling the aftermath of a racing heart, odd spurts of panic. She was grateful for the normality of his opening question.

Mahesh sat down on her bed. "So, Mrs. Mukherjee explained the situation," he said, clearing his throat.

Rumi waited.

"With regard to why you did not return with her on the night of the convention."

A silence followed. Although she was used to this tempo of meaningful words followed by long silences from Mahesh—it had formed the sound track to her life to this point, after all—this particular one felt insufferably long. There was something he wanted to say. She swallowed and waited.

"This . . . Jane Green," he said.

"Yes," said Rumi, with what she hoped was a respectful tone.

"I looked Jane Green up." He cleared his throat again, the sound a mixture of tentative breathing and throaty blast, like an engine revving.

"I noticed that Jane Green is . . . in this instance . . . another name for Johnny Green," he continued, his voice hardening and increasing in volume over the words "another name."

Rumi looked at her textbook, her face betraying her with a violent spill of red. Oh, God, she thought. This is too weird. Her heart felt like it might give way—unfit for all this complex pumping and bolting, these convoluted peaks and troughs.

"Do you think," said Mahesh, his words very deliberate, "that Jane Green is someone with whom you should be getting acquainted?"

A surprise collapse of wind found its way through Rumi's windpipe, a kind of sigh mixed with an ellipsis of complete shock.

"I know that you are wanting to make friends with new girls, who have had experiences like you. But my feeling is that this particular . . . girl is one to be avoided."

He got up and made his way to the door. "Do not place the bookshelf here," he said, at the door. "You are too old for such childish games with Nibu. I will ensure that he doesn't bother you, if that is really your anxiety."

He left the room and Rumi took a few moments to reorder her thoughts, angrily jabbing her desk with an old compass, trapping the spike in the sticky, pockmarked wood.

After about thirty seconds, Mahesh reappeared, without a knock. She jumped, as though she had been caught in a state of undress. "And another thing," he said. "You need to open your window and wear some summer clothing. You know that you are much too warm at present to concentrate. The same rules apply—you need to be at shivering point when you are studying to achieve true alertness. Don't forget the basics—they are key to your success." He paused meaningfully, awaiting her reaction. She looked him in the eye. This is like the game where you stare as long as you can without blinking, she thought, crushing her nails into her palms. "That is, if success is what you want," he said, moving the bookcase aside and closing the door so that it clicked into place.

ON THE DAY she arrived five minutes early, and arranged herself at a table in the far corner of the café. It was more like a restaurant-bar, chosen by Rumi for its sophistication—she had heard Serena talking about the jazz there, that it was in a huge converted church, and put it down with a time in the letter she'd sent him, confident that on the day she'd find her way there by asking. As it was, it took her a good seventy-three minutes to locate and get to the place, much longer than she had anticipated, but she was still five minutes early.

Rumi had recoiled at the sight of Freuds: the columns at the entrance, the vaulted, mammoth interior with its raised stage and glossy piano adding to her slip-sliding fear, familiar now after four days of constant highs and lows. She imagined sitting in the corner, hour after hour, preventing the waiters from removing the single cold coffee on her table. The very size of the place signaled a high probability that someone who knew her might turn up at any moment. This image of solitary humiliation alternated with another, more lucid, dream, in which he entered the hall and saw her across the room, increased his speed and almost cantered to her table, rushing to sweep himself round her and kiss her right there and then, his lust uncontrolled, their joy at seeing each other absolutely and wonderfully mutual.

Fifteen minutes in, halfway through a jug of tap water, and she was unprepared for the moment when he entered, dressed in the same biker jacket and light trousers, the distinguishing block of hair drawing her attention even over the distance. He walked through the various tables looking for her and she wanted to call out, sign him over, but was not courageous enough to surmount her immobility. Eventually he saw her and walked over. Her hand went to her hair and ran clumsily through it, as though she was trying to fulfill some flouncing notion of being on a date, the epitome of elegance. But there was no fun in it once she saw his face. He sat opposite, without kissing her cheek, drably pulling in his chair, avoiding eye contact with a heartbreaking formality.

"Hello," he said, in a clipped, posh accent—not one that Rumi associated with him in the variety of memories and fantasies that had accompanied her over the past four days.

"Hi," she said, trying a smile.

"You wanted to meet?" he said.

He reminded Rumi of her GP at home, Dr. Matthews, who always spoke like this when she walked into his room. You wanted an appointment? There is something you need to discuss? As though she had just walked in off the street and surprised him. "How are you?" she said.

"Very well," he said. "And yourself?"

"What's wrong?" she said, a plaintive note entering her voice against her will.

"Pardon?" he said, frowning.

"Parr-don," attempted Rumi, in an Indian accent, gambling on the shared reference.

"Sorry?" he said.

"What's wrong? Is something . . . is everything . . . OK?" she said.

"Um," he said, looking around the room and catching the eye of a waitress, who came over and asked for their order, her smile like a raspberry ripple of friendly charm. "I'll have a cappuccino, thanks," he said, using a notably warmer tone, then turning back to Rumi.

"Don't you think you should be answering that question?" he asked, pouring himself a glass of water and looking at her for the first time.

"What?"

"Don't you think there are a few things that might be worth mentioning?" he said.

Rumi watched him drink his water. Her stomach growled and she shifted position to try to cover the vulgarity of the sound. It felt so inappropriate, bitterly savage that at such an awful moment her body was doing something so mundane as demanding food. She had a packed lunch in her bag that she was supposed to rely on but hadn't been able to eat—and about thirty pence left. She didn't want to think about it.

"I'll help you, if you like," he said, taking the cappuccino and nodding at the waitress appreciatively.

"I'm . . . I don't . . ." stuttered Rumi.

"How about beginning with some basics?" he said. "Like some

basic lies. Your age, your life, your setup here, your whole deal, basically." He drank half of his coffee in a series of gulps. "Your age," he said. "Or did I mention that?"

A series of chords sounded at the piano, and the globular opening of some jazz tune filled the space round them. Rumi focused on his coffee cup, meditated on its glazed contours, following the green stripe that licked round the center of the cream china, praying that she wouldn't be subjected to her own tears. It was, quite simply, the end of everything. He must have seen an article. It was horrific. This was the definition of gruesome—appalling, wretched. All those words now took shape in the ashy coagulate of feeling in her throat.

"How did you . . ." she began, loathing the sound of her own voice.

"Oh, you don't have to worry about that," he said, draining the dregs from his cup. "I'm sure you can work it out. You enjoy a modicum of . . . 'celebrity' in this place, don't you?"

"But I . . ." said Rumi. "I really . . . I'm so sorry, I didn't realize."

"Oh, don't apologize, dear," he said, felling any hope of happiness with a swift blow as he stood up to leave.

"Don't go, please!" said Rumi, the tears now in her eyes, threatening to rain down her face in what she feared would be a terrible cliché of desperation.

"Come on, 'Rumika Vasi,'" he said, with a curt meticulousness as he pronounced her name. "I'm not one for underage fondlings." He grimaced briefly, and looked away, to the piano, which was now smoothly resounding with a fully bloomed tune. "I suppose I should say come back when you've grown up or something saucy like that but, truth be told, my appetite for flirting with you is kind of, well . . . gone."

He laughed, a short bark, again unfamiliar to her.

"I suppose the maths-nerd part shouldn't have been a surprise. But just quite how extreme—I mean, really, I suppose I should have known, worked it out, but I had no idea."

"Why are you being like this?" said Rumi, unable to keep the wail from her voice.

"Look, love," he said, using the word disparagingly, "it doesn't really turn me on. I get it, but it's not my scene. I'm twenty. How do you think I feel?"

He looked at her for a few moments, in a silence so long that she began to wonder at its meaning. He seemed almost tender now that he wasn't speaking. She stared back, asking for his forgiveness with her eyes. "You should have told me," he said.

He walked confidently, his back to her, through the maze of tables and chairs as he proceeded toward the bar. He paid the waitress there, genially dismissing the change she tried to give him. As he approached the front entrance, Rumi willed him to turn round, sent shock waves of mind-over-matter thoughts to create a schism in him that would make him look back against his will. Come on, she prayed. Come on, you can't just leave like that, forever. But he went, walking straight through the arch at the front with a light authority, as though he hadn't a care in the world.

22

Mahesh is sitting at his desk in the department at Swansea. He is wearing a thick V-necked sweater under his raincoat, which is grasped round him and buttoned fully, even though he is indoors. On his head, covering an oval island of hairless skin, is a flat cap, gray polyester, bought for him by Rumi as a birthday present only two months previously. It is late afternoon, and the dim light is throwing a cold glaze over the five pieces of paper on his desk. He is due to leave to pick Rumi up from Cardiff Central station in an hour and take her back to their home. As usual, she has been away for three days.

He can feel the end of autumn: the ruthless instability of winter is in the air, affecting his movements, preventing him from fully resting in his chair, edging everything with an insidious cold. He shivers, shudders violently: a disaffected movement in the face of events that he doesn't know how to control. These are events that have already happened, protected from reversal—impossible to undo. This is it, he thinks. The end of my sixteenth autumn in the United Kingdom, Rumi's fifteenth year. It is bitter indeed.

The five photocopied pieces of paper have been read by him several times, maybe fifty, maybe a hundred or more, over the past twenty-four hours. The originals are back in Rumi's desk. Shreene has read the stuff only once—she absorbed their detail and import almost instantaneously, not needing to look at them again. But he is different. Each time they have discussed the possible meanings, the roads ahead—him and Shreene—he has had to return to the sheets, take the words in again and feel the ensuing emotional damage as if for the first time. Even now, looking at them alone, he can't make sense of some of the phrases, because of her terminology and her handwriting. One thing is clear, though: each letter is a different approach to communicating with the same boy. That is one of the harsh facts—unwilling to be controlled or erased. The name of the boy.

Dear Fareed,

Strange, so strange to be writing to you like this, in words on a page when in a sense we don't really know each other so well yet. I feel like I do know you, in a way, though. Like there was something special between us when we kissed, some kind of poetry. What is it when two people fit together mentally and physically? How does it happen? Did that really happen to us? It's something I've thought about a lot since it happened. You're kind of like a fractal or something, so brilliantly sure of yourself, like that type of a fractal repeating pattern, if you know what I mean—a very definite person. But when we kissed, it was like there was a gap in the middle of the sequence, I thought. It was like I could see you through it.

I'm posting this from outside pigeon-post as I decided to visit my folks this weekend. Maybe we could hook up next week. I'll be at Freuds on Walton Street at 1:30 p.m. on Tuesday if you feel like having a coffee.

Rumi

Hey sexy,

All that rough-and-tumble in the park at Blenheim Palace has made me think about you in all sorts of ways.

I'm posting this from outside pigeon-post as I decided to visit my folks this weekend. Maybe we could hook up next week. I'll be at Freuds on Walton Street at 1:30 p.m. on Tuesday if you feel like having a coffee.

Rumi

For the joker of all jokers,

Having held your beautiful body against me, as requested, I do hope you'll do it again. This doesn't mean I'll surrender all innocence, of course.

As you said, I'm a "classy bird." You mentioned that e = mc
*squared as you left on Thursday. Thanks for that information. Maybe
you'd like to meet me at Freuds on Walton Street at 1:30 p.m. on
Tuesday, if you feel like having a coffee and telling me more about
your theories of relativity. I'll be there anyway.*

   Rumi

> *For you,*
>   *Sat in the shaky motion*
>   *Of your car, the whispering*
>   *Sound of Bob Dylan and his*
>   *Guitar messing our heads,*
>   *Big clouds crushing up*
>   *Our need to "fit"*
>   *In weird harmony.*
>
> *Freuds,*
> *Walton Street,*
> *Tuesday, 15 November,*
> *1:30 p.m.*
> *Rumi*

Hi, Fareed,
   *How are things? Hope all is well. Just a quick note to say it'd be
lovely to meet up as you suggested.*
   *I'm posting this from outside pigeon-post as I decided to visit
my folks this weekend. Maybe we could hook up next week. I'll be at
Freuds on Walton Street at 1:30 p.m. on Tuesday if you feel like
having a coffee.*
   Rumi

Mahesh looks at the name of his child, signed in a different way
for each note: five variations on "Rumi" that range from cocky
whirls to delicate embroidery in lighter ink. He feels a still lake of
sadness inside him, a lethal melancholy that doesn't move, doesn't

even ripple as he thinks or shifts in his seat. How could this happen? Why did she write this?

DURING THE JOURNEY home from the station Mahesh did not speak to Rumi, even though it took all of his energy to prevent himself lapsing. He almost let something out by accident, in a short jam by the Gabalfa roundabout, provoked by her shameless lack of interest in the cause of his anger, her seeming lack of guilt or fear that he wasn't speaking to her. She matched his silence with her own, infuriatingly preoccupied, lying in a slump with her face against the passenger window as though he wasn't there. On their arrival Shreene opened the door and Rumi walked in, hauling her rucksack in a bid to get up the stairs straightaway.

"Where are you going?" asked Shreene, stepping in her way.

Rumi looked at her with clear boredom, her expression tinged with a frown. Mahesh walked into the living room and composed himself. It was important to be a man, he thought. He had to do this correctly. For all of their sakes. He had to stay alert, be strong, but he felt as if it was going to kill him, this melancholy, seep into his veins like a sleep-inducing drug, gradually overdosing until the cumulative effect made him give way.

They came into the living room. Shreene sat next to him. Rumi positioned herself moodily on the edge of the second sofa, the seat farthest away from them. He could see she was anxious, confused by their quiet formality—that they were getting ready to talk to her together.

Shreene spoke first. "We want you to tell us something," she said, looking at Rumi across the room.

"What?" said Rumi, glancing at Mahesh.

"You know what it is," said Shreene.

Rumi moved awkwardly in her seat.

"We are giving you the chance to confess," said Shreene, her tone harsh and leading.

"I don't know what you mean," said Rumi, maintaining a dismissive politeness in her tone, but affected by the way in which Shreene was speaking.

"We know what you have been doing. It will be better for you if you confess," said Shreene.

"What do you mean?" said Rumi. "Is this about Jane Green?"

"What do you want to tell us about Jane Green?" said Mahesh.

"That I stayed at the convention and had dinner with her parents—" said Rumi.

"You liar," said Shreene. "You disgusting, dirty—"

"Stop it, Shreene," said Mahesh, pressing her arm down on the sofa. "Remember what we discussed?" he said.

Shreene did not respond. Her nostrils flared, eyes blazing with a livid sheen of moisture.

"What did you do that night?" Mahesh said to Rumi.

"I told you already," said Rumi. "I know I shouldn't have stayed out late but I thought it would be OK because her parents were there and it was . . . you know . . . the convention."

"LIAR!" shouted Shreene, reverberating as the word came out, as though her entire body had vocalized it. "KUTHIYA!" she screamed, letting the Hindi word for "bitch" vibrate like a spasm, pushing her hand into the air so that her palm pressed from a distance over the image of Rumi's face. "I WISH YOU HAD NEVER BEEN BORN!" she yelled, belting the words at the top of her range so that they broke in the air, a drop of spit collecting at the corner of her mouth. "Was it for this that I gave you birth? You—dirty, nasty, FILTHY, DISGUST-ING—"

"Shreene!" said Mahesh, cutting in with a guttural stamp of authority. "Stop it now. Right now. I will speak from now on. I am serious. Do not say another word."

He looked at his daughter. She was shaking, cowering away from them against the armrest of the sofa.

"We know what happened," he said. "I was in the locker room at the university tennis courts and I heard men talking about you. They were talking about what happened. Imagine how it felt for a man in my position to hear men talking about my daughter in such a demeaning and cheap way. Imagine what you have done to me. How it feels. To know that my daughter has been party to such corrupt behavior. Imagine that it even reached here, to my university, from Oxford, so famous are your exploits. I am giving you the chance now to tell us in your own words what happened."

He took a deep breath and surveyed the quantifiable shock in Rumi's eyes. At least the lie was over. It had felt insurmountable. He had been like a man losing oxygen on a mountain, stepping on and on through the words to get it over, but he had managed it, hidden his pain, got it out, been strong. The key thing was, any foolish idea that he had been untoward in looking through her drawer was not to confuse the issue. Shreene had agreed—Rumi was to understand the impact, the morality, of what she had done. It could not be confused by the irrelevant ethics of how he had found out.

Rumi looked at Shreene and then at Mahesh in open fear. She gulped, a horrible vulnerability in her breathing.

"I just—" she said. "I didn't . . . Nothing happened!"

"Stop LYING!" said Shreene. "You stupid girl, you don't realize what you have done. You have played football with your father's honor. You dirty little—"

"Shreene," said Mahesh, in a monotone this time.

"But she has to understand. Don't you realize?" said Shreene. She leaned forward in her chair. "In India we have a saying. 'A man wears his honor like a turban—a pugri—on his head.' You have taken that pugri from your father's head and played football like this, so carelessly, so selfishly." She kicked her foot out, miming an expression of dismissive cruelty, tossing her hand to the side.

"Mum, I didn't do anything!" said Rumi.

"Rumika, if you don't confess to this then things are going to get extremely bad for you," said Mahesh. He eyed her. "What you consider 'nothing' is something you need to understand is unforgivable," he said. "This is not a question of having fully debauched yourself with the ultimate final act. Whatever you have done, however far you have gone, those actions are also unforgivable. Can't you see that?"

He raised his voice: "You don't seem to realize how serious this situation is! You have no idea what is at stake!"

He watched Rumi for a reaction. She looked imploringly from him to Shreene, like an animal caught on a road, quivering in the moment before impact.

"I am going to give you till tomorrow to confess and make a promise in front of the guru's photo upstairs," he said. "You are to promise that you will never do this again. Witnessed by him. You will never get involved with a boy again. Not until after marriage. Otherwise I am afraid that we will have to terminate our relationship. You will be sixteen years old soon. We will have nothing more to do with you. Until your birthday you can live in this house but then . . . you can leave."

Rumi stared at him, without blinking, twitching, tears dripping down her face.

He found it intolerable—it made him so angry, this face of hers. He rose, went over and sat next to her on the sofa. She stopped shaking for a moment and looked at him, wonder in her eyes. Maybe she imagined he was going to hug her, he thought. Instead he did something he had only seen in films, iconic Indian family sagas where everything followed a system, every action had a reaction. He was outside his body as he did it, watching himself move like a puppet. "My family were raped by Muslims, you—you—" he said. He put his hands round Rumi's neck and held them there loosely, as though in preparation to strangle her. "If you ever—ever do this again," he said, holding his hands limply in a circle.

From the corner of his eye, he saw Shreene approach. She took away his hands—they came apart readily enough. It seemed appropriate. As though it was the natural way for the scene to end, for a dishonored family in this position. He left the room feeling faint, ready to close his eyes and be subsumed by the end of everything.

23

glass is coming at her now in rain. Rumi feels it spit on her face. Her skin is traced with the feathers of glass. The wet red inside her eye is levered by a piece. It is tiny and sharp. The eye looks out to the left, darts back to the center, struggles to expel the hurt. The lid blinks and flutters. Like the tongue of a bird licking and wiring itself round a piece of food, her eyeball rotates wildly round the piece. Her lower teeth bite her lip as she breathes. The picture of the kitchen around her is smudged. Her finger goes to her eye and presses the corners together till the glass flicks out. There must be blood in my tears, she thinks. That is the pain in my eye. Her body snaps, releases her to the floor and tips her away from the pile of glass onto her knees. The oven door is in pieces. It is the glass around her. The chair with which she broke it stands by the sink.

Her eyes open. She looks at the large pieces of glass on the kitchen floor. Some have the design of the oven printed in dark brown over opaque gray. Each piece is cut thickly, like a slab of hardened sugar. In her right hand there is now a piece. She sees her left arm uncovered. A thin line of down whispers over goose bumps down to her wrist. The fever in her head is now sweating through the pores where her skull hides under hair. The sweat follows her hairline like an oil slick, releasing a foul smell. Her body shakes again as her right hand presses the glass onto her arm, pulling it toward her chest. When the blood seeps out through the brown split, like a sweet line of red licorice, her heart deflates. The hand cuts through her skin again in a swift, deep movement. Five times later, her breathing is quiet and steady. She sits with her arm in her lap.

—

RUMI MANAGED TO clear up the mess, patch up her arm and put on a long-sleeved top in time for their return from the supermarket. It had been an odd morning alone, after a sleepless night in which she had lain trapped inside her body as though she was lying in a block of ice, waiting for it to melt. No matter how hot her tears, how maniacal the shaking, she did not dissolve into real feeling. By morning her conscious thought was destroyed. She had alternated between leaving and staying so many times that she couldn't think anymore. She heard Mahesh calling to Shreene from the car, and Nibu being fed in the kitchen, before the doors slammed and she was left at home alone.

If the idea was to give her a taste of life without them, it had worked. Devoid of a judging audience, she had built herself up into a pitch of insanity, screaming and throwing herself against the walls of her room. It was snowing outside, in a sludgy, soiled, Cardiff sort of a way—a snow that seemed to mix itself with all the different contaminants in the air before falling onto the windowsills or lawns she could see outside. Finally, in the kitchen, she had taken a chair and smashed it against the oven.

By the time they returned she had decided what she would do.

They seemed to take her explanation without comment: that the glass of the oven had cracked into pieces when she had shut the door too quickly while making "cheese toast" on the top level. Without the devastating visual evidence, the shower of brown glass that had flooded the floor—the wounded remnants of the pane that she'd demolished—it seemed a perfectly reasonable explanation. The oven looked fine without it, except that there was no way to keep things hot inside it now. Shreene had pursed her lips and gone upstairs to change Nibu's clothes. His request to throw snowballs with a group of three other boys down the road had been granted, and Shreene was going to wrap him up.

Rumi was left with Mahesh downstairs. He did not stay in the same room as her, fiddling with his coat in the hall. She listened to the sequence of his movements, the rub of the material as he arranged it round the lower knob of the banister, the jingle as he looked for the keys in his pocket.

"I'll do it," she said, standing in the kitchen.

The noises continued: a deep breath and the click of the store-room door as he replaced his umbrella, pushed it among the stacked shoes, the sacks of basmati rice and wholemeal chapatti flour. Up-stairs she heard a muffled series of thumps as Nibu was dressed in layer after layer of warm clothing. She walked out into the hall.

"I'll do it," she said, standing behind Mahesh, viewing his back with venom. You disgust me, not just the other way round, she thought. You didn't even have the guts to close the deal, tighten your grip when you put your hands round my neck.

Mahesh turned. His face was sorrowful, deadened with his new passivity. The rotund mass of his beard was wet with melting snow, and his eyes seemed dull, washed out. Don't look at me like that, she thought, as though I am the one who has killed you, turned you into a zombie, robbed you of your whole life. You can't make me hate myself any more.

"Do what?" he said.

"I'll confess and promise," said Rumi, then turned and walked up the stairs.

THE SHRINE FOR their guru was in Nibu's room: a padded space in-side a square wooden structure built on top of a chest of drawers. The photographs were surrounded by stocky cushions covered with ostentatious material: saffron silks encrusted with deep purple se-quins brushed up against the crackle of magenta satin. Mahesh and Shreene sat cross-legged in front of the shrine. Rumi sat a little to their side, facing the same way. Shreene covered her head and Rumi's with simple cotton shawls, then prepared the tray for prayer, sculpting a piece of cotton wool into a wick, dipping it into a diya of oil and lighting the tip. Rumi smelled the scent of the burning oil and cotton wool, a scent that had traditionally comforted her, signi-fying shared and happy family time on festival days or at the ashram in London. At this moment, instead, she felt a deep prick of hurt as she looked at the blank faces of her parents, like a puncture in her lungs, so that she hid her face under the veil of material like a demure maiden as the tears rolled.

They sang the Aarti song for prayer together. Rumi read the lyrics, written in English script in a booklet, as normal. But Nibu was not with them. She could not tease him with their shared portfolio of weird and wonderful grimaces. And Shreene and Mahesh sang in a quiet rush, as if they wanted to get that part over and done with. At the end they did the ten-minute meditation as per normal, Rumi scratching her left arm over the Band-Aids that covered her cuts as she waited. Then Mahesh spoke. "What would you like to say, Rumika?" he said.

She looked at the floor. "I'm sorry for what I did," she said.

"Can you stand up, please?" he said, his voice stern.

They did not look at each other. She stood with her back to them, replacing the scarf, which had fallen to her shoulders, on her head.

"Can you touch Guruji's feet?" said Mahesh.

Rumi did as he requested, avoiding eye contact with the man in the photo.

"I, Rumika Vasi . . ." said Mahesh.

"I, Rumika Vasi . . ." said Rumi, enunciating the words as though the name belonged to someone else.

". . . hereby promise," said Mahesh, "never to engage in this kind of activity ever again."

". . . hereby promise never to engage in this kind of activity ever again," said Rumi.

Shreene whispered something under her breath, a quicksilver tryst of words that Rumi couldn't hear. Her hands shook in her lap after she had spoken.

"Until marriage," Mahesh added.

"Until marriage," said Rumi, catching Guruji's eye in the photo, searching for signs of recognition, wondering if he knew that she was lying.

24

for the next two weeks Mahesh took Rumi to Oxford himself, re-arranging his tutorials and organizing cover for his lectures so that he could sit in the car and wait to drive her back at the end of the day. The silence in the car was monotonous, almost lulling him to sleep during the long drives back to Cardiff, the road threatening to suck him into loss of focus at the wheel. He was not sure how he felt about his daughter. In fact, Mahesh was experiencing a general absence of emotional sensation, except for the limitless melancholy that still refused to shift inside him, a constipated load of pain that he carried wherever he went.

They avoided connecting with words, found other ways to observe their duties. Once or twice during each drive, Mahesh would flick his head at a service-station sign, flashing the hazard lights over the green board as they drove past, indicating that he was willing to stop for a toilet break. Rumi shook her head briefly each time, turning to press her cheek hard against the window as though she was aiming to push open the door with her face and fall out, rattle to the ground. He did not react to this. Similarly, in Oxford, when Mahesh dropped Rumi outside the college, he demonstrated that he would park elsewhere and return to collect her at the end of the tutorial through a series of three discreet gestures: pointing at the steering wheel, using his finger to simulate a circle against the windscreen, and finally a sharp double tap on his watch accompanied by a frown. There was an agreement that this language of physical theater had to be respected by both parties—to ignore it would be perilous indeed: it would mean their forced deportation back into the land of speech.

—

BACK AT THE house Shreene too aimed to avoid conversation with Rumi, but was less successful at complete withdrawal than Mahesh. At mealtimes she found herself telling Rumi to get yogurt from the fridge and sometimes asked her, by accident, to take Nibu to wash his hands, tapering the commands into a terse silence as she remembered the status quo. Once, and only once, she lost control and battled to make Rumi respond to her. It was soon after the confession, just two days after Rumi had made her promise. Shreene was vacuuming in the corridor, wanting to finish before it was time to pick Nibu up from school. Mahesh was due home from work, and Rumi had decided to leave her room and watch television in the living room, lying on the sofa in comatose belligerence. Shreene entered, bringing with her the violent zoom of the vacuum cleaner. Rumi turned up the volume so that studio laughter and game-show guests bellowed in competition.

"Turn it down," said Shreene.

There was no response.

"Isn't it time to go back to your room?" said Shreene.

Even though it seemed hardly possible, Rumi turned up the sound even louder.

"Your father is coming home. He just telephoned to say he was leaving."

Rumi pressed the remote control so that the sound became oppressive, a blaring misfit of voices and distortion.

Shreene leaned over, the vacuum cleaner in one hand, speaking over the noise. "Give me that remote control," she said, her free hand reaching to take it.

Rumi got up and walked toward the door, holding it close to her. She stood there, her back to Shreene.

"What are you doing?" yelled Shreene, in the center of the room, enveloped in a wild soundscape. "This is how you respect me, is it?"

Rumi opened the door and walked out, taking the remote control with her. Shreene went after her, carrying the vacuum cleaner, the tube trailing along the floor, pipe vibrating in her hand. In the corridor she tried to stop Rumi starting up the stairs.

"What do you want?" said Shreene, pulling her daughter's shoulder. Rumi pushed the other way, opposing Shreene's hand, clutching the remote control even more tightly to her chest.

"What do you want?" said Shreene, her voice marked with a rising note of desperation. "What do you want?" she repeated.

Rumi let herself swing round.

"What do you want?" said Shreene again, with anger now, her grip tightening.

"Leave me alone," said Rumi, raising her top lip in an expression of unabashed disgust.

"What?" said Shreene, raising the vacuum cleaner pipe so that the rectangular suction pad hovered by her shins, the drone intensifying. "Even now you are so sure you are right? Even now? After everything?"

Rumi threw herself to the floor so that her face fell against Shreene's feet.

"Get lost!" she wailed at her mother. "Get lost! Get lost! Get lost!"

"What?" screamed Shreene, thrusting the pipe so that the flat suction pad rested over Rumi's face. "What do you want?"

"Get lost!" shouted Rumi, squirming and pushing her face so that it touched the pad, thrusting her nose against the bristles on the underside and shouting up the hole in the center, into the long tunnel of howling air. "Get lost!" she bellowed. "Get lost!"

"What do you want?" cried Shreene, controlling the pipe so that the pad forced itself against her daughter's cheek, thrusting Rumi to one side. "You want your Muslim boy, do you?" Shreene yelled, her eyes smarting with tears as she cuffed Rumi's cheek lightly once more. "Your Muslim boy? Is that what you want? You want to go to him?"

Rumi clutched at the pad with both hands and hit her head against it, ramming her forehead against the black plastic casing, harder each time, like a hammer on a block.

The sound of the machine ceased, leaving a wheezy collapse in its wake. Shreene looked down, following the lead, and saw Mahesh standing with the plug in his hand at the other end of the corridor.

"Don't do this," he said to Shreene, leaving the plug on the floor. "End it now."

He put his briefcase in the storeroom under the stairs and walked past them both to the kitchen.

THREE WEEKS AFTER the promise, Rumi returned to Oxford on her own. Mahesh was unable to get a stand-in for his lectures and had to acknowledge that he couldn't chauffeur Rumi everywhere as a permanent arrangement. In a way, he was relieved that there was no way round it. Although he had enforced twenty-four-hour supervision on Rumi, like a Band-Aid on the disaster, in the silent time they spent together he thought constantly about the facts of what had happened. A Band-Aid could only ever be a reminder of the wound it covered. There were only two weeks left before the end of term and he had no option but to let her go unattended. Shreene took care to communicate with Rumi about it. On the morning, she spoke to her in the kitchen as she prepared her packed lunch. "This means that we trust you," said Shreene, sealing the lunchbox with clingfilm and a blue plastic cover, then making space for it in Rumi's satchel.

Rumi nodded.

"What?" said Shreene. "Are you listening?"

"Yes," said Rumi, placidly.

Shreene bundled up her daughter, pulling the scarf round Rumi's neck, then sent her through the door to the car, where Mahesh was waiting to take her to the station.

"You understand what you should and shouldn't do?" she asked Rumi, as they stood at the porch in the moment before parting.

"Yes," said Rumi in a monotone.

"Just try not to touch any boys," said Shreene, lowering her voice and giving Rumi the briefest caress, brushing her fingers over her head, as though she was flicking some dust away.

25

It was the day before the Penal Collection. This fact lay unwrapped in Rumi's mind as she stared out of the window at a motorway flanked by fields in rain, honored with small details—a few coils of sheep, the occasional muddy hill path. I am going to do my Penal Collection tomorrow and nobody knows but me, she thought, her cheek against the window. It was a tart globule of thought, bitter as a gooseberry gobstopper, which she sucked, waiting for it to crack up into something she could chew, digest and understand.

At the coach station she bought three oversized bars of chocolate. Standing under a bus shelter, she ate each piece, listening to the tipsy rain on the plastic dome above her, feeling her rucksack shift on her back, the connecting straps buckled across her chest. Then she walked, making her way up the rising road of shops, cafés, travel agents, pubs, until she reached the main thoroughfare, a divergent sprouting of roads in front of her, each carrying its own immense blocks of history, buildings that were old to Rumi—old as could be. "Old" was the only word—just "old" was all she could summon to describe their power. She felt stupid, devoid as she was of vocabulary for history—architecture, epic battles, eras, wars, kings and queens—none of it understood. She did not know why but they made her feel like crying, these sandy old giant walls that made up a church, reaching to the skies, a fat golden theater to her right, the high fortress of a college ahead to her left. She looked at the arched opening of the college, shielded by a door, the wood nailed, set open just enough to hint at a clipped quadrangle of jade. For a moment she shut her eyes.

She felt her inferiority; the weight of her books and the clothes on her back seemed to deform her posture appropriately, forcing her to bend over like a true outcast, a hunchback huddling herself together as she stared at one of the most famous views of the town. Probably, even, one of the most famous pictures in the world, she thought. People photographed the scene as she watched, straggling away from guides to position themselves in front of different buildings with varying degrees of interest. She was not part of this family. It was too beautiful for fraud—too old and important to tolerate faithlessness, too hauntingly significant and romantic for her, a living museum of deep thoughts, housing people who understood, clean, relevant people, who were adding to a legacy with each moment of their lives. She imagined them walking in the grounds of these colleges, locking their bicycles in faculty grounds as they exchanged ideas, drinking in the pub at the end of the road ahead, these impossibly deep people exuding their intellectual brilliance like truth, reflecting the light from each other so that they shone like named stars in this galaxy of knowledge, sleeping and working in these buildings that she was watching now, as voyeuristically as the gang of Japanese tourists that had appeared just yards away from her.

That night Rumi opened the kilo bag of cumin seeds in her room and ate from it, slowly, until dawn. She had avoided dinner with Mrs. Minus, asking to take her meal in her room, throwing the ready-to-eat vegetable lasagne out of the window as soon as she was sure Mrs. Minus was asleep. At first the taste had been vile, the smell of broken, raw seeds causing a queasy backlash after seven weeks of absence. But within seconds the familiar movement of her tongue was bringing the seeds to her teeth for crushing, the indentation of a spray of new ones as she swallowed each round, and she settled into it. As she ate, she wrote, the hourly changing shows on Fox FM forming a stabilizing rail track for her journey through the night, marshaling the work she had to do so that she approached it methodically.

As she finished writing each line, copying a formula or equation from the book, she ripped it from the page, folding it over and over till it pressed into a tiny piece of about a single centimeter squared. Slowly, during the night, she built up row after row of these springy little items, which rose from their folds like tiny harmonicas. She dotted the top of each piece with an appropriate color for the subject area. Algebra was given turquoise, her favorite color, in an attempt to rebrand the fear it inspired in her. Geometry was allocated a highly visible red. Probability and stats, the least of her worries, were marked in a light and unremarkable yellow. Mechanics, brutally real and unforgiving to the end, received a purple makeover. By dawn she had created 673 squares, a tapestry of bite-sized information that lay on her table instead of in her head.

The exam was not until the afternoon, but Rumi was due to meet Whitefoot for lunch two hours before it began. It was an arrangement that had been made weeks previously, as soon as Mahesh had discovered that his friend would be in Oxford for a day-long conference. He had checked Rumi's timetable and booked Whitefoot. When Rumi had realized it was the same day as the Penal Collection, the best she could do was to say that she had a visiting lecturer that afternoon so they would have to be done by 12:30 p.m. Luckily, the lie had been convincing enough and Mahesh hadn't checked up. Although the Penal Collection was not a formal public examination, Mr. Mountford had decided to hold it in a small room in the Examination Schools on the high street. This seemingly perverse desire to make her take the procedure seriously also affected her attire: she was allowed to enter the buildings only in the traditional exam "sub-fusc" colors of black and white. She had put on as many layers as possible, beginning with her bra and knickers, covering them with an all-in-one leotard-style piece of black thermal underwear, rolling thick charcoal tights over her legs, then a long black "skirt" that divided into culottes, a thick white cotton shirt and a black cardigan over the shirt. In the pocket of the cardigan she put the thin black ribbon that she was required to wear as a kind of tie, ready to knot it round her neck just before she entered the building. A sleeveless academic gown formed the final layer.

Only when fully clothed did she consider where to hide the pieces of paper. She needed five distinct locations to keep the subject areas separate, placed with accordingly easy access. After a period of experimentation she settled on padding the area in the left-hand side of her bra for algebra, and stuffing the right cup full of mechanics as a priority subject. It took persistence, but once done, the cardigan seemed to cover the now uneven mounds of her breasts, although she could feel the sheer mass of paper shift and change shape each time she tried a practice run, thrusting her hand into her left breast to remove pieces of paper at random from a designated section of that part of her bra. She had transcribed too many formulae. The fear of not knowing anything had meant that she had not been selective. She was also subject to a general lack of control over access points. Although she had attempted to organize within each section (putting linear algebra under her breast, for example, and abstract algebra in a generally left direction within the cup), the bits had inevitably got mixed up. Still, she had no option but to continue. Geometry went into the left leg of her tights, crammed in along the front of her thigh, ending at the knee. Probability and stats went into the right leg in the same way, thankfully with much fewer pieces. She stood up and various parts of her body prickled in torturous unity, stabbing her with the squashed points of exercise-book paper. She walked to the mirror, feeling the piercing as she moved.

"Ow!" she hissed, as a large piece of algebra insinuated itself into the flesh of her left breast.

"Shit!" she said, crushing her teeth together, as some mechanics popped out of the right cup, bouncing down to rest in her cleavage. The front of her left thigh stung with a scraping pain, as though she was suffering from heat rash.

She spent the morning arranging and rearranging. By the time Mrs. Minus called her for the trip into town, it was bearable.

WHITEFOOT WAS SITTING at a small table by the window when Rumi entered the Queen's Lane coffeehouse, a place that seemed popular with tourists, judging by the number of times she had walked past and stopped to look at the cream-filled scones and chocolate tarts in the window. He nodded at her, a smile filling his face as recognizably as always. Sitting down, Rumi realized she had never met Whitefoot outside her own house, and never without Mahesh present. The fact that he was the same old Whitefoot was a source of some shock to her. Even though it had been years since he had done such a thing, when he put his hand into his pocket she expected him to produce a Sherbet Dab and slip it into her hand under the table. Instead he handed her a rain-drenched paper bag. "It's time you read this," he said, grinning. "Time for a real education, Ms. Fancy Vasi."

Rumi made a nervous sound, a forced laugh, and peeled back the brown paper, which had formed a wet skin over the book. "*In Defense of Marxism,*" she read, a loud trepidation in her voice. "By Leon Trotsky."

"That's right, my love," said Whitefoot, good-humoredly. "Read it from cover to cover, and we'll commence discussions during my next visit. I've got another of these conferences in January so I thought I'd get in early with yer Christmas reading."

"Thank you," said Rumi, formally. She looked at Whitefoot, and thought of everything: the Penal Collection, a broken oven, Shreene's hurt face, a vacuum cleaner pad, tears—Mahesh's uncried ones; wet and drugged eyes, a kiss, fingers on her breast, nails pinching like the paper daggers in her bra right now, red pen on newsprint, disgust, utter disgust. She thought of it all and bent forward, shame like a belt round her stomach, too tight to breathe. Whitefoot knew nothing, Rumi thought, holding her hands over her belly. He thought the world was about books to be read and discussed. Imagine a world like that, she thought. Imagine a world like that.

"What's wrong with you, girl?" laughed Whitefoot, pouring Rumi a cup of tea from a patterned china teapot, which clinked as he placed it back on the table. "And what's with this incredibly fancy getup? Since when did you start dressing twice yer age?"

"Since whenever," said Rumi, shaking her left leg under the table to try to disperse the prickle of the stuffing in her tights. She had removed the gown before she walked into the café, but that habit prevented Whitefoot noticing, it seemed.

"Oooh!" said Whitefoot. "Sorry, my dear. I didn't mean to offend you. I'm just an old fart. What do I know? Do they expect you to dress smart here for lectures and the like?"

"It's just . . . whatever you want," said Rumi, tapping her foot at an increased speed, jiggling her leg, which was now taken over with pins and needles. "It's just . . . whatever you want to wear."

Whitefoot leaned over the table and pressed his hand on Rumi's arm in an attempt to quell her nervous movement. "Look, kid," he said. "What's bothering you? Is everything OK? You're looking a bit peaky, I have to say. Just noticed it now I'm seeing you close up."

He peered at Rumi, with a joke frown as though he was waiting for her to confess to something. She raised her index fingers under her eyes in an involuntary movement, to hide her black circles, then moved her hands up so that the bases of the palms fully covered her eyes. Whitefoot laughed and shook his head. "Oh dear," he said. "Trust me to put my foot in my mouth again, eh?" He took a sip from his teacup. "Ignore me. What do you want to eat anyway, Roo?"

Rumi flinched at the unfamiliar nickname. "Where are your other conferences?" she asked.

"How do you mean?"

"As in, where are the other places you go for conferences?"

"Well, it varies. This year I've been to a good few—Manchester, Felixstowe, one in Geneva, which was great. Where else? Brighton, Coventry . . ."

"It's by the sea, isn't it?"

"Which one? Brighton?"

"Yes," she said, repeating her question. "It's by the sea, isn't it?"

"Oh, yeah, Brighton was great. I was in this funny little B-and-B, hear-the-ocean-at-night type of thing, no-frills landlady, you know. Lovely. Yeah, Brighton has a real sense of community, people who've decided to get back to being themselves. Turn on, tune in, drop out, all that. You don't find people killing themselves over their pay-checks in Brighton."

"Why don't you live there, then?"

Whitefoot snorted with laughter. "OK, good point," he said, nodding. "Yes, put my money where my mouth is."

"Do you know that Bob Dylan song?"

"Which one?"

"It goes 'Brighton girls are like the moon—Brighton girls are like the moon.' "

"You what? I haven't listened to him in years. You're definitely showing promise, though, I'll give you that. Who introduced you to him?"

"I just heard it somewhere," said Rumi.

"How does it go?"

" 'Brighton girls are like the moon—Brighton girls are like the moon.' "

"Not his most complicated lyric, then."

"You know it," said Rumi. "You must know it. Then he says something about the rain. 'Looks like nothing but rain.' Something like that, he says. 'Brighton girls are like the moon.' It's so beautiful. It's about these two people, they just go off together . . ."

Whitefoot chuckled quietly. "Aye. I wondered how long it would be," he said, in a murmur.

"How long for what?"

"Nothing," said Whitefoot. He called the waitress over with the menu, then looked Rumi in the eye. "What do you want me to say?" he said. "I just think . . . you need some time to work out what matters to you, what's in your bones, you know, the stuffing of you, the marrow, the central pulp that makes you up. You haven't been able to—"

"How long for what?" interrupted Rumi.

"Sorry?"

"You said you wondered how long it would be. How long for what?"

"How long before . . . Aw, this is tricky . . . I don't know what I'm getting into here." He tailed off, taking a long drink from the teacup, and gave Rumi a fraught look.

"What? You're scared of what my *dad* will think?" said Rumi, taunting. "My *beloved* father dearest." She bit her lower lip.

"Hey!"

"What do you think I should do?" Her eyes urged him with new tears. "Why can't you just say it? Why do you have to be so vague and just, like, messy like this, just as cowardly as the rest of them? Why do you lie and hide and deceive and pretend, all of you? All of you!"

The last word came out like an arrow, held in a whine, and louder than she had intended. Two middle-aged women at the table behind Whitefoot curbed their conversation, lowering their voices and raising their eyebrows.

"Come on, love," he said awkwardly, pressing his hand against her wrist on the table. He shuffled her fingers with a sentimental playfulness. "Come on, don't get upset, take it easy," he said, cajoling her.

"That's easy for you to say," said Rumi. "Easy for you to order from your high-up throne of—"

She leaned back abruptly in her chair, and pulled away as if she was going to stand up.

"Hang on!" said Whitefoot, pressing his hand against her wrist more firmly.

Rumi tried to snatch away her hand.

Whitefoot put his other on her free arm, urging her to calm down. "I hear you," he said, crinkling his forehead. "I've known you since you were a wee baby, Rumika. It upsets me to see you like this. I want you to be happy."

"Really?" Her voice was plaintive, suddenly young. "What should I do, then?"

Whitefoot took a breath, as though he was about to answer, then looked away, as if embarrassed by the intensity of her question.

"What?" she said. "What shall I do?"

"Come on, Roo," said Whitefoot. "It's not that bad. You'll be OK. It is natural to, er, feel insecure sometimes at your age. But yer father's very . . . proud of you and all that. You're a very accomplished young lady."

"Oh, just stop it!" said Rumi, putting her hands over her ears.

"What?" said Whitefoot, sounding genuinely shocked. He reached his hand up to her in a halfhearted gesture, then let it slip back to the table.

"Stop the same old . . . same old . . . same, same, same rubbish," said Rumi, loudly, over the muted background in her ears. "I've heard it all before."

THE EXAMINATION SCHOOLS were over the road from the café. Rumi stood outside and tied the ribbon round her neck, sweating under the layers of clothing. It had taken some time to shake off Whitefoot. She had been forced to go to the Bodleian with him, as though for private study, after their meal was over. And now she was at the Schools. The building was threateningly ornate. She could see a gargoyle-style scene carved above the entrance, featuring a row of men in long gowns and square hats kneeling before a seated elderly figure, similarly dressed. He seemed to be blessing one of them, in the manner of a guru with a deserving disciple, resting his hand on the man's head, which bowed before him. She winced, a droplet of sweat running into her eye and blurring her contact lens. There didn't seem to be any other students around, but there were plenty of smartly dressed people, presumably staff, who came in and out of the buildings. What do they do all year? thought Rumi. Exams were only in June, surely? How many people were there like her, disgraced into early entrance?

Inside, it was easy enough to find the room, which, in spite of the sacramental halls she walked past on the way, turned out to be a small office space with six desks and chairs, filing cabinets, books, the usual academic paraphernalia. She had a flashback to the maths building in Swansea, the ritually clocked exam time with her father inserting itself into those Saturday-night memories now with a nostalgic glow. Mr. Mountford was already there, reading through a sheaf of papers at a desk in the corner of the room.

"The examination is due to begin in two minutes' time," he said, looking up and pointing to a large clock on the wall. "I suggest you speed up your preparations."

Rumi saw the desk that was marked out for her, exactly opposite and to the left of Mr. Mountford. There were three papers on it, turned so that only white was visible, a sheet of lined examination paper next to them. She sat down, bra rustling, and realized how close to him she was in terms of physical space. He had been forced into taking a private exam with her alone. It seemed obscene. Imagine if she put her hand into her bra right now, to lucky-dip for some abstract algebra. He would see it all so clearly. Mr. Mountford raised his hand and brought it down—a sharp movement to signify the start of the exam.

She turned over the paper and looked at the questions. A fatuous laugh escaped her: a sliding whoosh of air, like a final, ghastly, death-bed sigh. Mr. Mountford looked up at her pointedly. She looked back down at the first page, holding her breath. It was beyond her. She recognized so much of it—the way that the figures and letters were strung together: she knew what they were after. But she couldn't do it. Another gush of deep-sounding air, like the emptying of bellows, as she opened her mouth.

"Is everything all right?" said Mr. Mountford, pushing his glasses down his nose so that he could look at her over the top, a terse frown demonstrating his annoyance.

Rumi nodded. This is not my life, she thought. This is not my life. The words gathered a hectic momentum, blurring in her head like the lines on a spinning top. She wasn't going to do this exam. She wasn't going to put her hand inside her tights and pray to find the answers. She was not going to beg for the intervention of God in this blind raffle of notes about her body.

"Ha-ha!" she said in a burst, as though she was clearing her throat.

Mr. Mountford sighed with exasperation. "I'm sorry?" he said, taking off his glasses, and placing them on the table. "Rumika, you really need to—"

"I need to go to the toilet," said Rumi, looking him in the eye, her voice challenging him to a duel.

"Rumika, really!" he said, no filter on his irritation. "You have to understand the importance! I mean, really, this is too much!"

"I am going to the toilet!" said Rumi gaily, getting up and edging to the door, picking up her rucksack with a hysterical titter. "Women's issues, you know!" she said, winking at him exaggeratedly as she jerked her head downward to explain why she was taking her bag.

"Rumika!" he said, pushing back his chair.

She had about thirty seconds on him before he realized, she estimated, as she ran through the corridors, speeding for her life, feeling muscles in her legs that she hadn't known she had. She even thought in gasps as she ran: one sec-ond, a heaving intake of breath and then two sec-ond, three sec-ond! The words leapfrogged through her mind. Her trouser-skirt flapped round her thighs, the rucksack shaking on her back as she sprinted, sucking the oxygen into her lungs, laughing through the sweat on her face as people turned to look at her. Two women stopped their hushed conversation in the connecting space before the entrance, as Rumi pushed past, hitting one against the elbow, feeling the papers nailing into her thighs as she ran.

"Sorry!" she shouted, throwing her voice backward over her shoulder, as though for good luck, like salt, as she ran down the steps out onto the high street, and raced across the road, imagining herself disappearing behind the large coaches like a girl in a film. She ran down Queen's Lane, feeling the gradient of her speed, unstoppable as she swerved round the corner like a motorcycle, emerging into a gaggle of tourists, Japanese yet again.

"Hey!" she said. They were gathered by the Bodleian Library, listening to the assured patter of an experienced guide.

Rumi put her hand into her bra and grabbed a huge handful of notes, crushing them in her fist and throwing them at the tourists as she ran past: maybe fifty pieces or more—paper scraps that floated on the wind like confetti, so sweet, almost edible as they fluttered down on the heads. The crowd turned en masse to watch her as she disappeared round another corner, releasing herself from the torture against her skin by grabbing at the hidden places for more offending items.

"Hello!" she said, giggling in hilarity as she doused a family with geometry: parents with two children of around five and eight, plus pushchair, suddenly covered with more multicolored paper that fell like petals all over them as Rumi continued to run, like Wonder Woman, with fire in her heels, a superpowered jet engine that carried her all the way to the station.

When she entered the space—such a familiar interface for all her arrivals and departures from her new life—she stopped in the center of the foyer and heaved for breath. What to do now? She waited, hoped for a secret sign, a portal that would open up like the false panel in the back of that famous wardrobe, in the books she'd loved as a child, and lead her through to the rest of her life. Her throat prickled with the threat of tears but she bounced the air out in a laugh, supporting her hands on her knees as she leaned over and attempted to regain her breath. What to do now? She needed to know what would happen next. After all the plans, the fantasies, the utterly complex dream scenarios she had created over the past few months, she was here, with an apple in her lunchbox, four tenpence pieces, the same old coins as always, and a rucksack full of useless maths books.

In the end she did it the old-fashioned way. She was a stowaway, someone who put their faith in chance, like a youthful spy or a detective in a book: almost accidental, almost innocent. She ran onto the platform and straight onto a waiting train, swift as could be, her feet not relenting until she got to the lavatory, locked the door, panting, and sat on the lid, waiting for the train to start.

epiLogue

ven here there is rain, she thought. They say Cardiff is the raini-
est place in the country, but even here it is the same.

Moisture saturated the sky like a peculiarly British incense: a
soggy odor of wetness dominating the air that Shreene breathed
now, as though she was actually sitting inside a big cloud, rather than
on a bench by the sea. Once, when she had been bathing Rumi (one
of the last times ever before Rumi started to do it herself), the water
had been particularly hot and the room extremely cold, causing
steam to rise in plumes. Rumi had been fascinated by the magical
haze, so tangible, pushing her face inside it and staring ahead with
absolute focus, as though she was seeing steam for the first time.

"Mummy, I can see all these little circles inside!" she had explained, a quiet ecstasy in her voice. "Mummy, I've discovered it—
look!" she had said, putting up her hand to pull Shreene down. "Is it
a discovery? I discovered it?"

The memory caused Shreene to shudder: a reaction to the word
"Mummy," a feeling of revulsion at Rumi's desire to please, the innocent ambition of her "discovery," and their easy intimacy at that
time. Was it before Bapu had died? Rumi's naked face, the color of
sieved wheat flour, her toylike spectacles on the side of the bath—
her first pair of spectacles, the one that had been responsible for
Shreene's tears when Rumi had come home in them, aged seven,
proud inheritor of her father's shortsightedness. Should she have
controlled herself then? Not cried like that for a daughter who was
to be eternally oppressed by glasses? It was easy now to look back
and make everything wrong.

"Tough love," he had called it. Mahesh had picked up the phrase
somewhere. But what was tough about it? He was so progressive
compared to her own father, his own father, even—they would have

never encouraged a girl to be so much, strive for so much, to try to fly like this. The love had never been in doubt. What was love, anyway? Everything, anything, all of it for her, and now nothing. Where to go to understand all this love? In this country, that is, where everything to do with love was topsy-turvy. Where you paddled and paddled, your feet under the water, just to stop yourself drowning, just to keep your dignity, stay alive as yourself, not someone else. Didn't she know, Rumi, her little one, the karmic outpouring of her own womb—didn't she know how easy it would have been to stop struggling for her? How selfish that would have been? How they would have wronged her if they had let her destroy her past, her future, with all her confusion? She was so bright, such a little harshly cut diamond of hope, sharp at the edges, glittering with so much promise.

THE PAST THREE weeks had been the longest run of daily pain in Shreene's life. She had never experienced pain so fierce and uncontrollable—the physical and mental combined. She ground her teeth through the nights and hobbled through the days. Not when Rumi was born had it hurt like this, not when Bapu died, even. None of it could equate to this feeling of ripped skin that she felt over her entire body, the sensation of chili powder rubbed into her sore brain from the moment she woke until after she had made sure Nibu had gone to sleep and was waiting for Mahesh to join her.

Everyone knew. Everyone had an opinion. From the snide family who ran the corner shop—the Gujarati mother, with her weasellike concern, wanting to get the full story from Shreene when she went in there to buy milk—to Nibu's class teacher, a patronizing stroke from her on Shreene's arm as she voiced her anxiety as to how "Nibu is bearing up" when she went to pick him up in the days after Rumi had left. Mahesh had it too: from people at uni, in his department, not just unknowns but his colleagues, fellow staff. Most humiliatingly, Professor Levinson himself had stopped in the corridor and inquired after Mahesh's "situation," a grave professionalism in his voice as he asked to be "kept updated," then walked away. They had been so private all these years, so alone, self-segregated through Mahesh's fear of outside influences, unable to trust people, and they were now totally public. Everyone knew their business.

Part of it was the shame. It was so visible. There was a tale about a boy who put his thumb in a big dam to stop it flooding—Rumi had loved it as a child. And now she had run away from them and left them to drown in a flood of hate. Shreene and Mahesh were subjected to a blast of judgment and hostility, an antipathy that Shreene hadn't really known was there. Or had she? It had certainly been hinted at in those early newspaper articles, but this level of fury? Had Rumi known about it?

All of the reports, the radio, TV and especially the newspapers, had linked arms in priggish outrage, an agreed ranting of the "truth." Some were more vociferous than others—sometimes the articles were just disapproving lists of the outer facts of the situation—but generally Mahesh and Shreene were portrayed as dangerous people. Shreene saw Mahesh morph publicly from a greedy, money-hungry immigrant, desperate to profit from his daughter's ability, into an aspiring terrorist, using his fiercely trained child as a weapon to subvert the freethinking traditions of the West.

And they were so alone with it. Rumi had gone and they were alone. They couldn't turn to the ashram in London because of the shame. Everyone in India carried on living their lives—what did they know? Mahesh and she had no one to cry before, even to laugh with about the horrific absurdities that formed their life. Instead they sat alone, dying together when Nibu was not around to force them to go on. Was she alive? They had to believe so. Hurt? Starving? Mistreated? How was she surviving out there, alone, so vulnerable? Who was she with? Shreene couldn't allow herself to think through the possibilities, let alone discuss them with Mahesh.

How to get her back when it was like this? How had their care and love made them villains? Even when Mahesh had done the first, and most regrettable, interview on television to ask for her safe return, they had massacred him in the newspapers for responding to a question about Rumi's supposed love interest. He had said that his daughter would never have run away with a boy, that if she had, it meant she had been brainwashed by some cult or tribe, and that he wanted his daughter back. He wanted her to come home. He was protecting her honor. Shreene knew what he meant. But they didn't. They thought they knew right from wrong, but how could they? They had a different system here: it was so obvious it made her weary to think it through, again like a drone with no sound of completion, a drone that was no good anymore. She had gone, she had left them, she didn't care. She didn't care about them, Rumi, their daughter. She had gone.

They were Indian people. Did they have to justify their origins? Their beliefs? Start from the beginning now with these people—when they had finally begun to let down their barriers? As though it was so simple, like a times table. The soul, the spiritual nature of sex, life-partners, commitment, marriage, families, purity of thought and action, society, Hinduism, karma, the next generation, children, heredity, love, you know love as a glue, the attempt to be a good person, all the basic values? Remaining true to yourself? So they could be laughed at? Just for that, so laughter could mix with their hate, had they asked Mahesh what he thought, those journalists? Had they expected him to say all this, share it with these people who came and scratched and scratched at them with their words like cats on their front door?

Every day Mahesh bought the papers, all of them. In a cruel parody of the police-camp procedures of their early married life, he sat with Shreene at the end of each day and found the articles, underlined them in demoralized wobbles of red, as though knowing what was out there would make it less unruly. Shreene felt her own loss of innocence as she sat in those bloody silences with her husband, devoid of the scrambling tiffs that had characterized the early newspaper tests, the youthful disagreements—the memory of her own ripe, freshly wed vigor twinging through her thoughts like a suicidal melody from a Guru Dutt film. Instead, they let death collect in the room around them—Nibu asleep upstairs, as though he didn't exist—as they sat after dinner at the kitchen table, trapped in their own home, and read about their child, two bereaved prisoners of war. Mahesh passed each paper to Shreene, marked up for her to read, as he continued through the pile. "The search continues," it said. "Police are searching the entire country for one of Britain's brainiest girls." "Last seen at Oxford's prestigious Examination Schools, fifteen-year-old Rumi Vasi is still incognito . . ." Sometimes they got Mahesh's job wrong, or Shreene's age. But generally the words were the same.

And then they found her. That phone call. They hadn't been ready for it. Who would have been prepared for it, though? That she would request, ask so officially, to be kept hidden from her parents. The shock of it brought back an unfamiliar emotion: their anger, buried in yearning and quiet over the previous six days. Mahesh continued to buy the papers, but they learned more—too much—from the police after that. Over the next two weeks the shocks came closer and closer together, like labor contractions: Rumi had managed to hide on a train to London, then get herself somehow to Brighton. They had found her after four days at some kind of refuge for battered women but then, and this was the humiliation of it—the fantastical part that made Shreene wonder if she and Mahesh had committed heinous acts in their past lives, acts that must have been disgusting beyond belief—her parents were not allowed to see her.

Instead, Rumi sent them a letter through the police explaining that she felt *abused* (such a harsh, adult word—who had told her to write it?) by her experience and needed to stay away for her health; she had asked to be taken into *care* (which meant, as Shreene later found, that she wanted to be looked after by strangers); her request was accepted. And then another shock, the worst of all: the police eased off contact with Mahesh and Shreene and they were referred to social workers, people who talked about beginning "a process of communication," which involved talking about "what had gone wrong." They said that Rumi did not want to see them for the indefinite future. They said it as though it had meaning. She had been placed with a foster family and, "for now," she did not want contact.

"She's angry! She's a child! Come on . . . Let's go and stop her being so silly. Let's go and get her . . ." Shreene had begged Mahesh, night after night, debasing herself with a rising and falling moan, a continual cry that fell hopelessly against his stillness.

"Come on," she pleaded. "She's just a little girl. If we write her a letter in love and ask her to come back she will do it. She is silly but she's fifteen years old only . . ."

But Mahesh ignored her. Even though his daughter was sleeping in a stranger's house, eating and drinking at a foreign table, apparently even going to school locally, as a "temporary stopgap," still Mahesh ignored Shreene. He stopped the newspaper ritual and slipped out of range, fell seamlessly into a new level of silence in which even his movements in the house became inaudible—deathly footsteps on the stairs leading to ghostly interactions with the bathroom. He came home at five forty-five each day, changing into pajama kurta as early as six to lie on their bed, over the quilt, eyes turned to the ceiling, glasses removed. He tuned the radio next to their bed to All-India MW and lay there each evening listening to the crackle and fudge of distant voices, interrupted by rough sitars, the strident crossings of abrupt strings.

Eventually Shreene wrote the letter herself, without telling Mahesh. And, in spite of the explanations she had been giving herself to keep sane—that this was just a test, that it wasn't real—still, the final shock after all the contractions of pain, it winded her. When she heard that Rumi had agreed to see her, alone, Shreene went to the shrine in Nibu's room and lay prostrate on the floor, crying, so that her tears ran down the side of her nose and into the nylon brush of the carpet, pressing her forehead hard on the floor, asking over and over again for the guidance, the strength and the knowledge to get her daughter back. She did not believe she had the ability to persuade her to come home. But she believed she could make Rumi remember who she was—touch her child again, be close to her in some way. She believed that Rumi would remember love.

—

SHREENE PULLED THE sleeves of her sweater down farther so that they came out from under her coat to cover the thin line of exposed wrist above each of her hands and join the border of her gloves. She sat on her bench and watched Rumi, farther up the beach, standing by the sea, kicking pebbles with her foot. Rumi was five minutes early. Although she was a little way off across the sand, her shape was unmistakable. She had a new jacket, black tights, her old trainers. A padded denim jacket with a sweatshirt hood sewn into the top. Her hair had grown a little so that it crawled half over her ears. She stood with her hands in her pockets, shoulders hunched in the cold, her head hooked over so that her chin almost skimmed her chest. As Shreene watched her, Rumi lifted her head and looked out across the expanse of water, shivering.

Shreene breathed lightly, repeating the oldest mantra in the world, all sounds of the universe together in a single round vowel of calm. Then she stood up and walked to her.

acknowledgments

I'd like to acknowledge the support of my family in writing this book: my father for his tenderness and intellectual warmth, my lovely mother, her lifelong master class in storytelling, and my brother for his true and absurd sweetness. There are several people I'd like to thank: my agent Andrew Wylie, and Tracy Bohan—your energy is infectious, as is your passion; I am lucky to be part of it. My editor Mary Mount, for her fine hand and generous spirit, also Jennifer Hershey and Hazel Orme.

My main readers at Bath Spa UC, where I wrote much of the book: especially Gerard, for his indefinable, precious effect; Richard Francis, Tim Liardet, and the soulful words of Tessa Hadley. Ian Breckon, for his patience and fortuitous ideas, Ros Cook, Mike Haughney, Jules Williams, Joachim Noreiko and Emma Hooper.

The friends who were also readers: Julia Miranda for her unique poetic, Krish Majumdar for the strength of his investment and belief, Nigel Singh, Doug M. Ray and Chris Hale. My dear mate Stephen, thank you for those diamond discussions on plot, honesty, and adolescence; similarly Susanna Howard and Bucymac—the invaluable exchange. Nirad Pragasam and Joanna Perry, you remain a constant source of inspiration and provocation. Also, Johanna Ekström, Suzy Jaffe, Camille Thoman, Owen Sheers, Simon Baker, Emily Woof, James Eaton, Kevin Conroy Scott, Alex Heminsley and Adam Wishart, for their advice and indulgence.

Indu and Chandra Mohan Sharma for their utter kindness and continually open door. Also Brij, Caroline and Gabriella Sharma.

Most of all I am indebted to Vik Sharma, who made me write this book, and is the true catalyst at the novel's heart. Thank you, my love, for showing me the "simple rip/in a curtain's shift/that reveals a window/that reveals the world."

gifted

nikita lalwani

A Reader's Guide

RANDOM HOUSE READER'S CIRCLE: Like Rumi, you grew up in Wales as the daughter of Indian immigrant parents. Do you empathize with Rumi's attachment to India, and why do you think she feels it so strongly?

NIKITA LALWANI: As a child, India was very much part of my identity at school as well as at home. Although it clearly demarcated me from the norm, it was something that I saw as quite epic, very exciting, as opposed to an embarrassment. As an idea, 'India' felt so abundant—it could be supernatural, exotic, melodramatic, so high on emotion and desirability: a place for which we were always nostalgic as a family. I think India represented an inherited and very romantic idea of a home-space. Rumi experiences freedom there on many levels as a child—freedom from academic rigor and playground politics, but also a sense of place and belonging. Of course, this relationship becomes more complicated—seedier, if you like, as she goes through adolescence and her belief structure morphs into something more ambiguous.

RHRC: Mahesh is determined to distinguish himself and his family in their adoptive country. Did you feel any similar pressures growing up in Cardiff?

NL: I remember our family was friends with another Asian family in a nearby town and their son actually was some kind of genius. He got his math O-levels in grade 8 and learned piano at an obscenely young age, and at dinner parties when we were sent to the kids room, I used to time him obsessively as he did the Rubik's cube over and over, and tried to beat the world record. What was all that about? We thought it was an entirely normal pursuit. When I was writing the book I kept coming back to this strange aspiration that I had for a while when I was around 8 years old, to be some kind of prodigy. This odd, and quite particular desire must have been linked to the need to stand out in some way, I'm sure to be less invisible, and math was the most useful thing I had in hand. As it was, I outgrew the idea within a few months and got on with being just academically decent at school, but the label 'gifted child' still interested me when I became a documentary maker as an adult—the whole nature versus nurture debate, and what was powering that particular kind of nurture in second-generation children.

RHRC: Her gift for mathematics causes Rumi to often feel isolated from her fellow students. Did your aptitude for math also mark you out as 'different.' How did you deal with this?

NL: Most of my love of math as a child was quite simple and tricky really. Just the sheer drama of mental arithmetic—acrobatics with straightforward sums. I didn't ever get beyond that to the deep stuff, but I'm sure while I experimented with being a human calculator, I was trying to turn some element of being different to my advantage. It was a chicken and egg situation though. As to which came first—was the feeling of otherness because of math or did the math fill the space created through being different by virtue of race? I think they fed each other. It is something I associate with early childhood though. As I got older, and nearer adolescence, that difference (and the math fascination) seemed to be much less apparent.

RHRC: Having gone to Oxford to study medicine, how did you come to be a writer?

NL: There was a moment at Oxford when we were all lined up at the end of our second term, and we were finally on to 'the head' in the dissecting lab. There were six students in our group and we had a tub of heads in front of us, all sliced in different ways to reveal different constituent parts. We each had to dunk a hand in and take out a head and name the parts that were exposed in the section. When it was my turn, I got a very small one, it must have been a child of about age 10. I thought to myself, I don't like this at all, but to make matters worse, I didn't have a clue what the major parts were when questioned. It was so much about the facts and at eighteen, I was just starting to desperately seek out everything that couldn't be quantified. I spent most of my time at Oxford writing for poetry magazines and trying to perform in dodgy theatre so I think it was only a matter of time before I got found out, and I was 'sent down' to use that wonderfully dramatic phrase, after a year of the course. It was, as my tutor predicted then, the luckiest thing to happen to me.

RHRC: Who are your favorite authors, and why?

NL: At the moment I'm very keen on the Belgian writer Amelie Nothomb, who has a very trenchant and bizarre humor married with real sensitivity. I recently read Tokyo Stories by Rana Dasgupta which is so relevant, ruthless and yet utterly heartwarming. I admire the absurd and the extravagant and so Rushdie has been my most longstanding literary involvement. I'm also a fan of Don Delillo and Kundera for the same reasons. Siri Hustvedt and Doris Lessing would be amongst the others.

READING GROUP QUESTIONS AND TOPICS FOR DISCUSSION

1. How does Rumi's focus on mathematics influence the structure of the novel and the way she processes the world?

2. Shreene's sister in India tells her she was "always the lucky one." Would you characterize Shreene as lucky? What are the grounds for Shreene's discontent and "desolation"? What similarities and disparities do you see between Shreene and her daughter?

3. "Nobody, not even the rain, has such small hands." Rumi cites this line from e.e. cummings during her first trip to India. What does rain, the moon, and the stars represent within *Gifted*? How do these elements surround Rumi's relationship with Bridgeman?

4. How do the characters in *Gifted* contend with cultural stereotypes?

5. Reflect on the conversations between Mahesh and Whitefoot while playing chess. What do we learn about Mahesh through their interactions?

6. Does Rumi ever transcend her self-described role as an "irrelevant . . . observer"? If so, how?

7. Discuss the importance of ritual for Rumi and Mahesh within Oxford University, Indian culture and Western society.

8. Rumi becomes increasingly impulsive and self-destructive as the novel progresses. What influences and perpetuates these tendencies? What do the cumin seeds represent for Rumi?

9. Shreene repeatedly admonishes Rumi for asking "shameful" questions about bras and sex, even telling Rumi "that is not how our babies are born. Only white people have sex." Why is Shreene so critical of Rumi's inquiries? How do her questions represent a lack of "decency" and "respect" to Shreene? How do their arguments progress?

10. Mahesh explains that "the label 'gifted' was meaningless to them as a family and . . . a damaging idea to perpetuate in the population as a whole." He believed that "any child could achieve this kind of knowledge and success rate, given the right developmental approach by the parents." Do you agree? Why or why not?

11. Discuss the presence of duality throughout *Gifted*: between right and wrong, thoughts and actions, perception and reality, and logic and emotion. How does Rumi embody these dualities?

12. Rumi insists that her strict regimen in the hopes of reaching Oxford "is what [she has] chosen . . . Until [she is] free." Her mother maintains that Mahesh "has given [her] too much freedom," while Mahesh is not "deluded enough to think that the world is full of choices." Discuss the manipulation of choice within *Gifted* and it's relation to freedom.

13. How do Rumi's perceptions of herself evolve throughout *Gifted*? What influences how she sees herself? Why does she decide to "walk in the valley of truth"?

14. Are Mahesh and Shreene perpetrators, victims, or both?

NIKITA LALWANI was born in Rajasthan, India, and raised in Cardiff, Wales. She directored documentaries at the BBC for several years before receiving her MA in creative writing at Bath Spa University. Lalwani lives in London, where she is at work on her second novel.

ABOUT THE TYPE

This book was set in Perpetua, a typeface designed by the English artist Eric Gill, and cut by The Monotype Corporation between 1928 and 1930. Perpetua is a contemporary face of original design, without any direct historical antecedents. The shapes of the roman letters are derived from the techniques of stonecutting. The larger display sizes are extremely elegant and form a most distinguished series of inscriptional letters.